'One of the UK's top
thriller writers'
Daily Express

'Like his creator, the ex-SAS
soldier turned uber-agent is
unstoppable'
Daily Mirror

'Could hardly be more topical'
Mail on Sunday

'Other thriller writers do
their research, but McNab
has actually been there'
Sunday Times

'Sometimes only the rollercoaster
ride of an action-packed thriller hits
the spot. No one delivers them as
professionally or as plentifully as
SAS soldier turned author McNab'
Guardian

'McNab's great asset
is that the heart of his
fiction is non-fiction'
Sunday Times

'Proceeds with a
testosterone surge'
Daily Telegraph

'When it comes to thrills, he's
Forsyth class'
Mail on Sunday

'Nick Stone is emerging as
one of the great all-action
characters of recent times'
Daily Mirror

'Andy McNab's books get
better and better'
Daily Express

ANDY McNAB

▲ **In 1984** he was 'badged' as a member of 22 SAS Regiment.

▲ **Over the course** of the next nine years he was at the centre of covert operations on five continents.

▲ **During the first** Gulf War he commanded Bravo Two Zero, a patrol that, in the words of his commanding officer, 'will remain in regimental history for ever'.

▲ **Awarded both** the Distinguished Conduct Medal (DCM) and Military Medal (MM) during his military career.

▲ **McNab** was the British Army's most highly decorated serving soldier when he finally left the SAS in February 1993.

▲ **He is a patron** of the *Help for Heroes* campaign.

▲ **He is now** the author of over twenty bestselling thrillers, as well as four Quick Read novels. Following the success of the perennial bestseller *Bravo Two Zero*, McNab continues to write non-fiction too. Most recently, he joined forces with Professor Kevin Dutton on *The Good Psychopath's Guide to Success* and *Sorted! The Good Psychopath's Guide to Bossing Your Life*.

BRAVO TWO ZERO

In 1991, Sergeant Andy McNab led eight members of the SAS regiment on a top-secret mission in Iraq that would send them deep behind enemy lines. Their call sign: Bravo Two Zero.

IMMEDIATE ACTION

The no-holds-barred account of an extraordinary life, from the day McNab was found on the steps of Guy's Hospital as a baby to the day he went to fight in the Gulf War.

SEVEN TROOP

The gripping true story of serving in the company of a remarkable band of brothers. But he who dares doesn't always win. Every man is pushed to breaking point, some beyond it.

THE GOOD PSYCHOPATH'S GUIDE TO SUCCESS

As diagnosed by Professor Kevin Dutton, McNab is what they call a 'Good Psychopath' – he's a psychopath but he's also a high-functioning member of society. Learn how to be successful the McNab way.

SORTED! THE GOOD PSYCHOPATH'S GUIDE TO BOSSING YOUR LIFE

Together, Andy McNab and Professor Kevin Dutton are here to show you how to dial up your inner 'Good Psychopath' to get more out of life.

THE NICK STONE SERIES

Ex-SAS trooper, now gun-for-hire working for the British government, Nick Stone is the perfect man for the dirtiest of jobs, doing whatever it takes by whatever means necessary...

REMOTE CONTROL

▲ WASHINGTON **DC, USA**
Stone is on the run with precious cargo, the only person who can identify a vicious killer – a seven-year-old girl.

CRISIS FOUR

▲ NORTH CAROLINA, **USA**
A beautiful young woman holds the key to a chilling conspiracy that will threaten the world as we know it.

FIREWALL

▲ FINLAND
At the heart of a global espionage network, Stone is faced with some of the most dangerous killers around.

LAST LIGHT

▲ PANAMA
Caught in the crossfire between Colombian mercenaries and Chinese businessmen, Stone isn't comfortable.

LIBERATION DAY

◢ CANNES, FRANCE

Behind the glamorous exterior, the city's seething underworld is the battleground for a very dirty drugs war.

DARK WINTER

◢ MALAYSIA

The War on Terror has Stone cornered: the life of someone he loves or the lives of millions he doesn't know?

DEEP BLACK

◢ BOSNIA

All too late, Stone sees he is being used as bait to lure into the open a man whom the West are desperate to destroy.

AGGRESSOR

◢ GEORGIA, FORMER SOVIET UNION

An old SAS comrade calls in a debt that will challenge Stone to risk everything in order to repay his friend.

RECOIL

◢ THE CONGO, AFRICA

A straightforward missing persons case quickly becomes a headlong rush from the past.

CROSSFIRE

◢ KABUL, AFGHANISTAN

The search for a kidnapped reporter takes Stone to Afghanistan – the modern-day Wild West.

BRUTE FORCE

◢ TRIPOLI, LIBYA

An undercover operation is about to have deadly long-term consequences.

EXIT WOUND

◢ DUBAI, UAE

This one's personal: Stone is out to track down the killer of two ex-SAS comrades.

ZERO HOUR

◢ AMSTERDAM, NETHERLANDS

A terrorist organization is within reach of immeasurable power – but not for long.

DEAD CENTRE

◢ SOMALIA

When his son is kidnapped by pirates, a Russian oligarch calls the only man he can think of, Nick Stone.

SILENCER

◢ HONG KONG

Stone must return to a world he thought he had left behind in order to protect his family.

FOR VALOUR

◢ HEREFORD, UK

Called to investigate a death at the SAS base, Stone finds himself in the killer's telescopic sights.

DETONATOR
◢ The Alps, Switzerland
When someone Stone loves is murdered, he can no longer take the pain. He wants vengeance at any cost.

COLD BLOOD
◢ The North Pole
Accompanying a group of veteran soldiers on an expedition to the North Pole, Stone learns quickly that it isn't just the cold that might kill him.

LINE OF FIRE
◢ London, UK
The Nick Stone series comes closer to home in more ways than one.

THE SERGEANT TOM BUCKINGHAM SERIES

RED NOTICE

Deep beneath the English Channel, Russian terrorists have seized control of the Eurostar to Paris and are holding four hundred hostages at gunpoint. But one man stands in their way. An off-duty SAS soldier is on the train; his name is Tom Buckingham.

FORTRESS

Ex-SAS and working for a billionaire with political ambition, Buckingham will have to decide where his loyalties lie as he is drawn into a spiral of terrorism, insurgency and, ultimately, assassination.

STATE OF EMERGENCY

Undercover inside a frighteningly real right-wing organization, Buckingham uncovers a plan to kill the party leader. But beneath that lies a far more devastating plot to change the political landscape of Europe for ever.

Andy McNab and Kym Jordan's novels trace the interwoven stories of one platoon's experience of warfare in the twenty-first century. Packed with the searing danger and high-octane excitement of modern combat, they also explore the impact of its aftershocks upon the soldiers themselves, and upon those who love them.

WAR TORN

Two tours of Iraq have shown Sergeant Dave Henley how modern battles are fought. But nothing could have prepared him for his posting to Afghanistan. This is a war zone like he's never seen before.

BATTLE LINES

Sergeant Dave Henley returns from Afghanistan to find that home can be an equally searing battlefield. The promise of another posting to Helmand is almost a relief for the soldiers but, for their families, it is another opportunity for their lives to be ripped apart.

ANDY
McNAB
LINE OF FIRE

CORGI BOOKS

TRANSWORLD PUBLISHERS
61–63 Uxbridge Road, London W5 5SA
www.penguin.co.uk

Transworld is part of the Penguin Random House group of companies
whose addresses can be found at global.penguinrandomhouse.com

Penguin
Random House
UK

First published in Great Britain in 2017 by Bantam Press
an imprint of Transworld Publishers
Corgi edition published 2018

A CIP catalogue record for this book
is available from the British Library.

ISBN
9780552174275 (B format)
9780552175340 (A format)

Typeset in 11/14pt Palatino by Falcon Oast Graphic Art Ltd.
Printed and bound by Clays Ltd, Bungay, Suffolk.

Penguin Random House is committed to a sustainable
future for our business, our readers and our planet. This book is made
from Forest Stewardship Council® certified paper.

MIX
Paper from
responsible sources
FSC® C018179

1 3 5 7 9 10 8 6 4 2

LINE OF FIRE

1

Zürich, Switzerland
3 May 2016

The heavy steel door, which the law dictated had to be thick enough to withstand the force of several Hiroshimas, had been nicely veneered in oak to make it look less intimidating. As it swung open, with a hydraulic sigh, I stood and turned to greet the woman coming through.

'Claudia.'

The door powered itself closed behind her, with a reassuring clunk. The clack of her heels on the shiny white tiles took over, and she approached with an extended hand. 'Mr Stone. Very nice to meet you at last. May I call you Nick?'

She was as I'd imagined her, early thirties, very smart, businesslike black skirt to just above the knee, big professional smile. Her hair was relaxed and pulled back in a bun.

She was probably running through the same evaluation process as I was and working hard to hide her disappointment.

'Of course. I thought we were old friends anyway.'

Her polite smile didn't exactly light up the room. She moved round to the other side of the desk and sat at the same time as I did, maintaining the smile of non-commitment to emotion.

She took a breath. 'Nick, I'm afraid there's still no progress on the release of the funds, if that's why you've come to see me.' Her English was every bit as perfect as, no doubt, her Russian, French, German and Italian were. 'We have not only the Russian fiscal and probate systems to deal with but also our own regulatory bodies here in Switzerland. They will need to be content with the process of the release, which, unfortunately, isn't yet a release. When your funds are eventually transferred, they will be held in escrow until we've conformed to both countries' regulations.'

She managed a slight widening of the smile that gave her already prominent cheekbones a little lift. She was West African, maybe Nigerian, but Claudia Nangel, I was sure, would never consider retiring there.

So, no change from what I'd been hearing for months now, not only from Claudia but also from my lawyer in Moscow. Her bank seemed to be making an absolute fortune – not that they were going to see any of it at the moment. 'You mean I have it, but I don't have it?'

Claudia rested her hands on her desk and leant forward. 'Nick, I'm so sorry for the loss of your partner and son. And I'm so sorry we can't do any more to help you right now. We will try hard to cut through

2

bureaucracy this end when your funds are released in Moscow, but . . .'

It sounded genuine.

She noticed the brown Jiffy bag I'd placed on the desk. 'Ah, I see. Is this why you're here?'

'Could I ask you to look after it for me?'

She opened the bag without a flicker of interest, concern, or even a smile, and produced a smaller one, white and the size of a CD, sealed, along with a folded sheet of A4. The brown Jiffy bag seemed far too messy for the room. I loved private banking.

'The three names on that piece of paper each have a different code statement next to them. If any of those individuals calls you and gives their statement, could you please courier the package to the address I've written on it? If I call in, that would make four of us who can independently authorize the move.'

She lifted the envelope a little to check the address.

'Do you need to know what's in there?'

'No, Nick, not at all. But there will be a charge for curation.'

'Ah. The problem for me, Claudia, is that I don't have any personal money left. I can't sell the apartment in Moscow because it was in Anna's name. And even if the court clears probate tomorrow, it clearly isn't going to be the end of the bureaucracy. I don't think I'll be able to find a way through without your help. So I'm skint.'

She eased herself back in the chair, her hands clasped together as if in prayer. Maybe her English wasn't as good as I'd thought it was.

'Skint?'

The diamond band with her wedding ring was on the fourth finger of her right hand. It looked like Claudia was German, not Swiss.

I had a flashback to the lesson I'd learnt the hard way as a young squaddie stationed in Minden. I was always getting into trouble trying to chat up women after a casual check of their left hand, but that changed the night I got filled in by a very pissed-off German husband outside a nightclub called Stiffshankers. He explained, in better English than I spoke, that in Germany married women wore a ring on the right hand instead of the left.

Not that my cultural lesson was going to help me today.

'No money at all. I'm going to have to start working for a living.'

Either the joke wasn't understood or she didn't like the idea of her clients soiling their hands. She smiled, a little less widely than even last time, and logged the word in the English dictionary inside her head, filing it with 'broke' and 'brassic'.

I knew what she was going to say before she said it. I'd heard it often enough before.

'I'm so sorry, Nick, but we can't help you in any way financially. We can't advance any sums of capital. It would be illegal.'

She smiled enough to display a perfect set of teeth. 'Not yet, of course. But we will hold your package for you and we can talk about our consideration in, say, two months?'

Why didn't banks talk about money? Maybe if you had to ask about costs you shouldn't be in that room.

Whenever I'd phoned, I'd pictured her gazing out of her window at some shimmering Swiss lake as she talked to me at all hours of the day and night.

The bank's foyer had kept the dream alive, a riot of beige and gold topped off with a crystal chandelier the size of a small planet. There hadn't been a cashier in sight. It wasn't the kind of set-up where you dropped in to deposit your pocket money. You either transferred it electronically or delivered it in a bulletproof attaché case handcuffed to a man mountain with biceps like wrecking balls.

But the lake view and opulence hadn't been for me today. I was sitting in the basement, surrounded by concrete walls painted white, glossy white floor tiles, no pictures, no plants. In front of me there was a smoked-glass desk and, behind that, what was probably the world's most expensive leather swivel chair. The desk was bare apart from the Jiffy bags and still folded sheet of A4. No telephones, no computers, not even a clock or a photo-frame. I was in the bank's confidentiality room.

'We should then, hopefully, be able to cast some light on your situation. We are working on it, Nick, believe me.'

I did, but I also knew it was the end of the conversation. So did the door, which began to open as if it had read her mind. We stood up.

'Shall I call you a taxi for the airport, Nick, or are you staying in Zürich?'

'No. I can't even afford to breathe the air.' I knew she wouldn't get the joke but thought I'd give it a try anyway. 'A taxi would be great, thanks.'

We came out into a windowless corridor of more white tiles and walls, and she walked me towards the shiny stainless-steel lift that would take me up to the ground floor and its sumptuous marble, leather and crystal.

The doors opened and I shook hands with my banking relationship manager for possibly the last time. At least now I had the fifth part of our security blanket in place for all four of us. My plan was to send the memory stick to the *New York Times*. They had a great system for whistle-blowers. I would also dump its contents with the papers in all the different ways they had ready and waiting, and all at once: WhatsApp, SecureDrop and Pretty Good Privacy. I would avoid the mailing address headed *Tips, New York Times*. That was where Claudia would send the white Jiffy bag.

2

Tulse Hill, London

I came out of the station in South London and got mugged by grime, decay, and air thick with diesel. Discarded copies of *Metro* swirled around my feet. There was still quite a lot of coverage in the broadsheets of the four coordinated Islamist suicide bombings in Brussels, which had left thirty-two dead and hundreds wounded, but these front pages were full of Brexit doom or joy and how some C-list celeb wanted us to vote. The chic spotlessness of Switzerland was five hundred miles away, an hour and forty minutes by plane.

I was heading for Rio's. He had bought an ex-council maisonette close to the station. Way back when I was fifteen, nicking money from gas meters and dreaming of owning a second-hand Ford Cortina, these places were the height of social mobility round here. My claim to fame was that a mate I used to bunk off school with lived in one.

There were only two comprehensive schools the kids from Brixton, Peckham and Tulse Hill went to, so if you went to school, you went to one of them. I didn't put in too many appearances, but I made a few mates along the way, and one, Pete, had lived on the same estate I was heading for now.

We were the same age but that was where any similarity between us ended. Pete had had all the kit – he'd worn his cuffs and butterfly collars outside his blazer, just like Jason King – and I'd thought he was smooth as fuck in his baggy trousers.

I put my card into an ATM on the main road and asked for five hundred quid. There should have been the best part of seven million US dollars tucked away in the Zürich account. Drug money, it had fallen into my hands years ago, and since no one had ever asked for it back, I considered it mine. I'd kept a few quid in reserve for my partner Anna and myself, but the lion's share had gone into a trust fund for our son, Nicolai. They'd been murdered two years ago, and the trust should revert to me after probate was granted. The problem was, my lawyers in Moscow had been more interested in dragging things out, maintaining their income stream.

The bank had issued me with a turbo-charged debit card when I joined it, the sleek black thing without any embossed numbers that the ATM was now spitting out. That shouldn't have been happening. The link between me and my bank vault was routed through a randomly selected, ever-changing configuration of about twenty-six separate servers, at the end of which I was guaranteed money at any ATM worldwide.

Except in Tulse Hill, it seemed. Maybe it was because a private Swiss bank card hadn't been shoved into any South London ATM before, but when I tried again, it fucked me off. I tried a third time. Nothing. I knew it wasn't going to happen, but it was worth a try.

It really did feel like I'd come full circle as I minced along the same pavement on the South Circular Road towards the same estate as I had back then. It was like I'd never left. The only difference was that the trucks screaming past just a few feet from us pedestrians were a more modern shape and had Polish plates.

Rio's house was on Coburg Crescent, just up on the left. Things hadn't been all bad back then. One Sunday afternoon when I turned up at Pete's he was out playing football and his mum and dad were at East Street Market, which left Fay, Pete's sister, at home. She was seventeen, willing and keen, but it was all very quick, and she made me promise not to tell anybody. I said I wouldn't, but as soon as I could, like the shit I was, I did.

3

I crossed what was left of the grass bank dividing the crescent from the South Circular, and wove through clumps of parked cars. Rio's place was one of the scores of narrow 1960s terraced houses with a garage each as the ground floor. From the number of vehicles clogging the street, nobody used them as garages any more. If they were anything like Rio, it was where they housed their freezer, washing-machine and tumble-drier, a set of wheels for a non-existent car, and bags of dog biscuits for a non-existent pitbull that would bite the arse off anyone who tried to break into the house. They had 'Buy One Get One Free' labels all over them, which was probably what had given Rio the idea that he needed a dog.

Every time I'd entered the house I'd felt sure it was Pete's old place. I'd gone into a familiar hall, then, almost by muscle memory, straight upstairs to the first floor where the living room, kitchen and toilet were, and up again to the three bedrooms and bathroom. A blue plaque on Fay's wall to commemorate our union would have sealed it.

I fished about in my jeans for the door keys. Rio had taken pity on me a couple of weeks ago when I had nowhere to live. He was one of the good guys: he'd wanted to help me and he really liked the idea of setting up a security firm for us four survivors to run. The Special Needs Service, as he liked to call it. He and the other two might not have the correct number of limbs for a private military company's line of work, but that didn't matter.

That was as far as it had gone. I'd forgotten about it, but Rio had got the bug. It would be right up his street because he'd be the ultimate undercover operator, a Rasta with only one good arm.

This being South London, there were so many keys in the set Rio had had cut for me that they filled my pocket. The uPVC-framed partly double-glazed door hadn't been there when I was a kid, but it was about the only thing that had changed. Within the glass was a grid of thin steel mesh and a 'Beware of the Dog' decal that Rio had picked up along with his dog-food bargain. Security was so much better now than it had been in my thieving days, when you knew you could just smash the unprotected float glass and grab a fistful of coins from the gas and electricity meters – and then probably take a dump in the sink for a laugh.

Rio was in: only the cylinder lock needed turning.

I pushed the door and entered the small hallway with the narrow stairs in front of me. The smell of vegetable soup was overpowering. The cans were stacked like an art installation against the wall. Above, on the first floor, there was a landing with two doors. The one on the left led into the open-plan living room and kitchen; to the right was the toilet.

I pushed upstairs. The swirly carpet was almost threadbare, and had probably been very smart when Pete's mum installed it. I shouted up, 'I remember the carpet pattern, mate. This is definitely the same house.'

Rio appeared in the living-room doorway, all smiles. 'Mate, don't believe you. Listen, we've got jack shit in. You want to go down to Maccy or get pizza? I'm fucking starving.'

He came down a couple of steps to meet me. On the safe phone he had tapped out a text. Now he held it in front of me. It said, 'Play safe.'

'Yeah, yeah. Maccy's great. Let me dump the bag first and have a piss, and I'm there, all right?'

He locked eyes on me and they weren't as happy as the voice had been.

4

Rio wasn't as house-proud as Pete's mum had been, that was for sure. A half-eaten bread roll sat on the glass coffee-table, along with a spoon and a bowl, both encrusted with dried soup. A week's worth of the *Metro* and the *Sun* were scattered on the old brown settee, most of them folded to the TV page to save us from Brexit and Islamic fundamentalism overload. If *Homes & Gardens* ever did a feature and asked Rio to describe the look he'd gone for, shabby chic wouldn't cut it. Freshly burgled would be closer.

'Hurry up!' Rio yelled after me. 'Fuck sake.'

I headed up to the second floor and dumped my daysack and mobile on the bed. I wanted it to look and sound normal, us not wanting to stay in the house any longer than necessary. If Rio wanted us out, then I wanted us out.

Play safe. OK, so who was watching? Who was listening? What was going on? Fortunately, I really did need a piss. I got it over and done with quickly and noisily by aiming into the water, as Rio shouted even louder, 'It'll be fucking closed if we don't get a move on. Come on!'

'Yeah, yeah, yeah.' I bounced down the stairs, through the living room and on down the last flight, taking them two at a time until I was through the front door and he could start on the three deadlocks.

As casually as I could, I checked for bodies in the sea of parked cars. It would have been difficult for anyone to sit out there for any prolonged period. Curtains would twitch. Residents wouldn't reckon on an assassin sitting in the car, they'd think it was someone from TV Licensing, watching for the glow of a screen, or the Social checking if someone claiming disability allowance was mowing the lawn or doing a spot of street dance. I checked, too, for anyone walking past or waiting at the bus stop across the road, lips moving as they gave the 'stand by, stand by' into their mics.

The answer was no, but that didn't mean we weren't being watched. Airborne optics would be able to pick us up from so far away we wouldn't be able to see the helicopter platform.

We strolled towards the station and McDonald's. His good arm swung freely. The other had done nothing but hang ever since an IED attack in Afghanistan. Just like the other two, Gabe and Jack, he was a casualty of the post-9/11 wars.

Rio was annoyingly taller than me, and far too slim, considering the amount of food he shoved down his neck. The dreadlocks had come on quite well since his medical discharge from the infantry four years ago. He reckoned it would be just another year or so before he had enough to bunch up into a woolly hat.

He looked at me and forced a smile to reassure anyone watching that we were just bantering, but I could hear the strain in his voice. 'You left your mobile?'

As if.

'What's happened?'

'I got back from picking the kids up from school, and the tell-tales had fallen, all three of the fuckers.'

The last man out had to put broken cocktail sticks on the two landing doors, and another on the one that led from the living room up to the bedrooms. They were wedged into the gap between the top of the door and the frame so that they were held vertical. If the door was opened, its stick fell and, being so small, would never be noticed.

'Shit. You're still controlling your memory stick?'

He looked at me like I was mad. 'Course.' His face clouded. 'We should do what we said we would if he tried to fuck us up. Let's get the story out there and fuck up the Owl!'

I'd guessed this was coming. 'No, mate, it's too early. We don't know anything about anything yet. The only time we dump that int out there is when we're about to lose everything. Otherwise we lose any protection we have. We have leverage while we hold the int, but don't think we're bulletproof.'

All four of us had a memory stick that held the intelligence the Owl so desperately wanted never to be released into the public domain. But he had a problem. None of us four memory-stick holders knew where the other three were hidden, and Claudia held the fifth copy that all four of us would soon have access to. So far, that had kept us alive.

'The girls, mate. Phase two was seeing if the missus would let me bring them to the house after school – you know, have their tea at mine, then I'd take them home later.'

Rio had been busting a gut to form a friendly relationship with Simone. His focus was on keeping her onside so he could see the kids. He called her his missus but, really, she was his ex-girlfriend and mother of his seven-year-old twins. These were early days for him trying to reconnect but he'd felt he was winning her round. She had agreed he could pick them up and drop them off at school, and he had been perfect so far.

That was now history.

We took a left. Rio rubbed his face. 'He's been bugging and videoing the fucking house ever since we got back, hasn't he?'

'Don't assume anything. Look, I'm with you – it's probably the Owl trying to fuck us up. But it wouldn't make sense to re-enter the house if there were devices already planted – why risk compromising something that's already been a success? It doesn't matter why anyone was in the house, just that they were. All that matters is what we do about it, okay?'

Rio nodded slowly. He enjoyed learning this stuff. It wasn't brain surgery: it was just stripping away the rubbish that meant nothing and didn't help in working out what had happened and what we were going to do about it.

'You have to think, So what? So what if someone's

been in the house? What does that mean to us right now, this minute?'

Rio didn't need time to think. 'We play safe and pretend we don't know.'

'Yes. We stay passive, for now. We need to find out who and why for certain, then get proactive and cut it out like a cancer. But that's for another day. All that matters now is making sure we're all safe, because we don't know what his or their next move is.'

Today's lesson on how to live life while constantly in the shit had got Rio past his wave of emotion. 'We've got to tell Gabe, yeah? We need to make him safe, make his family safe.'

We passed the station and the golden arches came into view further up the South Circular.

I shot him a glance. 'And Jack.'

He shook his head. 'Mate, he's still fucking us all off. He's doing his own thing. Tortured artist and all that.' He gave a hollow laugh.

I split left, he split right around a couple of young women with buggies, toddlers dragged along in their wake.

'We'll get Gabe to talk to him. He'll listen to Gabe.'

Rio pushed the glass doors as we entered the kingdom of Chicken Legends and fries. For me, anyway. Rio always went for double whatever was on offer, times two.

5

We ordered at the touch screen, grabbed a booth, and Rio put the receipt on the veneered table next to the safe phone. We'd bought two of them from a CeX for forty pounds each in cash, along with a couple of PAYG SIM cards. We used WhatsApp. Most apps only encrypted messages between the sender and the app provider, but WhatsApp's encryption was end-to-end. It ensured that only you and the person you were communicating with could read what was sent and nobody else, not even WhatsApp. No wonder it was the go-to choice of communication for drug dealers and terrorists. For now, anyway.

Gabe was in Edinburgh, trying to patch things up with his wife and kids. From what Rio was telling me, the patches weren't sticking.

Rio was still visibly shaken by what was going on at this end. His eyes darted to the large window every time a body walked past. The streetlights came on, and soon he was getting jumpy about shadows as well.

'Mate, it's all right. No harm's going to come to the girls. Look, if this *is* the Owl . . .'

Rio took a breath, but now wasn't the time for yeah-buts.

'Hear me out, mate. If this *is* the Owl, that would make him stupid, and he's not, is he? His priority is to find all five of the memory sticks and take control of them. Why would he do anything that would provoke us into exposing what we have on them, yeah? So, if we switch on, stay focused on the situation, we keep safe.'

'What if he does get them, Nick? What happens then? We're fucked, aren't we? We're dead like the rest of them.'

A skinny boy, with enough zits on his face to fill a bucket, hovered while Rio lifted the mobile, then placed a tray between us on the table. He left to deliver the second tray he was carrying to a group of kids in my old school uniform. The boys were trying to be hard and the girls were being cool. Nothing had changed, just the lack of big collars, flares and, of course, platforms.

Rio was right that we'd be fucked – but we weren't there yet. 'All we've got to do is be on top of our game and make sure they're not found. In time, he's going to see we aren't a threat.'

Rio wasn't convinced and neither was I. But we couldn't undo the situation we were in because we didn't know who was on our case: the Owl, his bit of the CIA-within-the-CIA or whoever the fuck it was he worked for, or someone else altogether. Right now, all we could do was control what was happening in our lives based on what we knew.

Rio lifted the bun to his face and, as he always did, nibbled the onions that stuck out. He gazed out of the window in a trance, probably worrying about his girls.

'Let's get back to the real world, mate. Hello?' I waved a hand in front of the bun. 'Before Gabe logs on, yeah?'

He sort of nodded and looked down at the screen to check there was still power and signal.

'I've got real-world news. There's no luck with the cash. The lawyers, bankers, everyone seems to be making money out of the money I can't get to – not for now, anyway.'

Rio sucked sauce off his thumbs. 'So no little start-up, then?'

I shook my head so there was no doubt. He wouldn't let go of the idea. Maybe it was because my non-existent cash would provide the funding.

'C'mon, Nick. The Special Needs Service. The world needs our super-powers, mate.'

It got a laugh out of me as I dipped a chip into the mayo oozing out of my bun.

Gabe, Rio and Jack had all received payouts and a pension from the government for injuries sustained in Afghanistan, but they weren't life-changing amounts. They still had mortgages or rent to pay, families to feed, McDonald's and Poundland to keep in business. There wasn't much going on out there for an amputee. People might love them turning up at fundraisers, but the goodwill soon disappears.

I had no idea of Jack's circumstances, but I knew for sure they'd be much better than ours. He had dropped out of the group, which was a worry. We really needed to be close, to look after each other even more now. Gabe and Rio certainly had to stand on their own two feet for cash. Well, Rio did. Gabe had only one foot left.

The mobile sparked up and Gabe was on WhatsApp. He delivered his normal welcome: 'You fuckers there?'

Rio didn't bother picking up the phone, just tapped with his middle finger, the only one that wasn't covered with sauce. He tapped the keyboard again to signal to Gabe that he should get out of his hotel room before we made voice comms. Gabe was in a Travelodge by the airport on some fifty-quid-a-night deal where the only breakfast included was a sachet of coffee and a little pot of UHT milk. It was cheaper to stay there than rent near the house he paid the mortgage for. I was hoping he would join Fathers4Justice so we could see him on his roof dressed as a one-legged Superman.

We got the word 'Two' in reply and went back to our food.

Rio was still looking about, but it was safe here in the crowd. It would be very bad skills for an operator to come in after us, especially as they had us contained. We were sitting by a window, and there was no other way out than the way in. It would be easy to get a trigger on us from outside, and remain out of the line of sight.

Rio licked his fingers and picked up the mobile as it vibrated. Gabe was a minute late. I leant in to hit the reply button.

Rio liked talking with his mate, even if it was to take the piss. 'You're late. There's no early, no late, just on time. You're late.'

He smiled at the 'Fuck off' he got in reply, then handed over the mobile. I put it to my ear, speaking into a cupped hand, Japanese-style. 'Rio's tell-tales have been moved. You still got your memory stick?'

'Yeah, safe.' His tone was serious now: it was work time.

'Good to know we're all looking after ourselves. Listen, we'll leave the house, but not to come north – keep this shit away from your doorstep. We need to meet up and sort out a plan.'

Gabe was ahead of me. 'What about Jack? He know yet?'

'We need you to do that. He still taking your calls?'

Gabe said exactly what I was thinking. 'He'll take this one, whether he likes it or not.'

'But will he listen?'

'He'll listen. Call back in two hours. I'll grip Jack and you grip the gimp, OK?' He didn't wait for a reply before closing down.

I handed back the phone and Rio pocketed it. 'Getting out of Dodge, are we?'

I shoved the last of the bun down my neck. 'Yup, let's sort this shit out.'

We headed for the disco lights of the South Circular. There was a small fire in a corporation litter bin, but no one was taking any notice of it, apart from a couple of schoolkids who'd been in McDonald's earlier.

Rio was waiting for a plan. 'Come on, mate. What?'

'We pack a bag, get away from here. But we do it casually. Back to the house and talk about where we're going out tonight. Then I'll suggest we go away for a few days, both our lives being shit and all that. We

22

meet up with Gabe and Jack and get proactive, work out exactly who, what, where, when and why. Then we make sure they don't get away with it.'

We crossed the grass and, as Rio pulled out his jailer-size set of keys, his front door opened and three bodies spilt out. They saw us and it was Rio who spotted their reaction. 'Gun!'

6

Two bodies loomed up front; a third hung back. I kept my eyes on the one to the left. It wasn't a gun in his right hand. It was a Taser.

'Rio, run. Go for it. Run! Run!'

My eyes were glued to the lump of yellow plastic. Rio ran and so did I – straight at the Taser to stop it coming into the aim.

The dark shape holding it swung the weapon up. I jumped the final couple of metres, arms outstretched, head down so I didn't knock myself out on his body. I rammed into him, throwing my arms to pinion his to his waist. I powered my toes into the tarmac and kept running, semi-stooped. My momentum was too much for him and he fell back on the path.

As he went down he attempted to tilt his wrist. The Taser popped and I braced for the zap. Nothing happened. The barbs bounced off the tarmac as we made contact with the ground, my knuckles taking the first contact.

I kept my grip, head down, burying myself in his bulk. He bucked, trying to wrench his arms free. I held on, knowing what would come a millisecond later. A flurry of punches from one of the others, still upright, rained into my head, arms and back as he tried to haul me off his mate. I squeezed in tight as the body below still bucked and heaved. I kept my head down and took what was piling into me.

The fact it was a Taser was a good sign: it meant they didn't want us dead. If all four of us were being lifted at the same time, and Rio got away, there would be a memory stick in circulation and whoever else survived the lift would have some leverage.

I held on as the breathing of the body above me became laboured, his hands pulling hard at my arms as he worked to get me off his mate. My face was buried so hard in the man's stomach I had to fight for breath. His abs tensed, and a second later went soft, then tensed again in his effort to disentangle himself.

The hands let go of my arms now their owner had realized he wasn't going to move me with them. Kicks thudded into my legs. I took a big dead leg on the right. It didn't matter: so long as these two were focused on me, only one could be running after Rio.

I took the pain and held on. The one I was gripping dug his heels into the path and pushed. My knuckles scraped along the tarmac again. He could do what he wanted: I wasn't letting go.

Still no verbal reaction. I wanted to hear their accents. I wanted some indication of who they were.

I tilted my head just enough to free my mouth from his stomach. 'That all you got?'

No reaction. All I could hear were grunts and laboured breathing. Somebody in one of the houses must have seen what was going on but round here people would turn a blind eye. So what if a dealer or the TV Licensing guy got filled in? Eventually somebody would call the police, and these guys knew that as well as I did. They wanted out of this as much as I did.

The standing one's hands grabbed the back of my jacket and pulled. I didn't let go of his mate. He pulled even harder and I suddenly released my grip and he flew backwards.

In that instant, I got what I wanted.

A voice, clearly American, clearly East Coast. 'You fuck!'

7

Now was my time. I grabbed the body on the ground and pulled myself up level with his head. Teeth wide apart, I launched my face at his. Anywhere it landed would do. He jerked away at the last second and my top teeth hit his cheekbone. The bottom set got a bit of lobe. I closed my jaw like a vice.

He shook his head in disbelief, but that just made my job easier. All I had to do was stay connected, and if he carried on he'd rip his own face apart.

He froze, and I bit down harder in an attempt to close my bite completely. Blood oozed into my mouth; warm, metallic. My top teeth scraped down the side of his cheekbone. If they met their mates, they'd take a big chunk of skin out of him. He knew it, too, and so did the guy above me. He got to work, punching hard and fast into my head and shoulders. There was urgency about it: they had to resolve this situation. We were just fifteen metres from the South Circular.

And then the punches stopped as suddenly as they

had started. A second later, he toppled onto my legs.

Rio stood with a knife in his good hand, seven inches of KA-BAR Tactical.

He brought down the knife once again and I saw a blur towards the side of a thigh below me. I heard it make entry, with a sound from him like a muffled squeak.

The body went rigid as the pain swept through it. He tried hard not to scream but he couldn't help it. 'Fuck!'

Even if sirens didn't sound immediately, I didn't want to have to start dragging bodies about and planning how to dispose of all the evidence. I unclenched my teeth and pulled myself away from the face. 'Don't kill 'em! Don't kill 'em!'

We might have been in the middle of a major drama but death would bring us all into the real world. Dead bodies on a walkway can't be ignored for long.

Rio waggled the knife and yanked it free. It must have embedded itself in bone.

I spat blood as I kicked myself free of the bodies and grabbed hold of Rio's shoulders. 'We've got to go, mate.'

The front door of the house was still open and light spilt out of the hallway. On the first-floor landing there was movement.

I hobbled to the door, my body not yet recovered. Number Three saw me: tall, short blond hair, side parted, taking the first steps down towards the door, hands full of wires and, behind him, the fuse box ripped apart.

I slammed the door. 'Rio! Keys!'

He joined me, offering them up before holding his KA-BAR at the ready.

I snatched them from him and shoved in the first lever key. It was the wrong one and Rio knew it.

'Fuck sake.'

I broke it into little stages, concentrated on what I was doing. I got the next key in just as the blond with the side parting got to the door and grabbed the handle. I locked it.

'Let's go. On me.'

8

Rio might live there now but this had been my turf since I was a kid. I was leading us towards a dark pool of safety in the middle of London. The council always used to close it at dusk to stop the druggies, doggers and generally fucked-up people having their own play space at night. They all went there anyway, so we'd just do what they did and jump the fence.

Rio was never more than a stride or two behind me as we sprinted down an alleyway. My legs were getting their lives back with the help of adrenalin. It wasn't just about getting as much distance as we could between ourselves and the drama that might still be following us. It's never about straight lines. I wanted to put in as many angles as possible. If we could come to a junction with four options, it would make their job more difficult: they'd have a larger area to cast about in and would have to split forces.

As soon as I got to the end of the alleyway I was going to chuck a left or a right, I didn't know which yet, and run as fast as I could until I hit another set of options.

We took the left at the end, then dived down another alleyway to the right.

Rio was lagging. 'Nick, hold up.'

We were between a couple of three-storey blocks of 1960s flats, and I took the chance to lean against the wall that made up the end of the terrace and bend down, arse against the brick, hands on knees, grabbing as much oxygen as I could. My face leaked sweat to mix with the blood around my mouth and chin.

Rio still had the knife in his hand. He grabbed a discarded Greggs bag and wiped it clean.

I pointed at the blade. 'What the fuck?'

'South London, mate. Every council-tax payer should be issued with one of these round here.'

He folded the paper to produce a clean bit and handed it to me. Sirens sounded in the distance, no doubt heading for whatever drama was left at the front of the house. If the two stabbed lads had a couple of brain cells between them, they would have dragged themselves into whatever they'd arrived in and made distance, just like us two. The blond one in the house would have switched the lights off and sat it out, unless he'd already jumped out of a first-floor window. His choice.

Rio had managed to get his breathing back to irregular rather than gasping. 'What the fuck they doing in the house?'

'Putting devices in. Maybe audio-visual. Who knows? But the third? He was trying to get them out when we turned up and compromised them. The first

31

entry, when they tripped the tell-tales, was the CTR, the second was placing the fucking things.'

I'd done quite a few close-target recces to place devices over the years, and it was never as easy as it should have been. Hiding them was hard enough because people moved things, broke things and, if they were aware, would be actively looking. But even when a good location was found, there was the question of powering the things. Batteries needed replacing, which meant more CTRs and the risk of compromise. Wiring them into the mains took time and had to be recced. If possible, it was always best to get power from an external source like the next-door neighbour, slowly drilling through the wall to expose their power lines. An aware target wouldn't moan about people not turning the immersion heater off at night because it was costing too much: they'd start looking for a device that was using power.

Rio still had a we're-in-the-shit face on that I had to change in case it progressed to stage two: outright flapping.

'But that's a good thing, mate. It means the other two aren't getting lifted. It's all about information. It's the Owl, it has to be, trying to find the memory sticks, not killing us. That would come after.'

As I wiped the blood off my face I could smell the greasy pastry or whatever had been wrapped in the bag. The raw skin of my knuckles stung like I'd stuck my hand in a wasps' nest, but I'd sort them out when there was time.

Rio was thinking instead of flapping. 'Mate, the best way is to cut through Brockwell Park, come out at Brixton.'

'Great minds. Use the dark.' From Brixton we could bus it, Tube it or train it out of the area. 'Then we call Gabe. We should meet up near Jack's. All of us need to keep safe, keep together, start getting proactive on the Owl. It has to be him.'

Rio just nodded, wanting to save what oxygen he had in him for moving.

It felt strange having to articulate what was in my head, after so many years of working alone, but it wasn't unwelcome. Maybe that was why I liked the three survivors. They understood the piss-taking, the vocab, and the mindset. The downside was having to be responsible for more than just myself – but if I got us all thinking the same way maybe it was an upside. Maybe it really was time to be part of something again.

The blue lights strobed the skyline, joining the rest of the light pollution over the rooftops around the area of Rio's house.

I threw the paper bag at him and got moving.

Rio grinned. 'I told you it was him, didn't I? You gotta listen to me, mate. I know shit.'

'That's right.' I grinned back. 'Shit is all you know.'

9

We dodged through the Challice Way housing estate.

The mass of red brick had been thrown up after the Second World War, and the vans with ladders padlocked on their roofs and signs on the back saying they held no tools overnight gave a hint about who lived there now. From the range of cars parked up, satellite-dish installation paid well.

We aimed next for the Cressingham Gardens estate, on the south-west corner of Brockwell Park. Once there, and over the fence, all we'd have to do was head up and over the grass hill to the safety of Brixton and its public transport.

It took only five minutes to cover the ground, and it was easy to find a section of fence with lumps missing. It was obviously a bit of a rat-run for the nightlife. I waited for Rio in the semi-gloom and he wasn't far behind. I held out a hand and he gripped it with his good one and scrambled over.

While we stood there for a few seconds catching our

breath, I wiped my hands on the dewy grass to clean the grit out of the wounds and let the clear liquid gunge oozing out of my grazed knuckles do whatever it did to wounds. Straight away, they were back in the wasps' nest.

The hum of traffic was perforated by an occasional scream or shout, just kids fucking about on the street. Then came a big hiss of air as a bus loaded and unloaded somewhere.

I gave Rio a couple more seconds to recover while I wiped my face clean with my jacket sleeve. 'You ready, mate?'

'Yep.'

'Right, let's go.'

I turned to cross the grass and pick up a path, but Rio grabbed my shoulder. 'This way, Nick. It's quicker.' He pointed. 'There's a strip of park behind some houses that leads right onto Brixton Water Lane – piece of piss.'

We reached the high ground and the whole of London unfolded below us. Bright lights burnt inside the Shard, the GPO Tower, the Gherkin, Canary Wharf and the Walkie-Talkie, the curved one the sun had reflected off, setting fire to the Jaguars parked nearby. Where we stood was like a location for spies to meet, rather than a couple of dickheads running for a getaway on a bus. Below us, millions of real people were heading home for the day or packing the bars. I wouldn't have minded joining them.

We started downhill, towards the streetlights of Brixton and red and white lights of nose-to-bumper traffic. I hadn't been to this bit of the park since I was fourteen or fifteen. My mates and I used to hang about the lido, one eye on the girls' bodies, the other on their handbags. The place was minging back then, everyone covered with baby lotion for a quick fry-up, their dog-ends bobbing up and down in the water. Not that many went in: it was far too cold.

Rio led the way towards the rear of the lido. His route took us past a group of teenagers smoking, drinking and generally pissing about. They didn't like the idea of two strangers invading their space.

'Fucking paedos, fuck off!'

We let them have their little victory and kept going.

There was a narrow strip of grass with a pathway, wrought-iron gates at the end, leading onto Brixton Water Lane. A bus trundled past; the pavement was busy.

Rio came right up close to me and stopped. 'Mate, I need to go and see the girls, tell them I won't be around for a while. Taking them to school's been working really well. I don't want to screw it up by just disappearing. Mate, they're only round the corner, I won't be long.'

He had manufactured the route for us to be at this gate. 'This where you bring them?'

He nodded – he knew that I knew.

'No problem. Just don't tell her anything. Remember, the Owl won't do anything to the girls. It's counter-productive involving the real world. And it'd turn you into a bigger problem, because then you're pissed off and can't be controlled, so neither can your memory stick.

'We'd do exactly the same, yeah? We wouldn't go out there and start involving the real world.'

A Polish truck's air brakes hissed and its driver screamed at a bunch of hoodies on BMXs who'd stopped in front of him. They had decided he was a wanker and started shouting that he'd get kicked out of the country immediately after the referendum.

I got us back to our world. 'So, where we going?'

'The estate. Effra Parade, just up the road – you know it?'

I did, but I issued a health warning. 'They'll be checking known locations now they've lost us. You know that, don't you?'

Rio was nearing another bit of rat-run fence, ready to jump over it. 'Yeah, but they won't hurt anyone but us, right?'

He'd take the chance regardless. Nothing I said would sway him.

10

This end of Effra Parade had never been as swanky as the name suggested, but as we went on, the houses that had been in a shit state when I was a kid were now double-glazed and freshly painted. The corner shop next to the butcher's had become a bathroom supplier with a roll-top tub in the window. People always moaned about a traditional area losing its character, but nine times out of ten they were the ones who'd taken the money and run.

Rio tugged my sleeve. 'Mate, listen. Thanks for getting your bollocks out back there – fronting up so I could do a runner.'

Serious never sounded right coming from him. I pulled away before the tug became a full-on hug. Or, rather, half a hug. 'No problem.'

He wasn't giving up. 'But you knew I wasn't gonna leg it, didn't you? You knew I'd back you, yeah?'

I nodded. 'But you still fucked up. It was all about keeping one of our memory sticks safe. If it was the other way round all you would have seen was the soles of my boots.'

It took a second to sink in, then he laughed. 'Yeah, fucked up there, didn't I?'

We were approaching a three-storey brown brick on the right and Rio's voice dropped to nervous. 'Nick, I won't be long – I can't be. The missus won't let me in the flat, and the boyfriend gets pissed off.'

He hit an intercom button and I held out a hand. 'Give us the mobile. I'll get hold of Gabe.'

He dug it out as a female voice answered suspiciously, 'Hello?'

Rio leant into the grille. 'It's me. Listen, I've got to—'

'You can't just turn up here like this. You don't live here any more.'

'I know. I'm away for a while. I've got some work. I just want to see the girls, say goodbye. I'll be five minutes. I can't take them to school. Just five minutes. Please, Simone.'

I'd met her once, and she'd seemed okay to me. Switched on, as you'd have to be to put up with three kids, Rio being one of them. The intercom still crackled but nothing was coming back from Simone.

I powered up the safe phone.

She came back on. 'Okay, five minutes. But you're not coming in. Go to the balcony.'

Rio didn't wait for her to change her mind. He jumped the fence and ran to the corner of the block. Simone's flat was on the ground floor. A steel grille was screwed into the brickwork to keep the kids in and, more to the point round here, to keep intruders out.

I hit WhatsApp and texted away: *You there, fuckhead?*

I'd found it easy to fall back into the military world of piss-taking and insults. If Gabe didn't open with an expletive, I'd be worried something was wrong. And, besides, I enjoyed it, a bit like running around South London this last couple of weeks. It felt like home.

'Daddy! Daddy!' The girls burst onto the elevated balcony. The grille between them made it look like a prison visit, except it was the girls who were caged up.

Simone stood guard in the doorway, keeping a wary eye on Rio, who was now on tiptoe to get level with the kids. Rio might be shit as a boyfriend, but he was one of the few men I knew who could instantly recall his kids' birthdays. The girls were in the same class at school, and he knew the name of their teacher. How many dads round here could you say that about?

I kept my distance for two reasons. The first was that Simone hadn't warmed to Rio's new mate the one time we'd met. Her exact words were 'You look like trouble.' I hadn't chatted much. I didn't want her to find out I came from round there and had maybe even gone to the same school as her girls, in case she took them away from the area to stop them growing up like me. The second was that I wanted to stand back and keep my eyes open, in case known locations really were being checked.

WhatsApp came back to me. *What you want, gimp? Nah, it's the other one. Call, but outside.*

I didn't have to wait long. 'Listen – we compromised a CTR at Rio's. They were placing a device. You okay?'

'All good. Nothing's happened here. I still can't go to the house so they wouldn't have bothered with that. A hotel, any fucker can come in and out. But I never make calls in the room – the walls are like fucking paper.'

I could see past Simone and into the flat, where a sixty-inch flat-screen filled a wall. In front of it a human landfill was slumped on a sofa with a party pack of Walkers. His shadow alone would have weighed at least two stone. Maybe Simone liked him for his personality.

'You still got your memory stick?'

Anything I ever said to Gabe was taken as an insult. 'Fuck off!'

'What about Jack? He all right?'

'Of course he's not. He sits there being arty with beer cans and thinking too much.'

'You get hold of him?'

'He knows we're coming but doesn't give a fuck. He doesn't want to meet. But I'll sort it. I'll meet you two in that poncy pub. You remember?'

I did. 'Don't tell him what happened at Rio's, okay? Let's not freak him out any more than he normally is.'

I stayed back for the last couple of moments of prison farewells before we headed for the Tube.

11

Elephant Hotel, Pangbourne

To Gabe the bar was poncy, but to the locals it was probably as perfect as a Sunday colour supplement. Perfect shops, perfect pubs, perfect boarding school up the road, perfect horses on pothole-free roads.

Rio sat the other side of the round pine table, guzzling his second bottle of Beck's and third packet of sea salt with a dash of balsamic. It should have been a Blue this time of the morning but he wouldn't hear of it. We'd finished breakfast a couple of hours ago.

We'd stayed there last night after catching the last train from Paddington. We travelled there separately on the Tube, and from two different stations. We didn't phone ahead to the hotel and we didn't get a cab from the station. Gabe didn't know it yet but he was paying for the rooms and, tactically, that made sense. It was better than drawing cash from an ATM, either here or back in Brixton, where CCTV cameras could have followed us all the way to Pangbourne. Until Gabe got there we had enough cash between us to buy a tube of toothpaste and a toothbrush each as soon as the shops opened. We'd frittered away our last reserves on beer and crisps.

Rio's party trick was tying a knot one-handed in the empty bags, then hurling them at the nearest target. The latest had landed in my lap.

'How many packets you going to eat? She's not going to take you back just because you've got a lard arse like that fat fucker.'

Rio sat back in his chair. 'If he fell down, he'd rock himself to sleep trying to get up.' He thought of another. 'He's so fat, when he goes to McDonald's they have to call Burger King for back-up.' He giggled, but you didn't have to be Jeremy Kyle to see it was hurting.

'Why's Simone with him?'

He reached forward and picked up the Beck's. 'Reliable, mate. That's what he is. He's got a job, doesn't go out on the piss, doesn't fuck about, doesn't do drugs.' He took a couple of gulps, but kept the bottle in his hand. 'She's had problems. A bit of dope, then coke. It was starting to fuck her up, fuck the girls up a bit, too, because they didn't like what it did to her.'

'So she's got the fat fuck instead of a therapist?'

He nodded. 'He's doing far better than I could, old Jamel. He's got her on chocolate instead of coke. He's steady, and that means the girls are at home and not in care. I know it's over with Simone . . . She's better off with him, and so are the girls. I just gotta get my head around it.' He studied the bottle in his hand, so intently I wondered if he was working out how to tie a knot in it. 'Rock steady. Something I suspect we're not, eh?'

The door opened behind me with a rush of wind, and Rio smiled. 'Including him.'

Gabe was wearing his default I've-got-the-hump face, as if someone had just crashed into his car. He'd shaved his head since I'd last seen him. Goodbye, acne-scarred ginger monk, hello, head-banger. With his prosthetic leg making all five foot five of him look as if he'd already had a few drinks, he waved a finger at the girl behind the bar. 'Stella, please, darling.'

Rio waved his bottle. 'Another of these, and a frothy one for the Cappuccino Queen here. And two more crisps.'

Gabe kept his black fleece jacket on as he dragged a chair beside me so we both faced Rio. He preferred to get hot and have something to complain about.

'When you two get in?'

I fished in my inside pocket for something I'd prepared once we'd arrived. 'Last night, mate. I even wrote you and him a love letter each.'

I passed them each an envelope. I'd found them among the stationery that sat on my desk next to the biscuit and the hotel pad and pen, and they both now contained a message. 'She's got the fifth memory stick. It's now in Zürich. Each of you has a different pass statement, which you keep to yourself – the same goes for Jack. So if life goes totally tits-up, we've got Claudia as back-up. If any of you ID yourself and give her your statement, she'll do the rest.'

I took the drinks as they were delivered.

'The statements are different for everyone. Memorize yours and give the paper back to me so I know they've been destroyed. Come on, you've seen the films.'

They were seven-word statements. Car registration plates and phone numbers are seven figures for a reason: our brains can take in seven items and remember them solidly, plus or minus two. A couple of thick people find seven too difficult, a couple of clever ones might be able to get an extra two, but seven really is life's lucky number.

Rio's was: *I quite like the vivid colour red.*

Gabe's was: *Blue always reminds me of the sea.*

They clinked their glasses in a toast they'd clearly used many times: 'Gives us something to blame everything on.'

I stirred my cappuccino with the finger of shortbread from the saucer, and let Gabe take a few swigs of his drink, then got back to the real world. 'So what did Jack say? He any better?'

Gabe put his glass down and his face clouded. 'Nah, mate. He's worse.'

12

Jack had changed his mind about the four of us keeping close, and had gone to live with his mother. Well, kind of.

Gabe started the next crisp-fest. Rio watched him for a while, then started a one-to-one. It didn't worry me: they had history, rehabilitating at Hedley Court with Jack, way before I'd fucked about with their lives a couple of months ago.

'You know the problem with Jack? Too much education.' He tapped the side of his head with a finger, leaving a couple of crisp crumbs behind. 'Makes him think too much.'

Gabe nodded, clearly wanting more.

'Now his dad's gone, no matter the reason, he should be feeling good – freer. The fucker, treating him like he wasn't good enough. Anyway, he's dead, and that's good for Jack, right?'

Gabe couldn't have agreed more.

Rio was waiting for a unanimous decision. 'I'm right, yeah?'

I'd thought the conversation was just between the two, but I agreed anyway. Rio liked that. 'See, you two should listen to me.' He tapped the side of his head again. 'I get what makes people tick, know what I mean?'

Now Jack was free of his father's overbearing ways, he should have been feeling like a weight had lifted. But he didn't, and his relationship with his mother wasn't any less fraught. Maybe she thought Jack resented her for not supporting him against his dad when he was younger. And then, when she was told that her husband was dead after an accident in the Arctic, the only way she could deal with it was to vent her anger and grief on her son. I didn't care about her. I just worried about Jack.

We all needed to stay tight.

I downed the last of the brew and turned to Gabe. 'So what did you say to him?'

'That we all needed to meet up somewhere neutral. But he fucked me off.' Gabe knew what I was about to say but kept going because I would have wasted my breath. 'Look, I told him about last night, okay? I had to – it got him to meet. But at his place.'

All I could do was shrug.

Rio turned to Gabe for another one-to-one. 'Last night was a fucker, mate. I checked the news and there wasn't a thing.'

Gabe nodded down to Rio's waist. 'You still carrying?'

'Dead right, mate, it's my other arm.'

'Dump it! Get a new one. Forensics! You never seen *CSI*?'

Rio sat back and laughed, a little too loudly for the

space. 'Yeah, yeah, but no. I'm not binning it. It's special. I swapped it for my nappy with a Yank marine in Bastion. Cost me both tiers.'

Rio was talking about the groin protection the army issued during the war. Tier One were boxers that looked like black cycling shorts but were made from ballistic material. They were ultra-lightweight but could stop most small pieces of shrapnel and dirt travelling at high velocity after a blast. Tier Two looked like the world's biggest camouflaged Pampers nappy and was worn over the trousers. When men get blown into the air the first thing they do when they come down is stick a hand inside to check they still have what's needed if they stay alive.

Gabe wasn't having any of it. 'I heard you didn't need your nappy anyway.' He turned to me in case I didn't get it. 'No bollocks.' He sat back and waited for the abuse to come from across the table. But none did, just a big smile and a knotted crisps packet.

I knew we'd be there all day if we didn't get things moving. 'So, what we need to worry about now is getting Jack on board with us, okay? We'll be better protected if we're stuck together like glue.'

Gabe picked up his glass to finish. 'Yeah, but what we going to do about this Falcon fuck?' He winked at Rio.

'Lads. It's not a falcon, it's the Owl. Let's wait until we're at Jack's and I'll explain. You two thick fucks just need to remember the shit on the paper. It'll give you enough of a headache for today.'

I looked at Gabe as I stood up. 'Seeing as I've spent all my cash on you two, Crisps Boy can't use his card, and you have a big fat pension . . .'

He wasn't impressed. 'The rooms as well? It just cost me a fortune driving down here to Gymkhana Land.'

Rio got to his feet. 'Shut up, you tight, mumbling midget. You just keep filling the tank and paying our way. You should be grateful we're here to protect you from the nasty men.' He grabbed my arm as he headed to the bar. 'Nick, all that talk about bollocks got me thinking. That Claudia. She married? Can you put in a word?'

13

Gabe steered us out of the town and it wasn't long before we were in a world of perfect hedgerows, grass and horses that looked like Grand National winners.

He drove a faded blue Jeep Cherokee, the square-shaped model. The T-reg four-litre engine drank fuel like there was a hole in the tank, which the Jock in him complained about non-stop. He had to put up with it, though. It was only the combination of it being left-hand drive, automatic and the right seat height that meant he was capable of driving the monster, and swinging his feet out easily and directly onto the pavement.

Now he was searching his pockets and we knew what was on its way. His pack had run out so as soon as he'd got to the Jeep he'd rummaged around in the crumpled collection of sweatshirts and socks in his daysack. At least he'd come to the pub prepared, but we'd made him stub it out before we got in the car. Even so, the inside reeked after his two-pack drive from Edinburgh.

Rio was in the front with him. He made a grab for the cigarette in Gabe's mouth and powered down his window. 'For fuck's sake, go ahead and die but don't take us with you.'

Gabe was too quick for him. He jerked his head, and smoke engulfed us. Then he powered up the windows. 'Whose fucking wagon is it?' The cigarette bobbed up and down in his mouth. 'Who's paying for the gas? It's you two's fault I started again so shut the fuck up. Besides . . .'

He took another lungful before emptying it once more into what was now an airlock of Jeep. 'If we're seen by the police with the windows down they'll have us as drug dealers, ready to dump the gear if we're followed. With Rambo and his knife in here, we don't exactly look like National Trust members, do we?'

Rio was up for it. 'Cos I can't afford to join, can I? All my money goes up north to pay for you Jocks' free prescriptions and university.'

I let the two of them eat each other as I worked out the best way to pitch them and Jack an idea that had been bubbling away.

Rio had another attempt at getting the offending object out of Gabe's mouth. 'Mate, I'm doing you a favour. Your missus won't have you back if you're sucking on that shit.' He gave up and sat back. 'So how's it going up there?'

A long sigh came out of Gabe's mouth, which sent an extra puff of smoke into the wagon. I tried to power down my window but the child lock was on.

'Hard work, mate. Hard fucking work. She says she wants to try again to become a family, but only if I

51

keep saying sorry for everything. It's not all me, is it?'

Rio couldn't restrain a chuckle. 'Course it is, you fucking midget. I told you, just agree with her, don't go on the piss, and smile. That's all you have to do. You need to learn from me and my wonderful domestic situation.'

After ten more minutes of them doing this, instead of memorizing Claudia's contact details and their statements, Gabe pulled up at a set of solid wooden gates with an intercom on a post level with the driver's window. He pressed and there was no answer. Ever the prime candidate for any job in the Diplomatic Corps, he pressed again and shouted, 'For fuck's sake, get a move on.'

The gates opened to usher us into a world of gravelled drives, with a Georgian manor house two hundred metres away. It was big and rectangular, with huge four-paned windows. There was even a peacock. We were in murder-mystery country.

We weren't going to the family pile, however, or what was left of it. Asset-rich, money-poor was the term that came to mind. About a hundred metres further on, the crunch of gravel stopped as we turned off into a concrete courtyard that was edged with newly reno-vated outbuildings. We parked up between a muddy fifteen-year-old Land Rover and a shiny 5-series BMW estate. Both vehicles had meshed fences at the back and we quickly saw what they were designed to keep in the boot. Two big brown Labradors with aged white muzzles ranged up to see what all the commotion was about, but it took them a while. They were not just old, they had eaten all the pies.

Once Rio had opened the rear door for me, because that was also child-locked, I climbed out of the Cherokee and its overflowing ashtray.

I pulled out the safe phone and threw it onto the back seat. 'Lads, have you got one with you? If so, better leave them here.'

They looked at each other and slowly shook their heads for effect. *What a dickhead.*

Looking down the driveway at the back of the house, I saw movement at one of the upstairs windows. A woman in her sixties was trying to stay in the shadows as she checked out the detectives. In a murder mystery, she would have gone straight onto the list of suspects. I definitely had to stop watching daytime TV.

There was no way Jack's mother would be coming out to greet us. She had a downer on us. She'd made it very plain to Jack that we were trouble. We were responsible for him going to the North Pole. On top of that we were responsible for the death of her husband – and probably for her blocked gutters as well. That was fine, as long as she didn't come out and confront us with it. Gabe needed more time to get the hang of 'agree, smile and move on'.

14

We walked across the concrete with the Labradors just about keeping up. Jack came towards us from the door of a long single-storey renovated barn, which was clearly where the dogs spent most of their day. In the open porch, there were water and food bowls, and a couple of big flat cushions with so much old dog hair on them they looked like roadkill.

Jack had put on quite a bit of lard to match the dogs. His hair was even more of a curly mat than it had always been. He needed a shave, and a sweater that didn't let his brown checked shirt escape at the elbows.

He was still only in his late twenties, but wore the look of someone much older. He wasn't alone in that – I'd seen it before on any number of once-fresh faces, after a bit of shot and shell, when their owners were facing a new set of battles back in so-called civilization. He'd been through a lot for someone so young and this drama wouldn't have been helping him.

I held back, letting Gabe and Rio be first in. Gabe

already had his hand out. 'How are you, big man?'

Jack had installed CCTV since we were last here, when he'd spoken nicely but basically fucked us off. He was in denial, thinking that if he cut away from our world, probably the whole world, all would be good.

Rio didn't follow Gabe's lead and shake hands. Instead he kicked the titanium under Jack's jeans hard enough for everyone to hear the clunk, then wrapped his arm around his mate.

Jack's replacement leg was a much better fit. What was probably the last of the family money and a trip to the world's top prosthetics designers in the States had seen to that. Not for him one of the NHS lumps of metal and plastic that Gabe had to fight with every time he wanted to fix it to his stump.

Rio released himself with a slap to Jack's face. 'Good to see you, mate. You getting the kettle on or what?'

Jack sort of nodded, then held out a hand to me. 'Last night – you two okay?'

We shook. 'Yeah, but Rio did all the work.'

Jack looked in worse shape close-up. There were dark bags under his eyes, and his hair and beard weren't anguished-artist or hippie-cum-hipster but pure neglect. He could have done with a couple of laps around the bath, and a squirt of Head & Shoulders.

I checked. 'The CCTV? It's online?'

He sighed. He knew what was coming next. 'No, and I'm not staying outside. Look, no one's been here, and I've got no sneaky-beaky watching or listening to me. You think I don't understand the shit we're in?' He turned back to the cameras covering the courtyard and porch. 'Nick, you're all here because Gabe said it was important, and what happened last night means it clearly is – but I'm not standing out here. It's safe, okay, so we go inside or you just leave.'

If the Owl was listening, it wouldn't be that damaging for him to hear what I was going to suggest to them. But I wanted us to keep control of the idea: knowledge is power, and all that.

'Okay, I get it, but all Wi-Fi, mobiles off, yeah?'

Jack nodded and Gabe started towards the door with Rio a step behind, leaning forward to get into Gabe's ear but making sure we all heard him anyway. 'I don't see the problem. He talks shite anyway.'

Gabe agreed. 'At least we can get a fucking brew on.'

I followed Jack inside, the two dogs slobbering at his heels. There was a strong smell of paint and canvas from all the half-finished works, but the studio wasn't exactly a hovel where rats roamed while Jack suffered for his art. Even the sculpture made out of beer cans had used San Miguel. I recognized the pose: *The Falling Soldier*. It was the one in the picture taken by Robert Capa during the Spanish Civil War. The Republican fighter was dropped with a single round and Capa snapped as he fell, both arms thrown open wide as the man's body was pushed back on impact and his rifle flew from his hand.

That was where the struggle ended. The long barn had sand-blasted oak beams and an oak floor, and the renovated walls were spotlessly white. There was a flat-screen TV on the wall that would have been the envy of Effra Parade, and a Mac laptop on a big oak table. In fact I counted three laptops, among discarded clothes on the floor next to an unmade bed. Maybe Tracey Emin was one of his influences.

A door was open into what was clearly the bathroom, a plastered square of stud wall in the far corner. Even the hinges on that were stainless steel, demonstrating there was no lack of provision here. His family had had it built while he was in rehab, but there'd been nothing they could do to stop him looking like a bag of shit with bad hair.

Rio disconnected the Wi-Fi cable from the wall jack, then checked the TV wasn't connected.

Gabe made his way over to the kitchen, a small, open-plan area that had all the gear, even down to a coffee machine George Clooney would have given the nod to. He filled the kettle from a water-purifier jug.

Jack might think I was paranoid, but anything online could be used as a microphone. On a phone, any mobile app with a mic option could be used as a listening device.

The old-fashioned ways were still popular, too. From an outside wall, ultra-sensitive drills were capable of auto-stopping just as the drill bit sensed the interior paint, so when a miniature mic was inserted into the wall it couldn't be seen from inside the building.

There were devices that could zoom into everyday items in a target room, a bag of crisps, a sheet of paper on a desk, vibrating as a conversation took place nearby; it could be used as an amplifier to listen to what was being said. I was right to be paranoid: there was nowhere a conversation could be covert if enough effort had been put in, and we were clearly at the top of the Owl's effort list.

The paintings were all dark, I thought, but Rio wasn't so restrained. He held out his hand and spun around to include them all in one question. 'Mate, what the fuck is all this about? You been inspired by George W.? He's just fucked everyone off and started painting to find his soul, repent for his sins or whatever.'

Jack smiled. What did we know? We weren't artistic and were never going to understand. He dragged himself across the room, shoulders slumped. It had nothing to do with his disability. He was physically exhausted. He put his arse on his bed and the dogs followed suit, collapsing on the floor at his feet and letting out a sigh. They'd had such a hard day, walking out to the cars.

Rio and I sat on a grey sofa facing him. Gabe carried on making the brews, opening the cupboards, rooting around. 'Fuck me, Jack – c'mon, where's the biscuits?'

He got no answer. Jack had decided to lie down, picking up his prosthetic leg and putting it down next to the good one, then pulling up his cargoes to get to the joint of metal and meat.

I thought we needed to get down to it. 'So, Jack, what about the house? Anything happened up there?'

He shook his head. 'Nothing. It's not as if I go up there or my mother comes here.' He flung out an arm and pointed at the desk. 'Before you ask, I've still got control of my stick. And I'm not going to tell you where it is because none of you wants to know. But look over there, at the desk. You see how the light is coming through? I'm doing what you told me, Nick. I'm using the dust.'

I could see Jack wasn't one for running round with a can of Pledge, and that was a good thing. He was doing exactly what I'd said. A tiny piece of Sellotape across a door, things arranged in a certain way inside a vehicle, the position of a mouse on a mouse-pad, a hair trapped in a drawer, whatever: if they were not as you'd left them, you'd have a rethink. But you could use dust, too, to see if anyone had been messing around. Sunlight on a TV screen or shelves could show if anything had been moved.

Jack continued as the leg came apart and he placed the amazing piece of technology beside the bed, next to the dogs. His stump wasn't red or worn the way that Gabe's sometimes was with his NHS special. Jack's looked more like the neatly tied end of an uncooked sausage. 'I don't use any other tell-tales because I don't go anywhere. It's not as if I take the dogs on long walks, is it? Or go out for romantic dinners.'

Gabe brought the mugs over to Rio and me, his face screwed up as he passed the dogs. 'For fuck's sake, man! Stop feeding them meat. Jesus. You can get your own brew – I'm not going back over there.' He shook his head, as if that would save him from the gas cloud, which, no doubt, was heading our way. At least it got a smile out of Jack, who had been staring at the ceiling.

Gabe perched himself on one of the kitchen stools dotted around the place. Jack wouldn't have been able to stand in the same spot all day, painting all this moody shit.

I picked up my 'Don't Panic, Carry on and Paint' mug, walked over to the bed and laid an Elephant Hotel envelope on his chest.

'The spare memory stick. Each of us now has her number, and a different statement to identify ourselves.

Once you've done that, she'll release the stick to the media. I need the paper back from you before we leave. But you're bright. It'll take those two longer to get it into their thick heads so they already have theirs.'

Jack's statement was *I think my favourite colour is yellow*, but judging by the canvases around the place, I should have chosen either black or navy. I headed back to the sofa, and the dogs went back into dream mode after their gas raid.

I sat on the edge, mug on my thigh. 'Look, the reason we're here is that we all have to keep together and get proactive, sort it out. The way out of this shit, gents, is to get close to the Owl. Close to the power . . .' I sat back, and prepared for the honk storm. 'We need to work for him.'

I didn't have long to wait.

15

Gabe was like a big bottle of Coke a kid had dropped a Mento into, then screwed the cap back on. An explosion was imminent.

'We should be staying well clear of that fuck, just keep protecting ourselves, getting on with our lives.' He turned on Rio with an accusing finger. 'This is your fault. SNS – shit idea. What an arsehole.'

'Thank you. You need arseholes like me or you'll never get shit done.' Rio sat back and smiled, hoping to get even more of a honk out of Gabe. He did.

Gabe's finger jutted at me now. 'You can tell the Falcon, or whatever the fuck he's called, if he doesn't back off . . .'

Rio couldn't help a smile and a slow nod. He liked the new name. Gabe now pointed his accuser at Jack, to make sure we were all involved. It finally came to rest on me. 'So, you go and tell him, if he doesn't fuck off and leave us alone, I'll be the one on the phone talking shite to Switzerland and taking that fucking information worldwide.'

Jack started the long procedure of getting up, and the dogs stirred too, suddenly very excited as they rolled onto their fat stomachs.

I expected Rio to weigh in, but he said nothing and concentrated on his brew. I tried to explain, as calmly as I could: 'We've been pushed into a corner. There's only one thing to do and that's to turn around and fight, but just with our heads.' I held a fist at Gabe. 'None of this – not yet, anyway.'

I dropped my hand to the sofa and continued, trying to get my points over as quickly as I could before they all decided I was mad and started to climb aboard me. 'The easiest way out of this is to get close to the Owl. We need to be in his tent, pissing out. All of us need to be working for him because then we show him we're not a threat. The SNS idea is a good way of doing that.'

Rio perked up, but I had to make one thing clear. 'We're not calling it that. Okay, back to it. We don't want a repeat of last night. If one of us, or them, lands up dead it'll mean more drama. And that is what we're trying to avoid, more fucking drama. I think we've got enough for now.

'Look, it's ninety-nine point nine per cent recurring that it's the Owl who's fucking us about, but we don't know for certain. That's another reason why we should approach him – because if it isn't, we've got another problem to sort out and we might need his help.

'All I'm talking about is a mutual contract with him, because we need to think about this shit from his point of view. I think he'd like the idea of having us close by, having us onside. We need him to feel comfortable. We need him to feel it's not worth his while trying to fuck us over.'

Gabe took a breath but I pushed on. 'At the same time, he still needs to understand that we can fuck him over. Think of it as a new Cold War. We are four independent nuclear deterrents, like four Trident subs, just floating about, not hurting anyone. We're ready to strike if ever one of us comes under attack, right? And on top of that, each of us has access to another Trident sub that will also attack if one of us gives the order.

'The Owl has two problems in getting the memory sticks back, then getting rid of us. First, he must make sure all of us are lifted at the same time so that none of us can attack by releasing the int. And second, even if he does lift us all at once he still doesn't control the memory sticks, and that's what he wants. The sticks first, then get rid of us.

'So what we're offering is assured mutual destruction and neither side wants that, right? And, icing on the cake, we'd get paid.

'Finally, what we all need is . . . a purpose. Look at you two.' I pointed at Rio and Gabe. 'You're scrubbing around, trying to grab onto your families, or bits of them, because you want some purpose, to feel loved and respected. I get it. It's what humans crave. But, deep down, you know that isn't going to happen without you changing, right? Those two women, they can see when a runaway train's coming towards them. That's why you were out on your arses in the first place, and that's why you're going to be out on your arses permanently unless there are changes.'

Jack had got himself upright on his bed, with his

only foot on the floor. The dogs were at his side, tails wagging, claws scrabbling on the oak as he bent down and picked up his prosthetic.

I nodded at him. 'That one is wallowing in his own misery, as if he's some kind of victim. Fuck knows what he's got stuck in his head, but the fact is, we're all deluding ourselves. Do sharks swim about feeling sorry for themselves? Of course they don't. They wake up, bite shit, chase stuff, look scary, and remind everyone they're a shark. We need to get our fingers out of our collective arses and do something. If we work for the Owl, we protect ourselves – and we get some dignity, self-respect back. I'm done with brown-nosing to bank managers. I want money in my pocket.'

I grinned at Gabe. 'Come on, mate, no job, no home, all you've got is a Jeep that stinks.'

Rio laughed and Gabe jabbed a finger at him. 'What you got to be so happy about? All you've got is some fat fuck sitting on the couch where your lard arse belongs.'

Rio shrugged and looked at Jack. 'At least I'm not making the world run out of black paint, like this fucker.'

Jack had appeared depressed as he was attaching his leg, but as he stood up he was suddenly laughing so much I thought he was going to fall over. The dogs took a couple of paces back while he assessed. 'Hmm, the Owl or my mother. Tough pick.'

I had eye-to-eye with each of them. 'We've got nothing to lose by approaching him. I'll do that. You know, love everyone but never sell your sword, yeah?'

Rio was the first to fire back. 'All good, Nick, but

what about you? It's not just about bank managers, is it?'

I shook my head. 'Mate, I find myself back being a fifteen-year-old. Square one. I've got no money, I doubt if I've got a future. I've even been walking up the same fucking road towards the same house I lost my virginity in. It's like I've never been away.

'I look at this as an opportunity. I can't worry about yesterday, because it's done. I'm not going to worry about tomorrow, because it hasn't happened yet. What I care about is today. I'm starting out again as a fifteen-year-old, but this time not fucking up.

'We've all got to think like that, lads. Clean slate. Fresh start. It's the only way we're going to get out of the shit we're in, financial, family, whatever.'

Rio had been looking around at the canvases and I wasn't sure if he had been listening or not. He pointed at one on an easel, with paint that looked wet. 'Jack, talking of shit, what the fuck is that when it's at home?'

I looked at the swirl of black, dark blue, dark red around what I thought was a woman in a Puritan trouser suit, if there was such a thing, with a big white collar. Her mouth was oversized, protruding, like a puppet's. In the background was what I thought was an onion. It was dark red, the layers had fallen off and were lying on the floor. The Puritan's hands were skinny and bony and raised, as if grabbing.

Jack came round the sofa to defend his work. 'That's my heart, lads.' He tapped the canvas a couple of times with a forefinger. It echoed like a drum. 'It's being ripped out by this bitch or whoever.'

Rio thought he'd got it. 'Mate, I know the feeling. But

what you've got to learn with women is that when they dump you—'

Jack's head was down, his hair falling over his face. 'She didn't dump me.' He looked up again, and this time his eyes were watery. 'She ripped me off and she ripped me apart.'

16

Gabe was quickest off the mark and looked like he was about to start a fight with her. 'She nicked money?'

'And then some.' Jack's shoulders slumped. 'I went on a dating site. I just wanted company, someone to talk to. I'm stuck here with the dogs, not talking to my mother, so I thought, Why not give it a go?' He tapped the canvas again and made a drumbeat. 'Her name is Kate. Divorced. She lived in Manchester but was working in Turkey. She had a son with her, a five-year-old, with a heart condition. A genetic disorder. We hit it off. Similar values. I was upfront about my injury and she wasn't put off. She got me to move off the site onto Snapchat. We were at it all day and night. She understood my injury because she'd been through the same sort of thing with her son's problems.'

He stopped and he was almost apologetic. 'I felt I knew her so well.'

Gabe had been nodding slowly. 'You never met her?'

Jack shook his head. 'Like I said, she was in Turkey.

We arranged to meet. She'd come here, she said, but not with the boy to start with. We'd take it gently. But two days before she was supposed to come, she said she'd been mugged in Turkey and couldn't make it. She had to pay for Freddie, who was now in hospital and needed surgery. He was in a bad way.'

Jack saw everybody's reaction. 'I know, I know. But what do you do? I was reluctant, but I kept thinking, What happens if it's true? This woman I feel I know so well, what happens if she really is the one for me?'

Gabe wanted to keep this on point. 'How much did you get fucked over for?'

'Just over four grand.'

Going by their expressions, the other two hadn't expected it to be so little either. Nobody said anything, though. Jack was on a roll, so we'd let him get it all out. This was probably the first time he'd been able to vent since it happened.

But Rio jumped in: 'That's not bad, mate. Lesson learnt, yeah, move on?'

Jack was resting his arse on a stool by the canvas so he could adjust the leg. 'I wish. That was the cash advance. Then came more medical fees, then it was money for food, money for rent while the boy was in hospital, money for a tax to get out of Turkey.'

He saw our expressions. 'I know, a tax, I know. Look, I wasn't comfortable with it but I'd got so far in I couldn't get myself out. I was in for over sixty grand, so I just kept going, hoping the feeling was wrong and maybe she was telling the truth. The minute I started to ask about the boy's treatment, could I talk to the doctors, maybe get the boy repatriated, all contact stopped. I got fucked over, and all I wanted was some company. Can you believe that? Embarrassing.'

I thought of the body standing in the window of the big house as we drove in. 'Have you told your mother?'

'You're joking, right? She'd lap it up. She'd even smile at me having the last of my compensation ripped off me. Even more proof I'm not right in the head.'

Rio sat back. 'Shit, that's harsh. All of it.'

Gabe stood up and got Jack his brew. 'Mate, you can have this after all. You deserve it. She send any pictures?'

Jack pointed at the bed. 'On the cabinet.'

Gabe took a hobble past the recollapsed Labradors. Jack put down his mug; he wasn't in the mood for tea. 'I doubt they were real anyway. You know what's really frightening? She got inside my head so quickly and easily. I must be really messed up for that to happen. I just feel so . . . brutalized.'

Gabe passed the two prints to Rio, who studied the images as he made an attempt at empathy. 'Mate, I would have shagged her. I would have fallen for it too. Us guys, we always stay with a lie rather than deal with a harsh truth. I read that.'

Rio's head jerked up. 'In a magazine, last time you were at the clap clinic?'

'Whatever. That's why we're all sitting here with just each other.'

It was my turn for the prints. The first one showed a very attractive thirty-something with long blonde hair, perfect teeth, perfect face. The problem was, it filled the frame: no indication of where or when it was taken. It could have been lifted from a modelling-agency portfolio, she was so perfect. The other was of her cuddling the boy, who was nothing like his mother. But that was Photoshop for you. I guessed when you were desperate and lonely you didn't bother with details. Jack had probably fantasized about this ready-made family he could look after and love. The kid being sick would only have added to the attraction. The moment the scammer found out about Jack's injuries, they would have decided this fictional woman should have a child who was ill.

Gabe had a plan. 'We should find these arseholes, get Jack's money and rip their heads off.'

Rio was up for it. 'But how, mate? You got some on-line detective super-power we don't know about? Wind your neck in or that bald head of yours'll get even more red and blotchy.'

Gabe couldn't let go entirely: 'It's not right – they can rip off whoever they want but not one of us.' Then he was heading for the great outdoors.

Rio grinned. 'Something I said, super-detective?'

Gabe fished a pack of cancer sticks from his pocket and gave it a shake at Jack. 'Want one? It's easy to start again.'

Jack didn't think twice as he hobbled towards the door. The two fat brown things got excited again and, very soon, their claws were clacking on the wood.

I stood up, mug in hand. Rio looked confused. 'Are we all taking it up?'

I waved my hand about, as if to gather them in. 'Wait. The reason we're here. Am I going for it with the Owl, or aren't I? I need to know.'

Jack was standing there, like a junkie, waiting for his

fix. Gabe tapped the pack so a cigarette fell forward. He shot me a glance. 'It'll end in tears, Nick. It'll not be the answer.'

I watched Jack take the cigarette and hold it between his fingers. 'Probably, but are you all in?'

Rio shrugged as the other two turned and headed for the door. Gabe pulled out his disposable. 'Yeah, mate. Course we're in. SNS. Who cares who the fuck wins?'

Rio had come up with a thought that I took as a yes. 'Only if we call him the Falcon. Owl sounds a bit Harry Potter, know what I mean?'

I ignored him. If I didn't, the Falcon would get a life just to annoy me.

I'd been hoping for a little more excitement out of them but I'd take what I was given. It was enough.

17

The pavements outside Notting Hill Tube station were rammed with tourists studying their smartphones, then looking around for the blue door from the Hugh Grant movie. It was about a mile away, on Portobello Road, so good luck with that one. I eased my way through them and started along the main drag towards Hyde Park and my RV with the Owl.

I twisted my fingers around the slim, coin-sized aluminium disc in the right-hand pocket of my leather bomber jacket. It contained more high-tech than was used on the Apollo missions. It wasn't going to take me to the moon, though: it was going to help me find the Owl and be able to grip him if things didn't go to plan.

It was a comfortable feeling, playing with the sliver of light alloy I'd bought at a CeX store as soon as I reached London. The days of improvisation had gone. There was so much technology out there to choose from, just a couple of clicks away, and this little guy, I hoped, would save what would otherwise have meant days, maybe weeks, of slog. There was still stuff that had to be done hands-on, of course, or the tech wouldn't get to where it was needed. Smart TVs could be used as listening devices but it wasn't like the Owl could just flick a switch to make that happen. A team would still need to make entry, attack the TV and insert a device for any surveillance to work. Rio had made sure Jack's flat-screen wasn't connected online by turning the thing off. He wouldn't have needed to do that in his own house because his TV was steam-driven from the Red Cross furniture shop. Many high-tech attacks were hands-on first so their counter-measures had to be the same. With hairs or bits of cocktail stick for tell-tales, there were no counter-measures beyond the skill of checking something before you opened it, using the Mark 1 Eyeball. Other than that, the only way to pro-tect was not to own anything that could go online, and if you did, never to take it out of its box.

I minced along the road. As I approached the meet-ing place, it didn't bother me that the Owl might be having me followed, ensuring that it was safe for him to make contact with me. I was doing exactly what we had agreed in the call. I'd phoned him as soon as Gabe had dropped me off at Pangbourne after his cigarette break with Jack. The other three were staying at the barn until I called them with the outcome. I would then head back and wait out with the rest of them to see what the Owl decided.

I had Rio's safe phone, and the others had Gabe's. Once I knew what was going on, so would they.

When I'd called the Owl, he was his normal plastic

cheery self, and even more so when I said I wanted to meet.

Why he'd specified this particular place, I had no idea. On the upside, it was just a couple of hundred from the Tube station, and it was starting to spit with rain.

I approached Café Diana. It was near Kensington Palace and made famous because the People's Princess had popped in once for a cup of coffee and a sticky bun, like an ordinary person, when the world's press just happened to be waiting outside to capture the moment.

I entered the shrine.

18

Press cuttings and pictures of her plastered the walls. A couple of tourists sat with cameras in front of them on the table, cross-checking it all with the menu to see if they could have what she'd been having. Three workmen in high-vis jackets and dusty boots, the leather of the toecaps worn away to show the safety steel, were tucking into tea and toast. The remaining occupants were the same lot you saw in any café offering free Wi-Fi, their laptops and phones plugged into the new banks of electric sockets.

I took a four-seater in the corner and a young woman with curly jet-black hair came over for my order, the pocket of her apron bulging with notepads and a card reader.

'Scrambled egg on toast and a large tea, please.'

'Would you care for white bread or wholemeal?' Her English was perfect, but with an East European accent.

'Whichever's bigger.'

As she disappeared, my thoughts went back to the

Owl. Ever since I'd first seen him, he'd waffled and weaved like a politician. All part of his job, I supposed, whatever that was.

I thought, too, about the problem he had with us. The information I had dangling around my neck in my memory stick was so dangerous to an already fractious relationship between the East and the West that the Owl was right to try to control it in whatever way he could.

But even aside from the minor detail that he would rather have us four survivors very dead to clean up the mess, I sort of liked him. His friend-next-door approach worked on me. Maybe it was just different from what I'd come up against over the years. I wasn't sure, but I wasn't going to agonize about it.

My tea arrived in a basic white mug with the teabag still in it and a little jug of milk, just the way Diana would have liked it. I took out my mobile and attached another purchase from CeX, a thumb-drive and ear-phones, while getting into my brew.

A few minutes later the food came. I grabbed the tomato sauce bottle. I hadn't had time to start squeezing when I heard a familiar voice.

'London rain, eh? Cats and dogs.'

I looked up to see Sam – at least, that was how he'd introduced himself to me the first time we'd met. But to me it was the Owl who was busy wrestling off his coat. He was like a driver caught in a narrow country lane, trying to reverse and getting the gears mixed up, putting the handbrake on when he shouldn't and ending up stalled. He finally managed to get his hand out of a sleeve so he could shake mine.

'Jeez, it's good to see you, Nick.'

The Owl's face was still baby smooth and without a hint of bristle, but he'd put on some weight. His neck was gripped by a light-blue shirt done all the way up, and the top two buttons above the V-neck of his jumper were straining to keep the cotton together. Life was clearly good, but it was making him look like a middle-aged mattress salesman rather than whatever he really was. But it was his big round face that had given him his name, especially those wide-apart dark brown eyes. Maybe that was why his nose looked too small.

He glanced around the walls, stage-struck. 'I love this place.'

He draped his coat on the back of a chair and sat down next to it. It was a three-quarter-length number with a thin fleece lining under a nylon shell, just the sort a mattress salesman would buy from Marks & Sparks because it was practical for this time of year: light yet protective, as the sleeve tag would no doubt have said when he'd bought it. Most importantly for my purposes, it had inside pockets. I could see a zip-up one at chest level among the folds of material. Further down, a slip of fleece would hold a mobile, but it was long and slim, designed for a Nokia in 2002.

He patted his light brown short-back-and-sides-with-side-parting, as if to clear off the rain. He looked at me, then at the walls again. 'The Queen of Hearts. Did you ever meet her, Nick?'

I shook my head, then thought, Why not? He had a big shock coming his way, so I might as well start on a good note. 'Just the once, when I was in the Regiment. See that picture?' I nodded at the framed shots of her with shiny mid-length princessy hair. 'That was when she arrived in Hereford. And that one?' I pointed further along to where she had a fashion-leading shorter cut. 'That was when she left. You're going to love this . . .

'She came down to Hereford with her husband, for familiarization with our methods, so if the shit hit the fan for them they'd know what to expect when the lads came screaming through the wall to rescue them.'

The waitress appeared and the Owl ordered a flat white.

She looked at me like I was his carer and she needed a translation.

'He's after regular black coffee with milk. Maybe a jug like the tea, so he can add his own, and hot if you've got it.'

She gave me a smile of pity, and left. When she came back, she'd probably ask me if he took sugar.

'So, the hair, Nick? I have to know about the hair.'

'Diana was in a room and we threw in a couple of flashbangs. There was a sudden smell of burnt hair and our army pensions didn't look too healthy.'

The Owl was a picture of concern.

'The only lasting damage was to her hair, which was badly singed. The next day, Diana was sporting a new hairdo that the whole world copied.'

The Owl was still smiling as he watched me take the memory stick from round my neck and shove it into the thumb-drive. I passed my phone across the table with one hand and presented the connected earphones with the other. 'Glad you like that story. Don't think you're going to like this one.'

The Owl held his hands up and away as if the mobile was toxic, but friendly toxic – he still had a big moon-faced smile. 'Jeez, Nick. Hey, no need for any more stories, all's good this end. No harm will ever come to you and the guys. I just need to know you'll always be on my side, that's all.'

If there was going to be harm done, he wouldn't be the one who was doing it. He wasn't the sort to do the dirty work – he didn't have it in him. I thought of him as living alone, surrounded by jam jars he was too weak to open by himself. His super-powers, I knew, were tucked away in his head. His body was just for getting that brain of his from one place to another to tell people to do shit. He didn't need strength: he had power.

I smiled back. After all, I wanted something from him. 'Of course it's good your end, mate, because we're on your side. You leave us alone, we leave you alone. But just so we really do understand each other, I'll say it one more time: if anyone gets dead, gets missing, or gets fucked up, all the information we have will be exposed. Every single name, event, location. Until then, we will control it responsibly. You don't have to worry, unless you give us a reason to worry.'

I waited to see his reaction and there was none, just that constant smile as he left the space between us empty. He waited for me to fill the void and I was willing to do so.

'Mate, again, to be very clear. Who we know, what we know, where it happened and when, the int'll be out there for everyone to see if at any time you or anyone else tries to fuck us over. Think of it as mutually assured destruction.'

The Owl didn't even acknowledge that. He just kept smiling and over-concentrating on the icons hanging on the walls around him. His default facial expression was a smile straight out of the fast-food guide to customer care, and I admired him for the way he appeared to breeze through drama as if he was just in a muddle. Smile, be friendly to people, but always consider how you're going to kill them: that's a skill. But it wasn't going to stop me.

'Even you can't hide a torpedoed ship, can you?'

At last he brought his Owl eyes down to me. 'So here's the thing, Nick. I'm good with you and the guys keeping what you know. I trust you. I trust the guys. We're all singing from the same sheet, am I right?'

I'd had eye-to-eye with him on more than one occasion and still didn't have a clue what that sheet was. His job description seemed to be made up on the fly.

'But there are others, Nick.' He turned his head and looked through the café window, like he expected them to ambush us from the pavement. 'The big kahunas. Dudes at the top table. They won't get what you're saying. They don't know you like I do, Nick. They don't know the guys. Their priority will be to make sure this never gets to see the light of day. You see where I'm going with this, Nick? I can't help you out with these guys. They're a law unto themselves.'

There wasn't much I could do but shrug. 'Mate, not my problem, I have no control of that. You need to convince all of them, your side, their side, anyone who'll listen, that we're good lads. There's no way we're going to be gobbing off about this shit – unless, of course, anyone comes for us.'

I lifted the earphones once more and offered them up.

He knew exactly what he was about to see. 'You making sure I know what you've got? That it isn't a bluff?'

He didn't need a reply, just a video show.

'Go on, you can press. I don't want to go to the pictures – I've already seen it.'

He kept his smile on and pressed play as I got back to my eggs.

'My name is Nick Stone,' the haggard face with bloodshot eyes and six days of growth would be telling him. 'I am an ex-serviceman of the British Army, and they can verify my identity. I am recording this on the twentieth of April 2016. I am recording this because, in the event of my death, I want the following facts, and therefore the identity of my probable killer and the reason for my death, to be known.

'I met the person we only knew as Sam on a Scandinavian Airlines flight from Oslo to Longyearbyen on the tenth of April 2016. I don't know Sam's last name, but it can be obtained from his association with a man called Munnelly, who was also on that flight. More about him later.

'I then flew north to Barnero ice station located at approximately eighty-nine degrees north with Jack Cauldwell's expedition. Jack is one of us four survivors and all three will also give their account of events after mine. Our names will be on the manifest. Once we got on the ice, three guides were waiting for us. They'd been provided by Jack's father.'

What the haggard face didn't add was that the

expedition was about more than skiing to the North Pole, dragging the pulks. It was to give the lives of five disabled ex-servicemen a purpose, to make them feel they weren't on the scrap-heap: they were still in the game.

I had said the same to the three survivors in Jack's barn. Nothing had changed, and that was one of the prime reasons I was there now.

19

The high-vis lads must have received a bollocking on the fattest one's mobile about getting back to work because their table suddenly looked like a scene from the *Mary Celeste*.

I got back to my breakfast of tomato sauce with scrambled egg underneath as the Owl kept up his perma-smile and continued to watch the film show.

He was about two minutes into the recording, so I knew what the haggard face was telling him now. That the team had set out north, with two of the guides placing monitors in the ice to measure climate change for an environmental pressure group – or so we'd thought. But it wasn't long before we were attacked by a heliborne team led by the Owl's mate Munnelly. Two of the guides, who were in control of the monitors, were executed and the monitors recovered by Munnelly's team. The rest of us were lifted onto the *Lisandro*, a US research ice-breaker, at gunpoint – and that was when the truth had come out.

It was all about the new Great Game, the new power play now that climate change had the ice melting, opening up access to the seabed and its vast mineral wealth. On top of that, the new sea-lanes cut thousands of miles off traditional routes, and the big players wanted control. The monitors were advanced Russian surveying devices, technology that was years ahead of anything the US had: they would predict sooner and with more certainty than ever before where and when the ice would start to disappear and the US wanted them. It was as simple as that.

That was when it really got fucked up. The Russians had to deny the US their technology and torpedoed the ship while the team and I were still aboard.

I took a long swig of hot tea while the Owl maintained his smile, just watched and listened.

The rest of our eight-pulk team were killed at different stages as we tried to escape.

I studied the Owl's face, because I knew the haggard one he was looking at was about to announce the one inescapable fact that would sink his own personal ship.

The Owl pressed hold and he stared across the table at me.

'The *Lisandro*?'

He was where I thought he was. 'Yes. It sank at latitude 89.4235, longitude 87.1141. It's in the vid and I'm sure it's still at the bottom of the Arctic Ocean, unless some scrap dealer has got wind of what happened.'

He looked like he was about to say something, but then he thought better of it. His jaw hardened, as much as good living would let it, and a podgy finger pressed play. Then, almost at once, he pressed hold again.

'Nick.' He pursed his lips. 'We had ourselves a situation. But, as you know, stuff happens.'

Stuff certainly did happen.

'You've got to remember the Russians respond very differently to problems. Russians, eh? What can you do?' He shrugged, like he was slagging off his mother-in-law, then raised his hands to the ceiling. 'Crazy world, crazy war, but there you have it.

'My job was, and still is, to pour oil on troubled waters. American waters, Russian waters, anywhere I see ripples. I clean things up before the world finds out, and if it does find out, I pour even more. Anything to stop our so-called leaders going to war with each other.'

I'd think another time about how that might work. If I couldn't influence or change something, why care or worry?

'You four survivors presented a problem, Nick. You raised the possibility that others might have survived when the *Lisandro* went down. Witnesses we didn't know about and couldn't control, when all we wanted to do was ensure that this little incident was forgotten . . . for ever. Is it, Nick? What do you say?'

I wasn't about to answer with anything he hadn't already heard from me. 'We just want to get our lives back and that's why I'm here.'

There was a smile and a friendly wink. 'And your digital witness here is a guarantee, right?'

I didn't have to answer but I wanted to anyway. 'Some would call it blackmail. I call it survival. Same meat, different gravy. We need protection from you, don't we? Crazy world, crazy war.'

I scraped up the last bit of scrambled egg and sat back with my mug as the Owl watched the last few seconds of the video. I couldn't work out his expression. Was he scared, angry, or couldn't give a fuck? It was impossible to read.

He leant across the table to pass me the mobile. The memory stick went back around my neck.

'Just so you know, there isn't anything further on that says about you having Jack's dad killed for organizing the monitor dig-in for the Russians. No need to get too personal about it, eh?'

It took him a long time but the big smile eventually came. 'It's okay, I get it.' He wagged a finger at me, as if he was telling me off for eating an extra biscuit. 'Now you make sure your team keeps a good hold of those little stick guys.'

He looked around the walls, taking in Diana's many faces. 'This is where we first met, you know.'

'You met her too?' I couldn't imagine him popping in for a coffee on exactly the same day she did. I couldn't imagine this as one of his places at all.

'No, my husband. He adores her. We had our first date here.' He twisted back to face me.

'Really, mate? On the first date I'd have wanted at least a tablecloth and the odd candle running around.'

He gave me a beaming emoji, full watts. 'Well, it kind of worked. I thought I'd come here again and see if anything had changed.' His arm gesture took in the whole room. 'But no! Can you believe it? I can't wait to tell him. He'll be so pleased.'

I wanted to get on with this but he had the brakes on. He loved small talk and I could handle that, but it was his smile I had a problem with. He smiled at everything and everyone but I could read his mind: *Be nice, but be ready to cut throats the first chance you get.* This man should have been in politics.

20

He'd settled down, hands on the table, like a line manager doing the Monday-morning pep talk. 'Nick, it's so nice to see you again, even though you brought along uncomfortable viewing. I was getting worried – you didn't call.'

I finished the last dregs of my tea. 'I had nothing to call you about, mate. We were just getting on with our lives. The endeavour of personal improvement and the pursuit of happiness, that sort of thing.'

He thought the last sentence was really heartfelt and approved it with a nod, as his eyes lifted briefly to the People's Princess. 'So, Nick, the call? You—'

His coffee arrived, at last. A couple of laptop rechargers came in behind the waitress and plugged themselves in at the next table.

I ordered another mug of tea and she nodded, but turned her attention to the newbies. I was the guy who liked tomato sauce more than her eggs; I'd lost her love.

I leant across the table to get the Owl's attention, and a better look at his raincoat. 'I want to talk to you about protecting us from the big kahunas.' I didn't even know if they existed. For all I knew, there might be just one, and I was talking to him. It felt like I knew more about the waitress than I did about this man.

'You betcha, Nick. We're both just the little guys making our way in life. Am I right?'

'Just the one little guy, mate, and he's sitting my side of the table. That's why I'm here. Last night, we had three fuckers at Rio's. They were installing devices. You know anything about that?'

He was either on another stream or just diverting the course of the conversation, I wasn't sure which. 'I try every day and every night, Nick, to make sure you four are safe. You know what those guys are like.' He held up his hands. 'Uncontrollable. Can you believe it?' The emojis went from worried face to shocked face and back to smiley. 'What can you do? Jeez, they can be a little scary at times.'

I was listening, but he was diverting. 'Mate, I don't believe that team playing electricians at Rio's wasn't working for you. But that's okay, I understand. What I don't get is who you actually work for. Who are these big kahunas? What's the set-up? Is it like some kind of international rescue, coming into the playground when everybody starts fighting, sorting it out before the teachers are told?'

The emojis spooled and morphed as the questions hit him, until they settled on one that looked like *I'd love to tell you, but . . .*

'Need to know – it's an important factor in our lives,

am I right? Hey, I'm sorry, but, hey, you know what? I've been thinking about you guys ever since you called. I really have, Nick. How I can help us all – you, me, even the big guys.'

He straightened his legs and stiffened his back, dug his left hand into his baggy jeans. 'I've got it somewhere.'

I carried on: 'So, at the house, a couple of them got badly hurt. From our point of view, it was all about getting away – all right? Just so they know, we don't want these fuckers coming back for retribution. Wrong place, wrong time for them, that's all it was. It's got to stop or both of us could lose people.'

He pulled his hand out. 'Nope, wrong pocket.' He changed hands and produced a cheap credit-card holder, the kind of thing that flops open, exposing slots to shove your plastic in, and handed it to me. I put it straight into my jacket pocket, feeling it had more than one card in it, then palmed the coin-sized piece of aluminium, my return gift to him.

'I've been thinking, Nick, on ways I can keep the big guys happy about your situation. I've got to tell you, I've had a hell of a time reassuring them – I really have.'

I wasn't buying it, but I liked the friendliness, even the bumbling buffoonery. I knew it was bullshit but it made the day much better. 'I guess us all having information to hit the real world with controls them a little bit, doesn't it?'

His head was down as he concentrated on pouring milk into his coffee drop by drop. 'Well, kinda, but anyhooo . . .'

Finally. The Owl's word for: Down to business.

'I've been thinking the way to keep everybody happy is for you guys to work with me.' He tested his brew, added another couple of drops, tried it again. 'That way, you're kind of close. You still have the leverage, of course, but it feels neat that we're all in the same tent, don't you think?'

I shrugged.

'But you guys, look, money and all, our vets, your vets, they don't get what they deserve. I'm guessing you wouldn't say no to a few bucks now and again. Just small jobs at first, and then who knows? Kinda makes sense for both sides, doesn't it? What do you think, Nick?' The cup came up in both hands, and he finally had a proper sip. He wasn't too pleased with it.

My tea arrived, and I waited for the woman to leave.

'So, what's the job?'

'Oh, just a simple thing. It wouldn't be difficult for you guys – a couple of days at the most. And eighty K sterling at the end. Not bad, eh?'

I tried not to look surprised because that wouldn't have helped me get more. 'That's exactly what I was going to ask you, and for the same reasons – to keep together and work together.'

I studied his reaction. Was this a coincidence or had he known? As I was expecting, the Owl's face gave nothing away so I got back to the job in hand.

'But at one sixty sterling. Now, that wouldn't be bad at all.'

No one ever paid anyone what they were worth in this game. Worth had to be defined and justified by the person getting paid. In this case, most of it would be bullshit because I didn't know what was required for the job to be successful.

His reply was far too quick, and what I wanted was far too easily given.

'Sure, Nick, why not?'

But the offer helped with other, more worrying, concerns, and I wasn't going to turn it down. 'Looks like we have a job, then. When?'

Later I could think about why he wanted us to work for him at all. Getting a little piece of alloy into that coat was the main item on my agenda now.

The Owl was a very happy mattress salesman. 'That's great, Nick. Today? It's all in the wallet. Nice and easy – a kind of trial run, a shakedown cruise. Find someone. She's young, maybe with a couple of guys. It shouldn't be hard.'

Then the other side of the Owl appeared, the one that could cause pain and death. 'Bring her to me intact. That's very important to me.'

I nodded a no-problem that gave him the reason to come back into emoji smiley-face mode. 'Our woman's in the UK, no foreign entry, easy-peasy. You deliver, I pay. Kind of like the US Postal Service.' He smiled. 'USPS, no? "We Deliver For You!"'

I nodded. 'Yeah, yeah. Good one. But why do you want her, and intact?'

He tapped his nose. 'Need to know, Nick. Let's just say you and I are keeping the wolves from the door, eh? Doesn't that make you feel warm inside?'

He could see it didn't. 'So, hey, look at it another way. During Liechtenstein's last military engagement in 1886, none of the eighty soldiers sent to fight were killed, and all eighty-one returned. Yup, eighty-one. They picked up a new Italian "friend" along the way. That's kinda what I do, make friends of the enemy. It's good for us all.' He pointed to the frame above me. 'She would have approved.'

I stood up. 'Mate, I've got to go to the toilet. Maybe she used the same one – what do you reckon?' I moved behind him and the coat.

'Nope. We checked. She never used the facilities.'

As I turned, I tugged at the raincoat, just enough to make it slip to the floor. 'Would have been good for business if she had, though, eh? Sorry, mate, it's got caught.'

I picked it up behind him, and brushed it down so he could see I was making good on my fuck-up. 'Think of the people lining up to sit on the same seat.'

His face turned up to mine. 'Oh, gross – come on.'

He'd already missed me slipping a bit of alloy into the Nokia pocket, and now he watched me place the coat back on the seat. I'd made a mental note of how it had folded over the chair and I slapped his shoulder gently. 'I'm going to pretend she was there anyway. I'll be back in a bit.'

The cubicle downstairs was narrow. I sat on the pan, elbows on my knees, worried face in my hands. Did the Owl already have a device in Jack's barn? How the fuck had he known that was what we were going to ask him for, and almost word for word? He'd even said 'tent', for fuck's sake.

It made sense. If he could discover where every-body's memory stick was hidden, he could seize them in a coordinated swoop and fuck us over. If they did

93

it all at once, maybe the message wouldn't get out to Claudia. The surveillance log must have registered that the fifth was with a woman. But that was all he would know. No phone number, no security statement spoken.

Did it matter? We'd achieved our aim, and we were working for him. We were getting close.

And then it hit me.

Fuck. Fuck. Fuck.

Worst possible scenario.

What if it wasn't surveillance?

What if it was one of the team?

No time to try to work out the whys, wheres and whens. What mattered was trying to remember if one of the other three had said or done something that would indicate they weren't even worth pissing on. I couldn't think of anything, but that didn't mean I wouldn't later on.

I pulled out the safe phone and punched in the dialling code and mobile number. The key to conjuring up regularly accessed data sequences was to crack on instinctively. Interrupting the process with rational thought only fucked things up. And because I never compromised my security – or anyone else's – by storing contact details, it had become second nature.

It rang four times, and when it was answered I imagined her glass-framed office overlooking a lake. One day I might get to see it.

'Oh, hello, Nick.'

21

'Claudia, listen, thanks for explaining the situation for me. I need a favour from you, and it's to do with the instructions I left.'

She was still *über*-efficient. 'Of course, Nick. What would you like me to do?'

'Cancel the instructions for now. Keep them, but there's a temporary hold. If anyone does ring in, take no action, keep the white Jiffy bag until I call you again to take off the temporary hold. That okay with you?'

'Of course, Nick. Remember, we need to revisit everything when we review your situation in a couple of months' time. Unless we get some good news in the meantime, yes?'

'That's perfect, Claudia. Thank you.'

I closed down the phone and left the toilet. I hadn't added that she might come into work one Monday to find a man-sized hole had been drilled into the bank safe and the only thing taken was a small white Jiffy.

Inspecting the coat folds to see if he'd had a little

check was now out of the question: the Owl was at the counter, paying the bill, coat on.

We headed for the door and the rain. I pointed to the right, the way I'd come. 'I'm going to the Tube.' That gave him the opportunity to tell me he was going the opposite way. We shook, and it was like we'd just had our first college reunion in years.

'Ah, Nick, that was fun, don't you think? You guys will be family. Kind of feels nice.'

I nodded. 'We've got a name. We're going to call ourselves SNS – the Special Needs Service.'

Rio had finally got his way.

I didn't get any emojis as he tried to work out what I was saying, which was a pity. I was watching for any giveaway that he'd already read the expression on the surveillance logs.

He thought for a second longer, then got it. 'Oh, my Lord, Nick, are you guys even allowed to say that kind of thing here?'

22

The Owl turned left and I turned right. The original plan to follow him had changed, now the SNS might have a mole. There was another way of finding out where he lived or worked, and I'd get on with that later. For now, priorities had changed.

On the plus side, I hadn't told the team about the tracker I'd planted in his coat. The Owl was right: need-to-know was important in our lives right now. I pulled out the cheap plastic wallet to reveal four pay-as-you-go Visa debit cards, a Post-it showing the PIN numbers, and a bright green USB card with a small fold-out connector.

I shoved it back into my pocket and pulled out my mobile to google an internet café. I didn't care if the Owl had guys following me: I was only doing what he'd expect of me. But, then, why would he need to? It looked like he already had someone in our tent.

'Mole' wasn't the right word to describe what this fuck actually was. 'Mole' felt almost quaint, something out of the 1950s when double-agents were recruited at Oxford or Cambridge with a tap on the shoulder and a G-and-T. Even when they were found out and exposed, no one wanted to do anything about it. Basically, they were 'one of us'.

The reality was much bloodier, and I was angry at the thought. For now it was only a suspicion that one of us was a traitor. But that didn't calm me down. It just made me want to find proof one way or the other.

At stake was my little fantasy about what this group represented to me: a new start, with people I'd thought I liked and, I'd thought, people I understood. Then I tried to justify it to myself. Maybe it was a good thing this had happened. I'd fallen into the trap of team players before. If this fantasy bubble of the SNS brotherhood was burst, it would knock me back into shape. The only person you can really trust, and even then only to a point, is yourself.

Rationalizing and justifying didn't help me cut away. Mole, informer, tout, stool-pigeon, grass: however it was dressed up, and whatever the reasons, incentives or coercion that had turned them, there was nothing worse than a traitor. No side liked them, even the one that was using them. They weren't respected. They were hated.

When I'd worked in Northern Ireland, source information was gathered from many different people for many different reasons. Some did it for money. I never really understood that because they'd never get more than they could naturally absorb into their lifestyle. That usually meant no more than five hundred a month – or most of them would have gone straight out and bought a brand new car, which might have looked a tad suspicious outside a minging council house. So why run the risk of being burnt alive or getting your head drilled for a couple of beer tokens each week?

Some became sources thinking they were protecting their husband, brother or whichever relation was in an active service unit. 'If I tell you what he's doing, can you stop it?'

I had contempt for them all.

They were helping us win the war, but they were traitors. I had no sympathy for them when their side caught them and the Black & Decker was plugged in.

Finally, there were touts who did it for ideological reasons. They were highly placed within the IRA and gave solid information: the most powerful weapon in any war.

But even words like 'tout', 'informer', 'source' – they all felt too tame when it was you being betrayed, when they were inside the tent, pissing in. The only word I could think of that felt good enough was 'snide'. When I was a kid, it had been worse than 'cunt'. It was the biggest insult on earth. 'Snide' was subhuman. And now that I'd pigeonholed whoever it was, even though it might turn out that the snide didn't exist, I felt a lot better because the snide would be about two things: giving control of the memory sticks to the Owl, and getting us dead.

Google gave me an internet café, and I turned round. It was only twenty or so metres back the way I'd come.

23

The café was rammed with people printing out visa applications, filling them in, cutting photos to size, stuff you'd expect when trying to comply with hours of bureaucracy for a visa. It was Embassy Central around there and I heard dozens of languages as I walked in, being shouted on Skype. Most of the speakers were pissed off because the sign on the counter announced that the bored-looking Indian guys behind it would witness documents for an extra charge of two pounds per signature.

I bought an hour online but didn't take a seat. The ones I was interested in were occupied, so while I waited I opened up the tracker app and hit the community option. The tracker was an American crowdfunded device, designed to be attached to keys, wallets, phones, even pets, or concealed in cars and bikes. Paired with the app on your phone and Bluetooth, you could quickly locate whatever you'd lost. My original plan had been to follow the Owl to the general area of his nest, checking I wasn't being followed myself, then to narrow down the search with the tracker later. It would work only if the device and I were in Bluetooth range, but that wasn't a problem because I had the tracker community to help me. Once you'd registered your device, you could ask every other user's phone to track it.

I'd registered the device as 'cat'. I decided that my cat was lost now, and the community was going to help me find it. If any of them was in Bluetooth range of Tiddles, had registered a device and had opted to join the worldwide team, a location alert would be sent to me automatically. The phone's owner wouldn't even know it had happened. The community was all about helping one another find stuff.

A girl in a hijab stood up from a corner screen. I jumped into her place before anyone decided they needed as much privacy as I did, and slipped in the USB.

The screen came to life once I'd double-clicked the attachment, and in front of me were a couple of pictures of a young woman. The first showed a page from a Belarus passport, which in itself meant nothing. It could be false, and no one ever looks the same on their passport photo anyway.

The name on the passport was Yulia Zyk. She had been born in '97, so I did a quick count on my fingers to work out her age. Her skin was white as porcelain, stretched over prominent cheekbones and framed by a mop of wavy, shoulder-length dark hair. I couldn't work out if the picture was a washed-out mugshot from an arrest folder, her pallor was genetic or if she just needed to get out into the sun a bit more. She could have done with lightening up in other ways, too. She certainly didn't look like a fellow citizen of the country's ever-beaming dictator, Aleksandr Lukashenko.

I understood enough about Belarus to know that no one should be fooled by the blow-dried hair and grand-dad perma-smile. Lukashenko ruled what the US called Europe's only remaining 'outpost of tyranny' with iron fists. The continent's last dictatorship had all the trappings you would expect: outrageous corruption; state control of the media; no social media; opponents disappearing; lavish spending on official residences and blow-dries while the population lived in shit. Russia had changed the name of their secret police to FSB to make them sound more cuddly, but their neighbour's lot were still called the KGB.

The country declared independence after the fall of the USSR, but Lukashenko made sure it was still joined at the hip to Russia. Just like Putin, he wasn't keen on gays so no one else in Belarus was either. The same went for beards. The country also had a problem with Islamic fundamentalism, and to add even more drama, Afghanistan was one of its neighbours. So, if the beloved dictator didn't like face hair, your passport photo had better show the most clean-shaven chin possible. Not that Yulia needed to worry about that.

The second picture had been taken on a beach, and showed Yulia with a bunch of lads about the same age. They were all standing with surfboards, but Yulia was so skinny that the one she was holding was twice as wide as she was. She needed a few plates of fish and chips but it was good to see that she'd got out in the sun at least once in her life.

I photographed both pictures with my mobile and double-clicked the Word document. It held very little information to add to what the Owl had already given me. Yulia was currently in Cornwall, surfing in the Sennen Cove region, and our job was to lift her. Once we'd got her, we'd contain her, contact the Owl, and arrange for her to be collected. Job done. A piece of piss at any other time, but not now, not today.

I could have lived with the possibility that the Owl really had thought of us working for him at exactly the same time as I did. After all, it was a perfectly reasonable idea, and hardly unique. Maybe this really could be the trial run for a beautiful relationship. But the thought of a snide turned all that on its head, and the hate bubbled up once more. I wasn't sure how, or why, or when, but it changed the way I needed to think about the job. We still had to prove we could be trusted and we still needed the money, but now I also needed to know if there *was* a snide. I had to find him.

So why not do the job, get paid, and when I found the snide, even let the Owl know his man had been exposed? Let him know that even though he'd been trying to fuck us up, we still wanted to work for him. Now, that was commitment to being in the same tent – and, on top of that, he might let us take the snide outside the tent and do whatever we wanted with him. No one liked them.

I called Gabe's safe phone, bending and snapping the data USB into pieces. It was answered in two rings by Jack. I didn't give him time to start waffling: I wanted to transmit information and get off the phone. There were things I had to do.

'Listen, we're on. We've got a job – he came up with the same idea before I got a chance to pitch him ours. As soon as I know what time I'll be at the station, I'll call so I can get a lift, okay? Here's a quick warning order. You'll all need passports and hand luggage for a temperate climate. Talk to you soon, mate.'

I closed down and headed towards the Tube station, then back to CeX for some more smartphones and other bits. Boring stuff, but important. Detail mattered.

At the first ATM I saw, I maxed out on each Visa card. We would deal only in cash.

I'd wait and see if any of the team said anything about needing passports. If they knew the job was in Cornwall, maybe they'd slip up.

I tried hard not to wonder who the snide might be – who would be the one to slip up.

24

Pangbourne Station

The rain had followed me from London and thumped onto the station roof as I watched the headlights crawling up the narrow approach road and stopping to collect commuters who weren't going to get wet until they had to. It was a difficult recognition task: every set belonged to either a Range Rover, Volvo or BMW.

Jack's Beamer pulled up and I jumped in beside him with my plastic bag full of mobiles and cables. The interior was warm and stank of fat furry brown things. They weren't with him this time but had been recently. Dog-biscuit crumbs filled the leather seat stitching.

Jack was full of questions. 'It sounds like they've given you an off-the-shelf job. What do you think? Maybe it's a test. Or a trap. I mean, coming out with the same idea at the same time?'

I gave a bit of a shrug. 'One of those two – or maybe he just thought of it at the same time we did. Like the sheep learning to roll over cattle grids in New Zealand at exactly the same time sheep were learning to do it in Yorkshire. Maybe there's a cosmic force out there. Who knows?'

Jack nodded hard. 'My mother's a birdwatcher. She told me it happened with blue tits, too. All within the same few days, all over Britain, they discovered how to peck open the top of a milk bottle, without any bird having done it before. They were too far away from each other to have communicated. Apparently it's called morphic resonance.'

'Yup, mate, that's the one. Sheep both sides of the planet came to the same conclusion at the same time. Weird, eh?'

He kept his eyes on the road as the automatic jumped gears, and the wipers kept the screen clear. He filled in the silent phase: 'I'm not going to ask what it is, because you'll just tell me to shut up and wait till we get back to the others. But what do you think? Are we good for it?' He tapped his empty leg.

'I think so, but only you lot can answer that one. So long as we keep away from any bang-bang. The more arms and legs you have, the better with that shit. But so what? We are where we are. We have a job.'

The indicators clicked as he slowed to take the last junction to the barn, though there wasn't another vehicle in sight. Maybe he wanted to warn the rabbits he was hanging a left.

At the solid wooden gates, he hit a fob and they swung open, the headlights penetrating the widening gap between.

If there was a snide, Jack was the most vulnerable. Betraying friends was seldom about cash, certainly over any length of time. If it was cash in Jack's case, he could easily dispose of it, maybe in a new roof to save having to donate the family seat to the National Trust.

But the cash thing just didn't feel right for Jack: he would have needed a stronger motive, an ideology, perhaps, or revenge, as a thank-you for something done on behalf of a loved one, maybe getting them medical care or out of trouble – or even into trouble. Maybe Jack just wanted the promise of freedom from his miserable situation. With luck, he wasn't that naive and would understand that if they got rid of us three they wouldn't just let their snide go, but when people are desperate, they'll latch onto anything. Rio was right: when people are in a shit situation, it's always good to hear the comforting lie rather than face the hard truth.

We drove through the gates and the headlights cast their arc over the gravel. I cut away from all that thinking.

I had to continue as if all was good in Camp SNS. I was going to brief them, give them a plan of sorts, and we'd be gone by the morning. Whether the Owl was listening via the TV, watching remotely via a laptop camera, or the snide was going to tell him later, it didn't matter. He would expect to see and hear what was going to happen.

As we drove up towards the barn on full beam, two sets of eyes reflected demonically and I soon saw the fat brown things waddling from side to side as fast as they could towards us. If they tried any harder, they'd topple over and die.

25

The barn

We sat around Jack's desk, the pictures he'd printed out from the phone spread in front of us. Every other spare inch of glass was covered with his entire collection of mugs, and islands of biscuit crumbs – Gabe had pressured him to stock up on the way to pick me up.

As I gathered up four dirties and took them to the sink, Gabe asked what else the Owl had told me.

'That's the lot. It's simple but, like everything that looks simple, it won't be. Never is, is it? We've got to get a plan together, but we're going to do it differently from your Green Army experience. It's going to be democratic . . . sort of. The way I need us to work is the only way the SNS is going to have any future. And at forty grand a pop it better had.'

Their faces had been a picture when I'd told them the size of our payday. Rio was looking even more pleased with himself now that his SNS creation had a life.

I filled the kettle and let the tap run onto the mugs in the sink while I turned and leant against the counter top.

'First, remember, we are just platforms to perform the mission, nothing more – and nothing matters but the mission. So, what is it? The mission is to lift the target, Yulia Zyk, and hand her over to the Owl. Got it?'

There were general nods, but I was going to say it again anyway. The mission is always repeated. 'To lift the target, Yulia Zyk, and hand her over to the Owl.

'We're in a safe area now. We've got time to plan and prepare. Now's the time for a Chinese parliament.'

I turned off the tap and grabbed a handful of tea-bags as the kettle started to bubble. It was strange going through the planning process with others, instead of just in my head. But now that others were involved I had to do it old-school.

The idea of a Chinese parliament was to come up with a plan. Everybody could contribute their ideas and rip to shreds those of others. Once there was a plan, we'd think of all the possible scenarios, which meant the ways that the plan could go wrong.

I carried on: 'Once we've all put in our twopence-worth, there will be a final decision – and that final decision will come from me.'

The kettle gave a mega-bubble and clicked off as I continued.

'There has to be a time when we stop waffling and get on with the mission. Otherwise, we're going to be walking round like all the fucking pencil necks out there, with their fingers up their arses and no idea what they're doing. You may not agree with what I come up with, but you've got to go with it. If you don't, we lose the integrity of the team – and that's when things get fucked up.'

I turned and jabbed the spoon at them. 'Because those fuckers out there, the pencil necks, their bottom line is their company's money, or their job, or they don't make it to Waitrose on time. For us, we might get our bodies fucked up.' I paused. 'Well, what's left of yours, anyway.'

It sort of got a laugh as I turned back to the kettle and poured.

'All agreed?'

I turned to see three nods.

If the shit hit the fan, decisions would have to be instant. There had to be a leader to take them and that leader had to know everyone would go with them. With the gift of hindsight, many decisions a leader had made perhaps should have been different. But on the ground all you can do is use your experience, knowledge, training, instinct – and the limited time available. Being in command is not a science: things always go to rat-shit. You're working against the elements; you're second-guessing the enemy. You can't dictate. You just have to do the best you can. But that wasn't the entirety of what all this leadership business was about. It also needs the followers to understand the system, because only then would they have a chance of success.

I had to assume we were being listened to by geeks who would hand the surveillance log to the Owl. Or maybe he'd get a much more personal report from one of these fuckers. It didn't matter: he'd still be expecting to hear this stuff and they needed to hear it even more.

'Lads, when we're out there and operating, there'll be no time for parliaments. Decisions have to be made there and then. So everyone needs to agree now that when I make a decision you'll go with it for the same reason you go with the plan in slow-time. If you don't, we put ourselves in danger because we lose traction as a team and fuck up. I might fuck it up anyway, but I guarantee there will be three other opinions on what to do if the shit hits the fan. But four people doing four different things? Won't work, lads. One voice and we carry out what it says.'

I squeezed the teabags against the mugs.

'Just platforms to fulfil the mission, remember. And that, lads, is the only way it's going to work. Get the job done, keep safe, get back, and spend our forty grand.'

I let that hang while I poured the milk, then grabbed two mugs in each hand. They could fetch the sugar themselves.

No one had sparked up.

'I take that as agreement. Any questions?'

Rio, of course, was the first. 'Yeah, Nick. Where the fuck is Sennen Grove?'

'It's Cove – and it's in Cornwall, south-west, down the bottom, somewhere near Land's End.'

Jack bent to connect the laptop as Rio reacted. 'Cornwall? All that pasty-and-*Poldark* shit?'

Gabe looked at him like he was crazy. He'd have to put in a few thousand more TV hours to catch up with his mate. 'What's the girl done or doing?'

I took a testing sip of the brew. It was far too hot.

'Don't know, mate. All the Owl said was that we're keeping the wolves from the door. But who gives a fuck? If we had to damage or even kill her that would be different. But we don't, so it doesn't matter.'

Jack had Google Maps up. 'There. Sennen Cove.'

We all looked at the small town right on the south-western peninsula of Cornwall. If you went any further south-west you'd land up in Massachusetts. That was why the Pilgrim Fathers had left from Plymouth.

Rio reached behind to the arse pocket in his jeans and pulled out his passport. 'What the fuck do we need these for, then?'

'It's part of the safety blanket, mate. You've got to carry your passports with you all the time. Always have the facility to get away from any drama.'

I fished mine out from the beige nylon middle-aged neck wallet under my sweatshirt to show I practised what I preached. Then I dipped into my jacket on the back of the chair and pulled out the wad of cash and three of the cash cards and threw it all on the table, along with the mess of chargers and mobiles that tumbled out of the plastic carrier.

'There's five hundred each – that's the twenty-four-hour limit on the prepaid Visas. There's two grand left on each card and you've all got a new mobile. We don't use the cards to purchase anything, just to withdraw cash. We want to minimize electronic tags.'

Jack picked up the cards, and dealt them like a Las Vegas croupier before starting to divvy up the money on the table.

'We'll set the mobiles up once we're on the move, and dump the old ones. Gabe, can you do that?'

Gabe shrugged and scooped up all the gear in his arms. 'At last all my years as an REME genius are being put to use.'

Rio glanced at his card and laughed. 'Melvin Spangler? I don't want to be Melvin fucking Spangler.' He grabbed Gabe's card before he'd had a chance to see it, which was a waste of time, but Rio didn't know it yet. 'Another Melvin fucking Spangler!'

I flashed my card at him. 'Yeah, we're all the same, mate. That's another reason I don't want to use them apart from getting the cash out. From today, we're all Melvins.'

Maybe the computer that had generated the cover name was in a funny mood.

The three of them started to sort out their cash. 'Any of you lot know Cornwall?'

They all shook their heads. 'Right. Does anyone know about her – she been in the news or something like that? Anything? There's nothing online.' I jabbed my finger at the printed-out Yulia. More shakes.

'Has anyone got anything about anything we're doing?'

Negative.

'Okay, so let's get our heads down for a couple of hours, then start driving to the cove. As soon as we can we hit an ATM for another five hundred each. Let's start checking out the area now, find out what the fuck's down there in the cove so we can stake the place out. Jack, can you do that?'

Rio picked up his mug and made for the sofa. 'It's all right for him, he's got a bed. I'm claiming this fucker.'

I let him get on with it as I tested the brew once more.

'We'll go down with Gabe and Rio in the Jeep, me and Jack in the Beamer.'

Rio had other ideas. 'Whoa, what about you and me, Nick, in the Beamer? I suit those fucking things. Those two smokers can kill themselves in the Jeep.'

'No. We need to stop them killing themselves. Besides, I've had enough of living with you.'

Rio put his mug on the floor before collapsing on the sofa, and I was finally able to take a mouthful of tea. 'Lads, one more thing. No contact with home until after the job. If you need to do anything now, do it on your own phones. We leave them here.'

I pointed at Gabe, who was already up and collecting cushions to get himself comfortable against the barn wall where the mobiles and wires now lay.

'Then nothing but work on those. Okay. One final thing, clothes. Gabe, you've got kit. Jack, we'll need a change of gear for me and Rio. You got anything other than jeans? We need to make sure we look different – have an appearance change, if needed. We'll get more later but start prepared.'

Jack tapped away and the printer began to bounce up and down. So did the fat brown things at his feet. Jack was already taking off his leg. 'What sizes are you?'

Rio couldn't help himself: it was a gift. 'We got no worries, mate. We'll both get into one of your jumpers. How many fucking Mars bars you having a day?'

Jack didn't dignify it with a response, just lay back on his mattress.

I turned for the door. 'I suppose the dog cushion's for me then?' I picked up my mug and walked. I wanted to be with Jack – not to stop him smoking: that was bollocks. I didn't care what he did with what was left of his body. I wanted to stay close and, I hoped, find out I was wrong about him being the snide.

26

Sainsbury's superstore service station, Penzance

I hit the unleaded nozzle and watched the display spin at warp speed as I joined lunch-time shoppers filling up. We were on the outskirts of town, where all the normal big stores congregated to sell everything from DIY stuff to sofas and windscreen wipers, and it had taken for ever to get here. The motorway had run out over a hundred miles ago at Exeter and the roads after that seemed to get narrower and narrower. The main in Cornwall was just the A30 dual carriageway, which cut through the middle of the county before changing back into a normal road with little stalls either side selling flowers or eggs. Maybe the *Poldark* lot had done it on purpose to keep the rest of the United Kingdom at bay.

Most of the locals seemed to want independence from the UK. Just about every vehicle carried a white cross on a black background in a window or on its number plates. Many displayed the pirates' skull and crossbones as well. I bet they were loving Brexit. All the fuel stations we'd stopped at had newspaper stands screaming front-page pictures of Boris or Cameron, depending on which way the paper leant. But these lads down here had only one view, judging by their window stickers, and that was Leave.

We'd taken the piss about the roads on the way down, but with just one fast escape route we could have problems. The A30 was the county's only arterial route in and out so a natural channelling point. It would be easy for anyone from the police to the Owl to cut us off if the job went wrong.

Rio was the other side of the pump, doing the same with the Jeep, while Jack and Gabe were inside to buy them out of Ginsters sausage rolls and pay for the fuel. From this point on, whenever there was an opportunity to fill up, we would. The same went for the new mobiles, which always had to be on charge when they were in the car. There was no telling where we might be going in our pursuit of Yulia.

Sennen Cove was about nine miles west of us, almost at Land's End. It had to be our starting point because it was Yulia's only known location – or, at least, the only one the Owl had given us. We had to find her, and then we had to contain her. Once we'd done that, we had to work out the best way of lifting her without third-party awareness or involvement. The third party were real people, like the ones filling up here, or spending their Nectar points, or, like the old lady in the silver Nissan Micra in front of the Jeep, just staring at Rio in disapproval. Maybe she'd never seen dreads.

Real people couldn't be part of anything we were about to do. They needed to be left alone to get on with their shopping and the rest of their lives so that they were never aware of what was going on around them. If they were, they'd do a number of things that could fuck us up. They could ignore what we were getting up to at the time, but later tell someone, who would tell someone else. Eventually it could lead to a series of events that would fuck us up at a later date. Or, if they were suspicious, they could do the good-citizen thing and call the police. Even worse than that, they could become a have-a-go hero.

One of the upsides of watching telly with Rio back in Tulse Hill was that he liked the occasional documentary. We'd watched one about the writer Paulo Coelho, which had included a great story about a young traveller in North Africa who'd received an offer of help from a Good Samaritan in a bar. The kind local was going to help him manoeuvre his way through the hustle and bustle of the souk, but the barman began shouting at the traveller in a language he didn't understand. He was happy to depend on his new best mate, and ignored the barman's warning that the man was dangerous. Obviously he got ripped off. It illustrated something I'd worked out for myself as a kid: the information the eyes and ears collect for the brain is one thing, but how the brain interprets it is another. People see the world in terms of what they'd like to see happen, not what actually does. They pull the wool over their own eyes about the world and the way it works. The traveller realized he should see the world as it was, rather than how he wanted it to be. It was the same with the third party

118

seeing and hearing things that didn't fit their normal experience, which they therefore couldn't make sense of. That was why they had to be kept out of our world, and stay in the real one for everyone's sake.

I put the nozzle back into the pump, and sat in the Beamer's left-hand seat as Gabe and Jack came out with armfuls of drinks, sandwiches and, in Gabe's case, something in shrink-wrapped plastic.

I caught Rio's eye in the passenger seat of the Jeep and he gave me a smile and the middle finger. Was he the snide? Why would he need to betray us? As far as I knew, he was an open book: didn't have much and didn't want much, apart from his arm back to normal, I supposed, and that was never going to happen. Was it to do with his girls? That was the only vulnerability I could think of. Had the Owl made promises about them? Schooling, maybe, a bright future? Or had he just threatened to fuck them up if Rio didn't do what he was told?

Gabe reached the Jeep and cut me away from my thoughts by tossing the package through the window at Rio. 'You drive this time.' He looked for support to Jack, who was climbing into the driver's side of the Beamer. 'He's done fuck-all since we left.'

Jack was too busy dumping the supplies on my lap to comment. We'd shared the driving down and it was my turn to navigate.

I could see Rio using his teeth to rip the plastic off what turned out to be a suicide spinner, the knob truck drivers attached to the steering wheel to help when driving slowly and parking one-handed. It wasn't a bad call of Gabe's.

I fastened my seatbelt and shouted through the window at Rio, who was busy clamping the suicide spinner to the bottom of the steering wheel. 'Ready?'

He powered up the Jeep, grabbed the wheel's new handle and gave it a turn. 'Got no choice now, have I? Never mind, my arse will find a way to pay him back.'

We headed out towards Sennen Cove. I wouldn't have thought it possible but on the other side of Penzance the roads got even narrower. Navigation was easy, though: we just followed the signs to Land's End.

Checking the Jeep was still behind us, I put in the earplugs I'd bought at CeX with the phones and dialled up Gabe.

He was his normal sociable self. 'What?'

'I know we've done it to death, but I'm going to run through our actions-on when we get to the cove, okay? When we turn off for the cove, you drive downhill to the beach. It's the only way into and out of the place. Then you turn right into the car park. We're going to carry on along the main that parallels the beach, to the other side of the village and the harbour car park. What me and you do then is de-bus. We walk along the main and see what we can see. If we find her, I'll sort out a trigger so we've got eyes on from then on. Remember, once we're eyes on, we must keep them on. You got it?'

He obviously thought I was insulting his memory. 'Course I got it.'

'Good. We're going to be turning off soon, so see you somewhere on the main.'

I closed down, and we turned right via a mini round-about onto a steep downhill road, just a car wide. The beach and the sea spread out below us. I could see it wasn't so much a main we were going to drive along as a track. The old fishing village had been given a new lease of life by the surf. If the news articles online were to be believed, this place had been ranked among the top ten places in the world to surf, alongside Bali, Hawaii and southern France, just not as exotic. Or as warm.

I could see bodies way out at sea, lying on their boards, waiting for the right wave. Some, closer in, were already going for it, then landing on the beach.

27

We got to the bottom of the road and hit the village. Google Maps showed only two ways to go from there: right, to a car park, or left, paralleling the beach and the row of buildings facing the sea, until another car park. It also showed the village had more parking spaces than houses.

We turned left and rolled past all the usual suspects on the left: a pub, a café, a fish-and-chip shop, surf outlets. Bodies wandered about with the tops of their wetsuits rolled down to their hips, and long-sleeve T-shirts or windproof jackets to keep out the cold. It might have been May, but the whitecaps on the water showed how windy it was out there. To round off the trendy surfer look, most heads were covered with woolly hats, and the hair beneath them was universally blond. A lot of dye had been involved but it didn't matter: they all looked as cool on the land as they did in the water.

It wasn't just surfers who populated the village. Very

smiley people who all seemed to be wearing baggy jumpers and multicoloured cheesecloth trousers sat along the sea wall, with signs telling everyone they'd braid your hair or teach you how to play a didgeridoo for a fiver.

We kept rolling slowly, playing the day tripper, eyes peeled for a Belarusian whose physique didn't fit. Even the surf thing didn't fit her. She came from a land-locked country that had been part of the Soviet Union until the nineties and they weren't exactly big-time surfers themselves. Maybe Yulia collected old videos of *Baywatch*.

We came to the far end of the village, and now I saw what all the parking spaces were for. Each one was taken by a camper van, predominantly VWs, with surf-boards on roof-racks or resting against them.

Jack nosy-parked in a disabled space and the mobile rang. It was Gabe. 'We've parked up, and Rio's tucked out of the way. He's not the blondest, the twat.'

I could hear Rio laughing in the background, and a very bad *Apocalypse Now* accent. 'Black men don't surf.'

I hoped they were focused. Even if we didn't see Yulia, we had to make sure she didn't see us, which was hard when everything the others knew about counter-surveillance came from watching American cop shows.

'Okay, we're parking up too. I'm going foxtrot. That means walking, remember?'

Gabe shot back, 'Shut the fuck up and get on with it. I'm going now. Going foxtrot.' He closed down.

I got out and a gale hit me. I zipped up my jacket, plunged my hands into my pockets, and started walking back the way we'd just come. Jack and Rio stayed put. There always had to be someone in the cars, ready to move, ready to run attackers over if the follow went very wrong.

The wind was even stronger as I followed the low stone sea wall and the Atlantic got whipped up to my left. A row of commercial boats was parked up on wooden cradles, with lads in wellies and blue overalls scraping stuff off or painting stuff on. I joined the brave few checking out the shops or getting their hair braided. No one had taken up the didgeridoo offer. I peered inside each shop as well as the cafés, but there was no sign of the target, and it wasn't long before I saw Gabe coming the other way, trying hard to disguise his limp.

We passed without acknowledging each other and I now rechecked his areas. Two sets of eyes were better than one. I also checked the bodies in the water as best I could, but the tide was out.

As I neared the other car park, I saw the Jeep first, then a clump of dreadlocks against the driver's window. Normally, I would have wanted the cars parked nose-out so they could drive away quickly, but there were two reasons why I hadn't wanted that to happen here. The first was that, under pressure, some drivers spend so much time backing in, or even trying to find a place to do so, that they end up compromising themselves. It wasn't as if everyone was going to look at them and say, 'Oh, look, there's an undercover operator.' But they might say, 'What the fuck's that twat doing?' which meant the target might see the car and everyone in it. Some people found it hard to do two things at once – in this case, look at the target and behave naturally behind the wheel. Nosy-parking was the answer: it was what the real world did. Anyway, these two vehicles had an advantage when it came to finding a space. They both had blue disability badges.

The second reason for nosy-parking was that it hid the driver a bit more than if they were facing out. Rio was wrong – I'd seen plenty of black men surfing, although they certainly weren't today – but those dreadlocks gave him a VDM, a visual distinguishing mark. I had enough of them in the team already.

This car park was about the same as ours, pretty much full, but there was one exception. It was dominated by a large, modern church building with a steel roof, very Norway-looking. At least, I thought it was a church: it had a new stained-glass window with the world's biggest cross on it, but all around were adverts for surf shops and lessons. Maybe it really was a religion after all.

I turned and started the tourist circuit again, wondering how we were going to stake this place out until she eventually turned up. I passed Gabe once more as he came out of the pub at the end of the main. The Old Success Inn: that was something we weren't having much of at the moment.

I approached the café and the crowd of half-wetsuited gods and goddesses having coffee outside, talking surf shit with their hands darting through pretend water. My phone vibrated. It was Rio. 'I've got her. She's in the car park. She's just come out of the water.'

'You sure it's the target?' If he wasn't, I'd have to confirm it.

125

'I'm telling you, it's her.'

'Okay, what's she doing? She about to leave? Is she in a vehicle?'

'No, mate. Just told you, coming out of the water. There's about four – no, one minute, there's five lads, big lads, older, with her. They're all getting out of the wetsuits, putting them back in a van.'

'What's the vehicle?'

'A blue VW camper. It's got a roof rack for the boards – they're strapping them down.'

'Can you see the reg?'

'No, the tailgate's up. Listen, she's got a big fuck-off tattoo on her neck. We ain't going to lose her in a hurry.'

'That's good, mate. Stay there and keep the trigger on the van. If it leaves with the target on board before we've got a proper stakeout on it, leave Gabe and just follow it. We'll pick him up, and then we'll back you, okay? If the target goes foxtrot, just tell me what direction and I'll take her. We'll sort our shit out from there. We need eyes on her all the time.'

'Got it.' His voice had gone where I wanted it to be, which was serious.

We closed down and I called Gabe. 'Mate, listen in. Rio's got her. She's got a neck full of tattoo and she's at the blue VW camper van in your car park. There's five lads with her. As you walk in, try to confirm that it's her. And get a reg of the van if you can. Rio knows what to do if you don't get back in time and they move. If that happens, we'll come and pick you up.'

'Roger that.'

Great. Both of them were now in work mode. I closed

down, got back to the Beamer and jumped in. 'Think we got her. We're waiting on Gabe.'

The phone vibrated and I put it on speaker. The wind battered the microphone as Gabe confirmed. 'It's definitely her and the tattoo covers all of her throat, not the neck. Those five lads, they've been hitting the weights, mate, and the tattoo parlours. If they're the wolves we're keeping from the door we need to get one fuck-off strong door.

'All the gear is going in the van and on the roof rack. The reg – I can't see much of it at the moment. All I've got is Whisky Kilo six four. Whisky Kilo six four.'

'Mate, that's excellent. Go back to the Jeep and keep the trigger on the van. If it goes mobile with the target, call me, and follow in slow time. They've only got one way out of here and just two ways to go at the top: left to Penzance, right to Land's End.'

I heard the Jeep door close, and the roar of the wind disappeared. There was just the rustle of clothes as he sorted himself out. 'I've got it. They're almost packed up.'

'Great, listen in. We'll get a trigger on the junction at the top of the hill, so we can give direction and take 'em – you can come up the hill in slow time and back us. Make sense?'

Jack had already fired up the ignition and was reversing out.

Gabe was on it. 'Yep, closing down now.'

As we drove out of the car park I looked at Jack. 'As we go through here, keep your eyes open, just in case we fucked up and it isn't Yulia. We'll go up to the junction and find a place to stake it out.'

We reached the end of the shops, then the pub, and came to the steep road up to our right. Yulia's car park was dead ahead. I tried to have a quick look. No luck. But we would at some stage today, or tomorrow if we screwed up today and lost her because this was the only known location we had for her.

The Beamer took the hill and the cove disappeared below us. I was concerned about the Wolves: it didn't sound like they were the Belarus surf team here training for the season.

28

We got to the junction at the top of the cliff and stopped at the mini-roundabout that helped the three bits of road sort themselves out. It must have been manic at the height of the season with caravans and all sorts snarled up.

I pointed left. 'Towards that school.' It was an old Victorian building with extensions out the back. Just beyond it was a car park where we could stop out of sight. 'Pull in, turn round, and we'll work out where to stop after that.'

To the left of the school there was a small electricity sub-station, with fields beyond. Good. It meant we'd be out of view not only of the van but also of the third party.

We turned at the bottom of the drive and parked just short of the substation. Jack switched the engine off, and I shifted the back of my seat down.

'We could be here some time, might as well get comfy. And it will make us less of a recognizable shape for anyone checking out the car. It might even look empty.'

The mobile vibrated. Jack got ready to move again, but it wasn't Gabe. It was the tracker. One of the community had walked past my cat.

'It's okay, mate, it's only Gabe wanting a call.'

I hit dial to cover myself, and would ask Gabe for a sit-rep, but he'd been about to call me anyway. 'All doors are closed. They're going to be off any minute.'

'Roger that.' I gave Jack a look so he'd know there was shit on. 'But is the target inside? Is she in the van?'

'She's in there with the rest of the fucks.'

'For definite she's in the van?'

'Yes! For fuck's sake.'

'All right, listen in. When they move, give them distance – don't get up their arse. Just make sure you know they're heading up the hill to the junction, all right? Keep the line open. I've got the trigger on the junction, and I'll tell you which way they went. Remember, we'll take them from the junction, you then back us.' I motioned for Jack to start the engine. 'You got that, Gabe?'

'Yep, here we go. They're leaving now.'

I jumped out of the Beamer and bent down to instruct Jack. 'Wait here till I move you up, okay?'

He nodded and I walked fast towards the road and the end of the school. 'Where are they, Gabe?' I could hear the Jeep's engine ticking over.

'They're moving uphill now, going up the road. We're still in the car park, just manoeuvring to get out.'

'Okay, stay online.'

I reached the corner of the school and could see the worn-out paint of the mini-roundabout about eighty metres away. A couple of cars were held there, coming up from the cove. Eventually I saw the blue VW joining the line. I could hardly miss it with all the surfboards strapped on top.

'Gabe, it's held at the junction, three vehicles back. No indicators on. Now that's two cars back. Still no indicators.'

I heard the Jeep's engine note rise. It would be at the bottom of the hill now, making its way up.

'Gabe. That's the van indicating . . . It's intending right, towards Land's End.'

I didn't move back yet. Until the van turned right, the indicators meant nothing. That was all they were. 'That's still two back, still indicating right.'

Gabe was on the ball. 'Roger that, I'm holding back.'

'Gabe. He's now at the junction. Wait. Wait. Okay, that's the van now turning right, towards Land's End.'

I waved for Jack to come forward, not looking back to check he saw me. My eyes needed to stay on the target. 'Gabe. That's now on the road towards Land's End.'

The Beamer pulled up next to me and I jumped in. 'Turn left, foot down, mate, catch the van up.'

Jack did as he was told, and as we passed the round-about I could see the Jeep approaching it from downhill. They were soon out of sight as we rounded the corner past a pub.

The camper van came into sight.

'Jack, close up to the car ahead. Let it give us some cover. We don't want to be too far back on these bendy roads.'

I held the plug mic closer to my mouth as the Beamer's revs climbed. 'Gabe, you there?'

'Yup.'

'We have the van, just past a pub on the left – he's slowing down. Wait, wait. He's indicating left. He's intending left. Wait. Okay, that's now gone left into Seaview Holiday Park – Seaview Holiday Park, on the left. Gabe, go in and park up so you have a trigger on the exit, then get out and see what they're up to. You got that?'

The Jeep's engine was gunning now to catch up with us and Gabe raised his voice to be heard. 'Got it, and closing down so I don't have to listen to you telling me how to wipe my arse.'

I laughed and indicated to Jack to continue along the road, taking a quick glance at the entrance to what I could now see was a big static caravan site.

Jack found an open five-bar gate into a field a few hundred metres further on and drove in, bouncing the Beamer over the grass to turn round. He sounded relieved. 'We wait until they get their heads down, and we take her?'

'We could do, mate, something like that if we're going to avoid those big fucks. But let's just wait here till Gabe tells us what's what. The van might be dropping someone off, picking someone up, just stopping for a piss and then out again – we don't know.'

It looked like Jack was going to stop with his bonnet sticking out of the gate ready to turn left or right.

'No, mate, behind the hedge. If she moves, Gabe will give us a direction.'

'But what if we miss her?'

'Then we miss her – but we'll have two places to check out later. Better than compromising ourselves on hour one, day one.'

I kept the mobile earplugs in and pointed to Jack's charging phone in one of the cup holders. 'Can you get maps up for us? I want to keep mine clear for Gabe.'

If Jack was reluctant to hand over control of his mobile, I couldn't tell: I was already out of the Beamer and leaning back in to take it from him after he'd entered his PIN.

'Just checking out what I can see over the fields towards the caravan site.'

I took off towards the gate, checking the satellite imagery of the area until I was out of sight of Jack. Then I hit the tracker app on my mobile, which came straight up on Google Maps and showed me that someone from the community and the Owl had been at the US Embassy in Grosvenor Square about fifteen minutes ago.

Gabe came back into my earplugs. 'Pass Reception, turn right, and they're parked up on the left about seventy down.'

'Good skills, Gabe. Can you see the target? Is she there?'

'No. Otherwise I would have told you so. They're unloading their kit, fuck-off black bags, the big vinyl adventure things. But I can't see where to – the place is full of caravans. They could be in any of the fuckers. I don't want to get too close.'

'Okay, mate. We'll come and take the trigger on the exit.' I checked the site map again as I spoke. 'It's the only one. Then you get back down to Penzance. We filled up by a big Halfords outside the town – get a couple of tents, sleeping bags, all that sort of shit, and give us a call once you've done it.'

I closed down and had one more job to do before getting back to the Beamer. I went into Jack's emails and texts to see if he was stupid enough to leave anything he'd sent to the Owl. There was nothing, but that didn't mean anything just yet.

Once in settings, I checked his battery usage. Fifty-three per cent of the battery life had been taken up on messages. A lot of waffling had been deleted,

I reverted the screen to maps as I ran back to the Beamer and jumped in. 'On to the road, turn left. We're going camping.'

I plugged both mobiles into the adaptor and glanced at Jack. Was there any concern on his face trying hard not to burst through?

29

The caravan site was coming up on the right and Jack hit the indicator.

'Don't acknowledge the Jeep if you see it. Just pull in somewhere like we're going to pick up a brochure or something.'

We crossed the A30 and drove in. Gabe and Rio were nosy-parked in the line of cars outside the reception building, which a sign said also housed a restaurant, bar, cinema, shop and bowling alley.

'Anywhere you want, engine off. I'll check out the van and try to find Yulia. All you need to do is adjust your mirrors, all three, so you can see behind you. If you spot the van leaving, you follow – without me, if you have to. All nice and slow, because that gives them time to get out of the junction and they don't see you manoeuvring.

'You don't want to be right up their arse – you just need to know which way they're going and start following. Call Gabe, then give me a shout. Just keep with the van because that's all we've got at the moment.'

Their job done for now, Gabe and Rio reversed out and headed for the main. I pocketed the phone, inserted my earphones, climbed out of the Beamer, closed the door with a cheery wave at Jack, thinking darker thoughts than my face showed, and set off in the direction of the van – right past Reception, about seventy down.

But first, I went into the shop and came out again a few minutes later with a children's cricket set under my arm.

Caravans stretched to the horizon. In and around them was the whole circle of life. Young couples kicked sponge footballs to their toddlers. Coming up on my right, older kids raced around a play park. Grey-haired couples sat outside on deckchairs, rugs over their legs as they drank tea. It was good cover having so many of the third party out and about, but if I found Yulia, it was also going to make it hard to get and keep eyes on her.

I passed the play park on the right. The Wolves' VW was parked on hardstanding a little further down on the left, just off the road and a metre or two before a bend, next to a couple of estate cars with luggage boxes on top and pushbike racks hanging off the tailgates. A sign for 'Nos 55 to 60' pointed up the grass to the left.

The camper van had been unloaded of boards, but I couldn't see inside it. The tailgate window was covered with a sheet of stick-on black film that had bubbled with age and heat. The sliding door didn't have a window and was closed. The only glimpse I got of the interior was the dashboard. The cans, empty Pringles tubes and car-park tickets were only what you'd expect.

I carried on and caught my first sighting of the Wolves between the first two caravans in the line beyond the car park. Not one of them was skinny with a mass of hair. No problem: I hoped to have a closer view in a second. The road continued in a big horse-shoe, and as I rounded the bend the two caravans were on the start of the straight, numbers fifty-five and fifty-six.

I followed the road, eyes fixed on a caravan in the mid-distance, a bit of a smile on my face at the prospect of playing cricket with my kids in a minute. I had a reason to be there, just like everyone else carrying shopping or ice creams, or the mother running towards the play park, shouting at her kids not to jump off the slide but use it the way it was designed.

The first thing that hit me as the caravans came into view was the music. Rap boomed out of fifty-six, which had the boards leant against it. Its flowery curtains were pulled shut, like they thought that would contain it. I got a good sighting of the Wolves in the gap between fifty-five and fifty-six, cartons of milk in hand and getting into what I assumed were protein bars. They had changed into fleeces, cargoes or jeans, and Gabe was right. They were massive. This was a fuck of a lot of muscle and not a lot of hair. They all had that white-walled cut with just a little more on top like a lot of gym rats had. Five colossal wetsuits hung on a line stretched between the two caravans, along with another that looked like it belonged to a ten-year-old. It was a good sign. A couple of large disposable barbecues had been lit and were already creating enough smoke to alert the Coastguard.

I tried hard to hear their accents or language but I was too far away, and so much bass was coming from the speakers that the tiles must have been flying off Reception's roof. Someone would surely say something soon. Or maybe they wouldn't, once they'd banged on the door to complain and one of the monsters stepped out.

As I came closer, the accents didn't matter because of what I could see. In Russian prisons, your life story is tattooed on your body. Pictures of bears shagging women, and rats with numbers above them tell anyone in the know the detention centres the owners have been to, and why. The Wolves were too young to have much of a story – they all looked in their late twenties, early thirties at most – but their first chapters were certainly written. On the back of the neck of one, who looked a bit older than the rest, there was a bird's head, blue and blurred, linking the collar of his fleece to his cropped hairline. Prison ink was normally improvised from a mixture of soot and piss, and injected into the skin with a sharpened guitar string attached to an electric shaver, which sometimes made the design hard to work out. Not this time. It could only have been a phoenix. The rest of the bird would cover his back as it flew out of the flames to each side of it, just like he would, along with thousands of others in prison who got the bird stamped on them.

The brightly flowered curtains were drawn in fifty-five as well, but as I moved past I saw that the window wasn't completely shut. A small grey rectangular plastic box, with two leads coming out of it, was suckered to the glass. No other caravan round here had one, just the normal dish arrangement. I wondered if Yulia was at the other end of those leads, doing whatever was so bad the Owl wanted a chat, but until one of us got eyes-on, baby wetsuit or not, I didn't even know one hundred per cent where she was.

I followed the road up towards my imminent cricket game with my kids. A few brave young souls were trying to enjoy the open-air swimming pool.

The Wolves looked like real surfers: their kit was worn. A couple of wetsuits had patches and the boards were well used, with dings underneath and lots of old wax on top. If they were there to protect Yulia while she did whatever she was doing, the surfing was a credible cover – and the area was probably overflowing with East European workers in the hotels and cafés, so it wasn't as if their accents would stick out.

Maybe Yulia and the Wolves really were from Belarus. There were ethnic Russians in the country and no doubt Putin planned an invasion to protect them very soon.

I got to the end of the pool and squinted through the fence as if I was rounding up my kids. They must have gone back to our caravan instead of waiting for me. I gave up and headed back down the road. The music still blared, the barbecues were getting smokier, and the lads were on their second round of protein bars.

Lifting Yulia, with that pack around her, was going to be a lot harder than I'd hoped. Maybe I'd strike lucky – maybe Jack was right: if she was caught short during the night and headed for the toilet all I'd have to do was grip her, bundle her into the back of the Beamer, and we'd all head for London while I put in a call to the Owl.

I carried on past numbers fifty-six and fifty-five, then the van. I had my sights set on the play park, wondering if I could get away with watching from the benches. Single male, sitting next to a kids' area, even with a cricket set under his arm? Nah, maybe not so much.

I got back to the Beamer and Jack powered down his window. 'I still can't see Yulia.' I wedged the cricket kit onto the back seat. 'She could be in one of the caravans – who knows? We've got to stake it out anyway, so it doesn't matter for now.'

I opened the door and motioned for Jack to get out. 'I'll take the trigger now and phone the others to tell them what's going on. I need you to go to Reception and book two pitches for the tents in the field next to the kids' play park. Get right up to the hedges and the bushes so we can hide the wagons from the parking area opposite the caravans – that's where their van is.

'From there, we can maybe get a trigger on the caravans – or the van – and find this little fucker.'

Jack clambered out, pleased for the stretch. 'What happens if we don't find her? If she's not there?'

'We'll just keep doing what we're doing, staying with the van. If the van moves, we move. Hopefully we'll see her getting into it, and if she isn't in it, hopefully the van will lead us to her. Hopefully the lads will go down to the cove, and hopefully we'll pick Yulia up like we did today.'

'Hope' is a good word to explain what you can't control, but that's all. Relying on hope gives pain and panic to events that were better worked at or not worried about. The Stoics had it right: be prepared for the worst, then anything good that happens is a bonus.

Jack pulled his mobile from its charger and set off for Reception and the club area like he had a girl waiting. Maybe he was bursting for a piss.

I jumped into the driver's seat and adjusted the mirrors, then checked the interior lights. Shit. These new cars all had integral units – there was no way I could take the cover off and disconnect the bulb.

I called Gabe and Rio to see how they were getting on and give them a sit-rep, along with some more odds and ends to add to our shopping list.

30

The caravan site

It was maybe two hours or so since dark o'clock and Rio was stretched out on a roll-mat behind me in the blue nylon dome tent, trying to get comfortable in a sleeping bag. Not that it was his: he and Gabe had their own tent but couldn't be arsed to move because this one was where the trigger on the camper van was and they would have to keep it later on. I sat cross-legged on a roll-mat of my own, inhaling the stink of the beef-flavour crisps and chocolate he and Gabe had bought on their way back from Halfords.

The ambient light from the site's streetlamps and the occasional car slowing for the U-bend glowed dully inside the tent, just enough for us to make out movement, not faces. The odd shriek still came from the play park to the left, but it was teenagers now, excited to be unsupervised so late at night. The vehicle traffic had died down after a bit of an exodus: a lot of guests had headed out, probably to the annoyance of the park owners who wanted their cash spent in the restaurant and bowling alley. We'd watched a stream of holidaymakers in towelling robes and flip-flops traipse to and from the ablutions block with their washbags.

I'd cut a small slit in the tent's inner and outer fabric and it worked well. The only trouble would come if anyone in the real world spotted it so close to the play park with an eye behind it. I could just make out the back of the van in the shadows cast by the lighting along the road. If it moved, I would know. With a bit of luck, I might get to see Yulia in a vehicle's headlights as she approached it.

Gabe was doing a walk-past of fifty-five and fifty-six, and I hoped – there was that word again – he'd remembered what I'd told him about keeping to the shadows. The big prize for us would be Gabe having a positive sighting of a skinny Belarusian.

As Rio fought with a nylon sleeping bag that didn't react well to just one hand pulling it about, Gabe appeared from the dead side of the VW camper van. There was a red glow and a trail of smoke as he sucked in his fix. He'd probably cut across the grass between the caravans after initially passing them on the road. I wondered where he was vulnerable if he was the snide. I didn't know too much about the situation with his wife, so all I could think of was his kids. I didn't feel he would have folded as easily as Rio if his kids were threatened. He would probably have done his fizzy Coke trick and overreacted by climbing aboard the Owl. Gabe did live his life on loud. Then again, it might have been carrot not stick. There was always the sweetener of a better life for the family, better education, social mobility, who knew? Almost certainly Gabe had a couple of skeletons lurking in his cupboard, like all of us, it was just his cupboard wasn't as transparent as Rio's.

It wasn't long before the zip was pulled down behind me and Gabe struggled inside, smelling like a teenager who'd had a smoke in the garden and thought his parents would never know. I wasn't going to look back: I had the trigger.

Gabe wrestled his way past the other body behind me. At least he spoke in low tones rather than a whisper, which would have carried. 'There are lights on in both caravans, but the curtains are pulled. No sign of Yulia. The antenna has been taken in.'

At last Rio had control of the mass of nylon and the zip was pulled – but not for long.

'Okay, Rio, you take the trigger. I need to check out the women's washroom.'

It took far longer than it would have done had there been the correct number of arms and legs in the tent, and on top of that there was Rio huffing and puffing as he tried to kick the rest of the bag off his legs while still keeping the trigger, but I eventually got out and headed off.

What the fuck had Jack been doing all this time? I had an idea, but needed to know for sure.

The washroom was divided in half for the sexes and the male side looked and smelt exactly as I'd expected, that damp scent of shampoo mixed with Lynx, and a wet but practical concrete floor. A couple of shower cubicles were in use, just beyond the row of toilets. The doors had generous gaps at the bottom to let the water flow away when they were hosed down.

I bent down to check the only toilet that was occupied and saw Jack's black Clarks boots. They weren't swamped with jeans – in fact, some of his high-tech titanium leg showed because his jeans were still pulled up.

I took the next cubicle and did what you were supposed to do. There was nothing from next door. I sat and listened. The only sound was a coughing fit from one of the bodies having a shower. Finally there was movement in the next cubicle. Jack's door opened and he left. No paper pulling, no zipping up, no flush.

I resisted the urge to do a Gabe and burst out to grab his throat. I gave him enough time to exit the block.

Gripping Jack wouldn't do us any good. For now, it didn't matter what the Owl knew because we were doing exactly what he was paying for. Jack could wait – I'd sort him out later. Maybe he'd fuck it up himself and the other two wouldn't have to be persuaded he had betrayed them by easing the way for the Owl to make them very dead.

Besides, I needed his help. We didn't have enough arms and legs to sort ourselves out in a tent, let alone lift someone.

I gave it another couple of minutes before zipping up and leaving the building to the shower boy, who needed to see a doctor about his lungs.

I poked my head into the tent just as Gabe ripped a crisp packet out of Rio's hand and started to munch. The tent amplified the noise.

'Everyone, stay where you are and I'll climb over and take the trigger.'

I scrambled over flesh and metal as Jack tried to help by moving a little. 'I had a walk round, seeing if there's somewhere one of us could trigger Yulia going for the washroom. Might be worth a punt in an hour or so, midnight.'

As I took over, Rio moved back, disrupting the set-up. Gabe had even more than that to honk about. 'You see 'em, Nick, those fuckers stuck in front of the TV watching Brexit shit? They're supposed to be on holiday! What's wrong with these people?'

I hated Jack even more for thinking he was getting away with being part of the group when he said, 'It's because it's important, isn't it, where the country goes from here? Don't you think?'

Gabe didn't. 'I don't give a shit. The only time I've ever voted was for independence from you lot.' He took a breath. 'We were so fucking close to winning. But I'm voting again. I want out. Fuck the English, fuck the French, and fuck the rest of them. Just leave us alone.'

Rio laughed. 'What you doing down here, then, Braveheart?'

Gabe wasn't having any of it. 'You can shove the EU. Which way you going to vote, Jack? You're the only one with a few brain cells in this fucking tent.'

Jack didn't miss a beat. 'Stay in, of course. Better the devil you know. We need to stay in for economic reasons – and social. I feel European.'

Rio wasn't going to be left out of this. 'Me, I don't care. They don't give a shit about me so why should I give a shit about them? No matter which way it goes, I've still got to live, work and play. Who gives a fuck? I don't believe either bunch of bullshit. Everyone's going to vote to stay in anyway, aren't they? What about you, Nick? You in or out?'

There was no time for an answer, not that I had one. I'd never voted so had never had to think about what I was supposed to be voting for. I kept it low to stop anyone getting excited: 'We have movement around the camper van. Just one voice now – mine. Listen in. Rio and Jack, get to the cars. Don't start them yet. Gabe, stay and listen.'

They moved a lot quicker exiting than they had coming in.

I carried on with the commentary to Gabe. 'I've got three big bodies at the front of the van. Too big for Yulia. There's more bodies coming but I can't see them in the dark. Wait. Wait. They're all now unsighted on the other side of the van. Wait. Wait. That's a door open, cab lights on. I've got two bodies getting in. One behind the wheel. The rest of them are now on the dead side of the van, the sliding-door side. That's lights on. Lights on.'

Decision time. Did I leave someone here to keep a trigger on the caravans? I didn't know if Yulia was in the van, but I also didn't know if she was in one of the caravans. The only thing I did know was that she was last seen at the van in the cove car park. Fuck it, stay with the van.

'Okay, here we go.'

I turned and scrambled over him. He didn't need to be out and heading for the Beamer as quick as I did for the Jeep. Jack and I had swapped vehicles because of its low-tech lights.

Jack fired the ignition as soon as he saw me and the headlights stayed off. I jumped in and the interior lights didn't come on. I had pulled them out. My nostrils filled with the nicotine embedded in the seat fabric as I saw the reversing light of the VW camper van cut out and its headlights begin to carve their way up to Reception. Jack was bent forward in his seat, his face almost against the windscreen.

'Okay, let's go – lights off for now. Watch out for kids.'

'What do you reckon, Nick? Maybe they're off clubbing.'

We passed their parking area and I glanced across at their caravans. All the lights were off. 'We're about to find out.'

31

We neared the reception area hardstanding. Jack wasn't too pleased about driving with the lights off, maybe because he was nervous about hitting somebody. I was going to have to talk him through everything. It would have been easier if I'd taken the wheel but there might be some running about to do if they went foxtrot.

'Jack, no brake lights. Just the handbrake if you need to slow.'

As we turned left into the parking area by Reception, I could see the glow of brake lights from the VW about thirty metres ahead, about to move out onto the main.

I shoved the second plug into my ear as I hit Gabe's number. 'You mobile?'

'Yup.'

'Great. The van's at the exit onto the main. No indication yet. Wait. Wait. That's now mobile, that's left towards Land's End. Gabe, keep well back, mate.'

The van disappeared onto the main. I kept it very clear, very simple. I wanted everyone to know who I was talking to.

'Jack, lights on, let's go.'

We exited onto the A30 and I could see the VW's lights about a hundred ahead. They were higher than the average car's, so that was a good VDM. At this time of night there was hardly any traffic, which was good – we could find the van quicker if we screwed up – but bad in that it could make us stick out.

'Gabe – that's still the van towards Land's End. No – wait. The light's disappeared left. He's turned left. Gabe, he's taken the first junction left. Signed Minack Theatre.'

Gabe also knew to keep it short and sharp. 'Roger that, Nick. We're now on the main.'

'Jack, turn left, get your foot down. Don't worry, you won't hit anything. It's a straight line. We're in the middle of nowhere. Just use the van lights ahead as a guide. You'll know when there's a bend. If you get too close I'll tell you.'

He needed to get into the zone but it wasn't happening. 'Jack, open your window, stick your head out, get your bearings from the hedge.'

For some people, a windscreen was a psychological barrier. So, too, was the spotter giving too much detail on a follow. Road names, details of houses or junctions don't work – too much information to take in and, on the move, it immediately changes. A simple picture for Gabe and Rio was best.

Jack needed to get a grip because the VW wouldn't wait for us.

'Gabe – that's brake lights on. Wait. Wait.'

Jack wobbled the Jeep a little as he tried to keep it in a straight line.

'Jack, foot off the gas. Let it slow on its own.'

Jack brought his head inside the Jeep. I kept my eyes on the lights in front.

'Gabe – that's now left. It's gone left. Wait. Wait.'

We covered the last twenty or so to the junction.

'Gabe – we're at a T-junction. He's gone left. Now towards Penzance. It's a B road.'

Gabe was still backing us. 'Roger that.'

I gave the VW another couple of seconds' distance before we had to continue. 'Jack, let's go – lights on now.'

The road meandered. No light either side.

As the VW's lights disappeared to the right without braking, we did the same. 'Jack – slow down now. It's open country. Let them get away and use their full beam. As long as we can see it, we're good.'

We passed a marker for the Beamer to use.

'Gabe – now passing a junction right. Signed Trevilley. The van's still towards Penzance on the B road.'

Their beam was about a hundred metres ahead of us when the rear lights disappeared.

'Jack – speed up. But remember, no brakes.'

It's difficult to judge headlights at night, especially how far behind you they are, and especially in rear-view mirrors. It's even harder when the road is winding. Brake lights, however, are a big giveaway. They give direction, distance and position much more than headlights because they're not constant so catch the eye. We had come to another marker for the Beamer.

'Gabe – that's now a sharp right-hand bend. Now a sharp left. Still on the B road to Penzance.'

We rounded the final corner and Jack almost jumped out of his skin. 'Shit! Fuck!' He hit the brakes. The VW was now moving at a snail's pace and the driver hit the left indicator.

'He's letting you pass. Just do it, normal stuff.'

We overtook them on the narrow road. This wasn't good. They now had our reg and make, if that was what they were after.

'Gabe – hold off, hold off. They're trailing in the road, we've just had to overtake them. I don't know what's going on.'

'Roger that.' He sounded bored, but that's how the military are taught. If your voice gets fast and excited, it's an infection that spreads. It can instil panic and you start stumbling over your words. Next, you're stumbling over your actions.

I was the same to Jack: monotone, reassuring. 'Jack. We'll carry on and look for a place on the left to turn off.'

We passed a junction signposted Skewjack Farm. 'Too close. Keep going. Take the bend.'

As we came out of the S there was a junction to the left. 'In there.'

It was the entrance to an industrial unit.

'Stop. Engine off, lights off, handbrake on.'

I pulled off my neck wallet and my earphones. My USB was already in the wallet. I had to go sterile.

'Jack, stay where you are. Keep looking back to the road. You should see my silhouette. I'm going to find out what the fuck they're up to. If I have a drama, you'll see. Come down and back me.'

I leapt out of the Jeep and passed the entrance to the industrial unit, legging it to the junction ten metres away. A vehicle was coming from the right. Its lights zigzagged through the S, and I threw myself into the hedgerow and waited.

A burst of red light bathed the trees either side of the road as the vehicle slowed for the bend. I stayed perfectly still, just one eye open as I buried the side of my face deep in the grass.

The VW slowed to a snail's pace again. Two lights shone from the open side door, searching the tarmac road. The van passed directly in front of me, and I could just make out the shapes of the torch bearers. One was kneeling, and there was a different set of arms below him, lying and holding out what looked like a mobile with its light on.

The van passed and I jumped out of the hedge and ran after it. The van crawled along the road, both lights still illuminating the tarmac to the side. It went another sixty or seventy metres, then its engine note rose and its full beam cut faster through the night sky.

I turned, sprinted back to the Jeep and jumped in. 'Lights on, let's go. Turn left, follow them – no brake lights.'

We hit the road. I necked my wallet and jammed my earphones in. The VW's beam was in the distance and over to the right.

'Gabe – get to Skewjack Farm. It's signposted on the left. See what they were checking on the tarmac. Then do the same for the next junction left, by an industrial building. From that junction, go past for another sixty to seventy. That make sense?'

'Yup, roger that. What the fuck they doing?'

'I think I saw them taking pictures or videos of the road. What I didn't see was Yulia.'

32

As we followed the lights I lifted the mic to my mouth. 'Gabe, you there?'

'Yup. Still checking the road.'

'The van's still on the main towards Penzance. We're at a village called Polgigga.'

'Come again?'

'P-O-L-G-I-G-G-A. You'll see a minor built-up area and warning signs for ducks crossing – coming to a sharp left-hand turn with a mud track on the right. Just past the duck sign.'

We were about to take the left-hander when Jack sparked up. 'They're at it again!'

'Pull over on the left, lights out.'

We bumped up onto the pavement between two cars parked outside a row of small stone cottages. We sat and waited as the red lights crawled along the road about 150 ahead.

'Gabe – I've got another for you to check out.'

'Roger that.'

I could hear Rio close to Gabe. 'You want pictures of these ones?'

I didn't have time to ask what he was on about. The torch lights went off and the VW began to move.

'Jack – let's go for it. No lights until we've lost them on a bend.'

The Jeep bounced off the kerb.

'Gabe – stand by. We're still on the main to Penzance, and there's a sign for Trethewey. Okay, marker for you, a lone stone bungalow on the right, nothing on the left, just fields.'

'Roger that.'

The VW was making distance and the Jeep swerved as Jack tried to manoeuvre in the dark.

'Jack, don't rush it. You can see their lights. Keep it in the middle of the road.'

His fists clenched the wheel as I got back to the Beamer. 'Gabe – now passing a war memorial on the right. There's a big gravel parking area.'

'Roger that.'

Rio was still in the background. 'Just doing one more.'

I left them to it as we had two problems ahead of us. 'Jack, cars coming up. You seen them?'

Two sets of lights were coming towards us. I wasn't sure what he had seen so far.

'Jack, foot off the gas, let it slow down under its own steam. Throw yourself left and park up. Only the handbrake.'

The two sets of white lights got closer and the red ones got further away after we had pulled in behind a couple of Transits. We had now lost the VW.

I jumped out and climbed onto the roof. What I hoped to see in the middle distance was a bubble of moving light. Instead, all I could see was a pinprick to my right. There was a minor road and we'd have trouble passing each other, but we had no option other than to follow.

I jumped back in the Jeep and pointed. 'To the right, lights on.'

I could see where we were going now and got my earpiece back in and mic to my mouth. 'Gabe?' I got nothing but the sound of the Beamer's engine and the tyres rumbling over the road. 'Gabe?'

'Yup. I'm checking out that bungalow area.'

'Okay. Listen, the van's unsighted – I do not have. We're going to check down the first junction right after the war memorial. It's signed for Porthcurno, Minack Theatre and the Porthcurno Telegraph Museum. It's a dead end.'

'Roger that.'

'Jack, get your foot down. Lights on.'

33

We screamed downhill to Porthcurno on a road that got narrower by the metre. The phone signal was falling off a cliff.

'Gabe? Gabe? Where are you?'

Finally: 'Still at the bungalow.'

The one bar of signal flickered. 'We might lose comms any second. I want you to stay up on the Penzance road and get the trigger on the junction to Porthcurno until we've checked it out down here.'

'No, Nick, I'm not going to do that. We've found something here that's much more important. I reckon she's in the van, and we know where they're staying. I need to do what I need to do here. I'll get the trigger when I'm finished.'

I didn't have the chance to tell him to do what the fuck he was told. Our headlights hit the signpost to the telegraph museum and beach, and a second later Jack had a hand off the wheel and was gesticulating. 'There, Nick!'

I saw it too. 'Keep going. Don't stop.'

The road went uphill and Jack rocked forwards as if that was going to help the Jeep climb.

'Gabe?'

The extra bit of altitude had brought another bar of signal.

'Yup.'

'We have the van. It's in the car park at the bottom of the valley, by the museum. Wait. Wait. Brake lights are on. That's now all lights off. They're static.'

I pulled off my earphones, then my neck wallet and I cut the phone. As long as our lights were moving, everything would look normal. It was brake lights that would give us away. Jack had done what he was told as I opened my door. 'Just keep moving.'

I collapsed out of the car onto the tarmac, chin into my chest, tucking in my elbows and knees, ready to accept the landing like a parachute jump that had fucked up when all you could see above you was a load of washing flapping rather than a fully opened canopy. My right shoulder-blade banged against a stone but that didn't matter: adrenalin would take over when I started running. I rolled again and thumped into the bank. I took a second to get my breath back, then jumped up and got running. My shoulder-blade felt like someone had taken an ice-pick to it, and my nicely healing knuckles were now scab-free and raw once more, but I'd have to suck it up. Pain was secondary to finding the target.

The VW's lights were still off, but others were flitting around.

A few metres short of the car park I slowed and

gulped in oxygen. A hedge paralleled the car park, and others ran into the space as dividers. I couldn't see the van now. I hugged the main hedge as I moved a couple of paces, crouched, stopped and listened. There was no light. I couldn't hear them; they couldn't hear me.

Another couple of bounds and I began to hear mumbling: no distinct language, just the drone of human speech. Down on my hands and knees I closed in, and the voices became more distinct. There were metallic sounds, too, but nothing I could identify.

The mumbling got louder. They were coming to me. Boots scuffed on the tarmac the other side of the hedge. I froze against the growth. Then I could make out the dull shapes of their boots on the other side, and the low mumblings became Russian. I spoke it well enough to know they were talking about 'which one was first', and I soon found out what they were on about. A torch shone a few inches off the tarmac on the other side of the hedge, revealing a fibre-optic cable that disappeared into the ground with the light. They couldn't have penetrated the tarmac, so there had to be a manhole.

Whatever they were doing, they were pleased with the results. There was a bit of backslapping as they left the equipment where it was and the boots moved back to the van. I gave them a few metres' start, then followed. Their noise would cover mine. They felt secure, so I needed to take advantage.

The roof came into view just above the hedge, and as I got closer I saw a dim light trying to burst through the greenery. Then more voices; also Russian. I saw the lights dotted around the car park, doing exactly the same as I'd just seen with the fibre-optic. I crawled on my elbows and knees slowly and deliberately so my boots didn't scrape the tarmac, until eventually I was opposite the van. I pushed my head into the hedgerow. The sliding door was open, and the dim light I'd seen came from a row of four laptop screens set up against the panel dividing the cab from the rear of the van. The one on the far left displayed whatever was under the manholes. It might have been interesting, but for now I didn't care: what mattered was a young woman, lots of hair, very skinny, on her knees in front of the screens, checking them out.

One of the Wolves came to the door and muttered to Yulia as he pointed at a screen. She turned to reply and I got a good side view of her face and neck. Her hair was the same messy mop, but there was a difference between her passport photo and what I was looking at now. There was a neck tattoo that really did cover all of her throat. I couldn't make out the pattern but, from the rest of her, it was going to be more hedge monkey than hipster. The feeds they were looking at were of deep, narrow, cobwebbed concrete chambers, with fixed ladders leading to the bottom, which was awash with gungy water.

The fibre-optic must have been an endoscope device, the sort used by border guards to check the contents of fuel tanks. The torch was to give extra light to penetrate the chamber.

About three metres down the chamber I could also make out thick cables, secured to the walls with ties, leading off to conduits either side of the manholes.

A Wolf went inside the van and brought out the antenna box I'd seen at the caravan park. He suckered it to the front passenger window as Yulia tapped away on a laptop. What the fuck were they checking for? I cut away. No time to think about that. Now was the time to work out how to lift Yulia and house her before first light. I crawled back to the road while they were still engrossed, then, covered by the hedge, I legged it up the hill.

The Wolves might have been covered with prison or gang tats but there was an order about them that worried me even more than their size. They knew what to do and when to do it, moving quietly as they got on with their tasks. I would have wanted the SNS to operate exactly the same. The Wolves were professional.

Easy-peasy, my arse.

Jack had stopped about three hundred up the hill in a car park for the Minack Theatre, which overlooked the sea. I jumped in and closed the door to the first click. I'd do the rest when we moved. There were houses up here and it was always good drills to do what might be needed all the time so there wouldn't be a fuck-up when it was actually needed.

I gulped air as I rehung my wallet round my neck, pushed in the earphones and pressed speed dial as Jack grabbed the nearest earplug and I leant across to help.

'Where are you, Gabe?'

'Just finished round the bungalow area. Nick, we gotta—'

'Wait, mate, let's get sorted first. Get to the junction for Porthcurno. We need the trigger. We've got the target – she's in the van. It's static in the car park. Lights still off. We'll trigger them away from here, and you can give direction from the junction. Okay?'

162

Gabe wasn't listening to the last part. He'd got it. He knew what he had to do. It was the first statement he liked. 'I fucking said she was in there! But did anyone listen?'

'That's for later, mate. We've got a problem.'

'Fucking right we do. We have one fucking big problem. We need to RV.'

Rio cut in: 'We gotta RV and right now, Nick. It's important.'

'Fuck the target.' Gabe's voice showed he meant it. 'This is major shit. If you don't RV we're gonna have to come to you, ram that fucking van and take 'em on right now. They gotta be stopped.'

Jack shuffled in his seat, trying to push the plug in deeper, as if he'd misheard.

'Okay, you get the trigger on the junction and we'll RV there. We'll let the van bounce around here. We'll be there in a couple. Keep the comms open.'

I turned to Jack and made sure I had his attention as I took the plug back. 'I want you to open and close the door in real time, slam it. Give it a couple of seconds before starting up and putting the lights on. Just as you would normally. Then drive as usual, okay? Don't worry about the brake lights now. Let them see lights belonging to real people.'

He nodded as we both opened our doors and gave them a slam. A few moments later the Beamer's lights cut across the high ground as we started downhill.

There were no pinpricks of light below us in the car park. They would have closed down until we passed.

What Gabe had to say had better be worth it.

34

We were about five hundred short of the junction at Trethewey so I gave the Beamer a warning. 'Gabe, you should see lights soon.'

'Roger that. Get to the junction, turn right. On the right in the line of vehicles.'

At the junction Jack turned right.

'Just throw it in on the left now, Jack. I want to get the lights off soon as – and we close the door just one click, yeah?'

It wasn't as if the locals would think there was an operation going on outside their homes, but there might have been burglaries that had heightened their awareness of car doors closing early in the morning. We needed the third party to stay asleep.

We got out of the Jeep, and the Beamer was parked in a row of vans and cars about forty metres away, facing the junction. The sting came back into my knuckles as I swung my arm, along with the thick clear liquid that started once again to ooze. I gave them a lick, but there was so much shit from the car park embedded that no homemade liquid was going to do the job.

We climbed into the back seats and no lights came on. The gaffer tape had done its job. Rio was in the driving seat, suicide spinner attached to the wheel, his eyes fixed on the road ahead.

Gabe swivelled towards us. His face said his brain was starting to fizz. 'The fucking road checks? They were inspecting manholes.' He jerked a finger downwards.

I almost laughed. 'So what? We're here to lift her, nothing more.'

Rio jumped in. 'You gotta listen, Nick. He knows what he's on about. He was posted to 14 Sigs for years.'

I knew 14 Signals Regiment was an electronic counter-measures unit that handled the military side of geeky surveillance, but I didn't have time to think about Gabe's posting.

He ploughed straight on. 'Down there, just a couple of fucking metres below us, is the whole world's inter-net traffic. When my kids use Facebook, the comms go to servers in the US, then bounce back. People think the internet is about satellites, but it isn't, it's physical. Satellites haven't been able to handle the volume of traffic since the early dotcom boom. There are under-sea cables connecting the whole fucking planet, and they landfall here. Every bit of traffic goes through Cornwall. We are on top of the most important and powerful telecommunications hub in the world. That's the fucking problem.'

The finger jabbed downwards once more as if I didn't

understand what he'd been saying and pointing would make it clearer.

'Right under our fucking arses, Nick, the planet's internet traffic. Kids googling, lawyers doing lawyer shit.' He took a breath to calm himself, then listed everyone who had ever been online. 'Now do you see? That skinny fuck is checking out the cables – and why? National security, Nick. That's what makes it a problem, and that's why we've got to do something.'

Rio jumped back in. 'Tell him what you said about the stations, mate.'

Gabe took a deep breath to keep a cap on the ever-building pressure. 'That first place you told us to look at? Skewjack Farm. That building has a dual-generator backup.'

Rio couldn't help himself. 'It's no pasty factory, Nick. It's one of the landing stations for the cables. There's stations all over the place. All the cables come into one, then go wherever they're going. That's what he says.'

Gabe jutted his head towards Rio, who didn't react – he was used to it. 'You gonna let me fucking finish or what?'

Rio shrugged. 'Remember what you need to tell him and get it in order. Do that and I don't have to cover your arse. Continue, Cable Boy.'

Gabe turned to face the rear of the Beamer once more. 'The manholes, they're everywhere. There's more steel on the roads round here than tarmac.' Gabe jabbed a finger back towards the junction. 'And that's no bungalow the other side of the war memorial. It's another landing station. It's Cable & Wireless's, hiding in plain sight.'

It wasn't that I didn't believe him. I just wanted to know why he knew so much. 'How do you know that?'

Gabe hit his mobile screen. 'Because I can read the signage on the manholes. Here, look.'

I took his phone and swiped at flash photography of manhole covers. Big names I recognized, like Verizon, were stamped into the steel, but there were a whole lot more that meant nothing to me – 'Route 4', 'MFSN' – along with a mass of information that might as well have been in Mandarin.

Gabe's finger stabbed the screen, like he was trying to goad it into a fight. 'All that shit on the top means something. See that one there?'

The main name said Telecom, along with other geeky shit. Two steel plates were welded on opposing sides.

'Those are locked covers, Nick. That means there's critical cables running through it. Look at that one.'

I stopped the swipe on a cover that said 'CATV'.

'That would normally cover cable TV lines, but I bet there's fuck-all cable down here. It wouldn't be economic to lay it – not enough customers. That's why I have a problem. Yulia is fucking about with important shit.'

Gabe waited for a reaction but it wasn't coming from me yet. I knew he hadn't finished.

Rio opened his mobile and did some swiping of his own. 'It isn't just external locks, Nick, there are thermal trips inside. As soon as you hit one of them fuckers, there's gonna be a quick-reaction force screaming down in their wagons from those landing stations.' He shoved his fist into Gabe. 'Show him the bungalow.'

Gabe was close to exploding as he snatched the phone off Rio, found what he was looking for and shoved it at me.

I was now staring at a satellite image of the bungalow. It showed a nice stone-faced building at the front, but the structure extended so far back it could have accommodated a couple of Olympic swimming pools.

'And now we've got a fucking geek from Belarus and a vanload of muscle crawling all over it. This is bigger than our job, Nick. Serious shit. The two busiest internet hubs on the planet are London and New York, and there's nine fucking cables that link them right underneath us.'

I handed back his mobile. 'So what do you think they're doing?' I could guess but it was better coming from him.

'They're looking for a way to get to the cables without triggering the alarms. Then they're going to blow the fucking things. We gotta stop them. Get hold of the security service, the police, the QRF, whatever. I don't give a shit who does it, but they need stopping. Right now, right this fucking minute.'

Gabe was too fizzed-up to see more than his part of the picture. 'I get it, mate, and you're probably right. But us lot are so far down the food chain we need to be careful. We don't know exactly what's happening out there. We could get fucked over just as much as that lot in the van would be if we gave them up without thinking.'

Gabe wasn't buying it and finally blew. 'Fuck Yulia, fuck the food chain. I'll ram that fucking van right now if I have to!'

Rio's hand came down on Gabe's shoulder. 'Calm, mate, calm. Don't want to wake the kids, know what I mean?'

Gabe pushed him away. 'Fuck off, and remember this moment. It's the reason I'm going to hurt you one of these days.' He came back at me hard as Rio just shrugged off the anger. 'Forget Facebook and porn. What if they're looking to hit something like the London and New York stock exchanges? If we leave Europe, London stays top dog because of instant trading with New York. They're the two biggest stock exchanges. They're like twins sharing the same umbilical cord. There's even computers now that trade between the two just working on algorithms rather than instincts. These things are now responsible for over a quarter of all trading already. Cut all that shit for just a day, and the world economy goes tits-up.'

Rio's thoughts on the situation were nearer to home. 'Including our pensions.'

Gabe didn't even bother giving him his normal look of contempt. 'Those fucks could be doing more damage down there than a Cruise missile attack!'

I'd learnt years ago never to underestimate a person's knowledge base, even if they were homeless or looked like they should be in prison, because I'd had a lifetime of people jumping to conclusions about me. But it had been a long time since I'd worked with other people, and I mentally thanked him for the kick in the head to remind me.

I kept my tone low and calm. 'Mate, I get it, believe me. But we have to stay focused to stop whatever they're doing. It's at the recce stage so we have time. If we start opening this thing up to the world, even just the QRF down the road, we have no idea what that will expose us to. Having the memory sticks only protects so far. That's why we're here, trying to keep onside. We're just minnows. We can still be disposed of if the decision is to clear the whole mess up. Do we want to take that risk without thinking about it first?'

A couple of nodding heads told me I was getting approval from Rio and Jack.

'We need to carry on with the mission, mate. That way we stop whatever is happening in that van, and we still lift Yulia. I'll call the Owl and tell him what's going on, yeah?'

I wanted at least to meet Gabe halfway. Besides, if I was right about the snide, the Owl would know soon enough anyway. Gabe's blank stare said he wasn't there yet.

'Mate, sometimes being the good guy gets you fucked over. Better to lift Yulia and stop whatever's happening without it being exposed to anyone. The more people that know, like the QRF, the more reasons there are to cover it up to stop even more people getting to know. Believe me, I've been here before. We all have. We're only breathing because we have those memory sticks.'

Beside me, Jack adjusted his leg. 'He's right, Gabe. We have to stop them, but we need to protect ourselves.'

Rio gave a nod too, but he had something else to say. 'Lads, the Chinese parliament has ended and there won't be any call to the Falcon. I got lights approaching the junction.'

35

Forward and left, the faint bubble of light moved up the hill to Trethewey.

Jack made to get out but I held him back.

'No, wait. They might turn right. Rio, trigger them away at the junction. Then we'll take whichever way they turn.'

Gabe scowled as he slid into the footwell. We all got down, apart from Rio, who had to keep his head just above the dashboard to keep the trigger and give us direction. I ended up on top of Jack, and a thought flashed through my mind. I shouldn't be covering his body to keep him out of sight: I should be covering his mouth and nose to keep him out of life.

I heard the faint sound of a vehicle.

Rio confirmed what I was hoping. 'It's the van.'

There was a pause.

'He's turning left, back towards the bungalow and Skewjack.'

I pushed myself up and, as I reached for the door, I

couldn't stop myself checking the interior lights. They didn't come on. The Halfords gaffer tape was still doing its job.

Rio wasn't happy. 'Hold up. Hold up.'

I turned towards the windscreen as he gave the commentary. 'Brake lights on – he's stopping. Just round the bend.'

I couldn't see the van but red light bathed the trees and a church over to the right. The light went out, then on again.

Gabe had his nose pressed to the windscreen. 'The war memorial. They're parking up.'

I pulled my wallet from my neck and chucked it to Jack along with my phone. 'Get back to the Jeep. Try to use the time while they're manoeuvring, before they go quiet. I'm going down there to see what the fuck they're up to.'

There wasn't time to wait for an answer. I was out and running at a low crouch, exploiting any patch of darkness among the red glow ahead of me. Half a dozen strides later I was close enough to hear the gravel grind under the tyres. They were still manoeuvring. They weren't just parking up, they were looking for somewhere specific. The lights went out and I crouched lower and used the hedge. Dead ahead, at the edge of the gravelled area, was a set of recycling bins on wheels. I got right down and crawled on my belly.

The side door clicked open and slid back very slowly. There were no voices. By the time I'd inched to the end of the row of bins and positioned myself to see through the gap between the last two, I was soaking with dew.

Once again, I saw slow, deliberate, professional actions happening. There'd be more room for fuck-ups and compromise if they rushed.

Boots crunched on the gravel, then two sets of knees came down to the ground. Two small fold-up shovels scraped away at the top layer, dimly lit by the glow from a laptop screen inside the van. I recognized the mass of hair in front of it.

The Wolves scraped some more, then became very happy at what they'd uncovered. Another two came over and did their job exactly the same as last time. Torchlight shone on top of the manhole cover before it focused on one of the keyholes to guide a lifting handle. The torch was then left lens down on the cover, and a fibre-optic cable went into another of the keyholes. This time the screen didn't display cobwebs, gunge and cables, but instead, about a metre down in the chamber, a chequered steel plate. It was clean, and each of the four sides was secured with a massive padlock, like shops use on their shutters so a cutter can't be got in to sever the shank. Whatever the Wolves were looking at, it was clearly the Holy Grail. There was gentle backslapping by the guys on the ground as they retrieved the fibre-optic from the manhole cover. I'd have to get moving before they finished. When the van manoeuvred, its lights would hit me.

I eased myself onto my elbows and toe tips and shuffled backwards, my knuckles oozing as the gravel dug in. The slightest sound would give me away. I managed to reach the grass and almost breathed a sigh of relief as I got up, stooped low and took a couple of strides towards the Jeep. I was now out in the open. Another couple of metres and I started to move faster, and that was when a big burst of red light washed over me.

Jack had silhouetted me to the Wolves.

There was another big burst of red, with my black shape caught in the middle of it – but no shouts. They were too switched on for that.

I broke into a run. I didn't look behind. I'd soon know if they'd seen me.

The red light was gone and I heard the first pounding of boots on the grass. A split second later, a body slammed into me from behind. Arms wrapped around my waist and slid down until they took away my footing. I hit the ground on my chest and chin. My head jerked back. More hands came round and grabbed at my face and forehead. I braced my neck. Both my arms were pulled behind me, my hands twisted to breaking point. They knew exactly what they were doing. All I could hear was three sets of heavy breathing. Then a hand closed over my eyes and I was dragged back towards the gravel.

It was pointless playing 'I'm looking for my dog' because they didn't even try to work out why I was there. Very soon they would know I wasn't third party anyway.

There were no commands, no anger. There was nothing but control. Through the fingers of the hand gripping my face, I could see the blur of the van, no lights on, just the gentle glow of the screens.

Boots crunched on gravel as we passed the wheelie bins. I knew they wouldn't start the engine and put the lights on until everyone was safely inside. They knew the danger of vehicle lights.

Unlike some.

But, then, that might have been why he'd done it.

36

Another two paces, and I was bundled into the van. Yulia jerked her feet away to make room for me, then fell onto a pile of the vinyl sports bags.

The two Wolves dragged me to the rear until my head banged against the tailgate and one jumped on top to control me. He pushed down on the back of my skull so my face was rammed into what felt and smelt like plastic roll-mats. My nose took the pressure, making my eyes water. Then knees weighed on my back and all the oxygen was forced out of my lungs as the second Wolf began to search me.

Hands ripped at my jacket, searching the prime places for weapons, then aggressively went everywhere else. If their hands weren't already wet they soon would be: my shirt was soaked with sweat and grass dew.

The sliding door closed and a voice ordered the driver, almost gently, to move. Gravel crunched beneath us as we slowly rumbled across the memorial park before turning left onto tarmac, back the way they had come, probably now passing the bungalow.

I couldn't see their faces. I was still being man-handled, like a rag doll, hands gripping me, knees pinning me down. It was pointless resisting. That would just cause me pain – and I might get enough of that later.

They knew I was fucked and were just maintaining me in that position as the search continued. I accepted I had no control over myself physically, but I still had control of my mind. There is always confusion in the heat of the moment; organization comes later. Pro-fessionalism is making sure that the gap between them takes a couple of breaths rather than hours.

I turned my head for a better view of what was hap-pening around me but a boot tapped the side of my face. I rested my chin back on the floor. I counted a few seconds, then lifted my eyes and tried to look around once more. I was trying to gather as much information as possible to help me escape and also to make me feel better because I knew stuff. I saw, heard and felt no scenes of frenzy; everybody seemed to know what they were doing. There was a lot of efficient movement. They'd taken prisoners before.

I analysed what I had seen. They were highly organized, and there were no panicked shouts or breathless orders, just heavy breathing from their exertions and my occasional grunt from their weight pinning me down.

I was turned onto my back and the jacket pulled apart as the Wolves continued to search. One pressed his knee into my stomach with all his weight. I tried lifting my head, only for it to be pushed down.

There was nothing I could do but try to keep breathing.

At least I could see a little more now. From what I could make out through watery eyes, Phoenix was on his knees, up at the front of the van alongside Yulia, stooped over the laptop screens, which I could see now were held off the floor a couple of feet by stacked plastic milk crates. His face was caught in their glow as he got right up to an A4-sized hatch in the cab panel to talk to the two up front. He glanced back and told Yulia to get the screens switched off, which was done by closing the lids, and very soon the only interior light came from a small Maglite fixed to the ceiling with a magnetic mount. The Wolf sitting astride me, with a leg either side to pin my arms, moved it to put me in the spotlight, turning his body above me into a fuzzy and overbearing silhouette.

Phoenix was still talking through the hatch, but I couldn't make out what was being said. As if to stop me listening, the Wolf above me pushed both hands against my face. The other dragged out my arms from under the legs. The short, sharp sound of ratcheting was accompanied by the pain of plastic tightening around my wrists. I didn't tense my forearms to bulk them out and give me wriggle room: I wanted the plastic as tight around my wrists as it would go if I was going to get out of this van in one piece. The owner of the hands bearing down on my face now shoved mine under his arse and adjusted himself across my hips, a knee still either side of me.

The vehicle came off tarmac and bounced and rumbled over rough ground. Maybe we were on the mud track before the sharp bend near the duck pond. The silhouettes above me rocked in time with each jolt.

Phoenix's voice came from near the closed-down laptops. It was louder, a clear command. He wanted to make sure the lads up front knew what was going on. 'Lights off. No brakes. Stop.'

Through blurred and juddery vision I could just about make out a sliver of windscreen through the hatch in the cab panel. Up near where the rear-view mirror would have been I saw a run of trees caught in the headlights, and then it was dark again. I heard the ratchet of the handbrake that was slowly decelerating us.

Nearer to me, Phoenix opened one of the vinyl bags Yulia had jumped on top of. They were Rip Curl surf-gear bags, another layer to their cover. The branding was where any connection with surfing ended, because he retrieved from it a futuristic-looking Vector 9mm submachine gun already loaded with a thirty-three-round mag. He checked the magazine extended out of its housing and was on securely, pulled back the working parts, then thrust a hand back into the bag to grab another mag. That went into the back pocket of his jeans as the Wolf who had plasticuffed me grabbed another Vector out of the bag and carried out the same drills as he joined Phoenix by the door.

Phoenix hit the overhead light. In total darkness, the side door was pulled back to let in a gloomy light as the wagon rolled to a stop. Jumping out, Phoenix was about to stand his ground. He wasn't flapping. He was accepting the situation and knew what to do about it. A man with a plan, and a weapon in the shoulder. He pointed it back towards the road as the second Wolf joined him. Both knew that if the sixty-six rounds they each had on them weren't enough to take anyone on they shouldn't have been doing the job.

My hands were already swelling beneath the plasti-cuffs, sandwiched between my stomach and an arse. I tried to lean up and forward to relieve the pain, but the bulk pinning me down quickly reminded me he was still there by pushing my head back down on the roll-mats. I realized that everything had gone quiet; all I could hear was breathing above me, and even that was controlled as he listened for any follow-up.

It wasn't just the wet wear that was on the top of its game, the hardware was, too. The Vectors were second-generation 9mm machine-guns, with a boxy chunk of green polymer and fat suppressors screwed to their muzzles, which made them look like they belonged on the set of *Star Wars*. They were deadly, and far more advanced than traditional automatic systems.

Instead of the working parts going back and forth horizontally as they fed a round into the chamber, fired it, then blew back, ejecting the empty case before the cycle started again, their working parts did the same job but not horizontally: instead, they moved downwards, behind the mag housing. Less recoil made the weapon more controllable and countered the tendency for it to walk upwards when it fired its six hundred rounds per minute. That meant these things could get a massive amount of controlled automatic fire down onto a target by playing about with Newton's theory.

Soon I could hear engine noise in the distance. There

was no flapping, no words exchanged between the two weapon platforms outside the van as they stood their ground. There had been a fuck-up, but they were dealing with it.

A dull white-light glow cut across the sky through the open side door. The engine noise got louder and the lights in the sky bolder, but the Wolves stood still, weapons in the shoulder, waiting for those headlights to come down the lane and illuminate us. The engine note decreased and the lights died. They were probably now illuminating the duck pond on the other side of the bend. A second vehicle was heading towards us, its dull lights getting brighter as it neared the bend. With the screech of a tyre or two the lights receded. So did the engine noise, and soon the van was surrounded by nothing but silence and gloom.

The Wolf pinning me to the mats leant towards the side door opening, which momentarily relieved a little of the pressure on my hands. He muttered to Phoenix in low, controlled tones. Phoenix took a step nearer the side door but was still checking the area as the other armed Wolf came back inside the van. The basic gist of the waffle was that I was sterile: I had nothing on me. Did that make me security? Police?

'Do I kill him now?'

His hands came down around my neck. I could feel his thumbs pressing into my throat, probing my windpipe below my Adam's apple. There was no point in trying to resist the already choking feeling as my windpipe partly collapsed, but I was still breathing. His voice was a little louder now so I could hear better.

'All of us might need to fight soon. I can't sit and fight. I'll kill him, yes?'

That was the drift. My Russian was enough for me to be concerned. I could hear Yulia, by the laptops, breathing nervously, her feet shuffling around as she made room for the incoming Wolf.

Phoenix's silhouette filled the side door opening, his head never leaving the direction of the road. The Vector was relaxed but still in the shoulder. 'It doesn't matter who he is. All that matters is the mission. We continue.'

The other armed Wolf had taken up station near my head, sitting with his back against the rear tailgate, knees bent, weapon cradled in the crease of his hips. 'But what do we do with him?'

Phoenix nodded across to the laptops and the mad hair kneeling by them. 'Ask him.'

Yulia was even more nervous now that she had been brought into the drama.

'Ask him who he works for, how many of them are out there, how many vehicles, what he was doing in the village. It's okay, he won't bite.'

Chances were, the computer geek was the only English speaker. Being a geek she would have to be.

Yulia did as she was asked and the hands relaxed around my neck a little. Her voice had a slightly lower pitch than I was expecting, but the Eastern European accent with an American slant was spot on.

Not that it got her anywhere, because I said nothing. It was clear to them I was a player, and I was hardly going to blurt out the truth. Phoenix was out to prove a point.

'Fuck him. We will report and will be told what to do with him. But he is better alive to find out what he knows, later. He and those others, they aren't police. They aren't security. Otherwise we'd have been hit by now. Who he is doesn't matter because we have no control of the others. If I think it is needed, I will give the command for him to go to the ground. But now, this moment, only the mission matters.' He gave a small laugh. 'We've had worse than this. Simferopol, no?'

There was a sprinkling of knowing laughs and the one sitting astride me found it so funny he shook. I couldn't hear anything from Yulia. Simferopol was at the epicentre of the 2014 annexation of Crimea. These lads had probably been very busy in that part of the world over the past few years, and I doubted it was on behalf of the Ukrainians who wanted to be part of the West.

Phoenix took one last look around, leaning into the darkness, ears cocked, then jumped back in and slid the door closed. The Wolf pinning me stretched up and the light came back on.

Phoenix thrust his head against the hatch. 'Lights on. Next checkpoint.'

The VW reversed onto the tarmac, but this time we turned right, back towards the bungalow, the war memorial and, after that, who knew?

37

The VW steadied, once its tyres were back on tarmac. The laptops were powered up once more, producing enough dull glow for me to get a better idea of what the fuck was going on.

The Wolf on top of me smelt of a mixture of sweat and cheap spray-on deodorant. I wondered if it was 007. East Europeans loved the Bond movies, and when I lived in Moscow, the half of the city that didn't stink of cooked cabbage and floor detergent reeked of the official range of spy fragrances. He was doing a good job pinning me to the floor, but at least my eyes were allowed to be open. It wasn't my bad joke about deodorants that made me smile to myself but the fact that I'd thought of it. I had processed the initial capture phase and the fact that 007 could have strangled me to death. Now I could get on with other stuff. No more smiling to myself or any expression apart from compliance. I wanted no indication that I understood enough of their language to make trouble for me. I was in enough already.

Yulia was back at the keyboards with Phoenix kneeling next to her, jabbing a finger at the mapping and satellite imagery. I could see where the plasticuffs had come from. A big bundle of them hung from the cab panel – they had been used to control the spaghetti of cables. Yulia looked back at the body beneath 007. Her face was ashen and beads of moisture glistened on her top lip. Her elbows were pressed into her sides, like she was trying to make her body even smaller than it already was. She reached for a water bottle and took a couple of big gulps. Phoenix got her back to work with a gentle reminder to focus on the screens, then passed her a power bar from a box next to the plastic-wrapped case of water and ripped one open for himself. These lads needed to keep up their food intake or they'd implode. Yulia just needed the energy – she had a lot going on. The screens were like PowerPoint visuals of Gabe's lecture in the Beamer. Superimposed on a large-scale sea navigation map of the south-west of England, thick pink lines ran into and out from the north and south coasts. On another screen, a map of the world showed hundreds of similar blue lines running from the UK to everywhere on the planet, west across the Atlantic to the States, east into Europe, south to Africa, south-east to Asia. The UK looked like a puppet-master with his hands full of strings heading to the USA, along with the rest of the world. The cables had exotic names like TAT 13, Apollo, Asia Africa Europe Gateway, and APNG-2, which whirled its way to Australia and Papua New Guinea. A mad-looking cable named CUCN seemed to dart all over the world, via Korea and the US, before heading to China, Japan and Guam. Exactly as Gabe had said, the hundreds of cables connecting the planet all came ashore into one of Cornwall's landing stations to be bounced off to wherever the next email or porn download had been clicked for from Cape Town to Riyadh to Anchorage.

Phoenix and Yulia were looking hard for something. They kept checking the onscreen mapping against a notebook, maybe of today's recces. The other two in the back were just as busy, 007 astride me, the other – I thought of him as Tailgate because that was where his back was resting – still cradling his weapon in the crease of his hips, ready to react if we got a drama from the occupants of the vehicle whose brake lights had betrayed me, the police or whatever other cavalry they called in. The only thing out of place in this extreme efficiency was Yulia, the geek, protected by the muscles and brains around her.

Could they be military? Not only was this group well squared away and switched on, there was a higher command and control. Unless my Russian was completely to fuck, Phoenix had said, 'We will report and will be told what to do with him.'

They and I had no control over what would happen next – and I had none over what Gabe and the others would do next. Were they going to make the situation worse by calling in the cavalry or continue looking for me? Fuck it. I was going to cut away from that. Don't worry about what you can't change.

Phoenix had said the mission was paramount, and he was absolutely correct. The body of *my* mission was now within spitting distance. I had given myself enough time to sort out my head and I needed to escape as soon as possible. The mission hadn't changed, just the way I needed to carry it out.

We were still on tarmac but not on a B road any more. I could hear vehicles coming from the opposite direction and the van didn't need to slow and push its way to the side to let them pass. There were very few wide roads to the west, towards Land's End, so maybe we were heading east towards Penzance. And all the while, I watched Yulia work under Phoenix's supervision, hitting the keyboards, making files of what they'd seen under the manholes, cross-referencing it with the mapping.

It must have been about thirty minutes later that we were about to make a right turn. We waited in the road, indicators clicking, as vehicles rushed past us from the opposite direction. A heavy truck rocked the van in its wake. Phoenix dived into one of the bags and pulled out the antenna box I'd seen on the caravan. He passed it through the cab hatch, keeping the two leads from it which he plugged into a laptop.

He stopped to look back at me, studying my face as his lips moved. Maybe he was describing me to someone, asking them what they wanted him to do with me because I affected their mission. I was one of those what-ifs: what if they were compromised? Was I a liability or a bargaining chip?

It got me thinking. What *was* their mission? It certainly felt like an attack. They had weapons, and they would use them at the drop of a hat to protect their recce. Why not an attack on the cables? Or on just one? Was that why they were doing so much looking and checking, because they needed to identify one specific cable to destroy? Taking down Gabe's kids' Facebook wouldn't bring the planet to a halt, but hitting the flow of information that linked two of the world's biggest stock exchanges certainly would.

Whatever they were up to, it wasn't a terrorist attack. This was too organized, too military, too determined.

A state actor must be controlling it.

And that, if true, made what was happening in the back of the van an act of war.

38

Sharp jabs on the brakes jerked my head from side to side as we travelled along a road that I guessed was narrowing.

I was still pinned down, hands still plasticuffed and a cushion under 007's arse as he leant back towards the Rip Curl weapons bag and pulled out a Vector, checked the thirty-three-round mag, interchangeable with a Glock pistol's, and made it ready. Throughout, he chatted in low, confident murmurs with Tailgate, who was still sitting with his back against his namesake. They agreed that I should have been dead by now. They knew Phoenix's decision was the right one, but that wasn't the point as far as they were concerned.

I got the feeling we were nearly there – wherever 'there' was.

The antenna was passed back through the hatch for Phoenix to pack away and secure: good military drills whether on a ship or in an armoured vehicle.

Phoenix had his mouth to the hatch once more as the

van came to a stop at his command. The engine stopped, and both front doors opened without the cab light sparking up. The doors closed on their first click.

Phoenix and Tailgate were weapons-ready to back the two outside if needed.

The Maglite attached to the ceiling was still on and I took the chance to look at Yulia, but all I could see was her mop of hair as she focused on the screen in front of her.

The cold steel of a fat suppressed barrel was shoved into my neck and made me hope that a number of things hadn't happened. First, that Gabe, Rio and Jack hadn't found us, followed, and were about to take action. Then that they hadn't warned anyone. And, finally, that the snide hadn't got a text to the Owl telling him what had happened. Any of those three things meant the VW would be found and compromised, and these lads would fight and had the means to do it – and before they did that, Phoenix would give the order to drop me. In his boots, I would.

After a minute or so of complete silence, there was a gentle double knock on the side door. Phoenix swivelled and slid it open. Slowly and deliberately, he stepped out and scanned around, then motioned for Tailgate to join him while 007 stayed where he was and maintained his Vector in place on my neck.

I soon saw what was up. As Tailgate clambered out, he had a torch with him on a length of paracord, and the fibre-optic device.

We weren't at a traditional war memorial this time, but some kind of granite Celtic cross set on top of a grassy mound, with a little railing around it and flowers in jars mounted on a lump of granite engraved with words I couldn't make out. I'd been hoping it would give me an indication of where I was. Maybe it was the meeting place for some weird Cornwall ley-line sect to honour those who'd got blown away to the spirit world.

One of the Wolves from the cab handed his Vector to his mate, then opened the shovel and began to dig at the base of the Celtic cross, slowly and carefully like he was probing for mines.

Yulia glanced across at the open side door and, in the dull glow of the laptop screens, I managed to get eye-to-eye. She tilted her head a little to be more face-on to me, and gave a fleeting smile. Fuck knew what it meant – maybe she was trying to tell me things were going to be okay. All I was concerned about was how to grab hold of her and get us both away from there. Nothing in my mind had changed, and I wouldn't let it. If you start worrying about the situations you're in rather than why you're there in the first place, then the whole situation starts to spiral out of control in your head . . . and that means you fuck up. So all I had to do was concentrate on the mission.

The Wolf had found what he was testing for. He used the shovel to peel back the turf, like a TV gardener creating a work of art for the Chelsea Flower Show. Tailgate got down on his knees with the torch and endoscope. Phoenix was on his way back.

I looked at the laptop screens in anticipation and, moments later, the three of us saw what I'd seen at the war memorial. No gungy water, no spiders, no cables, just a steel plate with a padlock on each side, and no doubt some thermal triggers in case anything bigger than a mole decided to tunnel past.

Yulia looked at Phoenix. 'Yes! Nigella!'

Either she was late answering a question about who her favourite celebrity chef was, or they had found the cable they were looking for and it had a name. Phoenix gave a sharp nod, then spun on his heel and walked the four or five paces back to the others. Tailgate was still on his knees controlling the endoscope and torch; the other two just stood there, weapons in the shoulder and covering. They were resting, but ready.

There was some murmuring I couldn't make out, but the tone told me it was still good news about the discovery. The torch was turned off and the endoscope was being withdrawn. The guy with the shovel got to his knees once more in preparation for returfing.

They'd obviously done well, but what did that mean? Were they going to detonate a device?

Then, as the turf was rolled back, I thought: Why have they done that? This still had to be a recce: that was why they were leaving no sign. Both memorials had steel plates covering what must be a critical cable. To come back and access 'Nigella' at two locations and detonate devices would really fuck it up big-time.

The turf was being gently patted down.

There was more to come. There was more of a plan.

39

The team ghosted aboard the VW and we rolled slowly back the way we had come, along what I presumed was the minor road.

Phoenix had already fed the antenna box through the gap in the cab panel, connected it to one of the laptops and was tapping away, no doubt explaining their success. More important to me was who was on the other end, what they wanted done now that they'd found Nigella and, the big one, what they wanted to do with me.

Fuck it. Time to cut away. No amount of second-guessing was going to help me get out of the back of this thing and grip Yulia. My only crumb of comfort was knowing that the jeans pinning down my hands were now just as wet as I was.

Phoenix was reading the laptops. His head blocked the screens so I couldn't make anything out on them – not that I could have done anyway from two or three metres away. Also, my spoken Russian was all right but I'd never been too clever on reading Cyrillic.

Phoenix laid a hand on Yulia's shoulder and muttered a few sentences she acknowledged with a nod. Then he pushed his face up against the panel hatch, issued instructions to the two in the front and the antenna was passed back. He immediately handed it to Yulia, who stowed it back in the Rip Curl.

Phoenix stayed on his knees and turned to address the other two Wolves. Tailgate sat with his knees astride me, his Vector resting on his thighs. 007's Vector was on my chest, still pointing at my chin and head. We were all waiting for what the commander had to say.

When the words came, they were very clear. 'We found it – we are withdrawing.'

He gave Yulia a congratulatory thump on the back that took her to the mat to join me. I remained looking confused and concerned, not that it was helping me. I was sure I didn't even come into their thought process. I was just hazardous cargo that was packed correctly, controlled and safe.

As Yulia pushed herself back up, showing neither embarrassment nor anger, 007 and the other two nodded their own approval, then laughed about her lack of back muscle.

Phoenix let the humour go on for a couple of seconds, then got back to business. 'It's a daylight pick-up. But we move in good order. The campsite, then home. Yulia, well done, an excellent job.'

Again she gave no reaction.

007 had a question I'd been waiting for. 'What about this one?' He jerked his head down as if no one knew what he was on about.

Phoenix's orders were clear. 'He comes with us. He

is the reason we exfiltrate as soon as possible because we do not know what problem he represents. They want to know how he affects phase two. Questions?'

There were none. Phoenix grabbed the bundle of plasticuff cables and shoved them into one of the Rip Curls.

My hands were really starting to swell and get painful under 007 but, fuck it, there was nothing I could do about that. All I could think about was this group and their good skills. They were leaving nothing behind, apart from Gabe and the crew, but they couldn't do anything about that.

Clearly, that was where I would come in later: they'd want to find out what was happening so they could adjust the plan for phase two, which had to be the attack. I was sure the small inconvenience of a carload of unknowns wouldn't stop it. I would have done exactly the same after a successful recce, making sure the decks were as clear as they could be for the next team, maybe this team.

The VW eventually stopped on the main and a couple of trucks powered past from right to left. If I had my directions correct, that would be west. We turned to follow them.

They were now on their exfiltration phase, and that was when many operations failed. Lesser-trained players became slack in their drills because they thought their job was done, so they fucked up and got killed. I wasn't expecting that from this lot, which was unfortunate: it would be even harder for me to get free of the van and make sure I was dragging Yulia with me.

The Maglite in the ceiling lit the controlled frenzy as

everything but the Vectors was stowed away in the Rip Curls. The laptops went into thick bubble-wrap sleeves and the cables were neatly coiled ready for reuse.

007 stayed where he was, clearly pissed off not to be part of this action. Yulia was helping after a fashion, but really it was only Phoenix and Tailgate who were doing anything. I wished my hands were coiling, packing, doing anything to get them working again, ready to make a run for it with Yulia. No way did I need the plasticuffs to be tighter now. My wrists had swollen and the fuckers were cutting in.

There was nothing I could do while the van was moving. The third party would be around us, which was good for me as it would provide witnesses and a sanctuary, but I had to assume the team wouldn't have any qualms about spreading the good news with their Vectors if anyone obstructed their mission – and that meant real people taking hits as they flip-flopped their way to the shower block.

40

I had no choice. I'd have to attack at the caravan site. The alternative would be wait, wait, wait for the perfect moment – and the perfect moment never comes. The only way you can say it's perfect is if you've done it and been successful. Until then it's just a punt. My mantra now was the old special-forces standby: react to the situation in front of you. Anything else meant shit.

The camper van picked up speed on the main drag.

Yulia had finished packing the bags and they were all zipped up. She lay on top of the pile, eyes closed, her hair covering her face.

I'd been trying to work out how she'd found herself on this job. Clearly, the team liked her, and they weren't holding her against her will, but something about her didn't fit.

Phoenix had finally got his back against the cab panel now the laptops were out of the way, and was in exactly the same pose as Tailgate, knees up with his

Vector in the crease of his hip. Not sleeping, but dozing.

I wished I could say the same about 007.

In a perverse way, I was glad Gabe and the others hadn't found me and decided to ram the vehicle or mount some other kind of heroics. It would have been bloody. Not that I was concerned about the individuals taking a risk: it was big boys' rules and they were big ugly lads. It was more to do with the feeling of responsibility I had for them: I didn't want them making a decision that would fuck them up even more than they already were. Apart from the snide, of course. I had plans for him.

There was a little part of me, too, just a little, that said this would be easier for me because I was on my own, only responsible for myself. If it went to rat-shit, there'd be nobody but myself to blame. It sort of put a damper on the thoughts I'd had about working with people while I was running from Rio's house. I cut away: navel-gazing wasn't going to help me out of this.

My hands were completely numb. I tried adjusting them and got a slap on the cheek from 007 and a wagging finger. 'No, no, no.' As if I needed any more indication that these lads were not only professional and competent but confident. There was no need for a big macho-slapping because it wasn't necessary. That might come if I didn't obey them, but again, I'd have only myself to blame.

There was a tap from the driver's side of the cab panel. It snapped Phoenix out of his doze. He turned and shoved his face to the gap. A set of keys was passed through to him, and whatever was said, it was good news. He got down on his knees again to give Yulia a shake, and his expression told them they all needed to get switched on.

41

Phoenix turned to Tailgate. 'Go with Foma, and take weapons. Bag them and use them only if you must.' He checked his watch as he glanced down at me. 'Just in case they have come looking.'

I'd lost all track of time. All I could see through the hatch and a small area of windscreen was headlights bathing trees and bushes either side of the narrow lane we were on. 'Forty-five. That is all you have.'

Tailgate peered at his watch, then grabbed the empty Rip Curl. He checked safe and slid his Vector inside. Then, keeping the zip open, he checked that the spare mag was tucked into his cargo pockets and concealed. He leant towards the doors. It had to be a recce of the caravan site. Good skills again. The exfil stage was always a nightmare: a good commander knew he had to grip his team to make sure everything was done correctly because this phase was more dangerous than the infil and doing the job.

Phoenix carried on: 'If you don't make it back in

time, the embassy will be at the emergency pick-up at zero three hundred hours every twenty-four hours for five days. You got that?'

I knew I had, and Tailgate gave a nod.

'Don't worry, we'll wait in-country – we're not going to leave you here. We all go home together.'

Tailgate waddled across to the side door on his knees. Phoenix gave the cab panel a couple of knocks and we slowed. A few seconds later we came to a gentle stop.

Tailgate nodded – 'It's all good' – at Phoenix, cut the Maglite and slid the door back. Simultaneously, the passenger door in the cab opened. I saw a fuzzy shape in the gloom that must have been Foma closing the cab door, then standing off the gravel layby in the treeline with his Vector at his side. That went inside the Rip Curl as Tailgate joined him, and Phoenix slid the door closed. The VW rumbled along the tarmac as Yulia hit the Maglite once more.

We took a sharper left and were soon bouncing up and down on rough ground. No doubt the recce would be taking place now. Foma would be checking out the campsite. He wouldn't be going through the main gate – he'd probably go in through a hedge, look and listen. Tailgate would have his back. Were there people in cars? People doing walk-pasts of the caravans? Was there sign in the dew going backwards and forwards near their two caravans, or even below the windows, when everywhere else at that time of the morning was untouched? They would look, move another bound, look, move another bound, look, move, then probably leave via the reception area, checking that out as well. Then they'd try to check the road. Speed was of the essence and there was a lot to do, but clearly they knew what they were about.

The campsite was a known location, and they'd have to factor in the possibility that it was covered now that they'd been compromised. That was what I would have done.

The van stopped again on the rough track, wherever that was, and this time the engine went off and they kept silent. Phoenix hit the Maglite button, putting us in darkness to make sure he wasn't bathed in light if the door had to be opened and the Vector had to come up into his shoulder to take on whatever was out there.

I listened to the engine settle down and stop its little taps as it cooled. Soon Phoenix was satisfied there had been enough silence and the light came back on.

'Okay, the caravan site.' He pointed at 007. 'Stay with him in here at all times. The rest of us will pack. I want to be in and out of there in minutes. All weapons will be concealed in the bags at all times. What the Brits see is just another day. Understand?'

007 nodded and there was a grunt from the front.

'Once we're packed, we leave for the pick-up point. No speeding, no violations. The embassy will take care of the vehicle and the weapons. Once we're picked up, mission over, we're on our way home.'

007 looked down at me, happy that we were all going home together. Then he put a damper on it. 'If we're attacked, what about him? Do I kill him and fight with you all?'

Phoenix saw the horror on Yulia's face. 'It's okay.' He rested a hand on her arm for comfort, then got back to

007. 'I'll tell you if things are going wrong. And then I'll tell you what I want you to do about it.'

Phoenix raised his voice so that the guy in the front could listen. 'Brief your partners when you get back.' As he pointed at Yulia, the driver made an 'understood' tap against the cab panel and 007 nodded.

Phoenix spoke very clearly, very slowly, his voice softened from command to request for her. 'We will drop you off at Reception, then go on to the caravans.' He paused so Yulia had time to understand what was being said. After all, she wasn't a Wolf. He gave it another second. 'Maybe no one will be at Reception – it's too early. But if someone is there, we may need your English again.' He dug into his jeans, held up a set of keys and dangled them in front of her face. 'If the place is empty, put these into the returned keys box. Write a nice note for them saying we had to go back to work early. Okay?'

Phoenix waited for Yulia to nod. 'Tell them we had a wonderful time and will be back as soon as we can because the surf here is so good. Okay?'

Yulia took the keys but it clearly wasn't okay. 'How will we be able to pack up if I've got the keys to the caravans? If we just leave and don't pay, won't they call the police?'

Phoenix smiled. 'We've all got keys. We had copies made because we all must have them. And the British, they always want everything paid in advance. They mistrust people even more than we do. Okay, so you know what to do?'

Yulia wrapped the keys inside a bony fist. The foreign baristas going back to their coffee machines.

That sorted out some of my guesswork. But fuck that. The embassy sorting out the VW and the weapons? I was actually witnessing an act of war between two sovereign states for the second time in less than two months.

No wonder the Owl was all over this like a wet dress – but why use us? That worried me. But unless I got away from this team – with Yulia – I wouldn't have to worry too much about anything because I'd be fucked.

Phoenix checked his watch and banged against the cab panel. A couple of seconds later the engine turned over.

42

We drove in complete silence. Everybody in the van knew what he or she was doing and how it was happening, apart from me. 007 adjusted himself again over my hands. He was probably as uncomfortable as I was, but without the pain.

After a while, the vehicle came to a halt and Phoenix slid open the side door. Tailgate jumped in with the weapons bag and I heard the door click in the front cab as Foma joined his battle partner. There was no need for any big briefing. All Phoenix got was a nod as Tailgate resumed his position at the back, knees up and resting, as the van moved off. 007 tried to feel he was part of it, adjusting himself to face him and waffling at warp speed about 'the plan'.

It was only now that I noticed Tailgate's nails or, rather, the lack of them. They were bitten to the quick, which was unusual for a lad so into his body.

Maybe five minutes later the VW slowed almost to a halt before turning sharp right, then rolling for maybe another fifteen metres or so, stopping with the engine running.

Phoenix stooped at the hatch and peered ahead through the windscreen, then turned back to Yulia. 'Wait outside and we'll pick you up – okay?' Once she'd nodded, he turned and got a hand on the sliding door, using the other to give her a pat on the back. 'Well done – we'll be home soon.'

The sliding door was pulled open and the slivers of first light exposed the line of cars by Reception where my team had parked up during the follow. With a guiding hand, he eased her out of the van.

That was good: it meant I just had to get myself free instead of having to drag her out of the immediate danger area as well.

The door was pulled back, and the van rumbled to the right and down the road past the play park. It pulled a sharp left and I knew it was time to focus. We stopped and I heard the handbrake go on, the engine turned off, and silence reigned until birds, doing their early-morning thing, filled the void. Phoenix had got up and was peering through the hatch, probably re-checking that no dew had been disturbed around the caravans and that no one was in any of the cars. Not because he didn't trust his team, but if the recce had been compromised, the Wolves could have been entering a world of shit as they climbed out.

Phoenix stayed where he was at the hatch and, after maybe thirty seconds, he turned his head to the side so he could address both groups. 'Remember – a normal day. If the giveaways are not there, we just turn and leave. Weapons only to come out on my order.' He pointed at 007. 'Remember, he stays alive. I'll tell you when he doesn't need to.'

Phoenix opened the side door gently and I heard the doors opening in the cab too. He stepped out, looking around casually but carefully as he waited for Tailgate to disembark with the weapons bag, then closed the door, shutting out those first slivers of light. We were back in the gloom but some feeble light now penetrated from the hatch.

The team had gone and 007's body language said he was pissed off he wasn't with them. He wanted to be with his mates, not babysitting me. He raised his arse a little, still with his knees on the mats controlling me, but twisted to try to check what was happening forward of him, finally raising himself an extra couple of centimetres so he could look through the hatch.

Shit or bust.

I bucked suddenly, pushing up with my arms and ballooned hands until they pressed against his arse, kicking out with my legs, twisting my body, anything to get him off balance. I kept twisting, kept bucking and pulling to get my hands free. He was silent, maybe in shock, maybe embarrassment, more likely because he was too professional to shout for help and risk alerting the third party.

My hands got free of his weight and, still cuffed together, I pushed them up against his head, trying to get his body back so I could reach up towards the roof. He swore under his breath in frustration and anger. I kept reaching up. I wasn't worried about 007's hands grabbing at my jacket to pull me to him to regain control. I just had to focus on what I needed to do. That was the way to stop 007 being successful. My numb fingers finally closed around the Maglite as best they could and, pulling it away from its mount, I brought it down on his head. I didn't know if it was the steel that hit him or my hands, because I couldn't feel a thing, but I pounded him again and again, bringing my hands up, arms as straight as I could make them so I got more power on the down-swing.

Eventually I heard the resounding thud of steel on skull and suddenly he was more concerned about his pain than he was about me. Fighting the numbness in my legs, I clambered onto my hands and knees and scrambled to the door. I had to drop the Maglite to free my numb fingers to scrabble at the handle, not feeling any resistance against it until it pulled back. As light poured in, hands came for me from behind, grabbing hold of me around the waist. I kicked behind me like a horse, not looking at him, twice, three times.

I staggered out onto the gravel. I didn't bother to find out what was happening with the rest of the Wolves, whether they were inside the caravans or not. It didn't matter. I was outside and I was moving.

43

I heard a muffled curse and turned. 007 was on his hands and knees, half in, half out of the van. He would recover soon. I ran the two paces back, grabbed the door and rammed it shut, yanking it along its rail with enough force to guillotine whatever was in the way. I didn't see where it had made contact but I didn't care. By then I was moving towards our tents. My legs took a time to get the blood pumping. It was more of a drunken stumble at first, and I was hoping against hope to see the team rolling out of the domes to back me as we headed for Yulia, then got the fuck out of there.

There was no Jeep, no Beamer. No domes.

But there was movement behind me. 007 wasn't giving up, and I hadn't expected him to. I turned left and headed for the toilet block. I needed to make distance and get into cover, then double back to lift Yulia.

It wasn't happening. 007 was making ground, and

he was still in control: no shouts; no compromise. I had to stop him.

I reached the block, circled it until I was in dead ground for a few precious seconds while I stopped, chest heaving, back against the concrete block, trying to suck oxygen into my lungs. My face was already drenched with sweat; my clothes clung to me.

Pushing out my right hip to create a platform, I raised my cuffed hands as high as they would go. They were so swollen that the skin either side had joined above the plastic, but that didn't matter. That was going to help me. It made the cuffs tighter. I swung them down, pulling my wrists apart as they hit my hip. It didn't happen. The restraining bracket in the little box of the cuffs didn't break. I lifted my arms again. Do it hard enough and it would happen, I knew. Up, deep breath, and I was just about to bring my arms down again as 007 turned the corner and rammed into me, arms out to take me down.

We went straight down onto the grass together, each scrambling about, trying to recover. I kicked out, bucked against his bulk, trying to get my arms over his head. I'd only survive this if I got him in a bear-hug with the plasticuffs still on.

Snot streamed from his nose in reaction to the effort.

I finally managed to wrap my legs around his body, and got my plasticuffed forearms either side of his head, my hands in front of his face. I pulled back with my bodyweight so the cuffs were against his throat, and pushed with my knees into his back. He knew what was happening but it was too late. I pulled back as hard as I could, opening my ballooned fingers as if that would help the plastic get closer to his throat. His hands shot up to try to pull them away. He'd done a bit of this himself. We both knew it wouldn't help him much, but it was a natural reaction that was hard to control.

I rolled onto my knees, pulling back my arms even more so I could get the back of his head against my chest. And then I switched direction, leaning forward, forcing his head down, while at the same time pulling back on my wrists so the plasticuffs dug into his windpipe. He wasn't going anywhere now. He could kick and jerk about all he wanted but the combination of my weight bearing down on the back of his head and the plasticuffs crushing his windpipe would keep him under me.

He didn't know it, but I wasn't going to kill him. There was no need, and it would use up precious time. I just needed to fuck him up enough so I could reach Yulia before Phoenix and his Wolves realized what was up. 007's legs jerked, his body spasmed, but he was under my control and his systems were closing down. It was enough. I was about to get up and run when I heard flip-flops the other side of the block. The sound faded as the holidaymaker went inside. I had to wait now for the sound of a shower or a flush before I started running.

I didn't get water. Instead I got Vanessa Feltz telling me I was listening to Radio 2, it was five seventeen, and she would be reviewing the front pages very soon. *But before that, this from Barry Manilow.*

I let go of his neck and staggered to my feet, just as a

blur of bodies surged round the corner. Whoever punched me took me down so hard I didn't get to hear Barry, and the next thing I felt was my body being picked up and thrown over Phoenix's shoulder in a fireman's lift.

My head thumped against his hip-bone as he ran. A vague blue shape closed in as we drew level with the entrance to the block, then the van door slid open to reveal Tailgate kneeling in the frame, weapon in the shoulder. He looked first at us and then to his left. I heard a tinny-sounding Barry behind us as Tailgate took aim. Phoenix gave a strangulated shout – 'Nyet!' – but it was too late. A dull suppressed double-tap came from Tailgate's Vector.

He jumped out to make way for me to be thrown in. Looking back, I caught a glimpse of the woman sprawled on her back, arms outstretched, two strike marks in her white towelling gown, centre mass, the circles of blood leaking out growing bigger.

No one shouted or panicked. Foma leapt from the cab and ran to the body as Phoenix hurled me into the van.

I landed between two surfboards. My jaw hit and rubbed against the lumpy wax of one and it was hard not to shout out.

I did a sort of press-up to relieve the pain and to see what was happening outside. Phoenix was bent over, scouring the grass, the first empty brass case in his hand.

007 jumped in after me, coughing and spluttering, scrabbling for the weapons bag, as Tailgate and Foma threw the woman inside. She landed on her back,

disturbing the boards that now smashed once again into my jaw as her towelling gown fell open to show her light blue pyjamas soaking up the blood pouring from two entry points.

Another wave of pain swept through my jaw, but it was nothing compared to the state she was in. Her life leaked onto the roll-mats as Tailgate ran back to the block, grabbed the radio, and jabbed at the buttons to switch Barry off mid-tune, then threw it into the van. Foma flung in the woman's flip-flops to join it as Tailgate jumped aboard. He stepped over the middle-aged, grey-haired corpse as if she was just another Rip Curl bag in his way.

Phoenix followed, tossing the two empty cases inside as the sliding door closed, the cab door closed, and we started up towards Reception.

It was then that I heard an ominous slurping noise in time with the woman's very shallow breathing. Air was being sucked into her chest cavity as she tried to breathe and collapsing the lung. She might even have taken a round into one to make it worse. She was on her way out.

44

Phoenix gave direction, and Tailgate jumped down beside her. He slapped the heel of one hand over the hole in her chest to reseal the cavity.

As the van negotiated a speed bump, which shook us all, Tailgate gathered up a fistful of robe with the other hand and jammed the fabric hard against the gut wound. He probably knew it was futile – far too much blood had already leaked out – but Phoenix dropped to his knees beside him and looked as if he was going to give it a go. There was no expression of concern on his face, no rushed or urgent movement, just matter-of-fact control as he grabbed her shoulders and pulled her over to check for exit wounds as Tailgate carried on with the business of keeping the two holes plugged. The back of her white robe had done what towelling did, soaking it all up, but at least there were no exit wounds that were also going to need plugging.

The worrying thing was that she didn't react to any of it, but it looked like Phoenix was going to try to save her. Otherwise, why check for exit wounds?

He'd already dropped her back to the mats, turned her head to one side and dug his fingers into her mouth, trying to clear her airway of blood and mucus. He tilted her head to keep the windpipe open and took a deep breath, his blood-stained hands around her jaw and behind her neck, keeping it in position as he then exhaled deeply into her mouth. Her chest rose with the lung inflations because Tailgate had the hole blocked.

The van stopped and the side door opened. Yulia had a self-satisfied look on her face and was just about to get into the van when she witnessed the bloodbath. Her face dropped its smile and she crumpled. Some people lose control of their body when they see blood. It's a protection mechanism. *Blood means death, maybe yours, so pretend you're already dead.* One of the Wolves might do the same if they watched a needle penetrate their skin.

Foma was out of the van in a flash as Yulia stumbled backwards and fell to the tarmac. He picked her up and threw her aboard for 007 to grab. She almost got dragged over Phoenix and Tailgate as they leant over the body, still working on her.

Foma slid the door and we were quickly on our way once more. 007 had gone back to his day job, weapon in hand and totally focused on me. He nodded over to the back of the van for a recovering Yulia to take Tailgate's coveted place.

Phoenix had both hands over the woman's sternum and half over Tailgate's blood-drenched fist, which provided the seal. He kept straight arms and gave short, sharp pumps.

We turned right on the main, towards Penzance, and

the VW raced through the gears in an effort to get up speed and make distance.

There wasn't much the two of them could do for the woman but plug the holes to stop her losing any more circulating body fluid and seal her chest cavity, fill her lungs, and squash her heart so it drove the oxygenated blood around her, keeping her alive.

Phoenix did about twenty pumps, then checked her carotid artery with his blood-stained fingers. Maybe there was a pulse, maybe there wasn't. His face gave nothing away. He was totally focused on what he was doing.

Checking that Tailgate's hand was still in position over the chest wound, he spat out a mouthful of the woman's blood and mucus that he had collected while inflating her chest, took a deep breath and exhaled into her once more, checking the chest for inflation.

All the while, Yulia was curled up in a ball with her hair covering her face, trying hard to cut out the world around her. She wasn't a coal-face worker.

Phoenix spat out yet more blood and pumped his patient's heart once more. The failing body bent under the force of his weight rapidly squashing her heart. He checked her carotid again and I still couldn't tell what he was thinking. But then, as he sat back on his arse, his spine against the sliding door, and Tailgate released his hands from the wounds and sat back on a blood-stained mat, I didn't need to.

But it wasn't the end of his world. He kicked at the weapons bag and told Tailgate to start getting them out.

45

Phoenix grabbed Yulia's attention as he checked the mag was secure on his Vector. They weren't going to let anything stop them.

'We are still going home. It's all good.'

007 didn't think so and let everyone know it. 'I told you all we should have killed him. There wouldn't have been any of this. He nearly compromised us.' He pointed down at me and kicked the side of the board. The shockwave fired straight into my jaw. I'd been dribbling because of the pain of swallowing, and a mouthful of saliva gushed down my chin. At least, I consoled myself, I was still alive and they didn't know I'd been after Yulia.

The board got another kick and my jaw felt like it had shattered. Phoenix cut in: 'No more.' His eyes burnt into 007's. He was pissed off with him for trying to deflect the blame onto me.

007 sat back on the bags.

Phoenix gave him a second or two to settle, then his

tone went back to professional. 'You are not angry with him, you are angry with yourself. You were careless enough to let him think he had a chance – and you nearly got killed because of it.'

He nodded down at the woman, her head now flopped to the side, eyes half closed. Her mouth was still open from the CPR and the blood around her lips had almost dried. 'So you must accept your mistake and your part in this situation. Learn by it, and make sure it never happens again. Do you understand?'

I flicked my eyes up to see 007 give the most reluctant of nods.

Tailgate knew he was next on the list and readied himself for whatever was coming his way. He would find it hard to justify what he had done.

Phoenix's face was expressionless. 'The mission. Does this affect it?' He gestured at the body as we rumbled over tarmac at speed – but not too fast: Phoenix wanted 'no speeding, no violations'.

We were on a straight road and going for it. 'I don't know yet, but it's a problem, a bigger problem than him. This is normal people. You understand that, don't you?'

Tailgate nodded. 'I saw movement. What if she had run? What if—'

Phoenix's raised hand stopped the waffle. 'You have a responsibility to us, to keep us safe. Just like we have to you but you overreacted. Just one breath – that's all it would have taken – and you would have had time to think. This isn't a fight that we're involved in. It's gentler than that. And now . . .' he picked up the woman's hand, covered with blood, to show Tailgate her wedding and engagement rings, the gold worn with age, '. . . a wife, a mother, maybe a grandmother. They will never know where she is, what has happened to her. They will never know if she is alive and, not knowing, they will eventually hope she is dead rather than suffering. But until then they will move the earth to find her. That is why we have a problem.'

Even if any of this shit-storm had been captured on the caravan site's CCTV, assuming there was any on the buildings, it wasn't going to help her family get any satisfaction. It wouldn't matter to them if they saw her shot or not. They would spend the rest of their days wondering why she'd taken a couple of rounds. Otherwise they would ask themselves if she'd been kidnapped, or had just disappeared. They would never find the answer.

'You have made this a problem, not her or him.' He nodded at me as he let her hand drop to the floor. 'Weapons are only as good as the brain firing them. Your brain.' He tapped his forehead, leaving red finger-marks behind. 'Use it.'

He let the van rumble along the tarmac in silence for a while as 007 and Tailgate digested the clever bollock-ing they'd just received.

I could see that Tailgate wasn't buying it, but he had to suck it up.

Phoenix trying to save her had had nothing to do with making the situation less dangerous for them. If she had survived, it would have been more of a prob-lem: what would have happened to her in Belarus? Problems like her always had to be cleaned up. But Phoenix wasn't about killing, not today, anyway. He

219

was about the mission, getting the job done. It wasn't that Phoenix thought naturally in black and white: it was simply because he had to.

All this practical thinking still couldn't absolve me of guilt. 007 was right: if I hadn't gone for it at the caravan site, all this shit wouldn't have happened. I'd taken a chance and fucked up. The result was now lying next to me. Collateral damage. We'd both have to live with it and I was sure this wasn't his first experience of a third-party fuck-up. It certainly wasn't mine, but I hoped it would be my last.

007 caught my eye and I immediately looked away, my face as passive as I could make it. I didn't want anything to indicate that I knew what was going on. I heard a loud snort, and a second later felt the contents of his sinuses land on the back of my head.

'Okay, there will be no more of it.'

Phoenix checked his watch again. Precious time had been lost. 'We've got to make the pick-up, and remember – we're doing that in daylight. It will be difficult, but we still have the mission to complete. And that includes this man going home with us.'

007 gazed down at me with clear plans in his head for when we arrived back in Belarus, but Phoenix had one more bit of his gripping-the-lads talk. 'If we encounter any problems before pick-up, only I will say if you put this man to the ground. Understand?'

There were reluctant nods from Tailgate and 007 but I wasn't sure their hearts were in it. As far as they were concerned, the only reason they'd received their bollocking was because of my actions.

As for Yulia, her response was to remain curled up

in a corner and keep facing the side panel to avoid any chance of seeing the blood now smeared about the van, like the floor of an abattoir. She was way out of all her comfort zones and Phoenix knew it. The commander put up a hand to attract her attention, along with a half-smile. 'We'll be home soon. All is good.'

She didn't look at him but her answer was surprisingly clear. 'I know.'

She might not like blood but she could certainly keep a grip of herself.

I closed my eyes. This lot might be going home soon, but it wasn't going to be with me, and it certainly wasn't going to be with Yulia.

It was going to be *Shit or Bust, the Sequel* very soon.

46

Phoenix had a lot on his plate, over and beyond the two problems on the floor behind him. He had to get all of the team to the pick-up point and make sure they were exfiltrated. Nothing else mattered.

The driver kept his foot down for the next ten minutes to get us out of the immediate area, but I knew he'd still be keeping it legal.

Phoenix was at the hatch, talking non-stop to the two in front, probably reminding them to check their mirrors and flanks, and as much of the sky as they could see. He couldn't see what they could, so he had to trust their input. It would have been easier for him to be up front, but that wasn't his job. Phoenix needed to be exactly where he was, able to communicate with whoever was on the end of that laptop. He had to trust his team. If the two up front said they were possibly being followed, that was a lot different from saying they were being followed. Different actions would be taken for different terminology – and getting it wrong would entail even more of the third party getting killed. One was enough. If the two up front said they were being followed, Phoenix would have to take action: they were so close to the pick-up point now. He would attack them. He had to stop it there and then before continuing to the pick-up and that was why all the weapons were out of their bags.

If the two up front were wrong and it was just a possible, not a definite follow, it didn't mean they were thinking over-aggressively, like Tailgate, or being slack, like 007. It meant they had to make a call. If they got it wrong, even more real people would be killed.

This business wasn't a science and that meant I might also join any collateral damage. If the police tried to stop us, I was one problem they could get rid of straight away, before focusing on the police, hosing them down and keeping on moving.

In his shoes, I wouldn't have hesitated in dropping me before taking down the local security if I had to get the team to a pick-up.

Phoenix unzipped one of the Rip Curls and retrieved a laptop, the antenna and a neatly coiled bundle of cables. Fuck knew how long we'd been driving. As far as I could tell we were still travelling in the same direction. We'd turned right out of the caravan site and were heading generally east, I was sure of that, towards the rest of the UK. Not that it really mattered: it just made me feel a little better that I knew something else the rest of them thought I didn't.

Phoenix didn't bother getting help from Yulia as he unfurled the cables. The geek was still curled up in a ball in her own little world, probably hoping it would all go away and that the horrible smell of blood and flesh would stop attacking her nostrils. In any event, for Phoenix, there was shit on. It would take time to explain what he wanted doing, so he might as well get on with it himself.

He linked the antenna lead into the laptop and passed it through the hatch to the front crew to attach to what I presumed was a mount on the dash or windscreen. He was soon tapping away and waiting for replies, maybe from the embassy. Whatever was going on, his bloodied fingers were busy. He was probably telling them I was still here and alive, but there was now a dead woman lying next to me: the killing might have been captured on CCTV, or there might be a witness, or the woman's family would raise the alarm very soon and call the police because she'd gone for a shower and not come back. Within a couple of hours something would be happening, if it wasn't already.

The VW braked hard and took a sudden sharp left. Our bodies lurched, and one of the boards banged into the side of my face, right on the jaw joint.

I wondered if we were moving off the main because we were being followed and were getting ready to take down the target, but Phoenix was happy. 'Good, good – go!' He checked his watch and I saw it for the first time: a Luminox. The military loved them because the dials' markers were gas-lit, so you could get an instant view of the time in the dark without the delay you experienced when you were looking at traditional luminous paint. So we weren't turning off because of a follow. It just made sense to quit the main once we'd made that initial distance, and put in some angles. If we'd been seen on CCTV or by a witness, the police would have the mains marked up. Not that there were many police in Cornwall, I was sure, but there might be cameras on the mains. On the downside, it meant a longer journey to wherever the pick-up point was, and the pressure would be on. That was good. They might start cutting corners and that might, just might, open up an opportunity for me.

The suppressed barrel dug into the side of my neck as we bounced around another corner, the driver churning up and down the gears to keep the wheels turning as fast as they could go. I checked the condition of the Vector's safety just to make sure that the next bump we hit didn't mean an accidental discharge into me. We all die sometime but I was hoping my death would be in bed with my boots off or, if not, in a blaze of glory rather than because the local council couldn't be arsed to repair their potholes. That would be even worse than being shot in the arse.

Phoenix stopped tapping and flipped down the lid. He moved up to the hatch – the engine was so noisy he had to shout through to the cab. We were being thrown around so much in the back that I couldn't hear what was happening, but they were orders. They were loud, they were short, and they were sharp. He came back and stuffed the antenna into the bag, followed by the laptop.

He pointed down at the woman and shouted so there would be no misunderstanding. 'She is staying. We leave everything, including the weapons. The embassy will clear up the mess. Everything stays apart from him.' He didn't care whether or not I understood he was talking about me. 'We need to know what he knows.'

A threat assessment would be made when they got home. Could phase two, the attack, be carried out with success after these two compromises? It was going to be hard for them to come to a decent assessment because I had no intention of being there to help them.

That probably wouldn't concern Phoenix too much. Sometimes the plan doesn't need a plan, you just need a pair of bollocks to get the job done, and maybe even after all this shit he would still come back to finish the job.

47

For the next thirty minutes we were on B roads, and
the Wolves got into their protein bars and water as we
slowed down or sometimes came to a halt to let larger
vehicles pass, then drove through a small built-up area.
I could hear voices and vehicle doors closing before we
stopped to let a bunch of chattering schoolkids cross
the road. Then we turned off tarmac and rumbled over
a rutted surface, stones ricocheting off the wheel arches.
Assuming the kids had been heading for school, it
must now be about eight o'clock or soon after.

It was maybe another fifteen before Tailgate got up
and climbed over the woman's body, checking his
weapon as he took up a position by the side door. Yulia
uncurled in the corner and pulled her hair back to
expose her face, desperate to get out of this van. She
was shooed back by 007. Not yet.

Phoenix concentrated on waffling to Tailgate as the
VW began to bounce cross-country, stones kicked up
by the wheels as the van negotiated the dips and bumps

that must have been a track. With the lurching and clattering it was difficult to hear what he was saying. Whatever it was, he got lots of nods in return.

The VW slowed. The driver would be wanting to keep the revs down so they didn't bumble into something too quickly to have time to react. We must be getting close.

The vehicle came to a very gentle halt. The engine was switched off, and I didn't hear the handbrake go on. The driver had probably kept his hand on the button to stop it ratcheting.

Phoenix eased the door open to reveal, framed in the doorway just two metres in front of us, a block of perfectly spaced commercial forestry firs. The sun was out and it was high enough to cast the camper van's shadow onto the scrub between us and the treeline.

Foma climbed out carefully to join Tailgate, both with their weapons in their hands, and they moved off, nothing else said, into the treeline and disappeared. They must be recceing. The pick-up point must be either on the other side of the block or within it.

Phoenix got out, checking the area with his weapon in his hand, not in the shoulder. He wasn't flapping, but he checked his watch more than seemed necessary. He looked left and right and around, even skyward, his mouth open, listening as if he were in the battle space. Then he took yet another glance at his watch.

Yulia's body faced the corpse on the floor but she kept her head turned to one side. There was no crying, fretting, or short, weak, nervous breathing. She was in control, almost rising above the carnage, just waiting for the moment it would end.

007 wasn't slack now: he was making sure the suppressed barrel was against my neck and aching for the order to drop me.

It was getting to shit or bust time again. Phoenix looked at his Luminox. Soon we'd have to be moved out of the van to whatever was picking us up. That would be the next time I was on my feet and could get my hands working. They were so swollen now that the plasticuffs were invisible. The scabs on my knuckles had split with the swelling and clear fluid was trying to form a seal over them but it wasn't working.

It was no more than fifteen minutes before Tailgate and Foma emerged from the treeline and Phoenix went to meet them for the sit-rep. There was too much hushed waffling for everything to be okay, that was for sure.

007 checked the scene as best he could but the barrel never budged from my neck and the first pad of his forefinger never strayed from the trigger. Even if I got out of the van with Yulia right now there were another three weapons outside. I would die out of breath, which was just as bad as a bumpy-road gunshot in the head.

Whatever was happening beyond the treeline, Phoenix had made a decision on how to deal with it. There was pointing at Tailgate and Foma, short words, then nods from all three before they came back to the wagon. Yet again, he checked his watch.

Tailgate and Phoenix boarded the rear, slowly but purposefully, and Foma climbed back into the cab. I heard subdued murmurs coming from up front, and Tailgate explained to 007 what was next. I couldn't hear a word. It had to be because of Yulia. They were sparing her something. Clearly she'd reacted badly to violence so far, and maybe something even worse was about to happen.

Soon the van was crawling along the track in first gear; Phoenix closed the sliding door onto one click. We travelled a few hundred metres, took a left for less than a hundred, then another left. We'd done three sides of a square.

Tailgate was on his knees at the side door, his Vector in the shoulder. He had his firing hand on the pistol grip and steadied himself against the VW with the other. Phoenix was on his knees, too, a hand poised on the door handle, ready to pull back.

We stopped and there was a voice, male, outside. The accent was northern, Manchester maybe. He was talking to the cab guys up close. I could hear it through the hatch: Foma's window must have been open. The voice was close and clear. 'It's okay, we can stay here. It's free land.'

Phoenix pulled back the door to reveal the talker at the cab window, but not for long.

'We have a right to—'

A double-tap went into his chest from Tailgate and he dropped like liquid.

Tailgate stepped out and leant down to him. Another two-round burst into his head. He had the Traveller's white-man dreadlocks, pulled back in a thick ponytail with some multi-coloured cloth that was now predominantly bright red.

Beyond him, framed in the doorway, was a big box van that looked at least twenty years old, hand-painted green, with a chimney sticking out of the top, smoking. A couple of candy-striped folding chairs were open at the rear, next to washing hanging from a rotary drier. There was movement inside. I could hear female sobs and screams. So could Tailgate. He already knew what was inside, of course, because he'd done the recce. That was why he hadn't stopped moving. As soon as he'd head-jobbed the guy, he took the first strides towards the box van, weapon up. The woman was now in the driver's seat, frantically scrabbling to turn the ignition key but flapping so much she probably hadn't even got it into the slot.

Her sobs penetrated to Yulia, who put her hands over her ears, brought her knees up and tried to bury her head in her chest. Two rapid shots gently clicked out of Tailgate's suppressed Vector and into the front cab of the hand-painted van. There were two dinks as the rounds drilled into the panels of the passenger door, and then even more double bursts and the safety glass shattered as she took a couple of rounds. She slumped sideways and disappeared down onto the passenger seat as Tailgate got right up to it and pulled at the door before leaning in to her for the head job.

Phoenix checked his watch and calmly made safe his weapon before it went into the bag along with his spare mag from the back pocket of his jeans. Tailgate headed our way. The cab crew got out and, as they started to dump their weapons and mags, we all heard the thump of rotors in the distance.

48

Phoenix punched a hand at the sky, urging events along. 'Come on, let's go! Come!'

007 leapt off me to allow Tailgate to drop his weapon just behind the dead body, then grab my swollen wrists at the plasticuff joint to drag me towards the door. I stumbled over the woman's head as 007 dumped his weapon next to Tailgate's and followed us. The rotors got louder.

Yulia was still in the rear, the last breathing body inside. My legs worked to stabilize themselves as I was pulled out of the van and onto the hard ground of the track. Tailgate didn't let up, my arms out straight like he'd lassoed me and was dragging me behind his horse.

My eyes were assaulted by bright sunlight as I did my best to take things in, and it was clear why this was a perfect daylight pick-up point. The forestry was in dead ground surrounded by rolling moorland: the heli could disappear below the skyline, then disappear even deeper behind the trees. There was an open area, maybe the size of a football pitch, before the gentle rise of the high ground again, more than enough for a helicopter to land.

The driver ran to the centre of that open space to become a marker and scanned the sky. He would make sure the pilot knew all was good as he looked down on the mess below him.

Phoenix and Foma were halfway between us and the heli marker, whose arms were vertical by now, still looking skyward, waiting to see or hear which direction the heli was going to come from. The rotor noise was much louder, but low-flying aircraft are difficult to locate, especially when they're ground-hopping below the skyline.

Tailgate kept dragging me. I checked behind me at the same time Phoenix did to see where everybody was. Just as I turned my head back the rotor blades roared above us, flying over the forestry block, no more than a couple of metres above the treeline. It swooped straight over the box van, then pivoted dramatically and flared out. The down-draught blasted the ground litter from the firs and the dust from the track, as the rotary clothes-drier spun as if it were in a hurricane and the candy-striped chairs flew at the dreadlocked head, bounced off it and crashed against the side of the VW, finally tumbling to the side and away.

The heli was red and white, an Agusta six-seater, more if the seats had been taken out of the back. 007 was coaxing Yulia towards the landing site. She bent forward, her mop of hair blowing about like she was in a wind tunnel. She was trying to keep the blast out of her face and avert her eyes from the body on the ground. In doing that, her eyes locked on the shot-out cab of the box van and what lay the other side of the open door, slumped in the driver's seat, the head lolling above a pool of blood that had poured from her mouth. Yulia's knees buckled and her hands dropped to her thighs. 007 fought to keep her upright and moving towards the Agusta as it descended in a deep flare. The rotors screamed in protest as it executed a tactical landing.

It was now or never.

Tailgate's arms were so straight as he dragged his reluctant prisoner that when I propelled myself at him I burst free of his grip. I turned and started running back towards the VW. I wasn't interested in what was happening behind me: my eyes were glued on 007 and Yulia, who were just a couple of metres away, making sure I could avoid 007 if he was quick enough and came for me.

I skirted the rear of the box van, my mind focused on the two Vectors the other side of the body in the VW. I'd passed 007 before he realized what was going on. Yulia looked up and there was horror on her face. Another killing? Maybe she wouldn't get home.

Some of the weapons had been made safe. No idea about 007's and Tailgate's. It didn't matter. All that did was getting my hands on one of the fuckers and making sure my balloon fingers could get the thing working.

Stuff must have been happening behind me but all I could hear was the deafening roar of rotors.

They would get Yulia on board but no one was going to leave without me.

I threw myself across the woman, the tops of my thighs grazing the door sill. My stomach landed on her chest, the rest of me on the boards; her body buckled and gas came out of her mouth.

My plasticuffed hands grappled for one of the Vectors. Would it be made ready or made safe? I'd soon find out. I grabbed the closest one and fumbled at the safety catch with my numb, swollen fingers. I had no sensation in them at all. I was working on visual as I pushed it down with the heel of my hand, not caring if it went to single shot, two-round burst, or full auto. I just wanted safety off.

I closed my conjoined hands around the pistol grip and willed the middle finger of my right hand into the trigger guard. I rolled over to see Tailgate less than five paces away. He wasn't stopping for anything.

I squeezed the trigger.

Fuck-all.

Tailgate knew it and screamed some kind of battle cry. I saw his mouth and eyes widen as he took the last couple of bounds to the van and I held the weapon out with straight arms, trying to create a hard barrier that he would collapse onto. It was all I could do before he gripped me.

As I got ready for the fight a blue blur crossed from right to left, one of the candy-striped chairs held against its grille as it bounced over the body on the ground, the bonnet then rising and smacking straight into Tailgate, hurling him up and away from the door frame, out of my vision. A split second later the chair and Tailgate came back into view, tumbling through the air. They landed on the ground just beneath the driver's door of the box van. The impact sent up a plume of congealing blood.

49

The Jeep screeched to a stop somewhere to the left at the same time as I leapt out of the VW's side door into a cloud of dust.

No more than five metres away, Rio was already out of the wagon and running towards me brandishing his KA-BAR like a claymore in a Highland charge. 'Nick, come on! Fuck sake!'

The Jeep's reverse light illuminated as I tried to make my fumbling balloon fingers lift the cocking handle that lay flush against the Vector to get the thing made ready. 'No – Yulia! Yulia!'

I waved the barrel in the direction of the Agusta, still on the ground, the din of its rotors overwhelming the bowl of dead ground. 007 still had hold of Yulia. 'Yulia! Get her!'

My eyes flicked to the other side of the box van as I finally cocked the weapon. Phoenix and Foma had seen what was happening and were sprinting back to fight.

I held up the Vector, my left hand trying to grab forward of the mechanism to give some support, but no luck. Not checking what Rio was doing, I screamed the same mantra: 'Yulia! Get Yulia!'

Phoenix and Foma had a mission to complete, and taking me was part of it. They saw the weapon come up into the aim, held in my straight arms, just like the old square-on-both-arms-out-straight pistol method, and immediately bomb-burst. They knew they had a good chance of one of them making the distance to me.

Both eyes open, I squeezed the trigger and a double-tap went forward to the closer one, before I swapped to the right, swivelling from my waist, and getting another double-tap burst down, this time at Phoenix. I needed as stable a platform as possible to get these rounds down accurately. I worked to keep control of the weapon as I gulped oxygen, knowing that adrenalin would compensate for fucked fingers.

They were about ten metres away as I fired left to right again. The iron sights were down flat so I just fired instinctively, swinging towards the centre mass of each moving target in turn, weapon up horizontal, staring straight down it. Double-taps left and right, left and right, keeping calm, keeping focused on what was in front of me. Flapping about the possibility of missing wasn't going to make me do the opposite. My feet were planted. There wasn't time to make the platform complete by moving them.

I loosed off another burst at the fast-moving centre mass of Foma and he went down. I didn't know if he was still breathing but who cared? I swung my arms to the right and Phoenix was now gone. Maybe he was behind the box van a few metres away. I stooped but couldn't see any boots the other side. He might be behind the wheels. He could even have passed the box van and already be moving through the treeline to get behind me. For sure, he wouldn't be running away. They had to get this done, because there was phase two.

I took a pace towards the box van, weapon still horizontal in my straight arms. The plasticuffs didn't hurt now. Adrenalin was seeing to that.

To my half-left and ahead, Rio was in trouble on the ground with 007 on top of him. In the mess of flailing limbs, I couldn't see who held the knife. Gabe was out of the Jeep and running as best he could, the cricket bat in his hands. Yulia was bent over, paralysed, neither help nor hindrance. I left them all to it. My problem was Phoenix.

I shouted to anyone who was listening. 'Yulia! Get Yulia!' I had no idea how many rounds were left but there was fuck-all I could do about it. Besides, all it would take was one round to sort this shit out when I found him – or he found me.

It wasn't long coming. He appeared from the side of the box van and I instinctively jerked my head to ride the punch but still took it in the neck and staggered to the left. His other hand would be wanting to grab the weapon. I pulled down my arms and turned away from him to present my back to cover the Vector, and from there maybe I could do a complete 180 and get the weapon into him. He knew it, and another hard punch went into my side, straight into the kidneys. It took the wind out of me and I dropped to my knees. All I could do was bring the weapon up to my stomach and then just fall on it. With luck he would make a decision to run to the VW to get another, and that would give me time to roll over and get some rounds into him. But it didn't happen. His boots rained into me and then his hands tried to lift me up and pull me over. Finally I felt his full weight on me. All I could do was keep covering the weapon with my front until I could get my blown-up finger back into the trigger guard.

From above me came hard, fast, controlled breathing as I kept my body tense, elbows in, head down, mantling the Vector between my body and the dust. Not many metres away, the rotors still churned; the heli was still on the ground. The rest of my world was pain.

Phoenix had obviously decided to fuck me up so much that he could either grab the weapon or buy himself enough time to run to the VW. I couldn't let that happen. No one was coming to help me. I could definitely hear Gabe shouting. There was nothing from Rio. Where the fuck was Jack?

I stopped trying to get my finger into the trigger guard and let go of the Vector. With both hands in the dirt I pushed up, trying to twist at the same time, like an alligator with its prey. Just a couple of seconds would do. His weight pushed down against my left shoulder and I pushed up with my right. It was enough to unbalance him momentarily. I punched out with both hands, not as much as I wanted to but it was enough. I slipped my arms over the back of his head, like I'd done with 007. He knew what I was doing, that I was trying to turn him around, get behind him and strangle him.

His hands went either side of me on the ground and he redoubled his efforts to grab the Vector under my back. I pulled down on the nape of his neck, dragging his face towards me and into my chest. He writhed about, kicking out, then using his toes to gain purchase in the dirt and push into me. He did almost a press-up in an attempt to lift me at the same time as he lifted himself. I closed my legs around him, pinning him, crushing my thighs against his as I heaved my wrists even harder against the back of his neck. It was all I could do: speed and surprise weren't going to turn him over. I caught a deep breath and used it to its full effect. 'Help! Fucking help!'

Phoenix did another push up before collapsing on his elbows, and I collapsed my whole bodyweight in the hope gravity would help me. 'Someone, get here!'

I opened my eyes to see Rio staggering above me, knife in hand. He dropped to his knees looking for a free place to stab into Phoenix's legs and not mine.

'Fuck that – kill him!'

He gripped the handle of the KA-BAR and raised it before ramming it down into Phoenix's back. There was an instant rigidness as he took the pain and tried to resist it. Rio yanked the blade out and slammed it back down. This time the body relaxed. I heard the last rasp of defiance as blood cascaded onto my chest and I let go. His head fell sideways. His eyes passed mine and they were still open, but already starting to glaze over. I kicked him off and grabbed the Vector.

Rio staggered to his feet. Behind his blood-stained features I could see he was getting ready to ask me a million and one questions. We had no time for that.

'Yulia?'

He nodded and came to me, KA-BAR ready to cut me free.

I shook my head. 'I'll sort it.'

I looked over to see Gabe dragging a physically incapacitated Yulia into the Jeep. He had a bloodied cricket bat in one hand from where he'd left the mush of 007's head on top of its lifeless body.

I waved the Vector at Rio. 'There's more of these in the VW. One behind the woman's body and some in a Rip Curl bag with mags. Don't forget the mags.'

I dropped the Vector to the ground before lifting my arms above my head and bringing them down hard against my stomach as I strained out with my wrists, putting the maximum pressure I could onto the restraining bracket. Nothing. The bracket still held the cuff's ratchet. The second time, I pulled down even harder, and the bracket broke under the pressure. I was free. It would have been easier for Rio just to cut the cuffs off me but I'd never tried it before and I wanted to know if it could have worked back at the toilet block. And, of course, I wanted to get free under my own steam, for no reason except that it felt better.

The heli pilot had clearly seen the fuck-up because the rotors were winding faster and faster and, within seconds, the aircraft was lifting and making dramatic turns to get out of the dead ground. The down-draught exploded into us.

I looked up to see the driver and two other faces peering out of the side windows, probably the embassy people who'd been sent to take the van and clean up the mess. They were surveying much more tidying up than they'd bargained for. They would already be radioing to wherever for new orders.

I picked up the Vector and tried to run towards the Jeep but it was more of a stumble. Gabe was in the driver's seat when I got there, with Yulia next to him, bent over, the hair in front of her face soaked with tears. As he checked her for weapons, mobiles, anything that could become a danger for us, her shoulders moved up and down in time with her sobs.

I jumped in behind them and the first thing I saw was the bull's-eyed windscreen. There was no blood in the crazed glass, but the indentation was so deep it looked like it had been made by a lead football, not Tailgate's head.

'Gabe – where the fuck's Jack?'

Gabe's face was splattered with blood. His hands on the wheel looked worse. 'It's all right. Soon. She's sterile, nothing on her.' He jerked a thumb at my hands. 'Where you learn that?'

'YouTube. Jedi Blade Channel. Let's go. Out of the danger area. Back on the road.'

There was no time for Chinese parliaments, just action that I was going to command. Now I'd see if they'd stuck to what they'd all agreed in Jack's barn: one voice, mine; they carried out what it said or we lost our way and lost everything.

Rio joined me in the back, throwing the weapons bag into the footwell, and the Jeep was soon bouncing back onto the track. He slumped against the side window, eyes closed, chest heaving as he pulled in oxygen. The KA-BAR rested on his lap, staining his jeans red.

His lips were swollen and bloodied, and there were rips at the neck of his sweatshirt.

'Rio, mate. Where are we?'

He was too fucked to open his eyes, let alone turn his head. 'Bodmin Moor, mate. The dead woman – what's the score with her?'

'Later.'

50

We careered along the track, shuddering left and right as the wheels hit ruts and bounced out again.

I leant forward to Yulia and shouted, above the noise, 'We're not going to hurt you. Okay?'

She didn't respond. Her head stayed down even when I tried to do up her seatbelt.

I looked around. 'Tech geek. She speaks English better than we do. Just think about what you say, yeah?'

Gabe took a more direct approach, banging a fist into her arm. 'You listening? We're not going to hurt you. For fuck's sake, look up, enjoy the view.'

It wasn't the warmest of invitations and she slumped even lower in her seat, sending tears rolling off her face and into the mop of hair. Eventually I got the belt across her and got her to click it in, hoping it had let her know we had her welfare at heart. 'Let's leave her alone, let her sort her own shit out.'

I'd had a hand resting on each of the two front seats,

but dropped them beside me to force some more blood through the veins. I should at least have been feeling pins and needles, but instead there was a total lack of sensation. They were going to be in a shit state for a couple of days, I knew.

We came to the end of the forestry block and turned right. At once the devastation was behind us and out of sight on the other side of the firs. The Beamer was parked by the track about fifty ahead, facing our direction of travel, and as we got closer I made out the shape of Jack's head above the driver's seat.

Gabe put his foot on the brake and the suspension jumped and creaked. He pulled in to the right, half on the track, half on the verge, his window level with Jack's. They powered them down together. Jack looked happy as he checked that all the faces in the Jeep were present and correct, but Gabe didn't give him time to offer any congratulations. 'You follow us, right?'

Jack nodded. 'Where to?'

I leant right forward so I could look left past Gabe. 'We're going to do a bound, dump the Jeep, find out what the fuck's going on from Yulia here, then hide up and sort ourselves out.'

I wanted to make sure we left as little as possible to connect us with the area in case it was compromised. There was bound to be DNA in the van to compromise me, but there wasn't a lot I could do about that.

Jack was looking at my hands and the banana fingers.

'Later. Give me your mobile.'

Gabe held his arm out of the window for Jack to do as he was told, while I sat back in my seat and focused on magicking the Owl's number into my head. Gabe passed the phone to me and was instantly impatient. 'For fuck's sake, let's get going. We might as well dump the Jeep and tell the world we've been here. We gotta get moving.'

'Not yet, mate, wait.'

The mobile was fully charged, just as it should have been, and had three bars: that was enough. I fumbled through Jack's call history. It was clean. I checked the texts for any messages. None. I next pressed the keys a couple of times trying to call the Owl, stopped, erased and started again. Once because I had got the number wrong, and twice because my finger wouldn't hit the right key.

Rio had been sprawled on most of the back seat. He opened his eyes. Gabe's impatience had spread. 'Nick, we've gotta go.'

'Yep, in a minute. This is important. It has to be done here. You know exactly where we are?'

Rio shrugged. 'On the moor, mate. We weren't exactly following the map, know what I mean?'

As I dialled, I got Gabe to retrieve my neck wallet and mobile from Jack. Three rings and the Owl answered with his usual front-of-house bonhomie. 'Good morning!'

'We've got what you want.'

'Great news. Is it intact?'

'Yes, but we've left a mess. Track this signal and find out what you need to clean up. Get a crew here or whatever it is you do – ASAP – to sort it out. Someone's going to find it. The mobile is staying for you to track.'

'Okay, will do. How many problems am I looking at here?'

'Three normal and three real big ones.'

'Sure. I can do that.' The perma-smile shone through. The fucker had probably been tracking Jack's mobile all along because the snide had given him the details. I hoped he had, anyway. It wouldn't have surprised me if he was already in the south-west, just waiting for a handover. 'Okay, Nick, so when are we going to meet up?'

'Not yet. Easy-peasy, my arse. This was way above our pay grade. Way above, and that worries us all, big-time.'

The Owl jumped in again: 'Hey, don't be like that. If it's about cash, I can—'

'Listen.' It was my turn, and minus the charm. 'Just get tracking, mop up the mess before the world sees it, then stand by for a call when I'm ready.'

'Hey, I kinda thought we had trust going on between us. Nick, I was just thinking . . .'

I left him to it and threw the mobile out onto the beds of pine needles just inside the treeline. 'Right, Gabe, wheels turning, mate.'

There wasn't any training manual to refer to when shit happened. It all boiled down to what I'd told them at the barn: experience, training and knowledge. Getting out of this wasn't a science: no side had complete control of what might happen. Just as Phoenix and his team had done, we had to accept that there was shit on, and work around it as best we could to protect ourselves.

I rested my forehead against the head restraint in

front of me and checked for Jack's reaction to losing his mobile. It wasn't what I expected. He didn't even do a double-take, just got on with the business of following.

Gabe powered up his window so we could hear each other a bit better as we rumbled forward. 'So I'm going to clear a couple of Ks and find somewhere to dump the Jeep, yeah?'

Rio's head rocked from side to side, eyes closed once more, his good hand still on the KA-BAR. 'Oi, midget. How you going to explain this one to Direct Line?' He laughed loudly at his own joke before remembering his lips were split and had to take the pain.

Gabe was thinking more practically. 'You lot will all be pitching in to buy me a new one.' He then had a thought that brought the situation back to focus. 'If we get out of this shite to collect the cash.'

Rio came back. 'Gladly, mate. Anything not to smell your nicotine shit.'

I leant forward again to check Yulia. She was still slumped in her seat crying, but that meant she was breathing, nothing was broken and all she was leaking was tears. Everything was good. Most important of all, she was compliant – and that worried me.

I tapped Gabe's shoulder. 'Mate, keep the sun on our right and we'll head north. No speeding, no violations. I want to keep away from the A30 and get rid of the wagon.'

Gabe nodded and his eyes never left the track. When I sat back, Rio was watching me. 'So aren't you going to ask us how we found you and saved your arse? Now it's all over, aren't you going to ask us how brilliant we were? Locate and confront, mate. Locate and confront.'

'All over? For fuck's sake, it's only just beginning. Remember what we spoke about last night in the Beamer before Jack fucked up? If we get the next bit wrong we're all going to be dead.'

That certainly got a reaction from Yulia.

51

We made it onto a B road that was so narrow and hemmed in by hedges and trees it felt like we were going down a tunnel.

Yulia was terrified of us. She whimpered, and took a deep, ragged breath. 'Please, don't hurt me. All I was doing was—'

I put a hand on her shoulder. 'Mate, it's okay. Do you know where the helicopter was going? To meet a plane, land on a ship?'

She shrugged and shook her mop of wet hair. 'I'm sorry, I . . .' Her voice trailed off.

'It's okay.'

Yulia would be as important to them as she was to us, and the fuckers might be up there thinking, You know what? It hasn't finished yet. The Agusta might have flown out of the area, then decided to come back – and they weren't the only ones we had to worry about. The Owl might have got something airborne, not only to go and clear up the mess but also to find us.

And that wasn't all. If the caravan site shooting had been compromised, the police could also be up and about, checking whatever they thought they had to. The fact was, I didn't know who could be out there, up there, looking for us. We had to get the Jeep off the road and concealed as quickly as we could to help us make distance.

I also needed to warm Yulia up to explain to us who, why, when and how. She needed to know that we were her friends; we weren't going to fuck her up. It was the people who'd sent us to lift her who were going to cause pain – but if she helped us, we could help her. Unless she didn't want to help us, of course, and then, for her, everything would very quickly change for the worse. I had a responsibility to the team to keep us all safe, and if that meant hurting Yulia until she helped me do that, it was her problem, not mine. She'd already seen the hard side of us, so for now she needed to see our understanding side and grasp that we were all worker bees together.

'Yulia, look at me, mate.'

She turned her head.

'Everything will be all right if you do what we say. Okay?' I tried to get eye-to-eye by bending forward through the seats.

She nodded a tear-wet face and I gave what I hoped was a soothing smile.

Gabe broke in: 'Here we go.' He'd found somewhere. He slowed, checked his rear-view for the Beamer, and turned into a car park. An earthy sign displayed a happy stickman family striding out for a day on the nature trail.

Rio was all eyes, checking for vehicles, checking for CCTV cameras. The car park had been dug out and lined with gravel, and the mountains of displaced earth sat in berms around the edges. The place was empty. It was too early in the day, and kids were at school anyway. There wasn't going to be any stickman family shit just yet.

I pointed to the far left-hand corner. 'The other side of those things, mate. Get as far in as you can.'

Gabe steered towards a row of plastic domes, big as church bells. Blue ones, green ones, white ones. He nosy-parked on the dead side of the recycling station until the front nudged against the berm. The mature trees on its other side spread out into the parking area so we had cover from the air. This wasn't about taking time and effort to conceal the Jeep for ever: it was just about hiding the wagon from the air.

As soon as the engine was off I got a grip. We needed to switch on, get ourselves sorted, before we got out of there. 'Listen in. The weapons, daysacks, tent stuff, and that cricket bat go into the Beamer. Then all three of us need to clean ourselves up, change of clothes – VDMs, remember?' I pointed at Rio's blood-stained jeans, then at Gabe. 'You looked in the mirror?'

He checked himself in the rear-view as Jack came up and nosy-parked beside us.

'While we clean ourselves up, Jack stays here to pack the Beamer, and we take Yulia with us. Go down that track. There's bound to be water – it's a nature trail. If not, we'll have to make do.'

Gabe nodded and jumped out to open the rest of the doors. Rio went to grab hold of Yulia, then opened the tailgate to get at the daysacks. He was doing his best to calm her but getting no reply. 'Yuli, stop flapping. Everything's all right.'

Jack had his door open and was helping his false leg out of the car. He looked up when he saw me coming, and his face said he was braced for a bollocking. 'Nick, I'm sorry, I fucked up. I shouldn't have . . .'

As he waffled I covered his exit by going right up to his door and putting my left hand on the top and the other on the roof, forcing him back into the seat. I lowered my head almost into the cab. 'Stop. There's no need. That was yesterday. Today's today. All that matters is now. We're all breathing and we have Yulia. Let's forget the history – there's not enough time. There's bigger stuff.'

He looked shocked. He'd probably rehearsed what he needed to say – whether it was a real fuck-up or on purpose – and he was backtracking. 'Thanks.'

'Good.' It really didn't matter to me whether he'd screwed up or not. This wasn't the time. It wouldn't get us out of this shit. I'd find out later if he was the snide and had done it on purpose, and then it *would* matter. But not now.

He came back with the only question he could ask. 'What happened?' He waved at the front of the Jeep, then at Rio as he began to walk Yulia towards the nature trail with our joint daysack over his shoulder containing the spare clothes we'd taken from Jack's barn. Yulia's slumped body language said she was thinking the worst, and it didn't help when Gabe lifted the weapons bag out of the back footwell. Her parents would have told her about all the times Stalin's men marched intellectuals into the forest and blew their brains out.

Rio was doing his best. 'Yuli, mate, I'm not taking you in there for a shag. Know what I mean? It's all right.' He took her arm but Yulia wasn't impressed. He still had the KA-BAR tucked into his waistband in taking-a-knife-to-school style.

Gabe dumped the weapons in the rear of the Beamer and I heard the clunk of the barrels. Squaddies all over the world would recognize that sound.

Jack looked up at me but didn't bother to ask.

'We're going to get out of sight and clean ourselves up. Hopefully there's some water down there.'

'What about the Owl?'

'All in good time. Just load up everything from the Jeep. Listen to the local BBC. If there's anything un-usual, like the roads have been closed because of an incident and they aren't saying what it is, or even closure because of an accident on one of the major arteries coming out of here, we need to know before we move. Also, keep an ear out for helis. All right?'

He nodded.

I double-tapped the roof. 'Done. See you in a bit.'

I walked away to join Gabe, who had now grabbed his own daysack, and we followed Rio and Yulia down the trail. I wanted to keep Yulia with me at all times. I'd got rid of Jack's phone, so there were going to be no communications telling the Owl where we were and what we planned to do. If he did as I'd told him, all well and good. If he didn't, I had no control of that. I just wanted him to think all was good and catch him sinning, let him hang himself, so there would be no doubt.

52

Rio was already changing. There was a small trickle of water off to the right about twenty metres down, and Yulia was standing beside him, her arms wrapped around herself as if she needed protection. She was keeping her eyes away from the blood. But it still didn't look right. The crying, poor-little-girl act on his drive from the moor? This wasn't the woman I had witnessed in the van. She watched Rio's withered arm do its best to help the good one struggle with his jeans. Rio laughed. 'Yuli, mate, you think this is weird? Wait till you see that fucker.'

Gabe ignored him as he pulled off his shirt and used it to soak up some water, then scrubbed his face.

I knelt down, splashed my hair and tried to flatten it, then patted at my face. The jaw joint on the right was swollen and painful.

Rio had put on some brown chinos and was easing his withered arm into a long-sleeved green T-shirt. Gabe finished wiping his face and threw the shirt at me to do the same, then got to grips with his bloodied jeans. Yulia had a close-up of what Rio had been on about, and looked confused.

It was the reaction Rio was hoping for. 'We're saving the world, one stump at a time.'

My face was aching now the adrenalin and cold water had worn off. I threw the wet shirt into one of the daysacks. Rio was deciding which hoodie to wear, the grey or the greyer. We both needed one to cover our faces as much as possible. He made his decision and I got the grey one.

We'd had our down time. 'Lads, we need to get a move on. We dump our mobiles here. Shove them in the water, in the mud, whatever. No mobiles with us. We move from here knowing we're as sterile as we can be.'

I dug my heel into the muddy bed of the trickle and shoved my mobile in, like I was planting a tulip bulb – if that was how you did it. The others were going into the water and being covered with stones.

Rio couldn't resist as we headed back to the vehicles: 'Aren't you going to ask us, Nick, how we saved your arse?'

'You're going to tell me anyway.'

Rio grinned, until his split lips stopped him. 'We fucked about for an hour or so, driving around the lanes like loonies trying to find you. The idea was to see if we could ram the van and take you.'

He'd forgotten something.

'And Yulia, of course.'

Gabe was up for that. 'Fucking right, and her. I got bills.' He studied her tattoo, trying to work out what it was. To me it looked like a dark blue bramble in a sea of more brambles. 'We should have taken them when I said.'

'Who's telling this fucking story? Anyway, Nick – last known locations, mate. We went back to Sennen Cove, had a look round, then packed up correctly and staked out the caravan site. Saw the recce, saw the van, saw Yulia get out, and decided to wait until we knew you were in the van.' He banged the side of his head with his good hand. 'Gimped up, but not fucking stupid. We learn. Know what I mean?' He didn't wait for a reply, which was just as well. I would only have said they should have grabbed Yulia and completed the mission.

'So we waited for Yulia here to be picked up, and followed. Then we saw all that shit happen when the heli came in and, fuck it, it was time. So in we came. I think we're up for a bonus, don't you?'

Gabe had other things on his mind. 'What about that woman in the van? What's the score there?'

I shrugged. 'Wrong place, mate, wrong time.'

Rio hadn't given up. 'Nick, not only have I saved the world today, but it's twice now that I've saved your arse. And I don't even get a thank-you, do I?'

Gabe turned to him. 'What about one for me too? You'd be lying there with the rest of them if it weren't for me and that fucking cricket bat. I don't even like the poncy English game.'

Rio did what he did best when it came to Gabe: he ignored him.

'Nick, we saved civilization as we know it. You think I'll get a knighthood as well as that bonus? The women would love it, know what I mean?'

We broke into the car park and I looked back. 'Let's find out what Yulia knows before we start emailing the Palace. Remember, we might be in as much shit as she is.' I checked to see if any reaction was coming from her. It wasn't.

I could hear the mumbles of a radio as we neared the Beamer. 'I'll take the front. She goes between you two – and, Rio, cover your face or at least your hair. Around here you're one big fucking VDM.' I opened the boot. 'A weapon each in the footwell. Check the mags – there's spares.'

Gabe was off on one. 'You telling us weapons drills now? Fucking Jedi Blade Channel shite. You'd be lying there with the rest of them if it wasn't for us.'

Jack had swivelled in his seat to watch the weapons come aboard. 'Not for you. You need to drive.' I tapped the roof with a forefinger. 'This is the biggest weapon we've got.' It could give us distance from danger, protection if we were in danger, and actually be used as a weapon of last resort. But there was something else. I didn't trust the snide. I wanted him driving and in a position where he'd fuck himself up if he tried to do anything to us. I didn't want anyone or anything aiding the Owl. I had to make sure I controlled Jack and, therefore, as much as I could, control our futures. We had probably stopped Phoenix's phase two happening – for now, anyway. But the phase two in our lives was just about to start. I didn't want it, but here it was anyway.

We buckled up, like good citizens, and I hit the satnav to check the routes north. The Hartland Heritage Coast was about twenty-five miles away. The map was a mass of green with not many place names dotted about. I pointed. 'That's where we're going. Plenty of cover to hide up until we sort out what we're going to do once she tells us exactly what, where and when.' This time Yulia did look up. 'And once she's done all that, we can decide what to do next. But, first, we need to find a place to do it.'

Jack put the Beamer into reverse, and we were soon rumbling out of the car park. 'Keep to the speed limit,' I reminded him. 'No violations. And you two in the back, you need to keep your eyes open up top,' I pointed skywards, 'while me and Yulia sort out how we're all going to spend the rest of our lives.'

53

The Beamer took us down narrow lanes, high hedges closing in either side, branches slapping against the metal-work. Whether Yulia liked it or not, it was information time.

I turned and pushed myself between the two front seats. 'Yulia, look at me.' I gave her a smile. It was good to start friendly, even if it didn't end that way. After what she had witnessed, I wanted to make her feel we were capable of being good lads, too.

'You've heard everything. You know we're not handing you over yet to that guy on the phone, not until we know what you know.' It was pointless checking she'd understood. Anyway, I'd find out soon enough. 'We need you to tell us everything you've been doing here, why you've been doing it, and what happens next.' I paused, but not for her to reply. I wanted it to sink in rather than release tears, but they started to roll down her cheeks anyway.

'And the reason we need you to tell us is because we

have to protect ourselves. You see, what we're doing here – capturing you, taking you to that guy on the other end of the mobile – it's too important a job for people like us to do. We're way down the food chain. Yulia?'

She wasn't looking. She might not have been listening.

'Yulia, look at me.'

She finally lifted her head enough for me to catch the tops of her eyes. It was clear she'd been listening very carefully indeed.

'That makes us suspicious. It makes us worried about our futures. As you should be. And that's where your incentive comes in to talk to us. If you tell us what we're involved with, if you help us, we'll try to help you, because I think you're also way down the food chain. We're all little people.'

Gabe watched the sky for helicopters but Rio looked down at her knowingly. 'Yuli, he's given you the aim, the incentive, and the reason why. Textbook. What more do you need? Worked on me when I was in. Got me doing all sorts of shit.' He smiled. 'Mate, like he said, we're just busy little bees, trying to make sure we don't get squashed. You understand that, don't you?'

Yulia understood every word. Her bottom lip trembled and her head dropped. Soon tears were soaking into the hair that touched her cheeks. 'What will happen to me?'

She was playing at it, turning the situation to her advantage, making it about her not us. But that was okay – for now, anyway.

I twisted from my waist to lean forward and get in

closer. My voice was gentler, more soothing now Rio had done his bit.

'It's all good, Yulia.' I thought of the way Phoenix had calmed her down, not that she'd needed it, but I wanted to go through the motions for a quicker result. 'All is good. You've just got to help us first, okay?'

All I got in return was a series of sniffs. 'Yulia, look up. Look up.'

Rio was about to impart another pearl of wisdom but I shook my head. It wasn't going to help: she had her own game plan.

'Yulia, it's okay. Look up, get some air.' It sort of worked. Her head lifted slowly, and a wrist came up to wipe her nose and clear some snot off a tear-soaked lip.

'You okay?'

She nodded under the mop.

'Okay, then, listen to what I have to say. You've found Nigella, so when is Nigella going to get blown up, destroyed? When do they plan to come back to attack?'

Her eyes widened, and her hands came up to her chest, like she was having a heart attack. 'No, no, no – I'm not a terrorist! I'm not blowing up Nigella! The man, the Owl, tell him I'm not a terrorist. Not a terrorist. I'm not blowing up any lines, no lines.'

Gabe came down from out of the sky and elbowed her in the side. 'Shut the fuck up. You hear me? Shut up.' He turned to me. 'She say Nigella? You say she found Nigella?'

I nodded. 'Found the cable.'

Gabe shook his head. 'Nigella is no fucking cable. It's a bigger problem than that.' He gave Yulia another elbow, trying to get a response. 'Oi, fuckhead.'

Yulia's tears stopped falling and her face stopped its wobbles. She cleared the hair from her face and her eyes filled with self-pity. Now there was nothing but cold fear. Gabe was good at creating that in people. This, at last, was the real Yulia.

'I wasn't blowing anything up. I'm just—'

Playing softly was over. 'Shut the fuck up.' I turned to Gabe. 'Nigella?'

He leant forward as if to exclude Yulia. 'It's not a cable. It's a GCHQ operational name. It's technology that covertly attacks the cables, sucking up all the internet traffic, sucking up all that data. Every bit of internet traffic running below us here, GCHQ have access to. The whole world's internet traffic, Nick, and this fucking thing here is trying to attack it.'

Yulia couldn't control herself. 'Please, I wasn't here to destroy any line, or destroy Nigella, just to find it. I was being made to hack into it, to hack into the UK's hack. That's all, I swear. I wasn't here to destroy but—'

Gabe wasn't listening to anything the geek had to say. 'WikiLeaks, Nick. Remember Snowden? That fucker dumped thousands of pages of information about this shit. No one knew about what was happening until—'

I raised a hand. 'In a minute, mate.' I turned back to Yulia. 'Stop grovelling, it doesn't suit you. Just nod, or shake your head. Is he right? Nigella isn't cables. It's GCHQ technology, sucking up the data flowing through them.' I pointed across to Gabe. 'Well, is he right?'

Yulia nodded. 'Not a line.'

'And you were here to find it and then you were going to hack into it?'

She nodded again.

'Have you hacked into Nigella yet?'

She shook her head.

'So phase two was coming back to hack into Nigella and not to blow up any cables?'

She nodded once more, but couldn't help herself. 'Please believe me. My job was just to hack into the tech flow, the data, not to hurt anyone. I was—'

Gabe took an exaggerated breath and put a finger over Yulia's mouth. 'Shut it.' He was very calm, which must have come across as even more sinister. 'Shut it or I'm going to shut it for you.' He turned his attention to me. This was important to him. 'Snowden, right?'

I nodded.

'Fucking traitor. He leaked about Nigella in 2014. I'm going to say it again so we all understand: Nigella is the ops name for the technical attack. GCHQ hoovers up everything that zaps around the world online. They sift through it, and share useful stuff with the American intelligence services. And that fucker's put lives at risk. I hope the Americans get hold of him and give him the electric chair.'

I turned back to Yulia, but my eyes took in Jack. I wanted to check his reaction to the word 'traitor'.

'Yulia, were you going to hack into Nigella to stop it, corrupt it, mess about with the information, turn it into disinformation, or just join in, sucking stuff up?'

'They want to capture the same data as GCHQ without them being aware the data's being intercepted.'

'Who are they? Belarus? KGB?'

She knew what was coming next.

'The Russians? FSB?'

Her hands covered her eyes, like she couldn't face reality, and she gave a slow nod. 'But they are not going to blow it up. I was going to write the code to give access. That is all, I promise.'

Scenarios flashed through my head of the ways that that data could help Russia do what it did around the world. The markets, trade negotiations, weapons procurement, not to mention their expansion into Ukraine, whatever they had planned next, and, of course, Syria. All politicians pirate-smiled, it was part of the job description, but knowing what the opposition were really thinking and doing? That would be a game-changer for Putin and a nightmare for us.

Rio looked down from the sky and didn't have any sympathy for her at all. 'Shut up with all the begs. They don't work here, mate. You got caught, you were out of your league, so accept it and get a grip of yourself. This is embarrassing.'

The tears stopped. Maybe I had given her too long at playing the frightened schoolgirl. But now we knew, and that was all that mattered.

Yulia was back to the woman I had seen in the van. 'What will happen to me now?'

Jack adjusted himself in the driver's seat. 'We're here.'

I put a hand on Yulia's shoulder. 'There's more to come, so no more bullshit tears. Help us and that will help you.'

I turned back to the windscreen and had a look at the larger scale map on the satnav. It was now all about finding a place to hide the car, and a place to hide us.

54

It was my turn on stag. I was lying under the tree canopy, on top of a folded-up tent we were using as insulation from the ground. A few feet away from me, in the real world, on the other side of the trees, the sun poked through the clouds every few minutes, but it never penetrated the gloom of the LUP. It was cold, and would get even colder after last light.

I bit into a coconut-flavoured power bar. When Rio had grabbed the weapons from the VW he'd also taken what he could of the water and bars. It had been hours since I'd eaten, like all the rest of them stretched out behind me in, or half in, their sleeping bags, each on top of a purple roll-mat and the second blue spread-out tent.

I looked downhill from our dip in the hillside into the valley. The Beamer was parked seventy or eighty metres below us, in a copse of trees just off the small tarmac road. It would be found if somebody walked past, but there was no reason for anyone to be doing that. There wasn't a track; the area was a dead end. And if people did find it, so what? There was nothing we could do about it.

The lying-up point was as high as we could make it without cutting the skyline. We were hidden from the ground and the air, but the spot wasn't perfect. I'd have preferred to be fifty feet underground with the world's supply of surveillance around us. We had weapons, though, and we had an escape route, and we weren't going to be there for long, now that Yulia had explained all. Rio's facts of life had soon made her see it was pointless continuing with the scared schoolgirl act. Apart from anything else, she had grown up in a country where even a rumour of terrorism meant arrest, torture and disappearance, no matter what the truth was. Her misconception of what would happen to her here had certainly helped her focus.

There had been a lot of waffle from her over the last four hours. She had detached herself from the Wolves, and we believed her. She was a geek, not an operator.

She was tough, but I wasn't sure she was mentally unscathed. This life wasn't on her job spec. Maybe that had helped me believe her. She was there for the ride, she said, the gig, the challenge, the excitement. What it seemed to boil down to was making the best of a bad situation, because when the FSB had come knocking at the door it wasn't as if a hacker like her could tell them to fuck off. But excitement had morphed into shit hitting the fan, and that was when she'd understood she was out of her depth. She'd said she felt good about being with the Wolves to start with – 'playing with the big boys' – but when it had gone wrong she was flailing. Rio was right. She was the same as us. We were all out of our league.

I wanted somebody on stag at all times so even if everybody else was awake and talking, there would always be one tasked with protecting the rest and, of course, keeping an eye on Yulia. Just like the rest of the planet, she was capable of changing her mind. There were enough sleeping bags and roll-mats to go round, because the one on stag would not be using any of that. He had to have the hardness of the ground and the cold to remind him he had a job to do. And, at the moment, that was me.

This Cornish operation, Yulia explained, had stemmed from the 2014 WikiLeaks dump. Included in the thousands of leaked documents was the state secret that GCHQ routinely tapped into the world's internet traffic in an operation called Nigella, and Snowden had posted that Nigella was based at Skewjack Farm. That was where we'd seen Phoenix's team take their first pictures of the road surface, hoping to ID any manhole covers that might indicate where Nigella was. Rio and Gabe had checked out what they were up to while Jack and I had carried on following the VW camper van.

'We were only covering the bases,' Yulia had said. 'I never thought Skewjack Farm was likely, because the landing station company that owned it wouldn't allow it. They weren't "access partners" – they weren't colluding with GCHQ. They would have lost all their business if it was known they were helping your spooks to pore over their customers' secrets.'

Yulia reckoned that Nigella would be located at the landing station bungalow down the road at Trethewey, because Cable & Wireless owned it, and Snowden had exposed them as 'access partners'. On top of that, FSB had shown her photographs that suggested the bungalow had had a big security upgrade after the Snowden leak. But even if she was right, she went on, she couldn't just walk into the building and make access to Nigella to enable FSB to access the same data as GCHQ, and do it in such a way that it would never be discovered.

'Hence the interest in the manhole covers and especially the covers at the war memorials?' I asked. It suddenly made sense why they were new and re-vamped. A war memorial was brilliant cover. Locals would notice if people began digging up or interfering with a site that many would consider sacred. 'That was what you were doing, going round the area, checking where Nigella could be accessed?'

She nodded. 'And we found it. They were the ones with a primary cover and a secondary steel plate beneath. We'd found Nigella.'

'What was the plan from then?'

'Just to leave them alone, go home and figure out how to gain access. And when I'd done that and access had been gained, FSB would know exactly what the UK and the USA knew.'

I couldn't work out which was the worst fuck-up-the-world option I'd heard in the last twenty-four hours. Gabe's destruction of the cables, and a world that immediately folded in on itself? Or Yulia's Nigella option that would have the same effect but take longer? I had to go with Gabe's option as it would at least get the pain over and done with.

As if on cue I heard the click of Gabe's lighter inside

his sleeping bag, a sound I'd been brought up on from the age of sixteen. Squaddies would go to any lengths to get a drag, and to keep the smoke undetected. I wasn't concerned about Gabe – it wasn't as if we were on hard routine, and at least he was trying to capture the smoke in his bag.

I looked back at the other two. Jack and Rio were crowding out Yulia to make sure she didn't have any ideas as they all sat or lay on the roll-mats. Jack opened the pack Gabe had thrown him and sat up, cigarette in one hand, lighter and a handful of sleeping bag in the other to keep it up to his chest. He took a lungful and leant down, his head now inside the bag, almost in synch with Gabe. When they lifted their heads, it looked like they were floating out of their bags on a cloud in some kind of stage show.

'Rio.' I kept my voice low, not a whisper. 'You're on.'

He unzipped the bag and mumbled, 'Great. I want to keep away from these two.' He waved his good hand like he was wafting smoke as he came up to me at the top of the dip and laid his Vector on the tent nylon.

I pointed down the hill. 'You see the Beamer? Okay, go left ten o'clock, and through the branches you'll just get catches here and there of tarmac. That's where any vehicles are going to come from. To the right is a dead end. I haven't noticed any tracks or movement. You've got two hours and then it's Jack, okay?'

He nodded as I rolled back to join the others and get into Rio's bag. It looked like an Indian peace-pipe convention, the three of them sitting in a tight circle, bagged up in cheap red and blue nylon as Gabe and Jack smoked and waffled.

55

I'd had two hours on stag, thinking about the situation, and had come up with a plan I hoped the rest of the team would agree with.

'So . . .' I let it hang to make sure I had everyone's attention, and thought of the Owl. He would have said 'anyhoo'.

Gabe's head had been buried in his sleeping bag but it popped up again, followed by a cloud of smoke. Everyone, including Yulia, had their eyes fixed on me.

'The way I've got it in my head is that the Owl is doing exactly the same as he did up in the Arctic. That's his job.' I glanced at Yulia. 'Before anybody talks about the Owl, remember, we've still got Yulia here.'

Gabe nodded, the cigarette still in his mouth.

'Jack?'

He agreed.

I half turned to face Rio's boots behind me. 'Rio?'

He lifted one and wiggled his foot.

'Okay, so let's just think about what happened up

north. It was all about the monitors. It was all about technology. The way I see it, Yulia's the monitors. She's the technology the Owl wants. He wants to suck out all the information she has tucked away in that head of hers. He wants to know how they planned to attack Nigella, because you know what? He's probably thinking he can reverse-engineer it and use it against the Russians – or the Iranians, or whoever. The point is, he wants the contents of her head. That's why he wants her, the monitors, all in one piece.'

I pointed to Yulia, who looked a mixture of confused and concerned. 'So she's the monitors, okay? And the ship – that was about coming to take the monitors at all costs, wasn't it? Today, that's us. We were sent to get the technology, to get the monitors at all costs. We're that ship.'

Gabe exhaled with a sigh. 'And the sub – who's the submarine, then?'

I wasn't sure if he was with me or just taking the piss, but it didn't matter. The analogy made everything clear in my head. 'The sub? That's the Wolves. They're the ones who would fight to deny anyone having control of the monitors, only this time they didn't. They didn't sink anything. We sank them. So we've got the technology. We've got her.' I pointed again. She was now looking just as confused but increasingly worried.

'So I reckon the Owl has exactly the same two objectives as he did in the Arctic. One, to get hold of technology that's better than anything the West has, and two, to stop any escalation between the countries involved by making sure nobody knows, cleaning up

273

the situation and killing anyone who would be seen as a loose end. He'll want to achieve both these aims before any government, politician or the media can start rattling sabres or cages.

'Make no mistake, what the Wolves were getting up to was still an act of war – simple as. And that's what the Owl does: he stops that. His job is pouring oil over troubled waters. American waters, Russian waters, he just pours that oil whenever he sees a ripple. It means nobody's aware, and we can all carry on watching daytime TV never knowing what scary shit went on that nearly led us to war. It's what the Owl did up north, and that's what he's doing here. Same meat, different gravy. So how does that affect us?'

Gabe came in to say what we were all thinking. 'This is a bigger fuck-up for us than we thought, isn't it?'

I shrugged. 'Yeah, but you know, lads, we still have the memory sticks, and we still have her.' I nodded as she reacted a second time to the mention of starting a war. 'Seeing as it's the same meat, different gravy for the Owl, I suggest it's the same for us. We do the same as we did a couple of days ago. I'll go and see him. We've got the leverage – the sticks and the geek – so why don't we stay here until dark o'clock, then drive back to the fat part of the UK where we have more options for hiding? I'll make contact with him, meet up and negotiate a way out of this mess. Lads, what do you think?'

There was a lull I wasn't expecting, certainly from Gabe. Surprisingly, Jack was the first. 'I'm in.' He took a drag of his cigarette and exhaled into his sleeping bag before his head came up. 'It feels like the best option. What else is there?'

It did feel like the best option, but so had the last time, except it had turned out the Owl knew what we were doing because we had a snide.

Rio had been kicking his toe into the ground to get attention and turned his head enough to be heard over the whisper. 'I'm in. Gabe?'

Gabe gave him a nod, pulled his sleeping bag over his shoulders and lay down. 'I'm in, but on one condition. If we get out of this shit in one piece, even if we don't make the money, you're still all pitching in for a new Jeep.'

56

Jack followed Gabe's lead in pulling his bag over his head and settling in, but Yulia stayed sitting upright, her bag around her waist. She had a question. She looked at me, then at the paraphernalia beside Gabe's bag. 'Can I have one?'

'Don't ask me, ask him.'

Gabe didn't bother moving his head out of its nylon shroud. 'Crack on.'

She leant down, picked up the pack and the lighter, shuffling her arse from side to side to bring the bag up to her shoulders so she could copy the others' smoking routine. She couldn't have had any idea why they did it, but she was trying to blend in.

It became clear there was an end-game. 'Nick, you didn't tell me what will happen to me. Do you know?'

Her head dipped into the bag to exhale.

There was no point bullshitting. In any event, people react better to the truth. 'For now, the guy on the end of the phone, the Owl, all he wants to know is when you're

276

going to access Nigella and how, as I said before. Then he'll want to know everything you know about FSB, what they're doing, who you met there, how you met, what you know, what you don't know. But after that I haven't got a clue. You'll probably be in the same boat as us, surplus to requirements.'

A cloud of smoke enveloped her head briefly, making her, too, look like she was levitating out of the bag.

'You know we are the best hackers in the world, don't you? Almost everybody I know is pretty great at what they do. But I am better – I am much better. I really am like those monitors. I'm far more advanced than what you have in the West.' She took another drag and dipped inside the bag to exhale.

'They all work for FSB like you?'

The reply was muffled as she didn't immediately bring her head out of the nylon. 'About half of them. No one works directly for FSB – just through other structures. So FSB are one step away from the action – and, of course, the government are even further away.'

She reappeared, and laughed, smoke escaping through her hair. 'I know how it all works because I'm not like the rest. The rest do drugs, lead antisocial lifestyles. They're just concerned about the money and the collection of data. That's all they do – collate data. They're very advanced, but they're stupid at the same time.'

She went to take another drag but paused, the cigarette halfway to her mouth. She didn't want to disappear this time: she wanted to make sure I was listening. 'I have moved away from that and I'm far more advanced. Tell this man, the Owl, I want to work for him, with him, it doesn't matter – I just want to work here in the West. Tell him he needs someone like me to show him why Russia leads the world. Why the West is so far behind. He stops wars? I can help him. We are already at war, Nick, and it's you who are losing.'

She finally took a drag so deep the cigarette tip flared like a firework. She savoured it in her lungs, then dipped down once more to exhale. This time smoke seeped out of the zipper line.

'Have you ever done bank fraud, Yulia? Credit-card fraud, that sort of thing?'

Her head stayed inside the nylon. Maybe that meant she got a double hit from the trapped nicotine.

'Yes, I've worked for the gangs. It was a very difficult period in my life. I really needed money. I was living on the street. But, Nick, I never did anything illegal – you must tell him that. All I did was collect data and write programs. What they did with them, I don't really know. I was doing it because I was paid.'

It was the best get-out clause I'd heard for years. She didn't actually steal money, just designed the means for someone else to do so. Fair one, I would have tried the same excuse in her shoes. Social mobility, Belarusian style. Her head didn't reappear. Maybe she wanted to give me more time to think about what she'd said.

'How come you're not all in prison? It's you guys that are ripping off the banks and us lot, left, right and centre?'

She reappeared, and flicked a few centimetres of ash. She'd finished the whole cigarette in about four drags. Jack and Gabe would have been proud. She gave a smile – a slight one, but it was the first I'd seen since we lifted her.

'You don't shit where you sleep, Nick. And, of course, there's no punishment for hacking outside Russia – only within Russia. So it's a free market. There's no police, no security services that try to stop it. Anybody can hire us. Ordinary people can. You just go to a cyber-fraud website and we're there. It's a free market. It's a job market. That is why we're the best – because the free market produces competition and competition produces excellence.' She locked her eyes on mine. 'We learnt that from you guys.' The smile broadened as she stubbed the butt into the ground, waiting for the next question.

'That's how you got into this? They offered you a job to come to the UK?'

She shook her head. 'Only sort of. I don't know that world very well, the world of strong men. I'm a well-mannered person. But it is a regular thing for FSB to approach hackers to work for them. They can't afford to employ hackers full-time so I was working for one of their troll farms – you know, spreading pro-Russia, anti-American news all around the world. We are considered patriots for joining in the fight against those speaking ill of Russia.'

She gave another smile, larger this time. 'It is so easy because you Westerners believe anything that is negative.' She studied my face for my reaction. I smiled back because she was right.

'We also targeted Turkey and Germany, Georgia, and then, of course, Crimea and Ukraine. If somebody asks me to do something, I'm not going to tell them to fuck off. I'm paid very well to collate data and produce code, but it isn't as if I have a choice.'

'You really from Belarus?'

Clearly she had been asked the same question before. 'Yes, but I'm Russian. Born Russian – Russian and Belarus passports. Just like Crimea, Estonia, South Ossetia. There are many of us out there who are always Russian.'

I gave a shrug. There wasn't much to say, and she hadn't finished pitching. She wanted this small diversion over and done with.

'Nick, would you please tell the Owl I am very good at what I do? The Russians think I'm the best, and that's why I'm here. But now I can't go back. They won't trust me – and I don't know what would happen to me. So I want to work for him – I want to work for the Owl, or the Owl's group, whatever it is. Because I'm really good at what I do. I can explain how I can access Nigella and collect anything they want. It's up to them how they use it. I can even tell them how to find Bogachev.'

'Who?'

She smiled at me, a parent to a kid displaying total ignorance. 'Bogachev, the gangs? The Business Club? The US have a three-million-dollar reward on his head. That's the largest ever for a cyber-criminal. That makes so many Russians proud.'

'I take it he's protected in Russia?'

'Bogachev is a legend. He has a great mind and, of course, it helps FSB. But I can find him for the Owl.'

That would count for nothing until I saw the Owl's eyes light up with excitement.

'Nick? Yes? Will you tell him? Tell him everything? What do you think he will say?'

I couldn't give her the answer she was hoping for. 'Look, all I can do is explain everything to him and he'll take it from there. I have no control over him.'

She was surprisingly upbeat about my less than positive reply. 'Please, just tell him. Yes?'

57

The waffle had stopped hours ago and we all felt the benefit of the bags. We had a long night ahead of us, getting into the fat part of the UK and hiding up. We would use the scenic-route setting on satnav to get us out of Cornwall on B roads, reducing our exposure to police, traffic cameras and habitation. Once we were well out of the county we could dump the Beamer and move on, like a snake shedding the last of its old skin. We not only had the Owl to worry about but also the aftermath of the woman's shooting – and what if the pick-up point had been compromised before the Owl had got there to clean up? I found myself thinking like Phoenix: I had a responsibility to the rest of them to make sure no one captured us. We had weapons and would fight, but what if it was the police? Would we have to use weapons and possibly kill them to make sure we kept safe? I cut away from that one and fell back yet again on 'react to the situation in front of me'.

That was why I would arrange to meet the Owl only

when we were another bound away from the area.

Gabe had done his two hours' stag and was climbing into the bag that Jack had left nice and warm for him. No doubt it stank of cigarettes, but Gabe would feel at home. It had been Gabe's second stag, and last light had fallen as he lay there protecting us and, of course, keeping an eye on Yulia.

I watched him sort himself out in the bag next to Rio, slowly and deliberately, no chat or loud zipping sounds. He knew better than that. The one thing he did do was nudge Rio to stop him snoring.

Since she had got her head down, there had been no snoring or even much movement from Yulia. I wondered if geeks ever slept in the open air. This one hadn't wasted any time getting her head down.

For my part, I'd been permanently on stag. I hadn't slept at all yet, but it wasn't because of the one little stone that always dug into your back but could never be found, no matter how much you moved around and tried to jiggle the leaf litter under you. It was because I was concerned about Jack, and particularly about Jack with a Vector. I didn't know what he was thinking, or if he had instructions about what to do in a situation like this. Maybe I was being paranoid but, still, he had to be watched.

After the change-over, I pulled the bag up to my face but kept my eyes nylon-free so I could watch the dark shape lying on stag. My weapon was next to my body, exactly as his should have been, but with one major exception. My safety catch was off. No fumbling with fat fingers next time.

I wasn't paranoid, I told myself. If it didn't feel right,

it probably wasn't right. That sixth sense, on top of what I'd seen, was enough: a snide was lying there on stag.

It wasn't much more than twenty minutes later that the shape shifted, turned onto the side with his good leg and spent a long time checking behind him. He did it far too slowly and carefully to be looking after us. He was studying the dark shapes for movement.

He rolled over very slowly and stood up even more slowly. It wasn't about his prosthetic. I'd seen him get up before. The movement was far too cautious and wary for that. He was making sure no one heard him.

After several more seconds, he took the first few steps out of the LUP, leaving his weapon where it was.

I let him disappear over the rise before I carefully unzipped and picked up my Vector. Fuck knew what I was going to meet the other side. It could be the Owl's clean-up squad, armed and with body bags.

I started moving, weapon in the shoulder, fat forefinger inside the trigger guard, mouth open to aid my hearing, each foot in turn lifting high to avoid anything on the ground that would make noise, eyes forward to the threat ahead.

Even if this was an innocent need of a piss, it was wrong. He'd left his weapon and he'd left his stag, putting us in danger. He should have given me a shake. I was the leader, and I would have stood in for him while he took care of himself. That was how it worked. He knew that.

But this wasn't about bad drills.

I reached the lip and peered over. Below me, defined by the faint ambient light from habitation kilometres away on the lower ground of the north coast, there was a dark silhouette. He was bent over, his back to me, and he was using a fold in the ground to give himself cover. Was he pissing, maybe vomiting?

I waited a couple of seconds, trying to work out what the fuck was going on, before Jack confirmed what I'd suspected all along.

The glow of a mobile screen spilt either side of his back and head.

I surged the last six strides, weapon in hand. When I was almost on top of him I stooped to drop the weapon. He heard me above the sound of his thumbs working the keypad and turned.

I wasn't going to give him a chance to breathe and talk. I bunched my still-swollen fingers into a fist and landed it in his face as hard as I could. He fell, and my hand felt like it was plugged into the mains. At least it meant sensation was coming back.

A split second after he hit the ground, the mobile joined him in the leaf litter and illuminated the area. In this little pool of light I focused on what was exposed of his face, and swung huge slaps with open hands. He screamed as I made contact with his face and then his skull. He tried to cover himself. I swung down into him more. I'd worry about my hands later on.

He recovered enough to curl most of his body into a ball, apart from his prosthetic leg, which lay out straight. I grabbed hold of it and twisted to open it up.

'Nick, Nick – please!'

Anger got the better of me. He had to pay for putting our lives at risk and for being a snide. I dropped to my knees and swung down again into his face.

It never landed. Hands grabbed me from behind.

Rio was at my ear. 'Mate – what the fuck? You've got to stop!'

Then there were two sets of hands, and Gabe was growling as he dragged me away.

Rio jumped between us. 'Nick, calm!'

Gabe couldn't bend down because of his false leg so he stood stooped, his arms around me in a bear-hug to stop mine swinging. I was on my arse by now and I could feel his stubble on the back of my neck.

I turned as best I could to the right. 'Yulia? Where's Yulia?'

She was with them, her face illuminated by the habitation lights and just paces from my Vector. She wasn't that interested in what was happening, just stared out towards the coast.

'Listen, I'm okay. Weapon, control my weapon. Get the weapon. Get the mobile. Check his fucking mobile.'

58

It was pointless struggling against Gabe. The argument wasn't with him. 'He's been telling the Owl what we've been doing.' I spat the words like poison. 'He's the Owl's man. He has been from the start. The fucking snide. Check the mobile. Think about it. The Owl offered us the job. I didn't have to say a word. Someone told him what the plan was. That fucking thing is a snide.'

Jack wiped blood from his face as he uncoiled himself. 'No – no! I haven't. Nick, you're wrong. Please!'

I waved at the mobile on the ground. 'Check the fucking thing – see who he moved off stag for.'

Rio gave Jack the death stare as he bent down and retrieved the device. 'Better not be prepping us to get dead.'

Jack watched him straighten with the phone in his good hand.

'Because if you are a disloyal cunt, I'll be ending your life right here.'

Gabe let go of me and passed me my Vector. Then he grabbed Rio's useless arm as he scrolled with the other. 'Make sure of this shit. If it's true, we'll both do him. You,' he jabbed a finger at Jack, 'you just keep shutting the fuck up and stay there.'

Rio was still thumbing as I got to my feet and stood over Jack. I ignored him: Rio's reaction to what he was reading was far more important. 'What's he been doing?'

Rio passed me the mobile, and Gabe stood at my shoulder as I flicked through the texts. Rio had bent down to Jack and was shaking his head. 'You're at it again, you stupid fuck.'

The texts were all to one number and, from the tone and little in-jokes, she was really getting to like Jack. She felt she knew where he was coming from, and really wanted to meet him when she returned from China.

Rio was already interrogating. 'What's she doing there?'

Jack was trying to explain through his sheer panic. 'She's a lawyer, she's working on a construction contract in Shanghai. I know what it looks like . . .'

Rio's response was more pity than piss-take. 'Mate? Really? What it looks like?'

Gabe and I were reading long-distance love, but it looked pretty much one-way traffic. Gabe was more angry than compassionate. 'What you doing? You met her yet? You given her any money yet? Don't you learn?'

Jack lay on his back, his head in the leaf litter. His eyes were on me. 'Nick, I'm sorry. I didn't mean to go against what we agreed. I just wanted to bring the mobile to keep contact with her. It's important to me. I want to see if it's for real.'

The course of true love wasn't my concern right now – but compromise was. 'Did you use the other phone to text her, the one I gave you? I checked and you'd used it. You sent texts. Were they to her?' I threw the mobile down to him. 'For all you know, this could be the Owl on the other end, you stupid bastard. Latching on to you, knowing you'd fucked up last time. He could be following us right now.'

Jack looked like he was going to make a grab for the mobile, then thought better of it. 'No, no.' His hands came up as if to shield himself from the hatred bearing down on him. 'He would have found us by now, wouldn't he? He wouldn't have left us all this time. We have Yulia – he isn't going to waste any time getting her, is he? Nick, think about it. The phone is clean, I swear.'

Annoyingly, he had a point.

'Nick, I swear I never used the work mobile, never. This is the mobile I had charging in the car when you used it by the caravan site, not the work one. Both the phones are the same. I've been texting till the battery ran low and I just put it in to charge it up. I know, I fucked up, but I've done nothing with our phones. The one back at the forestry block – that was our phone. This is my personal one. I got it a day before you came to the barn, just for her. I was being careful. After last time I thought I'd keep her at arm's length.'

Rio liked his conviction but still couldn't understand the logic. 'Really? Last time? And you know this is different. How do you know?'

Maybe Jack didn't hear. 'No one's had anything to do with it. I bought it second-hand. It's pay-as-you-go. No one knows, I swear.'

He finally picked up the mobile and offered it to me as if my taking it back and inspecting it would convince me.

'So you never used the work mobile to text anyone about anything?'

The phone was still in his hand, held up.

'I promise. Nick, I've never met the Owl. I don't even know what he looks like. I've never spoken to him. I know I shouldn't have brought the mobile to keep in contact with her, but I did and I'm sorry.'

Rio took the mobile off him because it was clear I wasn't going to, and started to work his thumb again. Gabe was unimpressed. 'For fuck's sake, stop begging. Put your arm down, get a grip.'

Rio was still flicking through, the screen lighting his face. 'Her name's Gail.'

Gabe's look said what we were all thinking.

Jack insisted, 'She's real, I know it.'

Rio threw the mobile back to him. 'All I'm reading is love shit to her or from her to him. Mate,' he looked down, 'you gotta switch on. Where did you find her, RipOffJack.com?'

Jack was like a broken record. 'Look, you have to believe me. I've done nothing. I don't know the Owl. No one's approached me. It was just to keep in contact with her. Please, I am your friend, you are my friends.'

He got no answer. The other two were waiting for me to reply, but I wanted him to keep bubbling away in case he tripped himself up.

'Look, I'm sorry I left my stag but I just needed to contact her. I swear she knows nothing about what we're doing. That's why I had to keep on texting, letting her believe I was still at the barn. I had no choice.'

I expected him to carry on with the same thing all night if we let him. It was now time for me.

'Okay, so why did the Owl suggest we work for him before I'd even said a word? Is that just coincidence, or what? Explain that.'

No answer came, and Rio jumped into the vacuum. 'Mate, they could have put a device in the barn. Think about it. They were putting one in my house – maybe they did his place first. Don't listen to what he says about the barn being clean when we got there. He's always got his artistic head stuck up his arse. How would he know?'

Jack looked between the two of us, trying to work out if Rio was his saviour. 'They could have, Nick. I'm sorry – I was just going to text Gail. Nothing more, I swear.'

Gabe was getting on board with Rio. 'You sure you're not getting ripped off? Are you sure she's for real?'

Jack nodded. 'She hasn't asked for anything. All we do is text. When she comes back we'll make contact properly. It feels right, Gabe.'

I took the mobile off Jack and offered it to Yulia. 'You know about these scams?'

She was still mesmerized by the coastal lights. 'Yes, of course. It's easy money.'

I handed over the mobile. 'Have a look at this, then. Can you tell from that if he's being scammed, ripped off?'

She scrolled at speed through the never-ending

stream of words and her answer took her less than a minute. 'Yes, it's a love-bomb pack. You can buy them on the dark web. They contain everything for a scam like this – photos, videos, texts, play sheets. Even false IDs. It's a scam. And it's a bad one, cheap.'

Gabe was pissed off with either Jack or himself, I couldn't work out which. Maybe both. 'Fuck, I knew it.'

Jack wouldn't believe it. 'I know I was ripped off last time, but this is different.'

She handed the mobile back to me and ignored everyone else. I was her point of contact. I was the one who would talk to the Owl about her. 'Of course it'll be different the second time round. Most men who've been scammed go back and try again. They just want to be loved. This was probably the same scammers, using Plan B. After that, they'll try a third time, Plan C. That's normally coming at you as online detectives who'll recover your money, at a cost that increases every time they come close, of course.

'All Gail does is reinforce what Jack has been talking about or asking. That way, he bonds to her quicker and even more intensely than he did the first time. The target will have less money or goods after the first attack, so to suck more, they need him to feel even more connected. There is still money to be had from men when they have no more in the bank. There are pensions, maybe a house to sell. They are so gullible – they will steal or even kill for you. It's simple with men.'

59

In spite of myself, I'd come over to the other way of thinking.

'Do not hide anything or lie to any of us again.' I'd forced it out. 'It will get us all fucked up. You understand?'

With slow apologetic nods he went to get up out of the leaf litter, but he had some problems with his false leg. 'Sorry again, everyone. I fucked up. Sorry.'

I held out a hand for him to pull himself upright.

He had pain in his stump, probably because I'd more or less pulled his prosthetic out of its joint. I had to help him down again so he could sort himself out.

'Thanks, Nick, thanks.'

Rio followed him down and started helping him sort his leg metal. 'For fuck's sake, mate, they're going to take your house. That's all your family's got left, isn't it?'

Jack didn't say anything, but his body language spoke for him. He was fast sinking into an abyss. Gabe noticed it too. 'Right, let's get on with this. I knew we should have gone and gripped them last time. Yulia, you know how to find these fucks?'

Her shrug became a nod.

'Okay, let's go and find them. Bring Gail to us, trap her, trap whoever, whatever it takes to fuck them up big-time.'

Gabe stared at me, waiting. I nodded back. 'I get it. But that's for another day. What about the Owl? The mission? We get ourselves safe by meeting the Owl, then delivering Yulia. Jack should just dump Gail and we all get on with what we need to do. We need to sort this out soon as. It's a health-and-safety matter, mate. Jack's problem is just anger.'

Rio was onside, but the wrong side. 'Mate, say they're in the UK. I'll take Gabe and Jack and we'll go and fuck 'em up.' He held up his Vector. 'Stick one of these in 'em and we'll get results – might even get cash out of 'em. Repay Jack and we'll be quids in. You and Yulia can sort our shit out with the Owl. You don't need us for that, do you? Two birds with one stone, easy.'

That wasn't going to happen.

'Too risky. We split up, we lose integrity and we fail. This can be done once we get ourselves safe. Say we do this and Yulia finds where they are. What if they're in another country? What do we do then? Nothing. We can't do anything until we've sorted ourselves out here. So what's the difference?'

Gabe must have known that was coming because the reply was instant. 'I'm angry with the scammers, and I'm angry with him over there. But so what? He might be soft in the head but he's a mate. We got history.' Gabe bent down and tapped his prosthetic. 'The poor fucker's been through enough already without all this shit annihilating him. It's killed his confidence and any chance of sorting himself out.

'Jack was the one who gripped us all to go to the Arctic. He was the one who gave us our dignity and confidence back when no one else gave a fuck. But now look at him.'

Gabe pointed as if we didn't know who he was talking about. But it wasn't for effect: this was coming from the heart, and it could cause a drama. You have to work with nature or you lose. I knew it was look-and-listen time.

'He's an emotional wreck. Why would you let that shit happen to you again? We, us three, we need to sort it out now. Because you know what? It could easily have been one of us sad fucks. I want retribution, simple as that.'

Rio was still on the wrong side. 'Nick, you get it, I know you do. That's what we do, don't we? We look out for each other. It's the only thing that distinguishes us from the pencil necks.

'Listen, if we fuck up with this Owl business and become history, I want to go down knowing I've done something good, something meaningful, for a mate. Shit, we know lads who got themselves killed saving their mates. We might be out of the army but is the army out of us?

'Chinese parliament, right? So, my twopence-worth is, fuck the Owl, fuck it all. Just get out there, find these scammers, and sort that shit out before anything else. This is more important, Nick. We all need to help him.

You need to get us to those bastards, then you can sort out the Owl. Priorities, mate.'

I checked out Gabe, who nodded, then added: 'Got to give Jack mates' rates.'

As Chinese parliaments went, it was a majority verdict. If I held out, would they go it alone? They were grown-ups: I didn't have any power over them. We had to keep together, no matter what, or we'd fail on all fronts and we knew what that would mean.

'Okay, you're on.'

There were nods from Gabe and Rio.

'But it's got to be about the cash. Let's get it back and stop them fucking up any more lives. So we'll find out who they are and where they are.' I turned to Yulia. 'You sure you can find them?'

She shrugged. 'Easy.'

She looked about as enthusiastic as Jack did. He must have felt drained at being ripped off yet again, and she was probably pissed off that her job interview with the Owl was on the back burner. But she had a glint in her eye that said she was going with it anyway – anything to help her achieve her aim.

'Okay, let's get back to the hide, sort ourselves out, and move on. We've made enough noise and light here.'

Everybody made a move, apart from Yulia. Her eyes had fixed themselves on the coastal lights again. I grabbed her arm. 'Come on.'

'You see those dishes, Nick?'

I looked down at the coast and the ribbon of light, and finally made out what she was talking about. Up till now there had been much more important things to look at.

'That's GCHQ's station at Bude. For people like me, that is Mecca.' She was transfixed.

I studied the collection of satellite dishes dotted over the area, like badly planted cauliflowers, red lights flashing on top of tall communication towers, all contained within a floodlit perimeter.

'That is where Nigella's data goes – as well as hundreds of millions of cell and landline calls every single day. All that data sucked up, more than even the NSA can collate. Ninety per cent of the entire planet's data has been generated in the past two years, Nick. What you're looking at there is the world's largest surveillance programme in human history.'

There was almost a religious tone in her voice, as if she really was looking at a holy place.

She turned to me. 'Nick, you are the world's information superpower, but there is so much data that you miss so much. I need to be part. I can help maximize that data. You will tell the Owl, won't you?'

60

It was just after 0100 and we were heading to the fat part of the UK. More people, more buildings, more places to hide. We had enough fuel to get us to Bristol. There would be no refuelling on this trip. Once we were safely in the city, Yulia would find out where Jack's scammers were located.

We'd packed everything into the back of the Beamer, Vectors in the footwells, and drove along the minors, biting into the last of the power bars.

We had all offered to take our turn driving but Jack insisted. Maybe it was his way of trying to make it up to us, to show he was still one of the group. I didn't know what was going on in his head but as long as it made him feel better why not let it continue? Besides, I reckoned he quite liked using the suicide spinner.

Yulia had concluded that, because the grammar was so bad, the scammers were probably Brits. Foreign spammers who learnt English at school usually strung sentences together correctly. It was a flaw. We would see. First we had to find them, and then we'd decide how to deal with them. I understood the loyalty between the three in the Beamer, even though I was a newcomer. It had been a long time since I'd worked with others and I'd forgotten the drive and devotion soldiers had to protect each other. It's what drives winners of the Victoria Cross. It was nothing to do with Queen, country or bravery. It was all about protecting their mates. I thanked Gabe and Rio silently for reminding me. The Owl would be out there right now looking for us, wanting to get his hands on Yulia. He had his mission to complete. And, of course, part of that mission was what he had planned for us four. Well, he would just have to wait.

Yulia was busy checking Gail's profile on Jack's mobile. She was still sure it was a set-up. It was the same style of picture that she would have used herself – an extreme close-up, with no background that could be checked. What I found most interesting was that Gail looked a lot like Claudia, except her hair wasn't in a bun – she had a wig on with a long ponytail falling over her right shoulder.

Rio had been impressed and had been digging into Jack for quite a while. 'Mate, if she was for real, you'd be punching well above your weight, know what I mean?'

I smiled to myself. If we got out of this in one piece, maybe I should set up Jack and Claudia on a blind date.

Jack still didn't look as if he was feeling good about himself. He was having a hard job trying to laugh along with the two in the back.

I leant across the central console. 'Mate, you've got to let it go. You texting the Owl? I fucked up, you fucked up, but that's history. This Gail shit? Soon that'll be history too.'

Gabe leant forward and gave Jack a shoulder tap over the driver's seat. 'You're one of us. Always have been, always will be. Don't worry, just like he says, we're going to get it sorted, no drama.'

Rio was more interested in Yulia than what was going on between Gabe and Jack. He stroked his throat with a forefinger and thumb. 'Why you got all that over your neck? We're the ones who are supposed to have tattoos and we ain't got one between us. I can't even make out what it is.'

She turned to him. There was no embarrassment, no excuses. 'Because I could decide to have it. It was my choice. What you people don't understand is that choice is a privilege. In my country there is no such thing. You have to take what you are given. But this,' she copied Rio's action with her thumb and forefinger, 'this is my choice. When FSB wanted me to work with them, I had no choice. But this I could choose. And it's a rose, growing out of a swamp.'

Rio wasn't convinced, not that he could see much of it in the gloom. 'Really? I think whoever did that tatt used a bit too much dark blue and black. I can't make it out.' He raised his voice as if we couldn't hear him up front anyway. 'There you go, Jack. After all this you should become a tattoo artist. All that black and blue – they love it.'

Yulia went back to busying herself with the 'woman' Jack had got himself embroiled with. Gabe and Rio kept an eye on what she was up to online. We had to remember she wasn't one of us.

I turned to face forward again, the hedges each side containing the headlights. I checked the satnav and made sure we were going east with a little touch of north. We wanted to keep off the main A30 that bisected the county. I turned back and watched her as she tapped away. 'Yulia?' Her face lifted. 'How did you get involved in this sort of thing, the troll farms? How did it all happen?'

She dropped her hands and the mobile onto her lap. 'It wasn't just the money, not at first. Some of the longest hacking forums are run by FSB. They almost turn the way the Soviet Union was into a romance, and they want Russia to be a superpower again, a country to be reckoned with. And being Russian speaking, and I've always thought of Russia as my home, I fell for it. Almost being a patriot – attacking the West.'

'So you see us and America as the enemy?'

'Of course. To hack the West is a heroic thing. The West was our former enemy, and you know what? It still is. You use your infrastructure to monopolize the internet for your own use and against us. So if we don't fight back and take the monopoly away, we lose.

'That was why I first worked at the troll farms, exposing a whoring politician on Capitol Hill or spreading stories to change policies in the US, Germany, wherever it was needed. You – you believe anything that is out there. But I was one of the stupid people who got the money and got into drugs, alcohol, became antisocial. I burnt out and dropped out.

'I lived on the street, just fucking myself up even

more. No money for drugs, no money for alcohol, doing anything I could to survive.'

Gabe had his sensible, almost compassionate, head on. It sounded really weird coming from him. 'So where are your parents? Why couldn't you go home?'

'They moved to Poland when the Soviet Union collapsed, like a lot of people. I stayed in Belarus. No one arrests you for hacking there. Like I said, it's a free market – and I got smart. I got cleaned up and decided to get myself onto that market and make money. I didn't sell anything or scam people, like these.' She held up the mobile. 'It takes too long. For me, it was all about raw data. Not compromising anyone, information on a whore and a politician, no. Just data. I collated data for whoever would pay for it.'

I took that with the pinch of salt it deserved, but I wasn't there to judge. It wasn't like I was a soldier in the Salvation Army. 'What are you doing working for FSB again?'

'I'm so good, they asked me. So therefore I had to. When we worked on a troll farm, techniques were needed to crack a site and various exploits, software programs, so a tool had to be developed. But when I came back into the game it became crystal clear to me that all data is open. You just need to be able to see it. That's why FSB came back to hire me. Because I can *see* Nigella. I can see a way of getting in. And that's why the Owl should employ me, not just question me.'

I had a feeling it might be more than just a questioning she would face if she didn't give up what she knew. 'And this Bogachev? That's where you learnt the scams?'

She nodded. 'That is how FSB got to me, for the troll farms. The gangs, they are like recruiting agents.'

Maybe she thought it wouldn't look good to the Owl on her CV.

Rio was impressed. 'Good pitch, mate! Nick, he should give her a job. What do you reckon?'

Jack announced: 'We're twenty away from Taunton.'

I played about with the satnav, closing the scale to see more of the country, then checked the fuel gauge.

Jack was ahead of me. 'We still have enough for Bristol.'

I turned back to Yulia. 'Can you google for a park-and-ride south-west of Bristol?'

She looked confused. 'Parkin who?'

Rio took the phone off her. 'No drama, Yuli. I'll do it.'

61

We were on the south-west edge of Bristol, following signs for Long Ashton park-and-ride, as I turned off the radio after listening to the four a.m. local BBC news. There had been plenty about Brexit and a couple of items about extremist attacks. Two sixteen-year-old German Islamists had been arrested in relation to a bombing in Essen earlier in the year, and two French soldiers protecting a railway station had been attacked by an Islamist with an axe. Brexit and terrorism were now the staples of the news, and there were no reports of any incidents around the forestry block, nothing about any major roads being closed. However, there was a mention of sixty-two-year-old Gloria Hadley, staying at Sennen with her husband and their grand-children. She had disappeared early yesterday morning from Seaview Holiday Park where they were enjoying a week's break. She was last seen dressed in blue pyjamas and a white dressing-gown. Police and the Coastguard were due to resume their search for her later that morning. I turned down the volume.

'Okay . . .'

Everybody except Jack was half dozing, but they stirred.

'This is a new bound. We're not going into the park-and-ride – we dump the Beamer off-site and everything stays, apart from the Vectors. We just use the public transport to get into the city. We'll leave the weapons in a hide to come back to after we've found out who's scamming Jack.'

The murmurs of agreement were sleepy. Jack had had the heater on full-blast because the warmth in the footwell helped his stump when he was sitting for so long.

'Yulia, a laptop or tablet, what do you need?'

She rubbed a face that looked as greasy and tired as the lads' and, no doubt, mine. 'It doesn't matter, but it has to be a Mac.' She pointed to the mobile charging on top of the centre console. 'So it's compatible. Personal hotspot.'

I hit Safari and checked if Bristol had a CeX. 'Jack, you got a pen and paper in here anywhere?'

Of course he did. There was an A5 drawing pad and a collection of numbered pencils in the glove compartment. I wrote down the address and we started to see signs for the park-and-ride.

'Jack, time for the small roads. Find somewhere to hide this and we'll walk back to the park-and-ride.' I checked the opening times on Safari. 'It's good from six.'

We turned left, out of the ambient glow of the city ahead of us, and almost straight away I saw signs for a golf club. 'That's the one. A Beamer estate, with a dog guard, all you need is a Barbour on the back seat and you've cracked it.

'Okay, everyone, switch on. We're going to be moving soon. Jack will dump us on the road just short of the golf club in case of CCTV.'

As everyone sorted themselves out, I pulled the mobile charger from the power jack and shoved it and the phone into my jacket. I checked safe on my Vector and passed it to Rio to bag up, then got back to Jack. 'Mate, we'll find a place just off the road and wait for you. Go in, park up as normal, keep your head down, then come out and walk back the way we've just come. We'll grab you. Okay?'

He nodded and slowed the Beamer so I could check the area to the left.

He was still trying to be in mega-helpful mode. 'What about the satnav, Nick? Should I smash it, take it out, so if they find the car they don't know where we've been?'

'Not a problem. They would have hit us by now if they'd been tracking us, and if they find the car, so what? It doesn't matter where we've been, it's where we're going that we need to keep to ourselves.'

We drove slowly alongside a continuous treeline and the entrance to the club was approaching. I checked behind me, between the two front seats, for headlights and to make sure the rest of them were ready. 'Just here, mate. No brake lights, just in case. And for us lot, remember, just the first click of the doors. Jack can sort that out when he parks up.'

The Beamer stopped on the hand-brake and the three in the rear climbed out. I leant across to Jack.

'Once you get on the road, count the paces to where we link up, okay?'

He gave me a thumbs-up. He knew there wasn't time for any questions.

While the Beamer rolled on to the club entrance, I took the weapons bag and gathered us a metre or so into the hedgerow to be clear of any headlights. I kept my voice low. 'We'll hide it around here – Rio, you take the stag for Jack, and I'll get on with this.' It wasn't as if we were going tens of metres away, but somebody had to be thinking about security while the job was done.

It was perfect ground for what we needed, a mess of brambles, bushes and fallen trees, and I was maybe five metres in when the ground dipped sharply to help us even more. I switched on the mobile screen for the next bit. You could hide something at night and come back in daylight to find it sticking out like a maypole, with a busy walking track right next to it.

In the faint glow I shoved the bag under a rotten fallen tree that had seen quite a few years of history by the size of it, then covered it as best I could with brambles and brush.

I went back to the others and gathered them in close. 'It's five metres directly behind here, in the big dip, under a massive trunk. Jack's going to count from the junction and give us a number. From the number count, chuck a right.'

Rio muttered, 'Got it,' and Gabe gave me a double-tap on the arm. Yulia didn't say anything. It was nothing to do with her and she knew when to shut up.

We stood in the treeline as a vehicle rumbled past, right to left, and it was several seconds before the dead quiet of the early morning resumed. I hoped Jack would get a move on. I wanted to be in habitation before first light so it wouldn't be suspicious that we were on foot.

It wasn't long before I heard him padding along the road and Rio brought him into the pack.

'The foot count is eighty-six.'

'Eighty-six – everybody got that?'

Obviously everyone's foot pattern was going to be different, but Jack's and Gabe's would probably be roughly the same because of their prosthetics. It would more or less work and that was all that mattered.

Now I wanted to crack on and find out one way or another if we could locate these scammers and sort out Jack, because we still had to sort the Owl before we landed up like Gloria Hadley.

'Okay, listen in. The plan. We need to split up when we get to the city. I'll go on my own – I need to recce a meeting place for the Owl. I want to bring him into our killing ground rather than the other way round. As soon as we sort out Jack's rip-off merchants, we can get on with our other business.

'Rio and Yulia,' I dug in my pocket and pushed the drawing paper into Rio's hand, 'CeX. Buy a laptop, whatever she needs for the job. The reason I want you two together is because you're going to blend in. You, a black man with dreadlocks in Bristol – they come in useful at last. And, Yulia, you're working at Pret, or you're an academic. Big student town, you've cracked it. But remember, take your time with your purchase because it's a big one. Make them check it out, ask questions, like you've been saving up for it for months.

'Gabe and Jack, soon as you're in town, start looking for a van. Gabe, you're the only one without a marked face. You might have a fucked-up accent but that doesn't matter. It's the face that counts. Take Jack along for a posh voice if it's really needed. It's got to be cash, and it's got to be private. White-van man, no windows. We might be living in it for a while. Did you get more cash out while you were running about looking for me?'

He was insulted, whether about the accent or not thinking of cash, I wasn't sure. 'Of course we fucking did.'

'Good. How much have we got?' I dug around my neck and brought out my wallet to pass over my cash to Gabe. 'So you got fifteen hundred, and I got out two grand. We spent a bit on fuel, tents, food, general shit, so Rio gets five hundred for Yulia's stuff. We all keep a hundred for ourselves and the rest is on the van. Does that make sense?'

Gabe nodded as he collected and divvied out the cash as best he could in the dark. 'I've got it.'

Rio had a thought that he couldn't wait to share with Gabe. 'Fuck me. That's over two grand you keep. That's more than the Jeep was worth. We've already paid up, mate – that's our money you got there and you're buying new wheels so that means we've pitched in for your new wagon. We're evens.'

Gabe scoffed. 'You wish.'

There was still more I needed Gabe to know.

'Also, mate, we need sleeping bags and mats. Just cheap old shit for the back of the van if we have to keep moving.'

Rio grabbed my arm. 'What if all these lads are abroad, Nick?'

'That's why I'm recceing for the Owl meet, just in case. If they're not here, the scammers become just another day for us – but at least we'll know where they are. Mate, you still got that knife with you? You've got to hand it over.'

'Why?'

'Like I said, you're coming in handy at last – black guy in Bristol with dreadlocks. All good. But with lips like split sausages, you're up for being stopped and searched. If they find that thing, you're fucked.'

He shrugged. 'Fair one.' He produced the KA-BAR in its sheath and I shoved it down my jeans exactly as he had, on the side, taking-a-knife-to-school style.

A car zoomed left to right, heading for the city, doing at least eighty along the empty road. No sooner had it appeared than it disappeared.

'Okay, any questions?'

There weren't any as Gabe handed me my share of the cash.

'Now the boring stuff. We leave here together for the first K and a bit, until we hit habitation. As soon as we're in streetlights we split up into our groups. Do your own thing, sort yourselves out, then head for the park-and-ride. It opens at six. You can normally buy tickets from the driver but pay with small notes if you can.

'Get a ride into town, have something to eat, start checking out vans, do whatever you need to do, but keep a low profile. The first RV will be at twelve thirty at the King Street Brew House. It's right at the end of King Street in the town centre, by the river. It's easy to find – it's full of pubs. Everyone goes there on the piss. The Brew House is one of those microbrewery places, lots of space. It'll be packed at lunchtime so we'll blend in. Any questions?'

There were none.

'Okay, now the ERV. If things get fucked up, the ERV is the Hippodrome. Every fucker knows where it is. It's the local music centre, large open spaces outside, bus stops, lots of footfall, places to sit and shops to lurk around. ERV time for the next two days is at seventeen hundred for two hours.' I said it again so there was no doubt. 'Seventeen hundred for two hours. If you have no luck, you're on your own. If anyone does get separated or there's a drama, you get yourself out of it and you link up at the ERV. No one's going to leave the city until the end of the ERV.'

Rio leant into Yulia's ear as I continued. 'He means emergency rendezvous. You know, meeting place.'

'Buy return tickets or it's going to look weird, but don't come back here. It might be the weapons or the Beamer that have compromised us, and whoever it is will be sitting here, waiting. Any questions?'

Gabe was still fumbling with the cash. 'How the fuck do you know Bristol so well? You lived here? Will you get recognized?'

'Hereford, mate. It's about an hour away and we used the city for urban surveillance training. Long hair, trainers, shooting around in fast cars. Got to know it really well.'

I wasn't expecting any more questions. There were few details to pick up on because it didn't need to be a detailed plan.

But Yulia had one. 'What about your cell? I need it to get online.'

'We'll do all that when we're together at the Brew House, twelve thirty.' I made sure my tone didn't invite a reply. 'One last thing. Rio, you'd better come with me and I'll show you the hide. If all goes to plan, and we van up, we'll come back for the weapons and it'll be one of us who'll collect. Those two will spend all day stumbling about and their legs are going to fall off as they fuck about in the dark. Gabe, can you explain to Jack what I said before he got here?'

I led Rio down into the dead ground and we both got onto our knees with the screen illuminating the trunk. I guided his hand underneath for the bag and the hard steel inside, then got right up close to his ear. There was another reason I wanted Rio on his own. 'Mate, keep an eye on her. Make sure she doesn't contact anyone. Buy whatever she needs, but make sure she's not on her own with it. If she goes for a piss, she hands you the machine. She is the most important thing in our lives right now, but she's also the most dangerous.'

'I get it. But we still have the memory sticks, right? They're still good?'

'Even more so now. Because we need to keep them – and her – secure for our futures. Just keep her safe, mate, yeah? You keep her safe, you keep us safe.'

We stood up and scrambled back to the rest of the team, then set off towards habitation and the park-and-ride.

62

I did what you normally do when you're watching people order breakfast in McDonald's from the other side of the street. I bit into the first of my two flaky sausage rolls from Greggs, then took a sip of flat white.

The shutters were still down at CeX, further up The Horsefair on the edge of what I used to know as the Broadmead shopping centre, but which signs were telling me was now called Bristol Shopping Quarter. No amount of name changes, though, could cheer up the planners' love of concrete.

The street called The Horsefair was on the edge of the shopping quarter, and was more Vape R Us than Planet Organic. From the amount of cardboard in the doorways, some with people still lying on it, a lot of homeless used the shops' overhangs for overnight shelter. Some even had pop-up tents and scabby dogs for early warning. Workers hurried past with paper coffee cups in their hands and earphones shoved in, all bent over in the wind. The area suited me, the way I felt and looked.

The sun wasn't playing today. It was dull and gusty, but at least it gave me a reason to have my hood up. My hands were recovering from the swelling, and the pins and needles told me that life was coming back to them.

There was no way I would ever have gone on a recce for the Owl meet. I was here to protect our main asset. It wasn't that I didn't trust Rio to do the job, but I needed to be one bound away from them, having an overview of what was going on around them so they could get on with it. If they'd known I was out there, they might have acted unnaturally. If I was part of the set-up, I would also be part of the problem. They needed to appear as normal as possible, just in case they were being followed. If anything happened, I was one step back and, with luck, could intervene.

It had been a straightforward journey into the city. The buses ran from the park-and-ride every ten to fifteen minutes, and for four pounds you got a return ticket. Not that all of us would be going back to the golf course: if Gabe and Jack managed to buy a van, which I was sure they would, it would be just me or Rio. It was a dangerous business going back to a hide. You never knew if it had been compromised, and if it had, whether or not the people you were trying to avoid had found it.

There was also an even bigger indicator that we were in the area, of course, and that was the Beamer. It was our link to Cornwall, so it didn't matter if it was parked at a golf course or shoved onto a treeline. It was the last bit of snakeskin we were trying to shed, the last connection to all that had happened further down in the south-west. The weapons were important to us. We didn't know what our futures were, and having some Vectors evened up the odds a little.

I finished off the first sausage roll, adding even more grease and crumbly bits to the fur coats my teeth were wearing after days of no brushing.

Rio and Yulia sat down with their trays and tucked into their coffee and food. I had seen Rio give Yulia a bollocking about her neck: like an over-concerned granny he had made sure that her fleece was zipped up to the top to cover as much of the ink as possible. Good skills.

I checked out The Horsefair. I didn't see anybody watching, repositioning themselves, doing anything other than getting on with life. Everyone had their heads down, bolting pastries as fast as they could as they made their way to another exciting day at work or school. The third party was just being third party.

There was a helicopter in the distance somewhere, but it was travelling, not static. It's only when helicopters stop that you need to worry.

I stood where I was, having a go at the second sausage roll. Traffic cruised past, fleets of taxis and buses – the occasional squad car did its stuff on blues and twos. A couple of police community support officers trundled past on the beat. All third party, all good.

Another fifteen minutes passed, then Rio and Yulia were on their feet and shovelling the waste off their trays into the bins. CeX opened at nine thirty. They came out of McDonald's and turned right.

I screwed up the Greggs bag and kept it in my hand. Litterbugs attract attention. Somebody might say something or grab the PCSOs and report me. Coffee cup in my right hand, I looked about and listened hard, in case some overexcited surveillance operator couldn't control the volume of their voice as they gobbed off into a concealed mic.

Rio and Yulia looked okay together. No one was giving them strange glances, and why would they? Everyone had their own dramas to deal with: kids, unhappy marriages, even unhappier mortgages.

The two of them were coming unsighted as The Horsefair curved to the left. I followed. I jettisoned the Greggs bag in a bin and took a sip of coffee.

The shutters were up and Rio and Yulia disappeared inside. I carried on past on the other side of the road, making no attempt to look in. There was no reason to. I kept my head down, walking with purpose, same as everybody else. We all had places to go.

Twenty metres further on I came to a smokers' convention in a series of doorways. It looked like the oversized windows had once belonged to a department store, but now it was Poundland and big green signs shouted about massive bargains inside. It would be a good place to stake out CeX from, but there were too many smokers. One would try to strike up a conversation, probably about why I wasn't smoking. Betfred was a bit further along: if they came out of CeX and turned right, I could nip inside for a minute or so until they were past.

I stood in the betting-office doorway, taking casual sips of coffee and wishing I'd bought four sausage rolls instead of two. The traffic rumbled past, the footfall continued, and then one thing was out of place.

He was normal height, normal build, normal haircut, short, side parting, nondescript blue fleece on blue jeans and trainers. He was wearing earphones, but so was almost everyone. The white leads disappeared into the chest pocket of the fleece. Nothing unusual. Everything perfectly normal as he crossed with purpose from my side of the road towards CeX and the bus stop immediately outside it, just as you do when you talk on your phone and you're crossing the road. But this third party wasn't checking the traffic as he dodged it: his eyes were fixed exclusively on the store, and as he spoke into the mic he pushed it closer to his mouth.

I cut away from him immediately because he was the possible known. I needed to know if there were unknowns. Were there others on foot, taking over the trigger, moving into another doorway ready to take Rio and Yulia as they left, or in vehicles parked up in the loading bays? Were cars suddenly pulling into the kerb? I strained my ears and eyes for any indication of the helicopter. Was it now a static dot in the sky, its optics bearing down on us?

There was none of that. And no police. Even the PCSOs had gone.

Keeping my hood up as I swigged the last of the flat white, I got back to Mr Bland. He'd reached the shop and was very interested in the window displays, all the mobiles and games gear, laptops and tablets.

A bus passed me left to right, a number fifty-four,

double-decker, its air brakes already on to slow it for the stop, and Mr Bland disappeared from view. Was he going to catch it? The bus stopped with the final hiss of brakes and the doors opened. Mr Bland reappeared, not sitting next to a bus window but emerging from behind the bus, walking along the pavement, heading back the way he, and we, had come. I checked for another stakeout. Had Mr Bland just been there to confirm they were inside before handing over to a trigger? Or maybe he didn't like the deals on offer and I was being paranoid again.

All I could see was the third party, all around, doing third-party stuff, and Mr Bland still walking away in the direction of McDonald's.

It was maybe another fifteen minutes before Rio came out of the shop with Yulia half a step behind. Rio was carrying a red plastic bag, and they turned left, back the way we had come. I stayed where I was until they became unsighted as they hit the curve on the right, waiting for the last possible moment to see if there was a trigger, if a follow was being initiated.

There wouldn't be vans screaming up, doors bursting open and men bundling them into the back. That was for Hollywood. They would wait. They would follow. They would be hoping to get us all together and deliver us as a job lot to the Owl.

I abandoned Betfred's doorway and followed them from the other side of the road. They carried on past McDonald's. Still nothing to indicate a follow. Fuck it: I wasn't paranoid, I was just conscientious. It didn't feel right, and that was the problem. If something didn't feel right, it normally wasn't. There was nothing I could do, apart from what I was doing now, because there was nothing to react to.

I followed them as they finished rounding the curve, and watched as they went into a newsagent's together.

63

I'd spent the last couple of hours hanging out in coffee shops in and around the shopping quarter, watching Yulia make roll-ups seemingly one-handed and join the other smokers standing outside the main shopping mall. Rio stayed with her at all times, and from his gestures, the waffle was nothing but complaints about her smoking and his having to be around it.

A band of Remainers had set up a gazebo and trestle table outside the main entrance and were trying to hand out leaflets on how wonderful it would be to stay in the EU. Then the Leavers turned up and did exactly the same thing, and the vast majority of people refused to take information from either.

I got the mobile up and downloaded the tracker app. I couldn't see anything to indicate surveillance, but what I'd seen still didn't feel right. Maybe if the Owl was round and about there was a slim chance one of the tracker community would pick him up, in Bristol, London, or wherever. Any form of indication of where he was would have been welcome. It would have been madness not to download the app and see if anything had happened.

It was nearly time to RV at the King Street Brew House. These two knew it too, and they checked the information-point map for about the third time, then headed towards the river. I fell in behind. It was a ten-minute walk at most, and I was back to watching and listening.

No Mr Bland. No helicopter. Nothing. I followed, yet still it didn't feel right.

King Street was Party Central, a partly pedestrian-ized area well known in the city for nights out. I remembered it as a good place to be in the summer. The Brew House was down at the end where the pedestrianized bit met the water. It was large, trendy, friendly and noisy, with big windows that looked out onto the road and river. It was perfect for us.

I watched from a distance as Rio and Yulia went in, and stayed outside for another ten minutes, all eyes and ears. It was only twelve twenty-five, so I took the time to double-check. I still had five minutes so I wouldn't have the team flapping, assuming Gabe and Jack were already there. I did a 360 around the cobble-stoned streets, and still nothing. It was time to move on. I'd soon know if I'd got it wrong.

The Brew House was a world of wood, green tiles and hipster barmen with the longest beards I'd seen this side of Kabul. It was busy with groups, perhaps work colleagues, because all the drinks looked like pints of Coke and lemonade and by twelve thirty they had already demolished most of their trendy burgers and salads.

I found all four of our group parked in a semi-circular booth, ordering from a woman who was tattooed all the way up her right arm. Yulia blended in perfectly.

I approached with a smile and a cheery 'Hello', then sat down with them. Jack was immediately to my left, with Yulia the other side of him, then Rio and Gabe, who faced me from the other side of the red leatherette horseshoe. Gabe had the local papers in front of him, open on the classifieds. He leant across. 'I couldn't wait. We ordered you a burger and a Coke. Did you get the meet sorted?'

I nodded, one eye on the road the other side of the floor-to-ceiling glass doors. 'Anybody checked the exits?'

Gabe looked disgusted. 'Course we fucking did. If you'd got here in time you would have seen.' He meant I should have met up at 12.25. That was army time for 12.30.

Rio gave me a disappointed shake of the head but couldn't help smiling. Then his lips cracked and his face went blank again.

Gabe tilted his head to his left. 'There's a fire escape on the way to the toilets, and another one signed through the back, the kitchen. It opens out onto a service and parking area at the side of the building.'

'Okay. You get the van?'

'We're seeing another this afternoon. Easton?'

I knew it.

'About three o'clock. Found it on Gumtree.' He lifted the papers. 'Still looking, just in case. Then we'll get the bags and the mats at Halfords, job lot again. Where have all the phone boxes gone?'

He sat back and Rio eased the laptop out of the plastic bag. They hadn't held back: the thirteen-inch MacBook Air was scratched and had more dinks in it than the Wolves' surfboards, along with a bunch of adhesive marks where stickers had once been, probably declaring war against meat-eating.

'Let's get on with it, then.'

Rio passed the lead to Yulia and she bent under the table to plug it in. I put the mobile on the table and pulled up the personal hotspot. Once both machines were ready, she tapped in the password and was good to go. The drinks arrived, all Cokes and orange juices. This was work.

Yulia adjusted her hands either side of the Mac, dragging it closer to her so the edge was nearly touching her chest. I leant forward and lifted the screen so at least Gabe and Jack could see what was happening. She read my mind. 'Do you really imagine I'd do anything to mess up my chance of staying here? I'm going to show you how good I am. I can find these amateurs in minutes. This is my world, not yours. They're my friends in there, not yours.'

'You going on the dark web?'

'Where else? But just me. This is what makes me special – and I'm not running a free tutorial.'

Rio had his hand on his Coke and sucked on the straw. 'Mate, let her get on with it. Protecting the assets – that's what we do, don't we? That's why she's sitting there. Why not her doing the same thing?'

He put his Coke on the table and sat back. He had said his piece, and he was right. I let her get on with it.

Yulia spent no time with any of us now: it was all about Jack. 'You need to text her now. Tell her you're sorry you didn't text last night, but you were busy. That will get her worried. Maybe she thinks you're losing interest. But don't worry, she'll answer. She always has answered, hasn't she?'

Jack already had the mobile in his hand.

'Of course she has,' Yulia went on. 'She's always desperate to talk to you, isn't she? That's because you understand her. You're the first man ever to understand her, aren't you? Yes?'

Jack didn't answer but the expression on his face meant he didn't have to. He carried on texting as she tapped on the laptop keyboard, clearly uncomfortable with her elbows pushed right back so she could keep the Mac close to her.

'Jack, tell her you're missing her, missing her texts. Don't worry, they're going to be standing by for you. They know what to say to take the relationship further. They will check the play sheets to see what stage they're at with you and what to do next.'

She continued her keyboard work. 'She'll come back and say she's busy, to build up your anticipation.' Yulia's eyes never left the screen, darting left and right. Her fingers were the only other part of her that moved. The rest was a waxwork.

Jack finished texting and kept the phone in his hand as the food arrived, carried by two very smiley women. Gabe took control before the inevitable questions about who wanted what. 'Just put them down. We'll sort them out ourselves. Thanks!'

Jack's head twitched. He hadn't had to wait long

before the return text. Yulia didn't move her eyes off the screen. 'What does it say?'

'She's at dinner with clients and thinking of me.'

That was good skills. Shanghai was normally seven or eight hours ahead, depending on the time of year.

'Okay, just reply as you would. Send a kiss, or what do you do?'

Jack tapped his response. 'I normally say, "Talk soon".'

'Okay.' She, too, was tapping away and spoke at the same time. 'Now we wait.'

She half closed the laptop lid and reached over for her plate. The rest of us followed and I checked again outside for Mr Bland, for anything that confirmed the bad feeling that was gnawing at my gut.

A couple of minutes later, Gail was back. Yulia lifted the lid again and craned her neck. 'What does she say?'

He read it: '"What a lovely surprise. I'm at dinner with clients and I'm hiding in the toilets. I missed you so much yesterday. Just great to talk to you."'

Yulia was in complete control, scanning her screen, only her hands and eyes moving. 'Tell her you missed her and ask her about work.'

Jack keyed it in. 'I'm asking, "How did the planning meeting go yesterday?"'

'That's good. Tell her you were thinking about her all day, wondering how it went.'

He read the reply without enthusiasm. '"It went so well – thank you for thinking about me. As I sat at the meeting I found myself dreaming about when we will meet up. Oh, I just remembered – would you be able to pick up a small parcel for me? A model cast of a project I will start when I'm back in the UK."'

Yulia's fingers froze and she scanned the screen. 'Tell her, no problem. Ask where you should pick it up.'

Jack did as he was told and Gail came straight back. '"I'm not sure yet, but as soon as I know I'll text you. You'll have to pay the charge, is that all right? I'll pay you back, of course. Send your details and I'll transfer."'

Yulia looked at Jack with a smug smile. 'Told you. Do they have your date of birth, address and bank details from last time?'

They did. I could almost see Jack's heart sink.

'You changed banks afterwards?'

Jack nodded a sorrowful positive, knowing it hadn't helped him one bit.

'It's okay, Jack, it doesn't mean they're going to strip out your bank account. They could sell your details on for fake ID. You get all the debt, somebody gets a mortgage or a loan. Or maybe they'll use your account for money-laundering. Cash would route through in just a couple of hours.'

Jack's shoulders slumped, following his heart into his seat. Yulia had no sympathy. In fact she didn't have anything – no anger, fun, emotion. It was just business.

'Okay, the good thing is, they haven't sold your details on to another group. If we stop them, we stop them for good. Tell her, no problem, you'll pay.'

Gabe stopped dunking his chips into a small pot of ketchup. 'But what if I say no? We're trying to get these fuckers, not give them more.'

326

Yulia glared at him. This was her world. 'Jack, please, just do it.'

Jack complied.

'She'll be back soon saying something like she doesn't want to take advantage.'

The mobile pinged as Yulia put the laptop fully on the table, opened the lid and sat back. Jack read: '"Thank you, but I want our relationship to start correctly because I want it to work. I've been hurt so many times by men who just want to take and I don't want you to think the same of me. I have to go now or they'll think I've fallen down the toilet! Thinking of you all the time. X."'

'Okay, do your normal sign-off.'

Jack hit the same key twice and placed the mobile on the table. He stared at it like it was an IED.

There was a moment's silence that Rio rightly ended. 'Well? You got 'em?'

Yulia was into her food, and clearly feeling pleased with herself. 'Yes, they're in the UK. Somewhere called Lie-sester.'

Gabe frowned. 'Lie who?'

She turned the laptop round to show a Google map and Gabe laughed. 'Leicester! They're in fucking Leicester!'

Yulia shot me an aren't-I-good? look.

Rio hit Jack's shoulder, a comfort gesture, as he was totally destroyed. 'Mate, no drama. We'll sort these fuckers out. They can't buy any of us off the shelf, mate – all right? Yuli here'll get your life back. She knows how to do it. She knows all this shit.' He bent a little to catch Yulia's eyes as she ate. 'Mate, you can do that, can't you? Get him offline, no ID rip-offs, all that sort of stuff? Come to think of it, you should get all of us offline, yeah?'

I'd kept my eyes on the crowd inside, which was growing, and the street. A grey Qashqai, two up, passed right to left, travelling just a bit too slowly.

Mr Bland, earphones in, was in the front passenger seat, looking and listening. A woman was driving.

'Lads – stop. Listen in, we've got a problem. Get everything packed up. Gabe, get another round of drinks in, mate. Make it look like we're staying, but ask for the bill at the same time.'

64

'There's a team outside. It's the Owl – it has to be.'

All I got was a sea of confused faces.

'Look, I don't know how – it could be the Beamer, the weapons, it doesn't matter. What does matter is that there's a team out there. So this is what we need to do. I'll draw the fire. You get out of here, bomb-burst into your two groups. Jack and Gabe, we really need the van. Rio, stick to Yulia like glue.'

My eyes were on her. She looked anxious, as well she might.

'Until we sort this, the life you want is fantasy. We're going to try to make it work for you, but you've got to stay with us.'

The tattooed arm came back to clear away our plates, and Gabe took the chance to order another round of drinks and get the bill.

Yulia stared down at her empty plate until it was whisked away. It was a while before she glanced up and nodded. My eyes flicked to Rio. 'Same thing I said at the weapons hide, mate. Do that and keep us safe.'

I looked at them all. 'Once you're out of here, you're on your own. Bomb-burst, then we RV with transport. Gabe – Easton, that's where you're going, right?'

He nodded as I checked Safari.

At last I found what I was looking for: an RV that was big, busy, easy to find and, most importantly, out of the city centre. I knew it from the old days but that wasn't good enough. I had to know it still existed.

'Okay, it's near the M32. That's where the RV's going to be. There's an IKEA and a twenty-four-hour Tesco there. So, nineteen hundred hours, in the Tesco car park. Gabe, Jack, just be there with a van. Wait fifteen minutes and pick up whoever has made the RV. If it's a no-go from any of our group, the ones at the RV have decisions to make. You have the memory sticks and you might have Yulia. Maybe you go back to the barn and start shouting for the Owl, saying you want a deal. You'll soon find out if there's a device in there or not.'

My eyes went back to Yulia. Her expression was hard to read, but inside that geek head of hers she had to be churning through her options. I knew I would have been. 'You really are better off with us for now – you understand that, don't you?'

'Yes.'

I wasn't sure she meant it.

Jack erupted. 'Let's just take them!'

Gabe looked proud of him. 'Let's front them up, all together!'

I almost laughed. 'Nice thought, but we'd lose. In any case, they want all of us together to take us down. They want control of the sticks and Yulia. Loose ends.'

The drinks came over and we waited once more. Gabe smiled at the waitress. 'Don't worry, I'll sort them all out.' He didn't smile at the bill lying on the tray, though. I put eighty next to it and waited for her to take it away.

'We keep to the plan, yeah? We get out of here, and we carry on with what we decided about the scammers. The new mission. If we don't, we really are like the pencil necks. So, let's help Jack, and then we help ourselves. Nineteen hundred hours, Tesco's, Easton.'

I took a couple of gulps, stood up and checked the mobile was clear before shoving it into my jeans. 'You know what? Me drawing fire for you lot is becoming a habit.'

Gabe grunted. 'That's because you're the only one with enough arms and legs.'

Yulia looked disgusted, but the others smiled.

Gabe got things moving. 'So you'd better start fucking using them.'

As Rio gathered the laptop into the plastic bag, I walked out onto the cobblestones and across the street, slowly enough for the trigger to be able to do their job, but not so slowly it looked like what it was. I glanced back through the doors, and the rest of them were starting their fresh drinks. I glanced left and right. I couldn't see the Qashqai; I couldn't see a trigger. I needed a target to draw the fire.

The nearest road junction was to the left. Maybe the trigger was out of sight, ready to pick us up as we came onto the junction. Only one way to find out.

I rounded the corner and there it was, in a parking bay about twenty metres down on the right, facing me on the narrow one-way. The grey Qashqai, still two up. I walked straight towards them, but they couldn't be sure of my intentions. Behind me was the river, to the left a restaurant and offices. Further along on my right there was a multi-storey car park, but they knew I didn't have a vehicle. Another fifty ahead of me was a crossroads. I kept going. I was going to pass them, a head-on encounter, something they would have wanted to avoid, but there wasn't a thing they could do. If they started their engine it would attract my attention. Even if they did get out from between the tightly packed trucks and cars, they would be driving towards me – and then I would be behind them as they drove away and they would lose sight of me. They would have to stay where they were and bluff, play the normal bland lunchtime couple, bland vehicle, bland Tupperware lunch.

I didn't check behind me. There wouldn't be anyone following. Mr and Mrs Bland could still be productive by checking in their mirrors as I passed and saying a left or right at the end of the junction. There would still be a trigger on the Brew House, and the leader of the team would have to establish whether they should stay or commit to this follow. The correct decision would be for them to stay eyes-on at the Brew House, but my job was to make sure that didn't happen. Gabe and Rio had been right about us never becoming pencil necks. We looked out for each other. We might all be out of the army but . . .

I was unsighted from the Qashqai as I walked along the side of a DHL truck parked about three vehicles in front of it. Now was the time to pull out the KA-BAR. I almost felt excited. Maybe the greatest freedom is having nothing to lose.

They saw me emerge from the rear of the truck, knife raised high. Mr Bland made to get out of the car and the driver waffled into her mic. Without a doubt, a mayday.

Mr Bland wasn't quick enough as I slammed the weapon into his window. The blade worked like a safety hammer and the shattering of the glass released the woman's voice. 'Attacked! Attacked!'

Mr Bland had bent down to take cover, but he didn't know I wasn't trying to kill him. I ran to the other side of the car, the KA-BAR up, and rammed it into her window. Mrs Bland thought I was going to stab her and ducked forward, but had the presence of mind to keep one hand above her on the ignition. Glass showered on her dark brown bushy hair as she tried frantically to fire the engine. Mr Bland stretched to get his legs and back as straight as he could as his hands shot to his waist. He was reaching for a weapon.

Through the smashed window I leant over the woman's back and jabbed the tip of the blade into the top of his arm. He screamed and recoiled as I extracted the knife, and then the engine turned over. I looked fast to my right, towards the river, at movement in my peripheral vision. Two bodies were running towards us. That was exactly what I wanted.

I turned left, shoving the knife under my left armpit inside my jacket, and ran the other way, up to the crossroads and right, away from the Brew House and the drama behind me. I ran into the multi-storey. They'd have to cover a lot of ground and vehicles to find me. I could have run further down the street and that would have drawn them away, but it would also have got the third party even more involved and someone would have called the police or, worse, had a go. I wanted to contain this. I wanted the drama to be between me and the surveillance team.

My mouth was dry and my lungs were heaving as I took the stairs two at a time, making distance, my hand grabbing the rail a metre or so ahead at each bound for extra momentum.

I finally burst through the door on the top floor and onto the roof-space parking area. It was open to the sky but the buildings next to it were taller. No chance of jumping onto them. It was stop, breathe, think.

65

I ran back through the door to the stairwell, panting, a pain at the back of my neck as I fought for more oxygen. My chest expanded close to bursting and my windpipe was so dry that each breath burnt my lungs.

Below, they were coming. I could hear the slap of their feet on the concrete stairs, the sounds bouncing off the narrow walls of the shaft with only two ways to travel. The echoes got louder and louder and soon I could hear the heaviness of their breathing. A head pushed out into the space below me and peered up, checking it was safe before the rest of him followed. Maybe he'd heard me breathing and wondered what a racehorse was doing on the stairs. It was the same short blond hair from Rio's house.

I burst back onto the top floor and headed for the ramp. They were coming up to me. Now was the time for me to get down and out. I had them where I wanted them. I heard vehicles moving, but gently – the third party doing its stuff.

I reached the floor below and kept running down. The Qashqai was coming up. Mr Bland saw me filling his windscreen and Mrs Bland revved the engine and screamed towards me. The ramp curved and the vehicle's wheels were committed by the kerbs either side. The alloys screeched against the concrete and the vehicle stopped. Mr Bland was moving to get out. His damaged arm must have made it hard to open the door, but he looked determined to grip me. I pulled out the knife as I jumped to the side, and rammed it vertically into the bulging sidewall of the offside tyre. There was a loud and sudden release of pressure, a massive fuck-off hiss.

The knife handle was ripped out of my hands as Mrs Bland put her foot down and the vehicle jumped forwards. I kept running down the ramp, hit the next floor, and carried on. I wasn't worrying about the third party, wasn't worrying about what was in front of or behind me. All I needed to do was keep moving.

The exit barrier was ahead. There was just enough room for me to squeeze past and back onto the road, take a left, then left again, back the way I had come, towards the river. It should be free of the Owl's team. If not, I was about to find out.

My throat was agony and my lungs were about to explode. Sweat poured down my face and neck as I passed the line of parked vehicles. At the river I turned right and ran along the cobblestones. A few metres short of the Brew House, I came to the service area Gabe had talked about. At the bottom there was a little car park for the workers, and a fire escape, but mostly crates full of empties, piles of packed-up cardboard, then rows and rows of wheelie bins.

I dumped the mobile into the first I came to and carried on to the end, sliding on the greasy ground. I burrowed in behind the bins, curled up and made myself as small as I could, using two flats of cardboard to give me a bit more cover. I took deep breaths as I tried to ease my lungs.

My face dripped sweat onto the cardboard. I didn't know if the rest of them had got away, but that wasn't my job. Drawing the fire was. If the surveillance team hadn't responded to Mrs Bland's mayday and had still been staking out the Brew House, I would have been picked up by now. My job was done. I just hoped the others had done theirs and managed to get away.

My breathing had calmed but my throat was so dry I could almost feel my Adam's apple creaking up and down. Like my jaw back in the forestry block, there was no oil in the joints.

I waited some more, and finally felt confident enough to move my head out from behind the cardboard. I could see right down to the river at the end of the service road and it was empty. I looked at my watch. I had nearly six hours until the RV. I decided to stay where I was and see if there was any movement from the Owl's team, particularly around that first bin with the mobile in it.

66

Tesco car park

I leant against the community bus stop, watching mums drag reluctant kids into the superstore and exit pushing trolleys laden with flat-screen TVs, school clothes and baked beans. Around me was a bunch of unhappy shoppers now the wind had picked up and the first few specks of rain were falling.

I had changed my last twenty to get a bus here and was now down to just two after buying a hoodie, an extra large Mars bar and a litre of milk. At least I looked good in my nice blue top. It had been worth shopping and getting exposed to CCTV to shed the VDM skin I'd had with the other.

The mobile I'd grabbed back out of the wheelie bin still had 30 per cent charge, and we could top that up once the van arrived. And the van *would* turn up. Thinking positively was always the answer. Never 'maybe' or 'if': the mind has to be certain. Only then can you start to think about what to do when things go wrong. You need a plan first, or everything becomes a heavy lift.

I had dumped the mobile to see if the Owl's team were tracking it and they weren't. I'd seen the blond man and Mrs Bland on foot, crossing my arc of view at the end of the service road where it met the cobblestones and the river beyond, but they had never been close to the wheelie. It must have been the Beamer or the weapons that had given us away – probably the Beamer. It didn't matter. This stuff happened and you should expect it. As long as we kept one step ahead, and shed our skins on the way, it would work out.

From my hiding place behind the cardboard there hadn't been any sight or sound of Gabe and the others, so I was expecting them to be here on time.

As the clock ticked on, I kept my eyes on Tesco's filling station and the approach road from the elevated M32.

I had a good view of the windscreens of the vehicles coming down so it wouldn't be too hard to ID their drivers, and it wasn't just the van and its driver I was looking for. I had to make sure they weren't being followed. As for Rio and Yulia, I didn't bother looking for them at all. I would soon find out who had made the RV.

At seven or eight minutes before the top of the hour I downed the last of the milk and, moments later, spotted Gabe, one up, at the wheel of a 10-reg Peugeot van. It had taken a few knocks, and where the metalwork had buckled and the paint had cracked, there were lines and layers of rust. But the wheels were going round, and that was all that mattered. The once-white van came into the car park and took a space fifty or sixty metres away, facing the superstore exits.

I set off towards it, and as I dumped the empty milk container in a bin, Rio and Yulia came into view on my right, weaving their way around the parked vehicles. That was a relief, and not just because we'd all made the RV. Once this scammer job was over and done with, we still had a lot to sort out.

Gabe saw us, but he looked beyond, left, right and behind, checking there wasn't the world's biggest drama following. Rio and Yulia reached the van first and as I came up level with the cab, the side door opened. I jumped in and Gabe got the van moving. The rest of the team looked at me, waiting for me to speak, wanting to know what I knew. 'Definitely the Owl.'

Rio sat on the floor, his back braced against the panelling as Gabe manoeuvred out of the car park. 'I knew it.'

'Yeah, mate, those lads at the house. One of them, for sure, was on the team.'

The van didn't have a dividing panel like the VW so it was easy to pass the mobile charger to Gabe to shove into the lighter socket, and the lead was long enough for the phone to lie between the cab seats and just a little bit into the back.

'Mate, the bad news is I lost your knife. Got ripped out of my hand. Sorry.'

Rio grinned. 'No drama. You can buy me a new one later. Plus a little bit more for the emotional distress. That was going to be a family heirloom. I was going to pass it on to the girls.'

We bounced about as Gabe negotiated the round-about to get onto the M32, and the van was soon fighting uphill onto the elevated slipway. There were no sleeping bags in the back, no packs of water, no mats. There hadn't been time for that. But at least the floor had a wooden base instead of us having to lie on bare metal.

Rio turned to Jack, who was lying on his back. It was the best way to rest his leg. 'Where the fuck's Leicester when it's at home?'

Jack tilted his head towards Yulia, who sat on the same side of the van as Rio, her knees up supporting the laptop, still in its carrier. 'Maybe we can google the target.'

She unpacked the Mac as Jack enlightened Rio a bit more. 'It's north-east of Birmingham. Gabe's taking us on the M5, round the bottom of Birmingham, then up. Maybe two hours, tops, depending on the traffic.'

Yulia was ready but she needed something from me. She gestured at the phone on the floor and had to raise her voice. 'Can I get online?'

I picked up the mobile as the tyres rumbled louder. Peugeot's production budget hadn't run to sound in-sulation and we'd joined the motorway. 'Yep.' I hit the personal hotspot button and Bluetooth so she could get a link, then let her get on with it. Once her eyes were fixed on the screen I nodded for Rio to keep an eye on what she was doing. He shuffled a little closer as she tapped.

He checked the screen. 'Nick, get this down, mate.'

I picked up the mobile again and opened email. Not that there was an account, but anything I typed would be saved.

'It's Loughborough Road, in Belgrave, just north of the city centre. Look.' Yulia turned the screen as Google Maps opened onto a satellite picture with its location pin on Loughborough Road, in the middle of what looked like an industrial estate.

She was happy with what she saw. 'This isn't precise, but when we get there I'll be able to pinpoint them.'

Jack rolled onto his stomach. 'That doesn't look like Shanghai, does it?'

I checked the imagery. 'Yulia, you sure?'

She seemed confused. 'Of course. Jack will start the conversation, and the rest is easy.'

I stared at the 3D satellite map, which showed the target area was in an old light-industrial area. At one time, before the M1 was built, it must have been on the main drag to Loughborough, which made its way north-west out of the city. This estate wasn't a collection of modern low-level steel-framed workshops and offices planned around a series of cul-de-sacs. It was much older and appeared to have grown up organically, the rows of terraced houses swamped by 1960s industrial squares of brick. Across Loughborough Road and opposite the target area was the new world: a cash-and-carry and a Lidl, steel-fabricated islands surrounded by car park.

Jack had seen enough. He rolled onto his back again and aimed the talk at Yulia. 'You said the pack they used on me was a cheap one. How much do they cost? How much do they make?'

She shrugged. 'Maybe two hundred, no more than two hundred and fifty dollars for at least four or five profiles. The British aren't as good as most because you're new to this big game. In the UK they're mostly criminals who see this as a new type of business venture. They don't understand it yet. They are muscle people, not brain people. They don't understand that the only thing new is the technology, the way to get to the money. Everything else is the oldest confidence trick, preying on human weakness. Love, hate, jealousy, stupidity. When people receive a malicious link and are told it's malicious, thirty per cent of you British will still click on the link.'

She paused for a second with a can-you-believe-it expression. 'But you British are getting better, because you have to. It's a free market. Market forces will dictate who makes the money, no matter where you are.'

Rio had other things on his mind. 'So, here's the thing, Yuli. Can you get Jack's money back? Maybe a little more out of them – I mean, it's free money, isn't it?'

She shook her head. 'The money will have been moved so many times now it would take for ever to find it. Even basic scammers know how to disappear money, these days.' She saw the disappointed faces. 'But if they're not so advanced, maybe there could be something we find that's going to help me.'

Jack liked that idea. His life had been drained but maybe at least he'd get a refund on the empties.

Gabe switched on the radio, and as he scanned the channels for the news, I handed the Mac back to Yulia.

'How did you and the Russians get into the UK in the first place?'

'I flew to London on a visitor's visa. I don't know about the rest of them, but they were already in the

UK. They met me at the airport with the camper van and I was told I was going to leave the same way. But, of course, all that changed. The helicopter was taking us to a ship. Maybe I was going home with them – who knows? They had many plans for if things went wrong.'

I had to agree with that. Phoenix would have had it all squared away, and a heli straight out to a ship in international waters sounded a good idea for when the shit hit the fan.

The radio was turned off, replaced by the slap of windscreen wipers. Gabe shouted over the engine noise, to Jack and Rio, 'Big ISIS car bomb went off in Kabul today, Afghan Army HQ. Twenty-four dead and another round of young lads with wooden legs.'

Jack muttered, 'Nightmare.'

All three of them would have worked with the Afghan National Army against the Taliban, which now had elements of ISIS fighting alongside it. They would have known the young lads who joined the ANA to support their families and had been killed or injured just like any other soldier who had been out there.

There was a minute or so of silence before Gabe shouted again: 'Yulia, you got any more of that baccy? I'm gagging up here.'

It seemed to lift the mood and put the team back on track.

Rio rolled his eyes as she dug into her jeans and brought out a pack of Drum. 'Oh, for fuck's sake.'

Jack nodded as she waved the pack at him. Rio didn't move away. Maybe being right up next to Yulia gave him something to moan about.

Clearly she had been rolling these things for years. The first one might have been straight from a packet as she passed it to me to hold up for Gabe, then started another for Jack.

She was being really helpful, not surprisingly. She was still hoping for that job interview, and at the moment I was her only referee. I pressed for more information while it lasted. 'So the picture we have of you surfing. You had to learn how to do that for the cover story, did you? A reason to be there?'

Some roll-up flake dropped onto the Mac. 'You British – you always think everything has to have a reason.' She licked a finger to pick up the escaped tobacco and flick it back where it belonged. 'It was just a picture taken on holiday years ago, on the Black Sea. There's no surf there but when FSB found it, they said I was a surfer so that would be the story. The others, they could surf. They live . . .' she thought about it '. . . lived in South Africa. They worked for FSB when they were needed.'

She passed Jack his roll-up, along with her disposable. It was clear from the cloud of smoke up front that Gabe had his own.

Rio was already enjoying complaining. 'Open the fucking window.'

It didn't happen.

Jack stayed on his back, enjoying his roll-up, which Rio and I had to endure.

Rio lay next to Yulia, the laptop almost level with his face. 'Smoke rises, yeah?'

There was a lull, broken by Jack after a few deep puffs. 'Nick?'

I looked over. He stared at the ceiling, his fingers at his lips as he took another drag, then picked some fallen leaf off his lips and rubbed his fingers together to get rid of it. 'The UK . . . information superpower. I think the EU would be really concerned if the UK did vote to leave. I'm sure they've got some sort of agreement in place for swapping information, but what would happen if that information to the EU was cut off? It could be a negotiating chip, couldn't it? I feel a bit better now if we do get out. We've got something Brussels needs.'

Rio wasn't having any of it. 'Mate, stop. It ain't happening, so there won't be any bargaining. Just suck on your cancer stick and make the most of your diminished life.'

67

We were maybe fifteen miles out of Leicester, on the M69, which took us there in virtually a straight line. It was dark, still raining hard, and the journey had taken a lot longer than Jack had estimated. The windscreen wipers struggled and their rhythmic slap filled the back of the van, merging with the steady whoosh of surface water getting jetted into the wheel arches.

Jack was still on his back, eyes closed, his fingers linked on his chest, like Dracula. Rio and Yulia sat with their backs against the panelling, and his cross-examination had been relentless.

'So what were you talking about, getting off the drugs? How did you do it? I mean, it's really hard, isn't it?'

His face was caught in the dull glow of the small rear light and I could almost see the cogs whirring inside his head. Maybe she'd say something about coming off drugs that would help Simone.

'Not when you're homeless in Belarus. You British

have no idea – you have welfare. A system that helps. Charities when it doesn't. But in my country there is nothing. Nobody is there to help, and nobody wants to help. You have to sleep and beg where you can, before the police come and beat you and move you on. You're not wanted, you're cast aside.

'For me, the choice was easy – stop the drugs, or die on the streets. So many do. I'd made some money, had lots of fun, but I'd let the fun take over. A bit like the guys who work in banks, and they all burn out. That's exactly what I did – but I landed up on the streets. And if you stay on the streets, you die on the streets.'

Rio's mind was in South London. 'You really had no one to help you? A boyfriend?'

Her answer was matter-of-fact, maybe a reflection of a hard life. 'I had a sister, but she is dead. Hepatitis from bad needles. It helped me understand I needed to get back into the big game, or I was going to join her.'

Rio didn't have an answer for that so he reverted to what he did best to try to counter any moment of perceived weakness. 'I don't think drugs are all that bad, really. I mean, they've taught an entire generation of American kids the metric system.'

She thought for a second and smiled, but not for long. 'Your arm, the legs, why are you like this? I have never seen so many people together like you.'

Rio had this covered, as all three did. I knew there wasn't going to be an in-depth analysis of how and why or anything that suggested they wanted sympathy.

'We all got fucked up in Afghanistan.'

She didn't register.

'The war, yeah? Jihadis coming from Pakistan joining the Taliban and using all that bomb-making shit they learnt at home to blow us up.'

She nodded slowly while she checked her memory banks. Why would she know instantly? It had had nothing to do with Belarus, and when the war had started she was still at school, then tucked away doing dark-web shit or off her head on the streets.

'Oh, you are soldiers?'

Rio laughed manically, to join in with Jack's more ironic attempt. 'No more. Once you've had bits of you fucked up you're out of any army. On the compost heap of life, mate.' He seized on the lull as Yulia let it all sink in. 'Anyway, back to the real world, eh? You going to get Jack's cash back, or what? You said you'd have a look and see.'

She shrugged. 'Maybe. Maybe I have to find how they move their money.'

'I know you will, and you're going to move a bit more, yeah? I think we need a bonus – and that Owl ain't going to give us one, is he?'

He looked at me and so did Yulia. Rio wanted a reaction; she wanted to ask a question. 'The Owl? Is that his name? Who is this man?'

It was my turn to shrug. 'You've been listening in since yesterday. You know as much as we do. All of us here are in the same boat.'

She didn't understand that one, but Rio was on hand. 'He means we're all the same. Like I said, we're just busy worker bees. Stick with us, Yuli, we'll sort you out good-style once we've dealt with these fuckers.'

Streetlights flickered in the back as we hit habitation

and Gabe shouted, 'I need some help here. Where the fuck am I going?'

I squeezed between the cab seats and opened the mobile on Maps.

'Loughborough Road, mate. Just north of the city centre. We're looking for Belgrave – the road cuts through it. Stay on the main drag and this'll be up in a minute.'

Like most post-industrial towns, this one had had its period of decay, but there seemed to be some regeneration going on, with new roundabouts and so many dedicated cycle lanes the locals must have had one each.

There were blue flags hanging from every other lamppost and Gabe could see my confusion. 'Nothing to do with Europe. Where the fuck you been, Nick? Football. Leicester City, they just won the Premiership?'

'Oh.'

He couldn't help himself as he shook his head in disbelief. 'And I hate English football, for fuck's sake.'

We came off the ring road, following signs to Belgrave, and drove past wall-to-wall sari and hijab shops, curry houses, Sikh temples and mosques.

Each side of us there were grid systems of two-uses, out-of-the-front-door-and-straight-onto-a-narrow-road types, lined with vehicles, just enough room left for one car at a time.

The map showed Loughborough Road was coming up. 'Here we are, mate. Chuck a left.'

He turned off onto a wider road and the terraced housing was gradually replaced by newer red-brick stock, alongside parades of old Victorian shops. We continued driving and Gabe was the first to see it. 'There you go, on the right. Every Lidl helps.'

'Keep going, up to the roundabout, and let's have a drive-past first.'

Gabe continued past the massive blue and yellow sign and then a much larger cash-and-carry, but I was checking left. The industrial estate was fronted by a 1960s rectangular brick building belonging to a construction firm. I shouted a warning into the back to wake up and get switched on.

68

We took the last exit at the roundabout, which brought us back down onto Loughborough Road, this time passing the cash-and-carry and Lidl on the left. The supermarket had closed half an hour ago so the scattering of vehicles in its car park probably belonged to staff. The construction company at the entrance to the industrial estate came up on the right.

'Gabe, mate, go past, hit the crossroads. Take a right. The road bends round and goes behind the estate.'

The thrash of windscreen wipers was soon joined by the click of indicators, but both were swamped by the hard drumming of rain on the roof as we waited at the junction. We turned right just after what looked like a stone-built Victorian school that was now a solicitor's, and the road ahead was lined with 1960s terraced homes, probably corporation housing before Thatcher sold them off.

We passed a pub and the road curved round to the right, then straightened once more, and we carried on with what looked like park railings on the left. I spotted warnings for traffic cameras ahead and then we were directly opposite the rear entrance to the industrial estate. 'Mate, stop here – no yellow lines.'

I leant back into the van and kept the tone low. 'The estate is over there.' I pointed. 'Behind us is a pub. Nobody's going to be out and about in this shit, but keep the noise down just in case.' I checked my door was locked and so did Gabe on his side. Jack got the hint and did the same to the rear doors. I unplugged the mobile and held it behind me for Rio to take and get online for Jack to start texting.

Yulia wanted more. 'Do you see any communication masts out there?'

I peered through the windscreen but it was a waste of time. I didn't need to tell Yulia: she was already tapping away. In the glow of the screen I saw her shoot an accusing glare at Rio. He backed away. 'All right, no need to chuck one.'

Yulia adjusted the laptop to make sure no one could see into her secret world, and was immediately busy. Her eyes were glued to the screen. 'Jack, text Gail. Tell her you're thinking about her and wanted to tell her so. It's her morning time, say sorry if you woke her.'

Jack got going, and Yulia supplied a running commentary.

'She's going to come back and say she's been doing the same – in reality they're working out whether you went cold last night because they asked for bank details. If they didn't hear anything for a couple of days they would cut you off and start again with someone else – or maybe even with you, with Plan C.'

'Gail's back. No problem, she was awake anyway, she can't sleep as she's been thinking about me.'

Yulia had been spot on. 'Okay, keep dialogue. Whatever you want, as long as you tell her you'll send her the bank details when you get home tonight. And thank her for her honesty in wanting to be straight about her experiences online. Tell her you've had really bad experiences, too. Open up to her. Okay? You're on your own for a couple of minutes – I've got to do this.'

Jack sent and answered texts, and Yulia typed, stopped, sighed, frowned, sighed again, typed again. The glow of the screen illuminated a face that wasn't showing progress.

Rio began to lean over to her but thought better of it. 'Can't find them? I thought that dark-web shit of yours held all the world's secrets.'

She breathed out and her chin sank to her chest, ignoring the challenge to her capabilities. 'They want money. The arseholes want money. I've helped them so many times.' She banged away at the keys. 'Fuckers.'

Gabe leant over to me, his eyes still diligently on the windscreen. 'Market forces, eh?'

Yulia muttered to herself in Russian, which translated into exactly what she'd said in English. They were all fuckers, and after all she'd done for them . . .

She stopped, looked up, then gave a heavy sigh. She carried on banging the keys in response to what was happening on the screen, and she wasn't happy not leading the dance.

Jack was in his own world, texting like he still believed in the fairy tale, but Rio was more grounded.

'If you can't find them can you just get hold of cash, Yulia? Can you get some now for all of us?'

Knees up, she slouched forward to cover the screen, sandwiching the laptop between thighs and chest, her elbows so far back they almost touched the panel behind her. I wasn't sure if she had even heard Rio. For several long seconds, only her fingers and eyes were moving, but she finally opened her mouth. 'I'm giving them codes that access the *Wall Street Journal* and the *Washington Post*. These guys are fringe – they don't care what they do, they just want to bring everything down. They're no longer my friends.' She hit the final key hard and pushed the laptop away. 'Fuckers!'

She closed the lid and turned to Jack as our world went dark.

'You're going to receive a text. Once it's arrived, I'll send them the second download.'

Jack twisted his phone to show her the screen. 'Is this it?'

She didn't answer, but reopened the laptop. 'Jack, you need to reply and tell Gail it's late. You've got to get home.'

She opened Google Maps so we could all see, but there was no pin. She stared at it and once again spat, 'Fuckers!'

Her fingers flew over the keys and she pressed send. The second set of access codes was on its way.

A couple of seconds later a pin popped up on the screen. 'There. That's where they are.'

Gabe clenched his fists. 'Right, let's get these fuckers.'

I shook my head. 'I'm with you, mate – but first

things first.' I looked around the group. 'We've got to find out exactly where they are – which building, which rooms. Then we've got to work out how to get in there, how to contain them and keep that place safe for us all while Yulia does her stuff to get Jack's money back. Remember, we're here for the cash and to stop them fucking anyone else up, nothing more.

'I'll go in and do a recce. Let's see if security pour out or the police turn up to check out an industrial-estate lurker.'

Jack couldn't suppress a grin as I threw my neck wallet at him to hold onto with the mobile he already had. 'Drawing fire again?'

'It's all I seem to do for you lot.'

It got its intended laugh.

'Okay, Yulia, keep the map open and pass over the laptop, while I give you lot the ERV for if I fuck up or you have to move.'

69

Sterile of anything that could identify me, and pockets empty of my two remaining pound coins and anything else that could make noise, I moved across the road and to the right of the rear entrance to the industrial estate. Rain came down like spears, and my new hoodie soon weighed heavy on my head.

The team had pooled their cash. They would be needing fuel if I fucked up and didn't make the ERV tomorrow, or they had to move because they felt they'd been compromised or I wasn't back with them in forty-five minutes.

The ERV was outside the cathedral at midday. I'd never been to Leicester, I didn't know what it was like, but it was a city and by definition it had to have a cathedral, and cathedrals had to be accessible. If I was a no-show they had to consider themselves on their own, go back to the barn and sort themselves out as best they could.

In a perfect world, Yulia would have been at my side

for the recce. People make instant decisions on what others are doing if it conforms to their norms. We all do it to make sure we're safe when we see other people in our space. So, a man and a woman in the rain in an area of isolation at night means only one thing, so is not a threat. In any event, there was housing, which might be accessible from within the estate and might help us to look the part.

That said, Yulia had to be protected so I was doing this on my own. The best way was just to get on with it and use the rain for what it was: cover. I needed a reason to be there and it was simple. This wasn't private land, there were houses nearby, and I was heading to one. Once I had a plan I would stick to it and act like anyone else going home after a night on the piss. The more you think about these things, the longer it takes, so there's more chance of compromise – and trying to blend in becomes the focus rather than what you're on the ground to do.

The first building I came to on the right housed a wrought-iron works, and directly across the road from it there was a double-glazing company.

I carried pictures of the estate's layout in my head after I had street-walked through as much of the area around the pin as I could, then studied the 3D view. The Google Maps van might have done its filming years ago, but the road layout wouldn't have changed.

I looked further down into the estate, towards where Lidl would be, to where a ring of dull yellow security lighting glistened in the rain. My hair was plastered to my face now the hoodie had given up, and my jeans clung to my legs like long-lost friends.

I moved on about twenty paces, hugging the wrought-iron factory until I was at a junction to my left. A couple of skips, overflowing with lumps and lengths of scrap plastic and metal from the double-glazers, stood on the corner.

I checked down the road that Google Street View had told me would have a row of terraced houses further down on the left, part of the area that the industrial estate had gobbled up as it expanded. Opposite them, on the other side of the road, was where the pin had dropped, and I saw rows of roller shutters accompanied by business signage identifying each unit, all set in a flat-roofed brick building that ran along most of that side of the road. There were no vehicles parked in front of any shutters or any light coming from windows set on the ground floor. On the left, curtains held most of it inside.

The only thing we'd learnt about the target was where the pin hit the map. The perfect recce to find out more would have asked a lot of questions. Was there physical security and, if so, were they young or old? Did they look switched on? Were they armed? If so, what with? If there was technical security, where were the devices, and were they powered up?

The best way of finding answers was just to observe the target for as long as possible. Some questions can be answered on site, but many only pop up once you're tucked up with a cup of cocoa and trying to come up with a plan. The longer you stayed there, the more information would sink into your unconscious for you to drag out later if you needed it. But that wasn't going to happen tonight. This was what was known in the trade as a smash-and-grab. Find the target, get in there, and react to the situation in front of you to get the job done and be out of the target area before anyone could even think about what had just happened. After all, if everything could be done with calm, control and a considered plan, what was the point of the SAS . . . or even the SNS? Who dares wins, right?

'I carried on and encountered a high fence and a gate that held the yellow island of light. The area beyond the security was an illuminated yard full of skips, trucks and stacks of shrink-wrapped bricks. It was the rear of the construction company that fronted onto Loughborough Road.

Immediately to my right there was more of the yard, and beyond that the line of 1960s terraced houses I had seen before the pub at the curve in the road. What I was interested in, however, lay in the other direction. The fence-line continued, protecting the goods in the yard to its right. The gap between the fence and the rear of the shuttered building that the pin had marked was an alley, tarmacked and just wide enough to take a van.

The rectangular two-storey lump of brick ran the full length of it, paralleling the fence, and the mapping had told me it was a dead end. I couldn't see any light at the front so the rear needed to be checked out.

Rain kept pummelling as I followed the alley. If anything, it was coming down harder. There were enough paddling pools on the tarmac to show where the drainage had died long ago. I could hear the faint drone of vehicles along Loughborough Road, maybe three hundred away on the other side of the security lighting to my right.

The rear of all the individual business units had two flights of steel fire-escape stairs leading to a second-floor escape door. A ladder fixed to the wall went up onto the flat roof, with safety hoops at intervals. The rear of the target building had windows on the top floor only, instead of on the lower level at the front. They were offset to the right of the fire-escape door, and therefore hard to get to. Even so, some were boarded up with metal anti-vandal sheeting, but all were dark.

Maybe two-thirds down the alleyway, looking, stopping, listening, I came level with the rear of a Ford Galaxy, nosy-parked under the final flight of a fire escape. I stood still, watched and listened, but there was no movement, no sounds. I opened my jaw a little, trying to pick up any noise from the houses, but heard nothing.

I wiped the rain from the passenger window, and had a good look inside. The first thing I saw, dangling from the rear-view, was a 786 pendant made out of a CD. These could be found all over India, Pakistan and, of course, Afghanistan – especially in vehicles. Preceding almost every chapter in the Koran were the words: *In the name of God, the most gracious, the most merciful.* The Arabic alphabet had numerical equivalents, and if you changed those words into their numerical equivalents, it added up to 786.

The distant traffic on Loughborough Road came back, fighting for air time over the rain. It was time to check out the possible. I placed my boot on the first step, as close as I could get to the wall supporting the fire escape to cut down on structural movement while

I checked there was nothing set as an alarm. Fishing line attached to hidden cans, infra-red, even motion-detection cameras. A trip to Maplin could buy you a lot of early warning.

It was like treading on ice, gently testing each step for creaks, always placing my feet to the inside edge, slowly and precisely, but I reached the steel-mesh landing and got up to the fire door. It was wooden-framed, but there'd been a partial repair with a steel sheet and nails. To the right of the doors, and beyond the landing's railings, were the unit's two windows. They weren't protected with steel anti-vandal sheeting but they were guarding the light inside the building. I could make out a tiny sliver penetrating through the gap of the drawn blinds.

I put my ear to the metal. Maybe I could work out how many were inside. A Galaxy carried a lot of bodies.

The faint sound of music came through with a constant beat, but no voices. I tried leaning over the rail to get a view through the narrowest of gaps between the window frame and blind, but without success. I balanced my waist against the railing and tilted forward over it to get a different angle of view. I finally had my boots off the steel and struggled to keep my balance, my not-so-functioning hands gripping the rail for all they were worth. What I saw wasn't much, but it was enough. No bodies, but a partial view of a table, deeper into the space, with three mobiles laid out in a line, their power cables trailing away from them, and a small stack of paper beneath each mobile.

Bringing myself slowly back onto the landing, I

carefully climbed up the ladder to the roof. Maybe there was a vent up there or a skylight for a better view, or even to make entry through. But as I got my head level with the flat roof, all I saw were more and larger pools of water than there had been in the alley. These 1960s buildings were thrown up cheap and not so cheerful.

It was time to get back to the team.

Once on the ground, I walked to the top of the alley and turned right – but I didn't go directly back. There was one slight detour. When I reached the shadow of the wrought-iron works, I crossed the road to the double-glazing skip and spent a couple of minutes picking out four of the biggest lumps of scrap metal I could find, tubular steel a foot or two long and about two inches square, then headed back to the van.

70

Half an hour later, with the team briefed on how the smash-and-grab needed to happen, we exited the van in the pounding rain and watched Gabe place the keys under the driver's seat with the rest of our gear to make sure we were sterile. Then, fuck it, we needed to get a move on.

I led the others into the estate, following exactly the same route I'd taken on the CTR. There was no tactical point in doing anything but heading for the target. Everyone had a job to do and everyone was in his or her own world now, just wanting to get on with it.

We passed the Galaxy and gathered under the steel stairs, which almost vibrated under the onslaught of rain.

I spoke in a voice so low the deluge almost drowned it. 'Yulia, you know what to do. Jack, immediately behind her. Yulia, remember, soon as Jack starts, get out of the way, just as I told you, until somebody tells you to come in. Yeah?'

She nodded, not too happily, as she brought her hands up to her chest with crossed wrists, as if that would protect her.

'Rio and Gabe, do your stuff, then back me. Rio, nobody in, nobody out. Remember, this is all about speed, aggression and surprise. Just take my steps on the way up, closest to the wall.'

They'd been pumped up and ready to go from the moment I'd outlined my plan.

I started to move, then stopped. They were maybe a little too pumped-up. 'Lads, one last thing. This is Leicester, not Libya. Keep a lid on it – control, yeah? It's the money and stopping these fuckers that's important.'

I set off up the fire escape with them close behind. A minute later I was at the door and Yulia came up next to me to take her position. Rain dripped down our faces as I spoke into her ear. 'You'll have to be loud. The door's thick, and they have music on – listen.'

As I left her she put an ear to the door and Jack raised his steel rod horizontally above her head, totally prepared, totally focused. He knew he had only one shot.

I carried on down past Gabe and Rio, both pressed hard against the wall behind Jack, and took up my position.

Last man in the line, first man through the door.

I knew that Yulia would now be looking back down the line through the rain, just as she had been told.

She was waiting for the thumbs-up from me, and she got it.

71

'Help! Help! Please help me!'

Yulia was going for an Oscar. She slammed her palm against the door, then tried the same plea for help, but this time in Russian.

There wasn't a reply, let alone an opening door.

She wasn't going to give up. They'd have to open soon just to get whoever it was to shut up.

'Help! Please! Help!' she screamed, against the door-jamb, forcing the sound through.

Finally the door cracked open a few millimetres and light spilt out into the rain. It opened a bit more to reveal a safety chain midway. That didn't matter to Jack. He rammed the steel into the gap before the face the other side had the chance to process what was happening. Yulia had done exactly what was required of her and moved back to the top of the stairs as Gabe and Rio ran hard at the door. Soon three hands were pulling at the structure, trying to wrench the chain off its mountings.

Jack improvised: he jumped to the side and levered

the steel against the door to help. It was my cue to move forward as the three grunted with each heave. As the wood creaked and the steel of the chain pulled tight I jerked my head left and right, up and down, trying to get a view of what I was going to run into. All I could see and smell was a solid haze of cigarette smoke.

There were shouts from two, maybe three bodies inside. Urdu, Punjabi, I didn't know. It didn't matter.

The chain's screws finally flew out of the frame and the door burst open, sending me charging and screaming into what I immediately took in as a large open-plan space.

'Stand still! Stand still! Stand still!'

There was a body to the right of me and it was moving. I bent down and spun round with my steel bar. It connected with a shin. I heard the thud and felt the crunch. Whoever it was, he collapsed in screams behind me as I carried on towards the other two targets, yelling at the top of my lungs, acting as a human flash-bang to add to the speed, aggression and surprise.

'Stand still! Stand still! Stand still!'

There were two trestle tables between us, and behind them, a door. On the tables sat maybe a dozen mobiles, each with a charging cable snaking off down to an extension lead on the floor. On the table, beneath each mobile, A4 sheets were neatly stacked.

The two targets stood their ground in the haze. Why didn't they run?

'Hands up! Hands! Hands!'

I waved the steel rod at them as I came round the other side of the tables to front them. They exchanged a scared glance, looked back at me, then at the mess I had left writhing on the floor. Both his hands now gripped his left shin. His grey tracksuit bottoms on that side were soaked with blood below the knee. It must have been fractured. I didn't give a fuck. I had to make sure I asserted control in the room and got these two geared up to the fact that if they didn't do precisely what I said they'd be getting some of the same.

I was right in their faces now. 'Stay where you are! Show me your hands! Hands up!'

I shouted behind me, 'Gabe, take control of these two. I'll check the other side of the door. Jack on me.'

I burst through it and into a corridor, not waiting for Jack. I knew he'd soon be there to cover me. The corridor was lit by two fluorescent lights, and there was another door ahead, outwards opening. I yanked it back. It was a toilet: one brush, a bottle of Toilet Duck, no window.

An ornamental garden gate and matching fencing either side, chained up and padlocked twice, blocked the end of the corridor. Downstairs had nothing to do with upstairs, for sure, and vice versa.

I ran back to the large room and into the haze. Add that to the bare walls and fluorescent lighting and the space was straight out of a 1970s office drama, even if the technology on display was not. The eighteen-inch HP laptop on another table against a wall looked new. The impression might have been of some ramshackle command and control centre, but it worked, as Jack's empty bank account testified.

Gabe had moved the two standers next to the guy I'd dropped. They were on their arses, their hands in the air.

'No English! No English!'

Gabe wasn't buying it. He bore down on them with his lump of steel. 'Shut the fuck up! We want our fucking money back!'

All three were maybe early to mid-thirties and overweight, two bald, one with a long beard. Their stomachs strained against their shirts.

'No English! No English!'

Gabe slammed his bar into the upper arm of the one nearest him. 'You'd better fucking learn some quick, then! We want our money back! Give us the money! You fucking speak English. Give us the money.'

Yulia was already sitting in a worn wooden dining chair and hitting the laptop's keys.

72

After the initial burst of excitement and mayhem, things were settling down. All I could hear was begging and sobbing, and the rattle of computer keys. Rio was outside the fire-escape door. The best way to protect us was beyond us – or the first we'd know of any drama heading our way was when it came bursting in.

I became aware of the faint sound of music and traced it to a little CD player off to the left. They must have turned the volume down when they heard the mad woman banging on the door.

Jack picked up one of the mobiles. 'This is me!' The name of each victim had been Sharpied onto silver duct tape and stuck to the trestle table beneath the phone. The paperwork was the play sheets, A4 printouts that were curling at the edges and stained with mug rings. I could imagine the fat fucks sitting back with a coffee and a cigarette as they texted messages of love to their victims. Two Costa cups overflowed with butts.

Jack went to read his play sheet.

'Mate, don't worry about that. It'll only get you sparked up. That's history now. Don't go back to it, all right? We'll take all these mobiles and the laptop. Make sure they can't fuck over anyone else. First, let's see if she can get the money.'

But he couldn't resist looking down at his love life, which had been reduced to a couple of sheets of A4, a series of boxes ticked off as they went down the list in readiness for the next part of the rip-off. He shook his head again. 'They were going to go for the new bank account.'

'Mate, bin it. Just get a grip of what we need to do. We've got to keep focused. We—'

We both spun round as three screams came in quick succession. Gabe rained down a flurry of blows. 'Money! We want the fucking money! Where's the money?'

The begging and sounds of pain were overboard. Of course it was hurting them, but Gabe was exercising restraint. If he'd brought his weapon down with real intent they would never have screamed again.

They carried on with the don't-speak-English thing but their eyes swivelled calculatingly between Gabe and Yulia, who had her back to them on the wooden chair as she continued to tap away.

Jack had found himself a bin-liner and was busy disconnecting the mobiles from their chargers and throwing them inside. Yulia stopped tapping and sat back, deep in thought, her elbows on the arms of the chair and her fingers together on her chin.

'You found something?'

Gabe shouted over the tables, not that it was needed, 'You got the money?'

She nodded very slowly, still staring at the screen as I went and stood next to her, bending down to look at what she had found. The screen was empty, just a solid wall of light blue.

'Yes, I found it. I know where they have sent it. '

She didn't sound as excited as I'd thought she might. She leant forward and hit a command.

A video hit the screen: loud, stirring Arabic music as bodies dressed in black paraded with weapons and jumped over burning tyres. A small black flag with Arabic lettering fluttered in the wind, top right of the screen. Then, dubbed in a northern English accent, a very angry and very young lad told the youth of the UK to join the jihad and attack whatever and whoever they could.

And, of course, to send donations.

She turned down the volume and the three held by Gabe had gone just as quiet.

'This is all about terrorism, Nick. This is all about funding ISIS. They're scamming for ISIS.'

Jack dropped the bin-liner and picked up his weapon, taking strides towards Gabe. 'Did you hear that? Did you hear where my money's gone? I'm bankrolling fucking jihadis! I'm paying for IEDs to blow legs off!'

Gabe looked stunned. He leant down and lifted the hem of his jeans to expose his prosthetic to the three lads. 'This was from fighting, you fucks.'

As one, they burst out laughing.

And then, finally, the English flowed. 'Fuck you! Fuck you, *kafir*!'

Gabe didn't need any further invitation. He let go of his jeans as Jack took the final step and thumped his weapon hard on the nearest of the three, getting him on the side of the trunk, right over the kidney. I heard the solid thwack from several metres away and then the gasp of agony as he went down.

The other two went straight into Islamist mode. *'Allahu Akbar! Allahu Akbar!'*

They stared up at Gabe defiantly, preparing for death, willing him to bring that bar down on their heads. He looked as if he was about to oblige. I had to get a grip. 'Stop! Don't kill them! Fuck them up but don't kill them! Leicester, not Libya, lads. They're better alive – information! We find a way to hand them over to get more of the fuckers!'

I let that sink in for a couple of seconds.

'Let's pack the kit, then get them and it into the van.'

The bodies on the floor restarted their chorus. *'Kafir! Kafir!'*

It might have been the biggest insult a Muslim could hurl at anybody, but it was water off a duck's back to those two. They'd had enough of it in Afghanistan to last a lifetime.

Gabe and Jack exchanged a look of agreement with me but still wanted at least to fuck them up. They turned and brought down the steel rods on their collar-bones to turn their chanting back into sobs. Why not? I wasn't going to try to stop them because it just wouldn't happen. They were in their own zones, their own personal battle spaces, thinking about their own fucked-up bodies and the mates who were no longer with them. I turned up the music to block out the screams for Yulia.

I continued to gather up the evidence and throw it into the bin-liner as Yulia continued to stare at the wall of light blue, not wanting to turn round.

'Get all the plugs and leads out, Yulia. We're taking it with us, yeah?'

She nodded, but she looked as if she was going to faint.

Gabe and Jack took a moment now, standing over the blood-soaked bodies on the floor. They were breathing; there was movement from two, anyway.

'Right, we're ready.'

I shoved the bag to Yulia and she gathered up the laptop and placed it with the mobiles. 'Look at me, Yulia. Keep looking at me. Just close your eyes and I'll take you to the door, okay?'

As I started to lead her, Rio burst through the fire-escape door. 'We got drama! Two vehicles coming down the alley!'

The fattest of the three turned his bloodied head towards us, suddenly all smiles and very happy. He started hollering, with blood spraying out of his swollen mouth.

'*Allahu Akbar! Allahu Akbar! Allahu Akbar!*'

73

I leapt down the stairs, stumbling and skidding as my feet landed on wet metal. Speed and aggression were our only help now that we had lost surprise. I had to take the fight to them, to draw the fire so Rio and Yulia could get away with the kit. She and that laptop were now as important as each other; both had to be got to the Owl, and that meant I had to get to the vehicles before they could stop and unload their bodies.

I needed to do my very best, with whatever I was about to get into the fight with, to give Gabe and Jack the chance to catch up and also start fighting like dogs. Those two would be bringing something else to the party, too. They would bring anger and a thirst for vengeance. There was more than enough of that behind me to compensate for the lack of legs.

I could hear their pounding boots above me, even over the thunder of rain on the fire-escape landings and the roofs of the vehicles below. I jumped the last half-flight and crashed into a deep puddle next to the

Galaxy. Weapon up, no time to think, I ran straight at the first vehicle's headlights as it rolled to a stop. They would have seen us by now and this was happening whether they liked it or not – whether we liked it or not. The only way out of a corner, mentally or physically, is to fight.

The vehicle pulled in behind the Galaxy as I closed. The other was still on the move, its lights bouncing up and down on the uneven alley, strobing the rain as it cut through the paddling pools and threw up mini tidal waves.

My eyes were fixed on the passenger door and it was just starting to open. Nothing else mattered: what was happening behind me, what was happening to my half-right with the other car. Just one target at a time. And after that get on to the next before they had time to react or even to breathe.

With my last stride I flung my body against the door and it slammed shut. He hadn't even got a leg out. I stepped back and swung the lump of steel against the glass like a baseball bat. It shattered into a thousand fragments.

I yanked the bar back but this time, instead of bringing it down in a swinging action, I used it like a knife and stabbed it through the shattered window into the side of a head. I stabbed again and connected again, but it was the third blow that did the damage. It caught him in the neck and blood gushed like a burst water main. He was fucked. He was leaving the fight.

Gabe and Jack shot past me on their way to the other vehicle, which had now stopped. I ran round to the driver's side of my vehicle. The door was opening. In the headlights behind I could see it was an MG saloon, and the driver was trying to break the world record for a vehicle decamp. He knew it was that or he was going to be joining his mate. He took one look at me and changed direction, now leaning across the central console to try to get out over the passenger.

I ran back to the passenger side and lunged in through the smashed-out window frame, grabbing his arm with my left hand and heaving him towards me over the mess that was now collapsed in the passenger seat. With the same stabbing motion I brought the steel into the top of his head. He fell forward onto the other body and I took my weapon as high as I could in the roof space and chopped hard into the back of his skull. Bone crunched and, moments later, his very long beard glistened in the headlights behind as blood and grey matter cascaded from his brain cavity.

As I pushed myself out of the window frame I cut my hand on the remaining glass. I heard more pounding feet and turned to see Rio and Yulia coming past the Galaxy. Rio was in front, his good arm around her, pushing her head into his chest as he worked at averting her gaze. 'Keep looking away! Keep going! We're going to turn right! All good, mate, all good.'

They hurried past me, Rio concentrating on her as she clutched the black bin-liner to her chest.

I was already at the second vehicle. There was a body on the ground behind it and I could see a couple of big shapes bearing down on it. It had to be one of the team. I caught a glimpse of prosthetic and heard a familiar growl. Gabe was taking the pain. Jack was virtually inside the vehicle. I could hear his screams – good or bad, I couldn't tell.

All I could do was charge at these shapes, aiming for the head, aiming for the face.

I took the three paces towards them, brandishing my steel like a claymore. I closed in, ignoring the one further back. The one I wanted was closest, his hand reaching inside his jacket. His face didn't register surprise or fear, just anger, and then he raised a knife.

My eyes were fixed on his face as I swung the steel downwards, and the point of contact was just above the cheekbone. His skin folded over below his eye, then split open. He fell with a scream, his body banging against my legs on the way down.

I heard, rather than saw, the dark shape from the right that was almost on top of me. Not bothering to turn and look, I lashed out wildly. The steel hammered against his skull twice, both times with such force that my arm jarred to a halt. I continued to rain blows onto the top of his head as he went down. Somewhere in the back of my mind I knew I'd lost it, but I didn't care. I was remembering the way, seconds ago, this fucker had been trying to kill my friend.

Three more times. There was a crunching, cracking sound as his skull gave way.

I raised my hand, ready to hit again, but stopped myself. I'd done enough. Thick blood oozed from his head wounds. He had lost function in his eyes and had a vacant stare, wide open and dull, pupils fully dilated. The blood spread beneath him, joining the puddles.

I turned to check the first guy. The knife was on the ground, and so was he, curled up, holding his face and moaning to himself. His legs flailed weakly.

Gulping air, trying to re-oxygenate, I didn't immediately see the one coming from behind me, but I took a swing. He jumped out of the way and swayed on his feet, another big guy. 'Fuck you, *kafir*! Fuck you!'

Jack materialized behind him and brought down his steel with both hands to force it into the back of his head. The crack resonated round the alley and he fell. No way would he have survived a hit like that.

We had bodies on the ground, some still moving, but they were no longer a threat.

'Come on, let's go! Let's go!'

I grabbed hold of Gabe with an outstretched arm to drag him out of the large puddle he was lying in, only for him to pick up his weapon and start beating the body nearest him. 'Fucking arsehole!'

'Mate, we've gotta go! That one's dead. There's no movement in the cars. This one, mate, you finished him. We've gotta go.'

Gabe stood there.

Jack did the same.

Neither moved, heavy rain falling from their faces and rinsing the blood from their weapons as they just stared down at the bodies about them. We needed to move.

'Lads, the agreement, one voice. Come on – Rio and Yulia, in case they're in the shit. We've got to make sure they're okay.'

The thing about command and control is that once you're fighting for your life, your senses narrow down to confront what is immediately in front of you. There can't be total control. The secret is to make sure control is regained once the fight has been won or you're losing it and need to get out of danger.

Both of them knew it, and Jack was the first to stir and follow me. He passed Gabe, who gave him an almost pastoral tweak of the face as he also turned and joined us. We ran as fast as we could with only four legs between us.

74

We could only move at the speed of the slowest man, and in this particular exfil it was Gabe. He'd taken a battering and was limping even more than usual.

As we hugged the wrought-iron works on our left and the van came into sight, there was still no sound of engines behind us or thunder of footsteps. I doubted anyone left behind was capable.

We came into the middle of the road to make sure Rio saw us and the engine was gunning as we crossed. As Gabe and Jack clambered into the back I ran up to Rio's window. 'Mate, I'll drive – both hands.'

He got that, and we swapped as I sucked a chunk of MG window out of the web of my right hand – it was catching on everything I gripped. My jeans stuck to me as I climbed into the driver's seat, soaked with rain and blood. My face was drenched with sweat and the down-pour that hammered into the van's roof.

As I threw the vehicle around in a three-point turn to get us heading back to the crossroads, I could hear heavy breathing behind me and the clunk of steel as weapons went onto the floor. There was a lot of sniffing and the noises of people generally sorting themselves out, but one thing there wasn't was celebration. We all knew we still had a lot to do.

I jerked my head round while feeling for our kit under my seat. We'd sort that out once we were safe. 'Rio, we got the laptop?'

'Yeah. And the phones.'

'Yulia?'

'What?'

'That's all I need to know.'

As we reached the left-hand bend with the pub on the right, I had to swerve hard over and bounce up onto the pavement as vehicle headlights in fast convoy cut the corner.

Everyone sparked up in the back as they took the bouncing of the van. 'What the fuck!'

I counted them past. 'We've got three vehicles. Hold on, we're going for it.'

The van rolled off to the left as it came off the pavement and I put my foot down. I looked in the mirror and saw a red haze of brake lights, then white as the first vehicle spun round.

I put my foot to the boards as Rio powered down the window and stuck his head out, his hand gripping the seat, trying to get a view behind.

'They're coming!'

I kept my foot down all the way to the lights, then hit the brakes hard. Rio was flung against the front of the window frame he was half hanging out of. The lights were telling me to wait but I strained my neck both ways and swung the wheel left.

The windscreen wipers were going mad; the rain hammered on the roof; the tyres roared on the road. I had to holler at the top of my voice. 'Listen in!' The gears crunched their way up. 'We need somewhere dark to lose them or we have to take them on. Stand by for the fight.'

Rio was still hanging out of the window, his face getting pebble-dashed with rain. 'I've got lights coming up to the junction.'

I put my foot down and screamed past Lidl in search of darkness. Gabe had wedged himself between the two front seats. I could see forward in the middle distance the other side of the roundabout. It was more habitation. I looked half right, the other side of the cash-and-carry, and spotted inky blackness. Once in it I would keep moving.

Just to the left of the cash-and-carry, a minor junction.

I hit the brakes and swung the van across the road, dousing the lights.

Rio shouted, making sure we all knew, 'They're turning! They saw us turn!'

Fuck it. Changing up a gear, I passed the cash-and-carry on the right, its security lighting giving me some help, and all of a sudden I saw what I didn't want to see. I braked so hard Gabe shot forward.

'Dead end!'

A barrier closed the road and behind it were piles of earth, mattresses and mountains of fly-tipped shit. I kept braking but the Peugeot's pads had given up the ghost on gripping their discs.

'Stand by for the fight!'

The wagon shuddered and broke into a skid.

I fought the controls and we came to a halt no more than a centimetre from the barrier. My right hand was already on the door and my left gripped my weapon.

'Let's fuck 'em up!'

I went to pull the handle but it was pushed from my grasp by an invisible force. There had been a massive shudder like we'd been torpedoed, then the deafening squeal of twisting steel. The van was hurled into the barrier by whatever had rammed us from behind and my head catapulted into the windscreen.

My world blurred. I saw flashes and starbursts.

I slumped into the footwell against Rio's legs. The poor fucker was still hanging out of the window.

I heard the screech of brakes, and now my world slowed into a kaleidoscope of shouts, lights and voices coming at me from every direction.

My door was wrenched open and as unseen hands grabbed at my jeans and dragged me out onto a carpet of stones and twigs and empty Coke cans, our passports tumbled from the cab onto my face. The Mac bounced off my chest and onto the tarmac.

Bodies criss-crossed frenziedly in front of headlights, and boots splashed in water. I instinctively tried to flip over to lie face down. But from nowhere, a pair of hands gripped me and flung me onto my back once more. Someone aimed a kick into my side. As I looked up I could see a silhouette in the headlights, and the silhouette had dark brown bushy hair. Expecting more, I curled up, and another kick came. I tried to move my head out of the way but Mrs Bland got me in the side of the face with her boot, exactly where Phoenix had punched me.

Starbursts did their best to black me out as pain scorched through my body. I could feel myself losing it, and I really couldn't let that happen. I worked hard to keep my eyes open. I was a bag of shit, but I knew I had to pull myself together if I had any chance of getting away with Yulia.

My jaw joint was grinding on itself – it felt dislocated. I probed with my tongue and discovered one of my teeth moving as a numb, swollen feeling developed on the right side of my face. I felt like I'd just had a session with a psychopathic dentist. I could hear other people dragging other bodies around, and then she was close to my ear. 'Fuck you, Stone.'

It was her parting shot. As suddenly as she had appeared, she was gone.

Okay, not so bad: I was still breathing, I was winning, but my celebration was cut short. On the tarmac, near my head somewhere, the mobile vibrated.

Two seconds later, the bottom of a raincoat came into my view, a three-quarter-length number with a thin fleece lining under a nylon shell, just the sort a mattress salesman would buy from Marks & Sparks because it was practical for this time of year: light yet protective, as the sleeve tag would no doubt have said when he bought it.

I didn't even bother looking up as more hands grabbed hold of me and dragged me back to one of the vehicles.

75

11.56 Thursday, 2 June

I was sitting at the same table, beneath the same picture. The People's Princess was looking down at me, probably wondering why it was taking so long for me to be served. I knew I was.

Nothing much had changed in the last month. The clientele was still the same plug-in-and-glug crowd, though today their *Metro*s and *Standard*s almost vibrated with excitement and anger all rolled into one about Brexit. It didn't matter to me: I'd be in Moscow or Zürich, sorting out that shit. The three lads had chipped in to fly and house me while I was away because that was what mates do.

The same jet-black curly-haired woman was running around with a serving apron full of notebooks and a card reader and was definitely ignoring me. Maybe she hadn't been too impressed by the tip last visit. Or maybe it was the state of my face after being rammed into a metal barrier, then Mr and Mrs Bland making merry.

I laughed to myself. But not too much: I was trying to stop the newly formed flesh on my lips splitting like Rio's had on Bodmin Moor.

The black-haired one should have seen the state of me three weeks ago. I wouldn't even have made it into the café because a concerned third party would have called the police. At least now the wounds were starting to scab up and I didn't look like I'd done a runner from an operating table.

I'd received the call from Mrs Bland last night to say the Owl wanted to meet me at midday, and that I had to be on time. He had only thirty minutes to spare – what for and what it meant wasn't explained. At least there was some movement. The only time I'd seen him since we were lifted was just over two weeks ago. He had put all four of us into an MPV and personally driven us to Brandon railway station before letting us loose on society once more.

It had been painful. Once they'd dragged us all out of the van in Leicester we were poured into the footwells of the team's vehicles and driven to Lakenheath, a USAF base in Suffolk, about a hundred miles east.

I was shoved into the back of the same one as Rio, who was in so much trouble with his back he had to grit his teeth and breathe through the pain every time the 4x4 lurched in a pothole or swung round a corner for the two hours it took. I muttered to him not to worry, but the moment we sailed unchallenged past the front gate of the USAF base, with its floodlights and uniforms and red and white flashing lights along the barrier, I knew we were fucked.

I was fully expecting us to be flown straight out of the UK to a black site somewhere either very hot or very cold, and then get gripped, but that didn't happen.

We were individually isolated on the airbase's medical wing, and it was there that we were treated for our damage, yet simultaneously exposed to what the military like to call TQ, tactical questioning. It was a euphemism, a bit like bombing a wedding party and calling it collateral damage.

Mr and Mrs Bland wanted to know the whole story, every single thing that had happened from the moment I'd left this café last time until she'd started kicking me. And not only what had happened, but also why. They were easy enough questions to answer, because there wasn't anything to hide. I wanted them to know every single detail so they could clean up behind us as fast as they could. Loose ends were going to affect our safety and the safety of the third party. They needed to lift the Vectors out of their hide. It might be a bunch of kids out playing who landed up zapping each other.

76

I had no worries about the other three giving away the location of their individual memory sticks. No one knew where each other's was, and no one knew anyone else's pass statement to Claudia. If just one of us held out, that would be enough to ensure the Owl couldn't clean up the mess.

But it was academic. I knew the team wouldn't let each other down. Not now, not ever. They were mates: that was what they did. If that hadn't been so, none of us would have been breathing. Just to make sure it continued, I called Claudia from the first phone I could find, which took for ever, and told her to reinstate the pass statements for the other three. I just hoped Rio and Gabe could remember them.

Of course, no one told me explicitly whether it was just the memory sticks keeping us alive, or that we had delivered Yulia, or that we had compromised an ISIS fundraising group. Maybe a combination of all three. It really didn't matter. We were still breathing, so we were still winning. For now, at least – but we were still loose ends.

I wasn't too sure what to think about this meeting so I told Rio, who was still putting me up in Tulse Hill. We then called Jack and Gabe, who were staying at Jack's, knowing full well that the Owl would be listening in. Jack and Rio had been proved right – the barn had been rigged up. The Owl explained during the road trip to Brandon how he had placed a technical attack on the barn first, then Rio's house was next. It just so happened we'd compromised that one, or they would have gone on to bug Gabe's hotel. That made sense. The hotel would have been the last attack because it was the easiest – but at the same time the easiest to be compromised.

His plan for using us to lift Yulia, the Owl explained, was simple. He knew FSB were recceing for a technical attack on Nigella. He also knew that Phoenix and his South Africa-based team were supporting Yulia on the recce. His only problem was that he couldn't do anything about it. The job was too sensitive even for him to pour oil over it as he would normally have done. He wasn't sure how to stop it without the real world's intelligence agencies finding out or, even worse, their politicians.

Fucking about on the ice, where there was no one to witness what was happening, was one thing, but in the UK? When he discovered I wanted to meet up with him and make a deal, his problems were solved. I wasn't sure how, exactly, because he didn't elaborate. All he did say was that it wasn't about wanting to fuck us up. He kept telling us: 'We have to have some trust now, don't we?'

I was still trying hard not to laugh to myself at those words when the black-haired one finally came over to take my order. Clearly it was the face that had held her back.

'Car crash. Tea, please, and lots of milk.'

I could read her mind. She was wondering how I was going to drink it without dribbling out of the side of my swollen lips. I already had a system.

'And a straw, please.'

She reached into the Aladdin's cave in her apron pocket and pulled out a bunch of napkins. I nodded my thanks. We both knew I'd be needing them.

I had seen Yulia just once as she got dragged off into Lakenheath's medical centre, but since then none of us had seen her. I asked Mr and Mrs Bland but didn't get a reply. All Mrs Bland did was smile, and tell me that really didn't concern me now. Then she did her favourite trick of positioning her fingers and thumb at either side of my jaw, and shaking my head, like I was a naughty schoolboy, only she squeezed just a bit too much and shook just a bit too hard. And then she rounded it off by telling me that she and her oppo had asked to be the ones to TQ me.

On the way to Brandon, Rio asked the Owl what had happened to her, and just got an 'All's kinda good' reply, with an emoji smiley face. Then, as if we had just been released from prison, he dumped us all at the railway station with fifty pounds each and told us to get on with it.

Then he explained that fifty pounds was all we were

going to get. No hundred and sixty grand: it had been hard enough for him persuading the guys at the top, the big kahunas, just to keep us alive.

At least we were out; we were a bit fucked up, but we were moving away from the problem, even if the train was seventeen minutes late. The delay gave the other three time to argue – he really did look like an owl.

The rest was for another day – and clearly that day was now.

77

The tea turned up and so did my little red and white plastic straw. I poured in all the milk and took a suck, but it was still too hot. The gap where a lower right molar used to be was still sensitive.

The Owl had told us on the way to the station that the Beamer parked at the golf course had led them to us in Bristol. He'd had a heli up, loaded with a team to clean up the mess at Phoenix's pick-up point, and as soon as that was being taken care of it had begun a sweep for us. They had found the Beamer without too much trouble. Then it was just a matter of clicking into the city's CCTV and its facial-recognition software. I imagined it wouldn't have taken long to confirm the Beamer belonged to the SNS. All it would have taken was a glance through the driver's window at the suicide spinner.

The lift wasn't going to happen in the city centre, so the plan had been to follow, then take the lot of us as soon as it was safe to do so. We were much better than his team, it turned out, but technology was on his side.

An older woman came into the café with what I supposed were her two small grandchildren to pay homage to the People's Princess. Her grey hair was shorter than Gloria Hadley's had been, but she was probably the same age. I thought about her, and what Phoenix had said about her family's pain at never knowing what had happened to her. He was right. Despite thirteen million CCTV cameras tracking us, PINs, credit rating, databases, social media, email, even GPS, up to twenty thousand people would vanish in the UK this year. Along with the box-van couple, Gloria was collateral damage. All three had just been folded into a statistic and forgotten.

Not even the Owl had been able to clear up the mess in Leicester. There wasn't time. The houses in the estate were straight on to the police once the fight had started in the alley.

There had been some deaths, three, in fact, then Special Branch had taken over and there had been further arrests; some of the survivors had cooperated. Being able to read about the spectacular success of the security service in smashing a terrorist fund-raising operation made a welcome change from Brexit boom or bust and the rest of the bullshit that was going on in preparation for the referendum.

Good for them – tea and medals all round. But what about us? What did the Owl want? He had summoned me here today for less than thirty minutes of what?

I was about to find out.

He walked in wearing a zip-up grey cardigan over a

blue checked shirt, button-down collar done up all the way to the top. He gave a big smile and a wave as he came over to take the same seat as last time, and placed his laptop bag strap over its back.

At least he had finally bought himself a shirt that fitted his new 'Life is good' size.

78

The Owl was all apologies. 'I'm so sorry I'm late, Nick. London, you know how it is. People. Traffic. It's crazy out there, isn't it?'

He smiled the fast-food welcome he'd maintained since he'd come through the door. He placed his well-manicured hands in front of him on the table and finally switched his expression to one of concern. 'It's good to see you, Nick. How are you?'

His head moved from left to right, surveying the damage. He really did look so much more like an owl now.

'I'm getting there. What's the agenda?'

His head tilted to the left. 'A couple of things. But first – I bet you really want to know why I asked you to take the job.'

I nodded as I sucked at my straw. I'd been waiting awhile and the tea was much cooler now.

He looked thrilled. 'I knew you would. I thought it was a kinda neat idea. Because, well, first, no one knows you guys. And the job had to be kept well under the radar.'

His hands came up in surrender in front of him. 'I admit it, and I'm sorry, but you guys wouldn't have been my first choice. But, like I told you, I couldn't risk a leak. It was far too important.'

His hands went back onto the table and he leant in to lessen the gap between us. 'You know what?' His voice dropped like this was some kind of conspiracy. I supposed it was, really. 'Between me and you, I thought you guys would fail. Become history. That would have been good for me, you know with the big kahunas wanting you all out of the way – and at the same time you'd have stopped what was going down there with Yulia and those guys just by turning up. Bit of a win-win. But guess what? I was wrong. I was wrong about you, and I was wrong about the guys. I've just got to say, well done, and thank you for the extra help you gave in the fight against you-know-who. You did good, Nick. You guys should feel very proud of yourselves.'

He gave me a short, reassuring nod to let me feel good about myself for a job well done. That was great, but I wasn't here for a pep talk.

'Look, mate, we're still breathing, that's good enough for us. So you hoped we'd be history, I get that. The job was all about the memory sticks, wanting us out of the way? Sorry to disappoint.'

The Owl sat back in his seat, nodding away and agreeing as he straightened his legs and fished his left hand into his trouser pocket.

'Hey, Nick, no need for sorry. I bet you would have

done the same, no?' He treated me to one of those we're-all-in-this-together type smiles. 'I know you would have.'

He became very happy with himself as he pulled out his hand. 'There it is.' He placed the coin-sized lump of alloy on the table and gave it a gentle tap with his forefinger. 'Now that, Nick, was a very neat idea. But you know what? That's what got you caught. My guys just kinda reverse-engineered. People are so clever, these days, don't you think? I only wish I'd found it earlier, but it didn't rain until that last evening. I grabbed my coat and out dropped this little fella.'

The black-haired one came over for the Owl's order and I went back to sucking up my tea.

'It's okay, I'll wait. Thank you.'

She turned and left. I gave her a few more steps away from us before getting back to business.

'The big kahunas – the ones you protect us from.'

He nodded.

'They don't exist, do they? You are the big everything. All the shit that happens comes from you, right?'

He smiled, thinking a little before letting out a big sigh that I didn't believe was submission. He leant forward again. 'No, Nick, they really do exist.' He tapped his forehead. 'But in here.'

He let his hand fall away.

'Maybe it's because I like somebody else to blame stuff on. It kinda works for me. You see, I'm one of the good guys, Nick – but sometimes I've got to do bad. So the big kahunas, my guys up there? They have a function. They're there to blame. You know, the guys making me do the bad thing.'

He gave a big grin. 'I know, I have shoulders like a Coke bottle, don't I just?'

I smiled back as much as my lips could manage, then took the last suck of tea. It wasn't that I was joining in the joke: it was that I'd liked what he'd said. He was the one voice, so he was the power, and it was always good to be close to that, especially when he was trying to fuck you over.

The Owl was keeping everything upbeat. 'And, hey, being the boss means I get to have a change of heart and do stuff like this.'

He unhooked the bag's shoulder strap from the back of his chair and placed it on the floor by my side of the table. It looked too bulky to hold just a laptop. 'Enjoy. You guys earned it.'

I left it where it was. 'It'll pay for part of my dental work.'

He put on his mock-concerned face. 'Sorry about that, but you know . . .' Then his expression changed because he'd just remembered something. 'Hey, something else I can make happen. Can you tell Rio she said she'll be in touch? It seems they kinda got a thing.'

I shrugged. 'News to me, but I'll pass it on.'

How the fuck did that happen? Maybe she'd promised to give up roll-ups or something.

'She okay?'

I had given the Owl, Mr and Mrs Bland and anyone else who would listen her sales pitch.

'Of course.'

He stopped, waiting for me to ask what she was doing so he could say, 'Nothing.' So that was what I did instead until he filled the void.

'So, anyways, what about you guys, the SNS? You staying together?'

He was waiting for the positive reaction.

For me it was an easy one. 'Yeah. We're mates.' I pointed to the state of my face, as if it needed to be demonstrated.

'We've got to sort our bodies out, then our personal admin.'

The Owl got that and slowly nodded in agreement, even though he wouldn't have understood the slang. 'I get where you're coming from.'

'Do you? Because what now happens to us? Where do we stand with you?'

He kept nodding, as if he was surprised the question had been asked. 'You know, Nick? You still have your little stick guys as digital witnesses. I guess they're still tucked away for a rainy day so maybe we really could work together. I think we're back to square one. We've all come full circle, don't you think?'

I couldn't have agreed with him more. 'You're right, in more ways than one.'

Gabe was back in Scotland trying to patch up his marriage. He'd find forty K did a lot of patching. He'd still be wanting money from us to pay for a new Jeep, though.

The other two had had some movement in their lives, too – well, ideas.

Jack was thinking of running residential painting classes. I knew it was because he was hoping the right woman would turn up and like what he did with dark blue and black.

Rio was the worry. It was good that he had finally

given up on Simone but not on the girls. The problem with him now was that he continually fantasized about the SNS getting out there and claiming the three-million-dollar bounty the US were offering for that Russian hacker Bogachev. Maybe that was the thing he had with Yulia. I felt very worried we might find out sooner rather than later.

As for me? Just like the Owl had said, back to square one, walking along the South Circular once again. Who knew what tomorrow would bring? Moscow might turn out to be a big bag of good news. But if not, so what? At least I could now afford my own airfare to get there, so fuck it.

The Owl's face went back to concerned.

'The thing is, Nick, do we have trust?'

I started laughing. I just couldn't help myself, and I now knew the pain Rio felt when he'd split his lips.

The Owl joined in and that was another worry. I grabbed a napkin to stop the blood trickle. He was still laughing when he stood up to greet the man who'd just come through the door.

'There you are! Come and meet Nick.'

The new arrival was early forties, clean-shaven, his salt-and-pepper hair very short and neat, combed all the way back. He had perfectly shaped eyebrows and was clearly American. If the light brown chinos with a sharp centre crease hadn't given it away, then the blue nylon windcheater certainly had. I didn't even know if you could buy them outside the US.

The Owl pulled out a chair for him. 'Nick, this is Tom, my husband. Tom, Nick.'

I stood to shake hands as he gave me a hello and did a double-take at the state of my face.

The Owl took care of that. 'Nick had an auto accident. He tells me it looks worse than it is.'

They both sat and I bent to pick up the laptop bag. 'Nice to meet you, Tom. I'll leave you both to it.'

The Owl wasn't having any of it. 'No, Nick, sit – please.'

He turned his attention to Tom. 'Nick here thinks I look like an owl. What say, Tom, what say?'

'Really?'

Tom checked between the two of us before studying the Owl. 'No, no way. I'm thinking more . . . eagle.'

The Owl liked that. He looked at me. 'You see? Eagle.'

The black-haired one came over and the Owl ordered two lots of coffee and carrot cake. 'And for you, Nick?'

'Gents, I'm going to make a move. Enjoy the cake.'

The Owl stared at me, this time with the look that only power gives somebody. 'Nick, sit. Please. Before you go, tell Tom your Diana hair story. He doesn't believe a word of it.'